WITH A KISS DUET
BOOK ONE

SINS *of* SORROW

A.R. ROSE

ISBN: 979-8-9882875-2-0

OTHER TITLES BY A.R. ROSE

Ridgewood Series
Between the Flames
Wicked Games We Play
Marked By Cain

Standalones
Wreck Me
Only One Night

Twisted Heroes
Siren

My only love sprung from my only hate!
Too early seen unknown, and known too late!
Prodigious birth of love it is to me,
That I must love a loathed enemy.

-William Shakespeare

*To all the readers who had their sexual awakening
when Leo came on screen as Romeo, this one's for you.*

Sins of Sorrow Playlist

Real - K-Si Yang
Dark Place - Sani Knight
Ur Perfect I Hate It - Micky Valen
Skin - Rihanna
Thinking About You - HANDS
Calling - Metro Boomin, Swae Lee
Special - ONZ
Heaven Sent - Sani Knight
Fill The Void - The Weeknd, Lily-Rose Depp
I Know Places - Taylor Swift

A Note from A.R. Rose

Sins of Sorrow is a contemporary romance novel created for adults. This story depicts dark adult scenes and situations.

Reader discretion is advised. Sins of Sorrow contains content that may be triggering for some.

Your mental health matters. For a full list of content warnings please visit www.authorarrose.com/content-warnings.

For those of you ready to begin, I hope you enjoy.

"*For never was a story of more woe
than this of Juliet and her Romeo.*"

Act 5, Scene 3 - Romeo & Juliet
William Shakespeare

Chapter 1

Sly

Age 9, Verona, Italy

"**P**apà! Mamma!"

The shrill sound of my six-year-old brother's laughter rises through the fragrant air as we run around my parents, playing a game of tag in the kitchen while my mother cooks. Mio padre sits at our kitchen table rubbing his temples as we race around him, my brother completely oblivious of the irritation that permeates off our father.

Tossing my hand out, I whip my fingers against his arm, just barely ghosting him as he lunges forward to avoid my touch.

"Ugh, Giulio! Sei un imbroglione!" *You're a cheater.*

He laughs again and keeps running, tripping over Mamma's feet. As he goes flying, skidding across the floor, she wags her finger at him. "I've told you the kitchen is not for playing, Giulio."

My brother stands and starts to run again until Papà stops him in his tracks.

"Enough!" Papà's voice booms as his fists hit the table. "My head is pounding, and your mother is cooking. Find somewhere else to play."

Papà is a doctor. A world-renowned surgeon, I've heard Mamma say. He works at the hospital that my bisnonno founded, and my nonno was a surgeon before my father. Nonno died when I was five, but his picture still hangs in the lobby of the hospital, alongside bisnonnos, and mio padres. Three generations of Lucchettis as doctors. *Surgeons.*

Papà says he looks forward to me becoming one, too.

Turning to my mother, his gaze softens as it lands on her. "Mia mogile, we have staff who can prepare the meals. You should be resting."

His gaze falls to where her hand rests on her stomach, rubbing where my youngest brother grows. "I love to cook, Antonio. You know this."

"Sì, bellissima. And you are so good at it. But your doctor—"

"Shh, shh. I know my body, and I will rest when it tells me to."

"C'mon, Sly, let's go upstairs!" Guilio pulls my attention from our parents as he retreats from the kitchen, his small, chubby hand beckoning for me to follow.

"No, grazie, I want to draw again." Taking the seat opposite my father, I pick up my charcoal and pull my sketch pad toward me, resuming the drawing I was working on before we started our game. I've always loved to sketch, and Mamma says I've been improving greatly.

Our black lab, Polpetta, is the perfect muse for me to practice. Mamma and Papà got her when I was two, and they say my favorite food was meatballs then, so the name stuck. Nowadays, she's old and lazy, looking as round as the food she is named after.

"It's looking well," Papà compliments as he watches me shadow the outline of her nose.

"Grazie, Papà."

A loud, abrupt ringing makes me jump, shifting my charcoal into a harsh line against my page. Frowning, I look at the mistake, my shoulders sagging in defeat.

"Pronto?" my mother singsongs into the telephone. The room falls silent as my father watches with intent while she nods her head, her hand flying over her mouth as she looks at my father. Pulling the phone away from her ear, she holds it out, signaling for him to come take it from her. "It's Gabriele."

My eyes perk up at the mention of Uncle Gabriele. He lives in America, in a city full of skyscrapers and twinkling lights. The photos he brought during his last visit were magnifico, and I long to go see it for myself.

I also wish to see my cousin Lorenzo, who is the same age as I am. It makes me sad that my best friend and playmate is across the ocean, and even though I ask a lot, Mamma and Papà still have not taken me and Giulio to see them.

"Gabriele," my father barks into the phone. "What is it this time?"

My father's expression morphs from irritated to infuriated, his golden-bronze skin turning red from his neck through his face.

"HOW?" he shouts, his eyes darting to Mamma before he lowers his tone. "How could you get yourself into *that* much trouble, Gabriele? I—no. *No.* Absolutely not."

He turns his back, cupping his hand over the place where he speaks as though to shield his words. I don't hear what he says before he slams the phone into where it rests on the wall.

"Sylvester, go to your room, please. Mamma and I need to speak alone." I can hear the anger in his tone, see the quake in his shoulders, but he doesn't look over at me as he commands my instructions. I know better than to argue, so I collect my sketchbook and shuffle out of the kitchen without a word.

For the next two hours, me and Guilio sit at the top of our home's staircase, listening to Mamma and Papà argue. The sounds of heightened yet muffled voices and Mamma's anguished sobs traveling through the polished surfaces of our house.

One of our housemaids tried to shoo us back to our bedrooms an hour ago, but instead, I tucked my younger brother under my arm and stayed put. We can't hear what our parents speak of, but a twisting in my stomach tells me nothing good will come of it.

A gulp of saliva catches in my throat as I tilt my head back and look at the giant stone mansion. Mamma tucks my hand into hers, ushering Guilio and me away from the car that brought us here while it idles against the curb.

"Boys, you are to be on your best behavior. This is a business visit for your Papà and Uncle Gabriele. You are to be seen and not heard—it is of much importance. Do you understand me?"

"Sì, Mamma," I answer for both of us.

It has been one week since we moved to America, and three weeks since the phone call from Uncle Gabriele that changed everything for our family.

That very same night Guilio and I listened to Mamma and Papà argue—they came into our rooms and told us Uncle Gabriele needed his family close and we would be moving to New York.

Eavesdropping on several of Papà's phone calls taught me Uncle Gabriele made some bad decisions and owed someone a lot of money. And if they didn't get it, they would do very bad things to him.

I still don't understand why we had to leave our country to go help him, but at least I get to see Lorenzo more.

The steps leading up to the house make me feel like I am climbing a mountain. The stone clicks beneath Mamma's pointy shoes and I look down at them for distraction. My heart races, and Papà's hand engulfs my shoulder as he comes to stand behind me while we wait for the door to be answered. Uncle Gabriele stands to his right, fidgeting, while Aunt Andrea squats to smooth the front of Lorenzo's jacket.

When the door opens, a tall man wearing a suit greets us with an unfriendly look on his face. Beyond him, I take in the elegance of the house. Shiny marble floors, a grand staircase, sculptures and artwork—this place could be a museum.

"Come in," the man says simply, then steps aside while holding the door.

I hear my uncle clear his throat as Mamma steps forward with me and my brother in tow. Once inside, a line of women in plain dresses stand, and one rushes to my mother.

Once the door closes, the loudness of the city disappears, and a cold silence takes its place.

"May I take your coat, ma'am?"

"Yes, grazie," she says, letting go of our hands to shrug out of her coat. Papà steps forward to help before removing his own and hands both to the lady waiting.

"Gabriele," a man says as he steps out of a nearby room. His hands are in the pockets of his pants as he moves slowly toward us, his eyes glued to my uncle. He walks like a hungry lion stalking a gazelle.

He looks mean. Scary.

Is this the man who is mad at my uncle? If he is, why are we here, at his house?

"Maurizio." My uncle's head dips as though he's bowing. "Thank you for having my family at your lovely home. This is my beautiful wife, Andrea, and son Lorenzo. As well as my brother, Antonio, and his family."

Giulio shuffles sideways until he's hidden behind Mamma's legs, but I stand straighter and move my shoulders back, trying not to seem as small as I feel.

The man my uncle introduced us to looks at us each and hums, scrunching his lips as he rubs his well-groomed beard.

My father clears his throat and takes a step forward, his hand extended. "Pleased to meet you, amico mio. Thank you for having us."

"I wasn't aware there was an *us* attending when I extended the invitation to Gabriele, but alas, our staff has prepared a large meal. We may as well break bread." He never takes Papà's hand.

I watch my father's eyes narrow before he quickly stows the look away and masks it with a smile. "I see. Well, I hope there is no trouble."

"Not at all," Maurizio clips and turns to one of the women standing along the wall. "Please see to it that the kitchen places…seven additional seats at the table."

"Certainly, Mr. Paladino." She practically runs through a set of doors just a few steps away.

The man turns to my mother and aunt, his tone softening as he speaks to them. "My wife, Leighton, should be down with our daughter any minute. You can wait in the sitting room while I take the men to my office. Should you need anything, Capaul can assist you."

"Thank you, Mr. Paladino," Aunt Andrea says as she ushers Lorenzo through the archway in the wall and into the room to our left. Mamma does the same, steering Giulio and me right behind her.

The room is bright from the sun, with plush couches and fluffy pillows, and a small table with a neat pile of children's books and grown-up magazines. It looks fancy, and immediately I am afraid to dirty it and get in trouble.

Lorenzo, on the other hand, takes a running leap onto the light gray sofa across the room, landing with a soft thud face down. His laugh is muffled as his mother scolds him.

"Enzo!" she hisses. "This is not the place for jokes!" Pulling him up, she pushes his small body until he's sitting on the couch as he should be.

Mamma's hand on my back urges me forward, and I sit on the bigger of the two couches as she and Giulio do the same. Handing us both a book, she passes another to my cousin. "Read these, boys. And keep quiet until we tell you otherwise. *Please*, behave." She shares a look with my aunt before I look down at my book.

The Giving Tree by Shel Silverstein.

I huff out an annoyed breath, not wanting to read this dumb book again but knowing if I don't, Mamma will be angry. The book is made for little kids, and I'm *nine*. But Mamma says the best way to practice my second language is through repetition.

Staring at the pages without reading the words, we

wait in the room for what feels like forever. Mamma and Aunt Andrea keep sharing looks. Guilio gets restless, sliding off the couch and onto the floor to crawl under the table. I sneak a peek at Enzo and see that he looks as though he's about to fall asleep with his arm propped up on the side of the couch.

What is taking so long?

More long minutes pass before the sound of footsteps pulls my attention and I glue my eyes to what I can see of the hallway. Moments later, a lady and a girl appear, both with smiles on their faces.

The girl looks to be about my age. She wears a puffy pink dress and her dark brown hair is long. I wonder if she has any brothers for me to play with.

Mamma and Aunt Andrea stand. Should I?

"Hello, ladies. Boys," the lady greets happily, walking over to us.

Sliding off the couch, I stand close to Mamma as the lady approaches and reaches for her hands.

"It's so nice to meet you! I'm Leighton, and this is my daughter, Vincenza. Come here, Vincenza."

The girl bounces over to her mother and waves at mine.

"I wasn't aware Gabriele was bringing his whole family for his meeting with my husband, or I never would have let my father take our boys this week for a hunting trip! They would have loved more little boys to play with."

"That's alright," Mamma affirms. "It seems as though our presence was a bit of a surprise. My name is Valentina, and these are my sons Sylvester and Giulio."

Aunt Andrea steps forward and extends a hand to shake with the lady, Lee-something. "Thank you for having us in your gorgeous home. I'm Andrea, Gabriele's wife. And this is our son Lorenzo."

"Ah, yes. I've met Gabriele a few times now! So nice to finally meet you." She gestures for everyone to sit, so we do, and she takes a seat in the armchair across from us. The girl settles on the floor by her mother's side with a chapter book on her lap.

"How old are your boys?" Aunt Andrea asks as she places her hand on Enzo's knee to keep him from wiggling.

"Luciano, my oldest, is fourteen. Then we have Joseph, who is eleven, Vincenza here, just turned nine, and Samuele, my baby, is four." She sighs. "They just grow so quickly. I can't believe I have a teenager." Looking over at my mother, she squeals, "And you! Look at that baby bump! When are you due?"

"Federico will be arriving in three to four months. Lord never knows with my boys, they come when they please. Sylvester was nearly two weeks late, but Giulio was a month early. I've stopped trying to guess when the Lucchetti boys may arrive." My eyes trace where my mother rubs my baby brother in her stomach, and she smiles warmly at me. "Sly is nine, Giulio is six."

"Oh, I understand that, honey. My kids were all over the place too." She smiles warmly at Enzo. "And you, sir? How old are you?"

Enzo shifts in his seat, sitting up taller as he proudly boasts, "I'm about to turn ten!"

"Such a little man you are!" Lee-whatever says affectionately.

Her sentence is barely finished when a woman wearing the same plain dress as all the other maids comes into the room.

"Your presence is requested in the dining room," she tells us and curtsies low before leaving.

It's very strange.

The grown-ups stand and Mamma pulls Giulio to his feet before we follow the lady out of the room. I watch as the girl bounces on her feet, skipping and twirling the whole way across the hall.

She's odd. So bouncy, and why is her dress so big?

When we enter through the open double doors of the dining room, Papà, Uncle Gabriele, and the scary man are already sitting at the table. They stand when they see us, and I follow Mamma over to the side where Papà sits.

She settles us, and once the room grows still, the scary man stands and clinks a knife against his short glass filled with a dark-golden liquid.

"I find myself to be a reasonable man. A *family* man. Which is why I'd like to welcome you all to my home this evening for dinner. Though unplanned, it seems fitting, as I have recently learned that things don't always go *as planned*. I hope that through this act of breaking bread and sharing time, minds will change before the night is over." His words trail off as he stares at my uncle, who I see gulp, the knob in his throat moving. "Now, please join me in prayer. Dear Heavenly Father, we ask that you bless our food and the guests we have here tonight to share it. May you offer your wisdom and guidance to those who may need it the most, and that you share your light by blessing our families, cultivating our relationships, and nurturing our businesses. In Jesus' name, Amen."

"Amen," I whisper, as everyone joins in.

Mamma and Papà exchange a look right before the sound of a loud snap echoes through the room.

With it, four people in black clothes walk forward and reach between us, pulling the shiny silver tops off the food sitting in the middle of the table.

Immediately, several scents hit me, and my stomach growls. Roasted chicken, steak, capellini pasta with Alfredo sauce, penne marinara, and fresh baked bread. My eyes bounce from dish to dish, skipping quickly over anything green—Mamma will make me eat my vegetables, but that doesn't mean I have to look forward to them.

With the clatter of dishes around us, I hear Mamma whisper to Papà, "Cosa significa che spera che le menti cambiano?" *What does he mean he hopes minds will change?*

"Shh, shh," Papà whispers, before painting on a smile and turning to the head of the table. "Everything looks delizioso, Maurizio. Grazie."

The scary man, Maurizio, begins to serve himself, and as soon as his wife does, the rest of the adults do the same.

When our plates and our mouths are full, I realize no one is speaking. A rarity for a meal with my family.

Looking around the table, I see the scary man sending mean looks in my uncle's direction, while his wife fusses over the girl, trying to get her to try the food on her plate.

I don't know why she wouldn't want to.

Shoveling my mouth full bite after bite, I clear my plate and lean back in my chair, my stomach protruding.

"That was delizioso!" I exclaim loudly, knowing I was to be seen and not heard tonight, but not liking the silence. We speak at dinner. Why is no one speaking?

The scary man turns his attention to me, and suddenly I wish I had kept quiet. I am surprised when his grumpy look wipes clean. "I am glad, piccolo Lucchetti."

His gaze sweeps along the table, and he turns to his wife. "Leighton, my dear, perhaps now that we have finished, the men can speak once more?"

"Sure, my love," she tells him, then leans over to kiss him—*ew*. "Ladies, kiddos, shall we?"

Standing, she helps her daughter pull out her chair while Mamma and Aunt Andrea help us. Mamma casts another look to Papà, who nods, and Aunt Andrea bends to kiss Uncle Gabriele.

Why is everyone kissing?

As we walk away, I slow my steps to eavesdrop. "Have you thought about my offer, Gabriele?"

"Maurizio, *please*, there must be another way I can—"

"You have stolen from me, Gabriele! I have given more than enough time and patience because at one time I called you my most loyal employee, but *now* I need an answer. Have we come to an understanding?"

I look over my shoulder in time to see my uncle shake his head no, and watch as the scary man stands, forcing my uncle to look up at him. "How disappointing. You abuse my patience, even after I am gracious enough to take in your family for a meal."

My mother turns and sees that I have completely stopped walking, and hurries back to grab my arm. As she pulls me toward the door, the scary man continues yelling at my uncle, without actually raising his voice. "I put my trust in you, Gabriele. It was misguided, and it won't be forgotten. Let this be a warning to you, Antonio, of what happens when you cross Maurizio Paladino." Maurizio's gaze lifts and he watches us as we near the door.

We hardly cross the threshold before their butler pulls both doors closed behind us, slamming them shut. They hardly click into place when the piercing sound of a gunshot rings out behind them.

"NO!" Aunt Andrea screams, charging toward the door, but the man blocking it holds her back.

The girl, Vincenza, whimpers at the sound and curls into her mother, burying her head into the fabric of her dress. Her mother's hand covers her own mouth as though she's surprised.

"I'm so sorry," she cries out, but she's already pushing her daughter down the hall and away from us.

They disappear quickly as Mamma rushes to Aunt Andrea, pulling her into her arms while she sobs louder than I've ever heard anyone cry before.

Seconds later the doorknobs twist loudly, and Papà appears, tossing open the doors and stepping through them. His eyes are wild and fearful as he looks at each one of us. "Come," he says hurriedly. "We must leave. *Now.*"

His eyes zero in on mine, speaking what he cannot say aloud. I nod in a silent understanding and grab the hands of my brother and my cousin, and pull them to the front door. Papà's footsteps are heavy behind mine as he guides Mamma and Aunt Andrea, leaning around me to open the front door when we reach it.

Once we're in the town car again, and our driver has made it safely away from the Paladino home, does the reality of what happened sink in.

Everything happened so quickly, and if I thought our lives were turned upside down before, I have a feeling I am sadly mistaken.

Aunt Andrea's loud sobs have turned into breathless hysteria as she cries into Mamma's bosom. Lorenzo is curled up on the seat, folded into himself with his head on his mother's lap. I can't tell if he's crying.

Papà hands Giulio his activity pack he brings with him on car rides to keep him occupied before looking at me.

It's then I see smatters of blood across his white

starched shirt. My stomach dips and I look away, out the window.

The city lights are bright, even through the darkened tint of the car, and it's only when the traffic begins to move and the lights begin to blur, do I allow a quiet stream of tears to fall.

There are two things I learned for certain today.

One: My uncle is dead.

And two: Never trust a Paladino.

Chapter 2

Vinnie

Age 13

"**R**emind me why I have to go to this stupid dinner?" I complain to my nanny, Cecilia, as I look at her through the reflection of my vanity mirror.

Cecilia is less of a nanny and more of an older sister figure. She's twenty-three, and even though she was hired on to care for me, she and I quickly bonded, and the formalities dropped. Cecilia helps me with everything: school, hair, makeup, *boys*. She accompanies me to almost every event I am forced by my parents to attend. She even lives here at the estate, although her room isn't on the same floor as mine.

"Because, it's a charity fundraiser at the mayor's house and anyone worth a damn is invited," she reprimands as she lets a curl loose from the wand, letting the hot strand bounce against her hand as it immediately starts to cool. She passes the handle of the curling wand to me so I can hold it while she sprays my hair with hairspray.

"The Townsends will be there," she continues with a coy smile. "I was talking to Esther today. She said Summer is ecstatic to go tonight."

I roll my eyes at the mention of Summer, and her keeper—I mean nanny—Esther.

Summer is three years younger than I am and tries desperately to act like she's my age. I only tolerate her presence at these dumb events because of her brother. Her brother makes my heart soar. I've had a crush on him since I was five.

I try to act casual as I ask Cecilia, "And Mason? Will he be there?"

She releases another curl and hands the wand back to me. Her lips turn up into a cheeky smile. "Maybe."

"Make sure my hair is perfect," I snap, but a smile plays against my lips as she narrows her eyes at me.

"I may be hired to be your nanny, young lady, but I'm still older than you. It'd behoove you to remember that."

"And it'd behoove *you* to remember that I'm your boss."

We stare at each other through the mirror for several seconds, our expressions hard, before we both burst into laughter.

She pokes my side with her freshly manicured fingernail. "You're a little princess, Vinnie. You're lucky I'm so fond of you."

"Mmmhmm," I hum and bring a tube of pink gloss

to my lips. Mom won't let me wear makeup yet, but she lets Cecilia style my hair however I want, and buys me a new lip gloss whenever I ask. This one tastes like cotton candy.

When my hair is done, I stand, and Cecilia grabs my dress from where it hangs nearby. It's beautiful. Ice-blue chiffon with a fitted bodice, and thick straps that tie on the top of my shoulders. It reminds me of a modern-day Cinderella, without the hoop skirt.

Shrugging from my robe, Cecilia slips the dress over my outstretched arms, careful as she brings it over my head, as to not ruin my hair or rub my gloss. Once I'm situated, she zips the back and turns me toward my mirror.

It's lovely. I can't wait for Mason to see me in it, and I wonder if he'll finally notice me as *more* than just a childhood playmate.

Mayor Conrad Moser's charity dinner is an absolute snoozefest. Nothing more than a four-course meal in their grand ballroom, packed with round tables for the most elite New York families to pretend like they care what each other has to say.

Mom insisted we attend tonight when Mayor Moser extended the invitation. This is their first social gathering in their new luxury 5th Avenue penthouse, since typically parties were thrown at their main residence, Gracie Mansion. Mom gushed about how close they live to the Met, if only part-time, and how she couldn't wait to see it because it was a tri-level penthouse—a unique rarity at this level of extravagance. So naturally, Father accepted the invitation, and here we are.

The auction was the most entertaining part of the evening, and even that was hardly bearable.

Leaning against my mother's shoulder, my finger traces along the extravagant beadwork on her tight champagne and gold gown. I was underdressed in comparison to her, but as she liked to remind me, "it's not your job to stand out, Vincenza."

Yet.

It's not my job to stand out, *yet*.

But I will, someday soon.

"Mom, can I go find the boys?" I ask, waiting until there is a lull in her conversation with Mayor Moser's wife, Elena. My brothers had slipped from the room ages ago and were probably exploring the grounds or playing with some of the other kids I saw earlier who have also disappeared. Who I really want to find, though, is Mason.

Looking around the ballroom, I realize I'm the only kid still sitting with their parents.

"Sure, sweetheart, but be careful wandering about on your own until you find them."

Smiling tightly, I stand and slightly bow my head as a sign of respect to Mrs. Moser. "Dinner was lovely. Thank you so much, Mrs. Moser."

"What a well-mannered daughter you have, Leighton," she praises. "A little not-so-well-kept secret, my dear. If you go through the main doors and up the staircase to the third floor, you'll find an access door to the roof. Somehow, all the children find a way to sneak into my rooftop hideaway. It's not much, but the view of the city is breathtaking."

"Thank you," I tell her, then spin on my heel and force every bone in my 'well-mannered' body to walk, *not run*, across the ballroom and to the stairs.

My nude sling-back kitten heels echo against the dark wooden staircase as I climb higher, craning my neck to see if anyone is on the second floor. It's quiet up here, so I turn immediately and climb the second staircase leading to the third floor.

Once at the top, I find the door Mrs. Moser mentioned will take me to the roof. For whatever reason though, I hesitate before stepping toward it.

My gaze sweeps over the ostentatious landing of the third floor and catches on a set of glass French doors that are slightly open. A light breeze ruffles the sheer curtains of the window next to it, the sounds of the bustling city pouring in.

I cross the space, drawn to the open doors, and push one just enough for me to slide through the gap.

Pressing my back against the door, it clicks into place, and the moment it does, a boy about my age slips out of the shadow cast by the wall of the balcony.

He wears simple black dress pants and a crisp white buttoned shirt, with a plain maroon tie hanging around his neck. But perhaps the most captivating thing this boy wears is his expression.

He looks sad, and angry, and above all, he looks lonely.

Something about his scowl makes me want to take his sadness away. I want to make him smile.

"Hi," I say shyly, tucking a lock of hair behind my ear.

"Hi," he replies, and takes a seat on the stone bench in the center of the balcony. From there, he stares straight out at the lights of the city.

"What are you doing up here?"

"Probably the same thing you are."

"Oh. Well, I was actually looking for my brothers."

"Haven't seen them," he says with boredom. It makes me deflate a little inside.

"Do you want company?" I ask as I take a step forward.

His head swings toward me, and he looks me up and down before turning back to the city. Nodding once, he says, "Sure, but can we not talk?"

"Okay."

Rounding the bench, I sit down next to him, leaving as much space between us as possible. I follow his line of sight and stare out at the twinkling skyscrapers. A few blocks over, a helicopter lands on the roof of Lenox Hill.

After several minutes, I can't take the silence. "Are you sitting up here alone because something made you sad?"

"I thought we agreed no talking."

My mouth opens, then closes again. There are so

many questions on the tip of my tongue. A large part of me thinks it may be wise to go leave and find Mason, or my brothers, after all.

The boy exhales and leans forward with his elbows pressed against his knees. "Sì," he sighs. "I miss my home. I wish to go back."

"I'm sure your family will be leaving soon. The auction has finished and everyone is just talking and dancing."

He laughs as I speak, turning to look at me. With his full attention, it feels like there is a spotlight shining down on me, the warmth of the light stifling. I squirm uncomfortably.

"I did not mean my house, I meant my *home*. Verona."

"As in Italy?"

"Sì. The one and only."

"Wow," I whisper to myself, before asking. "What's it like there? I've always dreamt of visiting. I'm half Italian, possibly a little more. My father is full, and my mother is half, mixed with Irish and French."

"It's very beautiful. A different beauty than New York has to offer." He looks back out to the skyline. His tone is a little more chipper when he eventually turns back to me. "Were you born here? You must have been —your accent is purely American."

"I was. Right here in New York, actually. My mom was born in Virginia and happened to meet my father when he was here for a summer abroad. They fell in love and he moved to the U.S. for her, and they settled here." It's more information than a teenage boy needs, but I love the story of my parents. Their love story gives me hope I'll find my own someday. If they could find their soulmate by chance, after living an ocean apart for so long, certainly destiny has plans for all of us.

"Romantic," he says, scrunching his nose slightly, though his voice holds no sarcasm.

"When did you move her—"

"Vincenza!" My mom stops my sentence, her voice carrying through the closed doors as she looks for me.

His gaze snaps back to mine when he hears my mom, and I swear I see his eyes widen for a moment.

I sigh with annoyance. I want to know more about this boy…hear more about growing up in Italy, and why he's here. How long he's lived here. But instead, I discreetly wipe my sweaty palms on the underside of my dress and stand.

"I have to go. Thank you for keeping me company." Smiling sweetly, I notice the way he stares blankly at me instead of returning the sentiment. It wipes the smile off my face, and I take steps backward to the door, not taking my eyes off him as he continues to stare at me with a cold look in his.

He glares at me as I twist the handle and step back into the penthouse, wondering where I went wrong.

Boys are so confusing.

"Oh, there you are, sweetheart! I was worried when your brothers showed back up at the table, but you weren't with them. It's time to go—your father's already sent for the car."

"Alright." I follow her to the staircase, and grab onto the railing, turning to glance over my shoulder one more time at where the boy sits alone again, cloaked in the night's darkness. I can just make out his silhouette, and I ignore my inner persuasion that begs for me to go back out there and find out what I did to offend him.

Back on the main floor of the penthouse, Mayor Moser's coat check attendant drapes my black coat over my shoulders. My father and brothers position their own coats, adjusting them while they talk amongst themselves.

When my mother ushers me into the waiting elevator and asks me if I had fun this evening, it's with the *ding* of the doors enclosing our family inside that I realize I never even got the boy's name.

Chapter 3

Vinnie

Age 17

I can feel the vibration of the bass before we make it to the top floor. My pulse races with every ascending number as the elevator climbs higher and higher.

This isn't the first party I've been to this year, but it's the biggest.

Asher Thomas's parents left for a long weekend trip to The Hamptons, and he decided to throw a pre-graduation rooftop rager the second they were gone, inviting not only the students of our schools, Agnes Parker's All-Girls Day School and Quincy Elliott's School for Boys, but the students of Kensington Academy as well. All three are on the Upper East Side, but rarely intermix.

Needless to say, knowing I'm about to be in a sea of faces I'm unfamiliar with is giving me a rush of adrenaline of both excitement and nerves.

Sensing I need an anchor, Raina, my best friend, reaches down and laces her fingers through mine. "I heard Christian broke up with his girlfriend, finally." She shakes my hand, a mischievous little smile coasting her lips. "Maybe he'll be DTF."

Snapping my head in her direction, I give her what I feel like is a completely baffled look. "Because *I* am? Just because I have a crush on the guy doesn't mean I'm going to give it up to him on Asher's *roof*, Raina."

She laughs and turns toward me, weaving her fingers through my hair and tousling it slightly to give it more volume. "I'm just playing! I know you wouldn't. But you didn't deny that you *want* to give it up to him."

"Whatever." Rolling my eyes, I adjust the hem of my black mini-dress, trying to give it more length than is physically possible. Raina talked me into wearing it, when the last thing I wanted was to bring more attention to myself.

Right now, I feel completely out of control of my body—an ugly duckling, if you will. Which isn't entirely true, but it's how I *feel*. Self-conscious and hyper-critical of my body. Teenage hormones haven't been kind to my skin, and I am counting down the days until my hideous braces get removed. Dolling me up in a skintight dress with pretty makeup and hair won't fix either of those things. No matter how much makeup she caked on my face.

"At least the Mason ship has sailed! You held onto that for far too long."

"He's cute."

"Mason Townsend is the physical definition of the word *settling*."

"Just because he isn't a bad boy doesn't mean he's boring!"

Her bubbly laughter fills the elevator as the doors open, she grins and pulls me through them. "You're the one who said he was boring, babe!"

Immediately we're hit with the cool New York air and a cloud of smoke—exhaled from a kid to my right, the lit joint extended as though he's passing it to me. Electronic dance music pulses through the huge speakers placed at all four corners of the rooftop, and all around us bodies gyrate. I watch as drinks get sloshed from cups spilling onto exposed skin, unnoticed by those completely lost in the music, or those too drunk to care.

"Looks like we're behind," Raina comments, pulling me to one of the two bars lined with liquor bottles.

Inwardly, I cringe.

I enjoy a party as much as the next person, but parties like *this*…they make my skin crawl.

And yes, I am aware of how incredibly stuck up that sounds.

I just hate when people can't hold their liquor, and I hate drugs even more. Ironic, considering what my father does, though if he knew *I* knew, he'd sugarcoat it with a bald-face lie and deny the truth.

To the world, my father is the single most profitable coffee importer in North America, with teams all around the world scouting the finest coffee beans and undiscovered growers. But behind that facade, my father is actually one of the most profitable drug smugglers this country has seen in decades.

It's only been two years since I found out, eavesdropping, when my two older brothers, Luciano and Joseph, were whispering in the men's parlor late one night. Joseph was praising my father's ventures, talking about how ingenious he was and how he couldn't wait to take over for him one day. Luciano, on the other hand, seemed quite irritated with the eagerness Joseph exuded.

Joseph was only seventeen at the time. He had his whole life ahead of him, and the brains and wealth to back him in whatever path he went down, but instead, he was *excited* to step into the shoes of a glorified drug dealer.

Since overhearing that conversation, I've kept a closer eye on Joseph, not that I needed to since he was always keeping an eye on *me*, constantly glaring at me with a look of malice hidden behind his toffee colored eyes. The last few years, intuition has reminded me to watch my back around my older brother. Joseph has a knack for making me feel like his prey, and while I want to think the best of my own flesh and blood, I'm not the only one who notices his strange behavior.

Raina hates being around him, too.

"Here," she says as she pushes a clear plastic cup in my hand, filled to the brim with amber liquid.

Bringing it to my nose, I smell what she's handed me, and take a sip when I smell the sugary scent of

Coke. But under the sweetness, are the unmistakable notes of rum, so I sip slowly. The combination explodes on my tongue and I can't fight the moan that escapes from the taste.

"Oh! Look," she squeals, and I lower my cup to follow her line of sight. "There's Brock Leclair. He's so freaking cute."

"Who's Brock Leclair?"

"He's the best attacker on Kensington's lacrosse team," Raina says with a deep sigh as she watches him from across the room. "I heard he plays hard both on *and* off the field."

Taking another sip of my drink, I scan the group of guys standing with Brock. I don't recognize any of them, but they're cute enough. "Do you want to go introduce yourself?"

"Introduce myself?" She rolls her eyes playfully at me. "We've been sexting for a week now, baby girl. I'm going to do more than *introduce* myself. C'mon!" Circling her fingers around my wrist, she pulls me again, and I have to hold my drink in front of me to avoid spilling it.

As we weave through people, I stop paying such close attention to my rum and Coke and look up at the countless faces around me. When we stop in front of the group, I give a shy smile, but let Raina do the talking. She doesn't hesitate.

"Hey, Brock. Recognize me?" she flirts, leaning into him a little.

He grins as she presses up on her tiptoes, her breasts

pushing against his bicep as she whispers something in his ear.

Raina is a pathological flirt. She thrives on male attention and has no care in the world about what other people think of her, but the hilarious reality of it is, she's still a virgin. And it's no secret, either. It's why the boys work so hard to get in her good graces—they're trying to be the one she finally gives it up to.

Little do they know, she'll never give it to any of them. Deep down, Raina is a hopeless romantic. We've had countless conversations about how she's saving herself until marriage simply because she knows if they've made it that far, he's worth giving it to.

"Introduce us to your friends," Raina urges as she trails her finger down Brock's arm. His eyes are hooded as he looks down at her, his arm braced above her head against the brick wall.

His head lowers slightly, never leaving Raina's orbit as he spouts off names. "Liam, Garrett, Ollie, Enzo, and Sly."

My eyes bounce around the half circle the guys have formed, most giving a wave or a nod as Brock says their names, but when my attention lands on the last one, Sly, my breath catches in my throat.

He's gorgeous, leaning against the wall in a black t-shirt and jeans with a look that could quite honestly kill. His hazel eyes bore into me with a look of anger, and I'm instantly confused as to why. I'm stuck on the sharp features of his face, the way his shirt hugs his muscles, and the way my body *begs* for me to move closer to him.

Conflicting emotions rage through me, alarm bells ringing in my head.

But the longer I stare at him—and at this point, I'm openly staring—the more a sense of familiarity builds in my chest. I've seen him before. I feel like I *know* who he is.

A faded memory flashes through my mind of me on a staircase, looking behind at a boy in the shadows…

"Have we met?" I blurt, taking a step closer although I'm not sure why.

My movement makes him straighten.

"I don't know, have we?" he counters, his voice deeper than I imagined.

"I'm Vinnie." I reach my hand out, but he doesn't take it.

"Vinnie is a guy's name."

His friends snicker. Heat rises in my cheeks, but I force the slight embarrassment it causes down and stand up a little taller.

"Afraid of a *female* with a guy's name? I understand. It can be a little disappointing when you realize females are the stronger sex *and* we get to use your names, too."

"*Ohhhhh*," his friends goad. All except Brock, who now has his tongue down Raina's throat.

I guess I'm on my own with this.

Pushing off the wall, he takes two steps toward me and suddenly there's only an inch of space between us. He's a full head taller than I am, so I tilt mine up to look at him.

The world falls away.

My pulse skyrockets as the light scent of his cologne and the darkness behind his eyes envelops me. His voice drops low as he leans in, careful not to actually touch me as he brings his lips to my ear.

"Paladinos are unworthy of my fear," he spits, then purposely bumps my shoulder as he pushes past me.

I'm rooted in place, my mouth hanging agape with shock. Speechless, I stand there, eyes bouncing to everyone in the circle, wondering if that seriously just happened. The looks on the guys' faces range from indifference to confusion, and it's clear they have no idea what just happened, either.

Except for one.

Enzo looks at me similarly to how Sly looked at me, but with even more malice. He's seething, hands balled into fists by his side as one of the other guys turns toward him, muttering something I can't quite make out.

Raina's glancing over at me from where she's caged against the wall, still making out with Brock as though the only air they can breathe is what the other's lungs expels. Her eyebrows lift in silent question, but I simply shake my head, looking down at the ground as my mind works overtime.

Before I can stop myself, I'm turning on my heel, scanning the party for where he went. Quickly, I spot him over at the makeshift bar.

As I approach, he's pouring himself four fingers of scotch and tossing it back—the exact opposite of how you're supposed to drink a scotch that expensive.

"How do you know who I am?" My voice comes out pitchy and slightly frantic, mirroring the beat of my heart.

Ignoring me, he pours himself another drink before bringing it to his lips and sipping it slowly. As he lowers the cheap plastic cup, his eyes meet mine. The feeling of recognition swirls in my chest, but I still can't place him.

"I—" I begin, but the moment the sound leaves my lips, he turns and walks away again.

This time, I act faster and take off after him, my heels clicking against the rooftop as I quicken my pace to catch up.

Why am I even following him?

The last thing this guy deserves is my time and attention, but I'm desperate to know how he knows who I am, and why he clearly dislikes me so much.

That other guy had the same look on his face…

But I couldn't care less about the other guy.

"You know, this is extremely immature of you. You act like you know me even though we *just met*, and instead of doing the decent thing and explaining why, you're ignoring me and literally running away."

This gets his attention, and faster than I can slow, he turns around, causing me to crash into him. Our bodies press together, my face against the soft cotton of his shirt, and I'm disarmed by the scent of him again— sweet citrus, amber, bergamot, and…something I can't place.

Something that's uniquely him.

He doesn't take a step back and instead leans down again, his lips ghosting my ear. "If you don't recognize me, *principessa*, that is your issue, not mine."

"So we have met, then?"

Stepping back, a dark laugh bubbles from his lips, and he shakes his head. "Unbelievable."

Taking a step to walk away again, I stop him, my hand grabbing his wrist. He looks down at where we're connected.

"Just tell me how you know who I am."

I watch his Adam's apple bob, and I narrow my eyes, confused more than ever.

Why do I even care so much? I can't explain why it's bothering me that he knows who I am, or why I care about him finding repulsion in that knowledge.

I have a list a mile long of people who hate me simply because I'm a Paladino—the last name comes with many caveats. My father's power and control within the city isn't something people take lightly, and simply being his daughter is both a blessing and a curse.

And don't get me started on my brothers and the strife they've caused over the years.

But the reaction Sly and Enzo gave me when they simply laid eyes on me was something I've never experienced before. Their hatred of my family clearly runs deep, and I want to know why.

Searching his eyes, I find no answers, but feel myself getting lost within them.

Neither of us says anything, but neither of us looks away, either.

Moments later, a girl stumbles over to us, her cup of white liquid sloshing over the rim, splashing on my shoe. I jump back to avoid more of her spill as she flings her arm awkwardly over Sly's shoulder, practically hitting him in the face as she does because she's too short to fully reach his shoulder.

Whining his name, she takes a large drink and sways into him.

"Angie, please control yourself. This is incredibly sloppy of you." He physically removes her arm from him and takes a step back, just as she tries to kiss him. "Where is Ollie? *He's* the one who should be caring for you."

Sly glances at me, then walks away from us both, disappearing through the crowd.

"Slut," the girl, Angie, mutters not-so-under her breath as she looks me up and down.

Rolling my eyes, I walk away too, back to where I left Raina. Thankfully, she's detached herself from Brock, and is looking out into the party. When she spots me, she visibly relaxes.

"Oh thank *God*," she says, pulling me in for a hug. "Where did you go?"

"To get some answers. Can we go?"

"Already?"

"Yeah, I'm not feeling it anymore, but if you're not ready, it's fine. I'll just call Tyson and have him pick me up." As I'm talking, I pull out my phone from my black sequined crossbody, and start writing a text to my father's driver.

"No, no, it's fine. We can go. My driver's still here—you know my father doesn't let him actually leave."

"Are you sure?"

"Absolutely, babes." She turns to Brock, pressing up on her tiptoes so he can hear her over the party's music, which has gotten louder over the last few minutes. He shakes his head at whatever she says, then immediately sticks his tongue down her throat again.

Thankfully, this kiss is much quicker than the last one, and when they break apart, I can practically see the hearts in her eyes.

She grins widely, then bounces over to where I'm standing a few feet away. "Okay, let's go!"

Back in her town car, I watch the city lights pass as we weave through the cars that are still on Madison Avenue.

"So, are you going to tell me what happened?" Raina asks. From my periphery, I can see her looking over at me as her fingers continue to sweep across the keyboard of her phone.

"I'm just not in the mood for a party," I lie, even though she already knew I *was* looking forward to the party.

She studies my face, and I turn away again, leaning my head against the cool window. "I call bull. You didn't like how Sly and Enzo reacted to meeting you. I know you hate when people don't like you, but did you seriously expect *they'd* react differently, Vins?"

My head snaps to her, and in that moment, I know I'm missing something.

Something big.

If my *best friend* knows why they hate me, why haven't I been clued in?

My head shakes with annoyance, and I lift my hand, swiping it through the air. "Care to share, since you obviously know?"

"Oh, baby girl, sometimes you really do live in your own world, don't you? This is why you have me. One of us has to know how to keep track of who's who around this city, and I like to consider myself a master at social media stalking." She laughs at herself while I continue to stare, waiting for her to get to the point. It takes everything I have to bite my tongue and not snap at her to hurry up. She sighs dramatically. "That was Sly and Enzo *Lucchetti*. As in—"

The color drains from my face as I hear *that* name and suddenly everything makes perfect sense. The anger, the disgust. Sly's words.

Years ago, rumors of how my father killed a man right in our home circulated, and how the crime was swept under the rug with the help of the mayor.

Rumors I now know to be true after learning of who my father truly is.

Repressed memories resurfaced when I overheard my brothers whispering about my father's true business dealings two years ago, the pieces of the puzzle falling into place.

A single gunshot ricocheting through my mind.

Faded memories of three faceless little boys in my home.

A teenage boy's wide-eyes when he heard my name from where we sat on a darkened balcony.

The so-called rumors of him murdering a man became a reality after the memories of that night flooded back to me. It took a long time to grapple with the lies I'd been fed my entire life, and even longer to come to terms with them.

Never in my wildest dreams did I think I'd ever see that boy again. And I wasn't sure how to feel now that I have.

Lucchetti. I repeat in my mind, the lump in my throat thick and stifling.

Swallowing it down, I look at my best friend in shock, finishing her sentence and wondering how I wasn't able to figure it out on my own. "As in, Gabriele Lucchetti. The man my father killed."

Chapter 4

Vinnie

Present day

How much would you spend for the opportunity to marry the daughter of one of the most powerful men in New York? Is there a business negotiation too big for you to consider? A price too high?

What piece of your soul would you sell for the chance to become a part of the Paladino family?

My father is currently accepting offers for my hand in marriage, although his wording is much more eloquent.

He thinks it's time I begin thinking about marriage and a family—strongly encouraging me to select a man with an impressive pedigree and a high yield savings account.

A son-in-law that would be impressive both on paper and *in* the papers.

Someone who will take care of me and give me the life I've grown accustomed to.

I'm twenty-six years old and while I hold a comparative literature degree from Columbia, have started my own independent publishing house, and live in a beautiful apartment in Central Park Tower, I *still* need a man to take care of me.

At least, according to my father.

And he means well, I know he does. Despite me finding out some things about him that part of me wishes I'd never learned, I am still daddy's little girl. Which is why I attend every single ball, gala, and fundraiser he suggests I attend.

It's why I let man after man sweep me across the dance floor, twirling me, and dipping me, as I pretend to enjoy their attention.

Catching Raina's eye across the room, she winks at me, the ghost of a smirk pulling at her lips as she cradles her martini in her perfectly manicured hand. She laughs at something the bartender says and waves him off, sauntering over to a nearby group to mingle.

"You look absolutely stunning tonight, Vinnie," Mason Townsend compliments, his hand tightening on my hip as muscle memory takes us through our waltz.

For almost twelve years, I was held in the mercy of a soul-crushing infatuation with Mason until teenage hormones ran rampant and turned my infatuation to a new guy every few weeks.

At age twenty, we dated briefly, but I quickly learned the attraction I'd once had for him completely faded and we were better off as friends. But these days, I can't help but feel like I'm twenty again and Mason is trying to court me.

His attention used to make me feel like I was the luckiest girl in the world. Now, it just feels so disingenuous.

"I'm wearing a mask, Mason," I counter, feeling slightly guilty for the hint of attitude I've given him. At least his hands aren't attempting to wander like the last man I danced with.

The blood-red off-the-shoulder gown I'm wearing protects my backside from being groped as it has been in the past, and I am thankful for the layers. The most I've had to worry about tonight is wandering eyes at the deep v of the bodice and the slight brush of the back of a hand against the side of my breast.

Men can be such pigs.

Leaning down, his hand brushes my immaculately curled hair away from my ear, and he whispers, "Even still, you are the most gorgeous girl in the room."

Girl.

He still sees me as a child.

Thankfully, the song ends and I pull from his embrace, giving him a small curtsy. He bows, as upbringing taught him to do, and before he can say another word, another man cuts in.

"May I have this dance, Miss Paladino?"

He's an older gentleman wearing a black satin mask over his eyes, so simple in comparison to the one covering mine. The intricate beadwork and feathers are the same shade as my dress, complementing its design.

"Of course," I reply hesitantly as the next song begins. Sometimes the older men were the most degrading, whispering filthy things they think will make me weak in the knees. I'd been to enough masquerade balls to know that men felt bold behind a mask, thinking it gave them anonymity, and they dared to speak that way despite knowing who my father is.

Perhaps if the words came from someone thirty years their junior, I would be interested in being told I was going to be fucked within an inch of my life like the dirty slut I was, but alas, coming from a man old enough to be my grandfather, it was revolting.

Placing my hand in his, he pulls me close, but still leaves a respectable distance between us.

"You looked like you could use a break from the young men," he tells me. "I asked my wife if I could give you a little reprieve. I hope you don't mind." He smiles over my shoulder, presumably at his wife, and I sigh with relief.

"That's very kind of you, Mr...."

"Emmons. But you can call me Ansel."

"Well thank you, Ansel. You were right—I *do* need a break from the young men. They're exhausting."

Ansel chuckles and spins me outward before pulling me back in.

As we dance, we maintain casual conversation, and it's the most relaxed I've felt all evening.

With the song coming to an end, I decide to ask Mr.

Emmons for one more dance. Graciously, he accepts, and we continue dancing.

Halfway through our Vietnamese waltz, I catch sight of my brother and his slimy friend, August, leaning against the wall, their eyes pinned to me. The disgruntled sneers on their faces make every nerve ending in my body prickle with awareness.

I try to shake it off as Ansel turns us, changing my line of sight. The relationship between me and my brother, Joseph, has gotten progressively more tumultuous as the years have gone on. It's no secret that he hates me, but his efforts to hide it have completely vanished, and though he's never actually made any moves to physically harm me, his emotional and mental persecutions have only intensified.

You'd think with age and distance, he'd choose to simply remove himself from my life, but he's done the opposite. He considers our family to be New York royalty, and despite him being the second-born son, he has plans to take over our father's empire.

The underground empire, that is. He couldn't care less about the coffee business.

As for why he won't leave me alone, time has proven that it's pure, spiteful jealousy. We're the closest in age, but we couldn't be further apart in personality. And as the only daughter, I'm doted on by both of our parents —not that I ask for it.

On the contrary, I'd rather be ignored from time to time. I'll happily share the attention I've never asked for. But Joseph doesn't see it that way. He feels like I've robbed him of something and clearly has a vendetta against me.

"Is everything okay, Miss Paladino?" Ansel asks as we slow with the music.

Pulling myself from my thoughts, I nod and smile politely. "Yes, I apologize. The music carried my thoughts away." Stepping back, I curtsey, and Mr. Emmons bows as low as his body will allow.

He reaches for my hand and places a gentle kiss on top of it. "Thank you for the pleasure of not one, but two dances."

"The pleasure has been mine."

I watch as he walks back to his table, the music starting again with a melody to carry a tango.

Fitting that a dance that tends to highlight the attention of a male would begin just as the devil himself steps into my line of sight.

Roughly, he grabs hold of my hand and my waist, not giving me the option of refusing, and starts to guide us across the dance floor.

Chapter 5

Sly

The last thing I want to do tonight is sit at a masquerade ball pretending to care about what the people around me are saying. Somehow, though, I let Sully swindle me into accompanying him. He was here on behalf of his father; his attendance was mandatory.

And to Sully, that meant mine was too.

Sullivan 'Sully' Rochester is the son of an oil tycoon and my closest amico—aside from my cousin Enzo—despite my trying to cut ties with him a time or two over the years. Not that I would actually want to end our friendship, but sometimes the man had an immature streak rivaling a prepubescent boy.

Particularly when it came to women.

But he makes for an excellent travel partner and is up for any adventure I throw his way. Which is why, when I suggested we move to Europe for a much-needed break from New York, he didn't hesitate to follow me across the globe.

We just returned to the States after two and a half years abroad, traveling and moving to different countries every couple of months. Over the course of our journey, Sully worked remotely for his father, and I… well, I had plenty to keep me afloat, and to pass the time, I took on odd jobs as I found them and as they interested me.

Shortly after I turned twenty, Mamma successfully talked me into medical school. After years of rigorous studying, around-the-clock rotations, and incredibly challenging tests, I passed the board exam. I'd never seen as much joy in my mother's eyes as the day I received my test results. Then, that joy quickly diminished when I told her I wouldn't be accepting a residency and instead, was leaving to live abroad.

To visit Verona.

I needed a fresh start, if only for a while.

I vividly recall the way she lightly cradled my face in her hand and said, "Farai grandi cose, non importa dove scegli di vivere." *You will do great things no matter where you choose to live.*

Whether I had done great things while abroad was up for debate.

Now that I am back, my questionable practices have followed.

And apparently, my acceptance of commitments is also questionable.

Leaning back in my chair, I bring my bourbon to

my lips and sip it slowly, taking in the crowd as I do. Clinking glasses, boisterous laughs, and the ear-numbing tone of overlapping chatter fill the room.

According to Sully, those with the deepest pockets and the most power in the state are in attendance. Though it is difficult to recognize some beneath their masks, I can see he was accurate in his assessment.

Much to my dismay, I have also stumbled my gaze upon a few faces I'd be happy to never see again in my lifetime.

Especially one.

Joseph Paladino.

Second son of Maurizio Paladino, the man who killed my uncle. Years of hatred have simmered between my family and theirs.

After the murder of my uncle, Papà was successful in avoiding Maurizio, but the feud never settled. In fact, it intensified when Enzo and I reached our teenage years. Though that was because we finally came head to head with Maurizio's sons, and when Enzo got into a fistfight with Joseph at a party, I didn't hesitate to involve myself.

Coincidentally, or perhaps not, that was also the first time I had laid eyes on their sister since running into her at a dinner party at the mayor's house years prior.

Having already been riled from my run-in with her, not appreciating how my body perked up at the sight of the enemy, I was all too happy to take my aggressions out on a Paladino. No matter how much my hatred burned, I would never lay a hand on a female, so her brother showing up when he did was like a gift from God.

In hindsight, two-on-one was not an honorable fight, but it was one Enzo and I both desperately craved.

Together we broke two of his ribs, split his lip, and gave him a nasty black eye we heard took weeks to fade.

At the moment, it was everything we had been waiting years for, but the aftermath was less than desirable.

Maurizio paid Papà a visit the very next day, escalating the feud between families.

A clear line was drawn, and both men made it clear there would be bloodshed if it were ever crossed.

Papà could be ruthless when provoked. Something I had seen very little of in my years, but did not doubt for a moment.

Part of the reason I left the country after upholding Mamma's wishes of medical school was because I didn't trust myself not to cross the line.

For Papà.

For Uncle Gabriele.

We had laid docile for long enough, and I was tired of letting the Paladinos think they had the upper hand.

Joseph Paladino had been running the Lucchetti name through the mud our entire youth, and I was at my wit's end listening to Papà when he said to do nothing.

Nothing was the *opposite* of what Enzo and I wanted to do.

My fists against him felt *good*. Necessary.

But the Lucchetti-Paladino war was deeper than me or Enzo, or even Joseph, and Papà insisted that I stand down. Until Papà was physically unable to protect our family, or the Paladinos crossed that line, I *needed* to stand down.

As the years passed, it became harder and harder to obey his wishes. Even with the distraction of medical school and focusing on mia famiglia and friends.

I knew what needed to be done.

Leaving allowed me to stand down.

And now that I've returned, I continue to stand down.

Still, it doesn't stop my hands from balling into fists at the sight of Joseph leaning against the wall of the ballroom, deep in conversation with a man I can't place. I study them for long moments, willing myself to stay calm despite the anger that stirs within.

Rubbing my hand along my short beard, I follow their line of sight, my breath catching in my throat at the sight of the most breathtakingly bellimessa woman I have ever seen.

She dances with an older man, the crimson of her gown billowing behind her as he twirls her effortlessly. Her laugh carries, piercing through the mindless chatter throughout the ballroom.

Even behind her mask, I can see the way her eyes glow, a stark contrast to the darkness of her brown hair swept back into a mass of intricate curls.

She's sensational.

Mesmerizing.

A growl sparks through my chest when Sully steps into view with a cocky smile on his polished face. Leaning forward, I press my palm against his leg to shift him as I support my elbows on my knees, continuing to watch the dark-haired angel.

"Did you hear me?" Sully asks, trying to garner my attention, but I'm transfixed on the dance floor.

"No," I bark in his direction.

He chuckles, slapping my shoulder. "I said, I just got the heiress of Centennial Hotels to give me her number. *And* she agreed to meet me later."

"How wonderful for you."

"Sly, I expect a little more excitement from my wingman—"

"I'm not your wingman."

"Fine, a little more excitement from my date to this lovely ev—"

"I'm not your *date*, amico."

Sully laughs again when my eyes flicker to his for the briefest of moments. Pulling the chair out next to me, he rotates it to face the direction I'm looking in and takes a seat. For a moment, he's quiet, and I assume he's people-watching.

"She's beautiful, isn't she?" he asks, amusement dancing through his tone. Clearly, he has figured out who I can't stop staring at.

My eyes narrow. "Sì," I say. I give him my attention this time, sensing he has more to say.

Grinning widely, Sully relaxes in his chair, draping his arm across the back. "Beautiful. Delicate. *Forbidden*."

I look back to the woman who's captured my curiosity, watching as she now dances with Joseph's friend. A scowl rests on her beautiful features, and she looks stiff in his arms.

Uncomfortable.

Her body language causes me to straighten.

"What do you mean, forbidden?"

Sully smirks and goes silent and watches those who are on the dance floor, taking in the sea of tuxedos and ball gowns. Moments later, he asks, "You really don't know?"

I don't bother answering, instead keeping my focus on the most beautiful woman in the room, watching the expressions on her face change. I'm trying to figure out what the man she dances with could possibly be saying to etch the clear signs of disgust and hatred on her face, when Sully places his hand on my shoulder and pulls me toward him, leaning his own body so he meets me halfway. Lowering his voice, he tells me the one thing that could shatter this feeling harbored in my chest. "She's a Paladino. *Vinnie* Paladino."

The room fades away as his words ricochet in my mind, ringing out against the sound of the blood rushing to my ears. The room around her becomes a blur, but she moves with perfect clarity as my eyes trail her.

She's a Paladino.

Vinnie Paladino.

How could I not recognize her? Even with the mask that conceals so little.

Fury erupts within me, squashing the flickers of desire that had begun to grow.

Meeting Sully's eyes, I shake my head in disbelief. "How?"

"What do you mean, *how*?"

"How is *that* Vinnie Paladino? How could I not recognize her?"

Sully looks at me like I'm the most ignorant person in New York before he rolls his eyes and laughs loudly. "Oh, Sly. Buddy. Because only you—well, you and maybe Enzo—would be so buried in hatred for that family that you'd turn a blind eye to how smokin' hot she's become."

I turn my gaze back to her—I can't help it—and watch her dance. Her expression has turned to sadness, and the look on her face makes something tug in my chest.

"Who is she dancing with?" I ask, knowing he'll know.

Sully is one of the most charming men in the city. There's not a woman or man who doesn't fawn over him. Even when their motives are not genuine, he still gets bathed in attention.

He scoffs in a way that tells me he isn't a fan of the man, either. "August St. Jean."

Ah, yes. August St. Jean. Coined New York's most eligible bachelor. He's a favorite in the papers right now, known for his philanthropy, deep pockets, and good looks. I'm surprised I didn't recognize him, though I haven't seen him since before I left the country, and even then, it was in passing.

From what I hear, most women would be overjoyed to be in the arms of August, so I am unclear as to why *she* looks so unhappy.

"Any idea why she looks like she'd rather chew her own arm off than be in his?" I try to mask the curiosity in my voice, but I can feel it come through.

Sully pays it no mind and instead stares down at his phone as he sends a text. He's biting his lip, so presumably, he's sent it to the hotel heiress from earlier.

Vinnie steals my attention yet again, and this time as August turns their bodies, I notice the way he looks over her shoulder at her brother. His expression turns sinister for a fleeting moment before the mask of magnetism blankets his face again. Though Joseph is not so quick to hide his intentions, the smirk playing across his lips lingers for all to see.

He's enjoying his sister's discomfort. Whatever look just passed between him and August was one of intention.

And for some reason, that ignites a rage in me so powerful it catches me off guard.

The melody of the song comes to an end, and as Vinnie tries to pull away, August curls his fingers at her waist so tightly I can see the fabric crumpling in his grasp. Her hands press against his arms to push him away, but he is unrelenting, leaning down to whisper something in her ear. She stills, and though I can only see the profile of her face from their angle, I don't miss the way her body freezes, and her mouth drops slightly in what I imagine is shock. Then he releases her.

August is all smiles as he bows like a gentleman before walking away, leaving her noticeably upset.

I should feel satisfaction at the hurt of a Paladino, even if the pain is emotional, but the feeling that pangs in my chest is anything but merriment.

Another song begins, and the couples begin to waltz as though they've waited their entire lives for these dances. For many, they have. But as I watch Vinnie stand in the middle of the dance floor, her body begins to move, but not with the music. No, her body begins to visibly shake, trembling, whether with tears or with rage, I'm unsure.

Instinct pulls me from my chair, and as I stand, Vinnie snaps out of her daze and practically runs toward the eastern double doors of the ballroom.

Before I can fathom what is happening, I move through the crowd, following after her.

"Sly!" Sully calls from behind me, but I ignore him, politely moving through the groups of people conversing, drinking, and laughing.

I'm a little more than halfway to the doors when I see Joseph slip through them first, and suddenly the world turns red.

Speeding up, I push through a circle of young women who gasp at my sudden intrusion, slinking into the large foyer of the ballroom of the Centennial Hotel.

When the doors close behind me, cutting off the

music and the noise of the guests, I seem to pull myself from my own daze.

What am I doing out here? Why am I chasing after a *Paladino?*

And why does it feel like I would burn this whole hotel to the ground just to find her and make sure she's okay?

I'm debating on which way to go when hushed voices suddenly come from somewhere on my right.

Moving as quietly as I can, I walk toward them, straining to hear what they're saying. Off the foyer is a hallway, and as I turn the corner, I see there are two more alcoves that likely lead to more. From so far away, I have no way of knowing if it even is Vinnie and her brother or just another pair who needed a moment away from the masquerade.

Quietly, I keep walking, careful with my steps until the voice becomes clear, and with it, my caution goes out the window. That red ball of rage inside me flickers to life when I hear her exasperated voice say, "Get away from me, Joseph."

Then I practically run.

Chapter 6

Vinnie

"**G**et away from me, Joseph," I say through gritted teeth, willing everything I have in me not to scream.

I *know* he's the one behind August's sudden interest in me; feeding him lies laced with promises he can't keep.

August is a disgusting man. He puts on quite the facade for the newspapers, but behind that is a selfish, degrading, and pigheaded man.

A shudder rolls through me, his words replaying in my mind.

"Smile, Vinnie, you're dancing with the city's most desired man."

"What's the matter, Vinnie? You'd be lucky to have my cock inside you."

"Just you wait, Vinnie. One day I'll make you my wife, and you'll have no choice in the matter. Didn't you hear? Your father

has pretty much promised you to me, thanks to the suggestion of your brother."

Father wouldn't dare…would he?

"What's the matter, Vinnie?" Joseph sneers, his words echoing August's. "You didn't enjoy your time dancing with August?"

Turning to face him, I lift my hand, pointing my finger in his face. "Don't you dare, Joseph. You *know* he makes my skin crawl."

Catching my finger, he squeezes as he pulls it away from his face. "And don't *you* dare, dear sister. August is his own man. If he wants to pursue you, who am I to stop him?"

"And his insane idea of marriage? That wasn't your suggestion? *Your* disgusting idea?"

He smirks maliciously, his gray-blue eyes that match my own growing darker with the hatred within him. "Oh no, baby sis. That absolutely was my idea. I'd love to see you with a man like August. Someone who will put you in your place and keep you there."

"How can your hatred for your own flesh and blood be so deep?" I yell, throwing both hands into the air.

"You lower your tone," he seethes, his jaw tightening with force.

As much as it kills me to obey, I do. With a softer voice, I continue. "What have I ever done to earn the way you treat me, Joseph? I'm your *sister*. The sibling closest in age to you. We used to be best friends…"

"I was a fool back then, but now I see you for what you truly are, Vincenza."

"For what I truly am? And what exactly am I, Joey?"

"Do not call me Joey," he snaps, taking a step toward me.

I watch as his hand balls into a fist, and it causes me to take a step back.

My brother has never physically harmed me, but I've also never seen him act like he is now. He's scaring me, but I try not to let it show on my face.

"Joseph—"

His lip curls upward as though his name on my lips is the foulest thing in the universe. The second of silence is all it takes before we hear footsteps rounding the corner. Someone is coming, and the breath catches in my chest, wondering if it's August.

Joseph starts to walk away, but before he moves too far, he stops and says, "I can't wait to make your life a living hell, sister."

And then he leaves.

As he disappears down the corridor, the shadow of someone behind me appears.

Turning, I'm surprised to see a man, his shoulder pressed against the wall as he leans into it. His arms are crossed over his chest, and he looks past me down to where my brother went.

He's exceptionally handsome in his all-black tuxedo, looking lethal as he stares daggers down the empty hallway. His dark hair is short and well-styled, as is his well-groomed facial hair.

But his hazel eyes...they're piercing. Colors swirl

together, hues of green and brown, and there's something about them that sparks recognition.

"Did he hurt you?" he asks, his Italian accent thick through his words.

"Not physically," I tell him. "That was my brother."

"It is clear that family relationships mean nothing to Joseph Paladino. Has he ever hurt you?"

My eyes narrow on him, my lips pursing as I work to solve the puzzle of how I know this man and why he finds it appropriate to ask such a personal question. "Not physically," I repeat. "You know who I am?"

"Sì, and you know who I am, so let's save ourselves the back and forth we went through many years ago, Vincenza."

He reaches around and unties his masquerade mask, and just like that, I'm transported back in time, knowing exactly who this man is. Once the realization hits, I *see* him.

Beneath the features of a man, I see the boy who I met so briefly but who made such an impact.

"I thought you were out of the country," I question, knowing it's quite possibly the lamest thing I could have come up with, but still, the words trickled out of my mouth quicker than I could stop them.

"Keeping tabs on me?"

"The maids talk."

My heart is hammering in my chest at the smirk that dusts his lips as he pushes off the wall and takes two steps toward me. Now that he's closer, his scent floods my senses and smells better than I remember it.

I've been raised to hate this man—hate his family—to the depths of my being, yet just being in his presence makes me weak in the knees.

Lifting my chin, I stare him down. My arms cross over my chest as he comes closer, crowding my space just like he did all those years ago. The memory of that night is still vivid. It took years before my imagination stopped creating scenarios of *more*.

"I hate to be the one to tell you this," he says with sarcasm as he places his palm against the wall behind me, caging me in with one arm. "Your brother is dirt on the bottom of my shoe—the scum that walks this earth. He is the reason things go bump in the night, and children have nightmares of monsters under the bed. He makes your father look like a saint when we both know he's anything but."

"I'm under no illusion that my father nor my brother are upstanding men. Why are you here, Sly? Felt like reliving the past and being an ass to a woman who has nothing to do with the grudge you hold against my family?"

He laughs, and the sound is so beautiful I have to force myself not to smile at it—to remember that while he clearly doesn't like me, I don't like him either.

"A grudge? Bella ragazza, this is more than a grudge. Your father murdered my blood, *my uncle*, and has threatened my family for more than a decade."

"It has nothing to do with me."

"It has everything to do with you. You're a Paladino."

"I may be a Paladino, but I was a *child* when my father did what he did. Your feud is with my father, not me."

"It is with anyone who has your surname," he scoffs.

Exhaling a breathy laugh, I push my hand against his chest to distance him. He backs up without any hesitation or lingering, which I can't help but find refreshing. Most men would have pushed back or stepped closer, but with the simple gesture, he took the hint and gave me the space I wordlessly asked for.

"I get it—you hate me and anyone with my family name. So I'll repeat my question, Sly. Why are you here?"

His eyes flare, then he turns on his heel, facing away from me. I watch him push his fingers through his hair in frustration, then swipe them down his face.

I stay silent, watching him closely. His reaction. His body language. He seems as confused as I feel.

Looking over his shoulder, his eyes sweep over me slowly, as though committing me to memory. "I don't know," he answers. "I shouldn't have followed you out here, but I saw him and needed to know he wouldn't harm you. The way he looked at you in the ballroom was not how a brother looks at a sister. It is how someone looks at an enemy. A threat."

His answer slams into my chest, the admission softening the anger I've been clinging to for the last several minutes, yet it also puts me on edge.

I'm at a loss for words. And it seems like he is too, because before I can think of an appropriate response, he shakes his head, runs his hand through his hair again, and then walks away.

Silently, I watch him leave, following the same path he came.

I think about calling out to him. Chasing after him. Asking him to stay.

But for what?

It doesn't matter that I'm still just as interested in learning more about him as I was when we were younger. It makes no difference that we're adults and should be free to make our own choices. Or that his words were truthful and honest, and I wanted more of them.

My curiosity about him doesn't matter.

The attraction I'm feeling is a moot point.

Because at the end of the day, I'm a Paladino, and he's a Lucchetti, and I'm confident if my father were to find out about the conflict I'm feeling about a man I've been raised to hate, he'd disown me.

And if my father didn't disown me, I have no doubts my brother would find a way to *kill* me.

Chapter 7

Sly

The door slams closed behind me, rattling on its hinges as I enter my dark apartment. Tugging at the buttons on my black dress shirt, the lights above me flicker to life as I walk through the open concept, the motion sensors doing almost too good of a job.

It's jarring, getting used to a new home. New sounds, the layout. What few personal belongings I moved out of storage hardly made a dent, most still sitting in the cardboard boxes I haven't bothered to unpack.

This space is too big for my liking, but I didn't have time to ask Mamma to tour it prior to digitally signing the lease. At almost three-thousand square feet, the four bedroom, four and a half bathroom luxury apartment is ostentatious and everything I don't desire in a home.

Cold.

Empty.

Outrageously modern and state-of-the-art.

But I recognize the need to maintain appearances, especially when behind closed doors what I will be doing with my time is less than ethical.

The Kenna was the perfect choice in buildings. Being a firm believer in everything happens for a reason, I jumped at the opportunity when I saw an availability. This building rarely had vacancies.

It's also walking distance from the other space I rent.

Four blocks away, adjacent to one of the Upper East Side's most popular markets, lies a descending staircase to an unmarked door, taking you deep beneath the ground.

Early in my European travels, I had the realization that not all were privileged to afford healthcare. I knew this—I was not naïve to it prior, but *seeing* it…*thinking* about it…so many are plagued with hardships.

Hardships no family should struggle through. Access to medical care shouldn't be considered a *luxury*.

We are all humans.

The only thing that makes us different from one another is wealth.

It's why I began offering my knowledge—my *services* —to those in need.

I've spent years in the hospital with Papà—practically from the time I could toddle down the hallways— and in college, studying. My surname gives me privilege in Papà's hospital, both here in New York and in Italy, where I have access to medications many cannot afford.

During my years in Europe, through unofficial

house calls and meetings in less than desirable places, I helped many patients. And I will continue to help.

Returning to the States and entering a residency program held no interest for me, but this—this is something I can be proud of. Something I can do with my knowledge for the good of others.

Illegal, yes.

But worthwhile.

Removing my gun from the holster in the back of my slacks, I punch in the code to the safe concealed in the coat closet. As I set the firearm on the shelf, my phone vibrates.

Securing the safe, I remove my phone and converse with my friends through text message as I continue to my kitchen in search of something to eat.

ENZO

So how was your date last night? Which one of you wore the dress?

SULLY

Sly did, and it was gorgeous. Dark green. Really brought out his eyes.

ENZO

I hope you wore a tie that matched, like a gentleman would.

Hilarious.

SULLY

Enzo, you know Sly isn't the best of planners. He told me he was wearing red, so I wore a red tie. We looked like Christmas.

ENZO

A little premature since it's July.

SULLY

Hey, Christmas in July is a thing.

Are you two finished yet?

SULLY

Never.

ENZO

How was it, actually?

SULLY

Fine until my date caught sight of a
beautiful woman and chased her out of
the ballroom.

Swiping out of the group message and into my indi-
vidual message with Sully, I pound my fingers on the
screen quickly and press send.

Silenzo, Sully. I swear to all that is holy
if you continue with that story, I will
end you.

Whoa, whoa, whoa, hound dog. I take it
things didn't go well with Vinnie?

There was nothing to go well. I didn't
follow her out. I merely left at the same
time.

I can smell your bullshit from here, and
it's really stinky.

Toggling back over to the group message, I scowl at the screen.

ENZO

What do you mean? Who was she?

I didn't chase anyone out of the ballroom. I just happened to leave at the same time as others did.

SULLY

You didn't even give me a goodnight kiss.

You were a terrible date.

ENZO

So no one got laid last night?

SULLY

Who's to say I didn't?

Sully went home with the Centennial Hotel heiress' phone number.

SULLY

Maybe I went home with her, too.

ENZO

Did you?

SULLY

No.

SULLY

But that's only because she didn't want to ditch her date.

ENZO

Ouch.

SULLY

Her date was her cousin.

> We all know you're into some
> interesting endeavors, but even you
> have to draw the line at incest.

SULLY

Her FEMALE cousin, asshat.

ENZO

Well, this conversation is wildly
disappointing.

> Anyone want to meet for dinner? I'm
> craving Mamma's spaghetti, and it's too
> late to bother her for some. I'm going to
> go down to Di Mercutio.

SULLY

Aw, you asking me out on another date,
Sylvester?

ENZO

You have a strange obsession with that
restaurant.

> Eating there is like an old amico's
> embrace.

ENZO

I'll be there in thirty.

SULLY

Gotta sit this one out, fellas. The heiress
and I have a sexting date tonight.

ENZO

So you have a date with your hand, then?

SULLY

Yep.

That was more than I ever hoped to know.

ENZO

See you soon, Sly.

Di Mercutio is nestled on the corner of 99th and 3rd, next to a Jiu Jitzu gym and a Thai restaurant—walking distance from my new building.

In the few weeks since I've been back, I've eaten here at least twice a week. The staff is beginning to know me well. So well, in fact, they secure me the same table next to a window, so when I dine alone, I can people-watch. It's also open late, which I appreciate on nights like these.

The cuisine is home-style Italian with an upscale aesthetic, which really just means they use white linens and overcharge for their wine. But the food is delizioso, and the waitstaff is friendly, so I frequent the establishment.

As I walk in tonight, a hostess by the name of Hattie greets me with a warm smile. The scent of garlic and rich sauces permeates the air, reminding me how hungry I am.

"Welcome back, Mr. Lucchetti. Your table is waiting. Will anyone be joining you tonight?"

"Sì, grazie. My cousin is on his way."

"Very well. Let me show you to your table."

She leads me through the restaurant, which is still very busy for such a late hour. The patrons range from families to couples, to small friend groups, and though everyone chats amongst themselves, the restaurant maintains a relaxed and semi-quiet atmosphere.

With my menu in hand, I thank the hostess and she retreats to her podium while I wait for the server. Nearly fifteen minutes later, after I have ordered myself a glass of merlot and my spaghetti and meatballs, Enzo slips into the seat across from me.

Picking up his menu, he skims it and mutters his greeting. "Sorry I'm late."

"On the contrary," I say as the waiter approaches again to take Enzo's drink order. "You told me thirty minutes, and you are practically right on the dot."

"Eggplant bolognese and sparkling water, please," Enzo tells the waiter before focusing his attention on me. "How's the new apartment treating you?"

"It's too large and too empty," I reply blandly, picking up my glass and swirling my merlot that the waiter places in front of me.

"I offered you my extra room."

"Sì, but you know I prefer to live alone."

"I know. I'm just saying."

A tension settles in the air between us, and I glance

out the window as a couple passes by. His arm is around her shoulders, resting below the fur of her parka.

Tourists.

I can tell by their attire. It is still summer, and yet she is cold.

I hear Enzo sigh, but don't look at him. It's what he wants—to talk. And I'm not sure I'm ready, but I know it's time.

Although he is still one of my closest friends, our relationship has been strained for many years. I'd like to say it happened when I left, but truly, it happened many years before, when Mamma pushed me into medical school. She tried her antics on Enzo as well, but instead, he chose a different path.

Enzo is incredibly intelligent, so much so that he began investing small amounts of money as a teenager and was able to grow it into a substantial savings that he used to purchase a failing hedge fund company, turning it into one of the fastest scaling businesses New York has seen in decades.

Still, he fears this isn't good enough. He looks up to Papà after he stepped into a father-figure role when Uncle Gabriele passed, and he thinks because he did not become a doctor, he has failed mia mamma e mio papà.

And that is simply untrue.

When I left the country and took Sully with me, it created a larger rift between us. Looking back, I can see he felt abandoned. We were his best friends, and we left together, and though Enzo knows *why* I left, I know now that it still hurt him deeply.

But I don't know how to apologize to him for something I do not regret doing. My time away shaped me into the man I am now, and for that, I am grateful.

"It was no easy choice, Lorenzo."

Turning, our eyes meet, and behind his I can see the pain of the boy he has all but buried deep within. The boy that's still healing.

"There was a monster within that was clawing his way out. He sought vengeance and blood, and though I worked to keep him hidden, I was failing. My choices were black and white. Stay and risk our family, or remove myself."

"You ran," he accuses, his voice low and gravelly.

"I left to protect our family." Raising my wine to my lips, I take a sip and let the flavors settle on my tongue.

Enzo scoffs and looks out the window to avoid my stare. "You took the coward's way out and left me here to figure it out on my own."

His words enrage me, but I don't let it show. I bite my tongue, swallowing the words I long to say to my cousin. Instead, I give him the watered-down version. "I would have killed him, Lorenzo. Joseph Paladino would have died by my hand and we both know it. It was only a matter of time."

"And now?"

"And now my monster lies dormant. While I was in my country, and throughout my travels, I learned everything there was to know about myself. Who I am. Who

I want to be. How to control my emotions and turn them from negative to positive. How to let go of my *rage*. I was able to use my schooling in a way that allowed me to help others in a meaningful way. I do not regret leaving, Enzo. It created me, and the man who shares this meal with you tonight is not the same man who left. And that is a good thing."

As I finish my statement and exhale a shaky breath, the waiter arrives with our dinners and sets them down in front of us. He takes his time grating parmesan over both plates and ensures everything is to our satisfaction.

Once he is gone, we both begin to eat. The spaghetti is everything I hoped it'd be, and after a few bites, I set my fork down and reach for my wine.

After sipping it, I stare at its rich burgundy shade and give it a small swirl for good measure before placing it down. When I look back up at my cousin, my eyes wander behind him to a table where three women sit. There's a blonde with her back to me and as she shifts slightly, I catch sight of the most beautiful face I can never admit to enjoying the sight of.

With a mass of curled dark-brown hair and a wide smile, she shines radiantly, lighting up the whole restaurant with her effervescence.

Vincenza.

The joy she exudes puts a scowl on my face. What a waste it is that all that beauty would be bestowed on a Paladino.

Immediately, I look out the window, trying not to

remember her sweet scent of cherry blossoms, or the way her eyes sparkled when she looked up at me.

It has been less than twenty-four hours since I've seen her, yet it feels like all the wonders of the first time.

I hate it.

Hate that her beauty captivates me, and that *something* about her calls to me. I need to squash the feeling and banish her back to the depths of my mind, where she is nothing.

No one.

Just a name connected to the family I loathe.

But seeing her *here*, in my favorite restaurant, makes her existence all the more real.

That feeling in my chest stirs again—the same one I felt a flicker of last night—and I can't help but bring my fist up to my sternum and rub it with my knuckles to dull the ache.

Sparing another glance, I take her in. The light pink sweater she wears. The movement of her thumb along the stem of her wine glass. The way she gives her friends her full attention and listens intently.

Last night, I convinced myself it was the party—the seduction of a masquerade—that had my pulse racing and my curiosity piqued, but now I'm not so sure. Her words echo through my mind, *"It has nothing to do with me."*

And maybe it doesn't. We were both just children, after all. But still, it does not change the fact that she's a *Paladino*.

Looking away, I take another bite of my dinner and

change the subject with Enzo. "How is Leah? You haven't mentioned her lately."

"Out of the picture. When the elevator security system catches the woman you're dating on the phone boasting about how much money you have, it's time to pull the plug."

"I'm sorry," I say, and I mean it. My cousin has been lonely for a long time. A nice woman would suit him, but instead he attracts the ones who care about his money more than his heart.

He chews his food and as he does, like a magnet, my eyes find their way to Vinnie again. She's laughing, cradling a glass of white wine in her hand as she leans forward, engaged in her conversation.

What is it about her that I can't seem to ignore? She is quite literally the last person on earth I should have a fascination toward. Gritting my teeth, I pull my gaze and use my fork to move my spaghetti around the plate.

"I'm not." Enzo brings my attention to him again. "What about you? Meet anyone while abroad?" He takes another bite.

I sneak a look back over his shoulder at Vinnie. *No, but it seems as though I've met someone here who's unfortunately piqued my interest.*

"No. A few enjoyable flings, but nothing serious. Sully fell in love every other weekend, however."

This makes Enzo laugh, and his laughter makes me smile. His face brightens when he is happy, and I realize how much I miss the more carefree side of him. "Of course he did. The guy still hasn't learned the difference between his heart and his dick yet."

"One day he will. It will take the right woman to sneak up on him."

A comfortable silence settles between us as we finish our meals, and I take the opportunity to continue sneaking glances over his shoulder at Vinnie. She hasn't noticed me yet, and I hope to keep it that way.

The women finish off their drinks and pay their bill, and as they stand to leave, a busboy takes his cue, hurrying over to remove their empty plates from the table.

For some reason unbeknownst to me, my heart rate quickens while watching Vinnie shrug on her cream-colored shawl, her hand sweeping beneath her hair to free it from where the fabric covers her shoulders.

The urge to stand and go to her claws at me.

I want to know she's okay—that her brother didn't further harass her last night. Her smile tells me she is, but I know all too well how easy it is to mask your pain.

Reaching to the chair next to her, she grabs her handbag and settles it on her forearm, turning back to the blonde woman to say something. As she does, she scans the room and it takes mere seconds for her gaze to connect with mine. Her eyes widen as her pink-painted lips part in surprise.

Satisfaction slips through me at her reaction. Still, I school my expression, making sure my features stay neutral so she doesn't see the amusement I'm feeling.

In return, she glares at me. It's difficult to imagine what she might be thinking.

I simply smirk.

With the least remarkable timing, the waiter reappears with our check, breaking my focus as I reach for it. When I look back up, Vinnie is already gone.

Opening the check-sleeve, I skim the total as I pull out my card and hand everything back to the waiter.

Enzo and I stopped arguing over who would be the one to pay many years ago. We now hold an unspoken agreement that whoever reaches for the bill first takes care of it.

"Thanks," he says, dabbing at his mouth with his napkin before placing it back down.

Nodding my head, I remove my own napkin from my lap and place it onto the table. Pushing backward in my chair, I stand, ready to leave. "Anytime, cousin."

As we pass by the hostess podium, I thank the woman before reaching for the door and holding it open for Enzo to pass through. The moment I pull it back, the cool New York air contrasts against the warmth of the restaurant, and nearby, a car's horn sounds.

Just outside the restaurant, a black town car idles, and Enzo nods to it. "Want a ride?"

It's tempting, but I know the walk will do me well. I need to clear my head, because as much as I want to deny it, seeing Vinnie again has messed with my thoughts.

Shaking my head, I tell him, "I'm happy to walk, but thank you for having dinner with me."

"Always happy to meet you for a bite—just tell me when and where," he says in earnest, pulling me by the shoulder into a hug. We embrace, then he climbs into the backseat and shuts the door, enclosing himself inside.

The tint is too dark to see him, but as the driver pulls away from the curb, I lift my hand to wave good-bye, watching him go.

Turning to head home, I hardly take three steps before sensing I am not alone, and within seconds, I feel a soft hand wrap around my wrist, pulling me into the shadows of the building.

Chapter 8

Vinnie

"**D**id you follow me here?" I accuse from the shadows. My hand around his wrist slows his steps, and as he turns to look at me, eyes flaring, the air constricts in my lungs.

Using my strength, I pull him closer to the building and into the darkness of it, away from prying eyes.

Dinner with Raina and Evelyn was everything my soul needed after the day I'd had, and the last thing I expected was to look over and see *him*.

Sly Lucchetti had gotten under my skin last night, which is *exactly* where he doesn't belong.

After my driver took me back to my apartment, I stormed in, slamming my clutch down on the oversized kitchen island, which startled Cecilia.

My former nanny turned "maid" moved to my new apartment with me, which makes my mother feel better about me living alone. I use the term maid lightly because, yes, she helps me with just about every aspect of my life, but I don't treat her like most people treat their staff. I treat her like a friend because that's exactly what she is—she just also happily accepts the paycheck my father gives her each week.

Last night, she listened while I went through the events of my entire night, telling her about the awkward dance with Mason, every despicable word August said, and about the strange encounter with Sly. I spared no detail, knowing she would never breathe a word.

Her advice for me was to just forget about the run-in with Sly. We'd made it how many years since we saw each other since the party when we were teens? It was a one-off—a fluke.

Well, I must have the worst luck in the entire world.

Pointing my French manicured fingernail into the middle of his chest, I ask again. "Seriously, why are you following me?"

His laugh is husky as he steps into me, forcing *me* to step back, but there's nowhere to go. My back nudges against the wall.

Refusing to cower, I tilt my head up.

He leans down, his presence looming over me. "Now why would I follow you, *principessa*? I have dined here many times and have never seen you. So perhaps I should be worried about *you* following *me*."

"You're delusional," I hiss, annoyed by the sheer audacity of his accusation.

"And you're wasting my time." His eyes narrow, but he doesn't back away or make any move to leave.

Instead, he pins me with his stare, and it feels like

time stands still. The noise of the city fades, and the cars and people who pass us zoom by in a blur. Before I realize what's happening, my chest is rising and falling with heavy breaths, mirroring his. The magnetism is palatable, crackling in the air between us.

Until a car horn blares, pulling us both back to reality.

What on earth was that?

Sly steps back quickly, like he's been electrocuted, putting distance between us.

"Stop following me," I sneer, pushing past him as I pull out my phone. A simple text lights up the screen.

ROSS

I'm idling outside of the market on E. 97th, Miss Paladino.

While walking out of the restaurant, I texted my driver, Ross, to meet me a few streets over, claiming I needed a light walk. It doesn't surprise me he's already there waiting.

Turning onto 3rd, I cross my arms and make my way toward Haven Market. My black suede stilettos click against the pavement, but they do little to mask the recognizable sound of footsteps following me.

Ignoring them, I hold my head high and keep walking, wishing my legs would carry me a little faster.

For every three of my steps, he takes one, and as his footsteps close in on me, I huff in annoyance. "Who's following who again?"

"It's not my fault you chose to walk in the direction

I need to go." His voice is thick with boredom, but surprisingly, I sense no irritation.

Which is all well and fine considering I have enough for the both of us.

It takes everything in me not to spin on my heel and tell him off—just the audacity of him following me is enough to make my blood boil.

Over my shoulder, I say, "You know, there are tons of other directions you could have taken and still ended up in the same place."

It's dumb and hardly makes sense, but accurate. He could have walked up a block and still ended up wherever he is going.

Reaching the corner of E. 98th, I stare at the red hand illuminated on the crosswalk indicator and wait for it to change. Sly's footsteps stop some distance behind me, and I blow out a frustrated breath, still refusing to give him the satisfaction of looking over my shoulder.

He never answered me either, not that there was anything to really say.

Pulling out my phone, I send a text to my driver.

Almost there.

The indicator begins to beep, and I fumble with my clutch, trying to put my phone back inside. But I'm distracted knowing he's standing behind me, watching me. My hands are shaky, and rather than letting him watch me struggle, I end up keeping a hold of my phone.

"Green means go," Sly's sultry words breeze past me as he steps off the curb, crossing the street with purpose.

A rumble of a groan reverberates in my chest as I step off after him, making sure to stay a few steps behind.

Which is a mistake, because now I have a perfect view of the way his cigarette pants hug his hips and butt. Inwardly, I groan again, for noticing.

Another block, and he stops at the crosswalk, and I'm forced to do the same. "Are you planning on following me home, *principessa?*" he scoffs, not bothering to turn around.

Home.

He lives around here?

Caught off-guard by his words, my eyes snap up from my phone, and it's then I realize I'm in front of Haven Market. Choosing to ignore him, I walk closer so I can peer to my right as I look for my town car.

Ross is standing on the curb, waiting for me.

Before I go to it, though, I gather the nerves that are balled up in my stomach and push them away, lifting my chin. "Never in your wildest dreams will a woman like me follow you home."

I'm not sure where the confidence comes from, or how the shake in my voice doesn't shine through, but I deliver that sentence—which really wasn't even a great comeback—and turn on my heel.

As I approach, Ross straightens and opens my door, greeting me with a warm hello. A curt smile is all I can muster before I look back over my shoulder, seeing Sly watching from the distance. His expression is stone, but despite the incessant beeping of the crosswalk indicator, he stares me down, watching as I get in the car.

When we pull away from the curb, I tell myself the windows are tinted so he won't see if I look over my shoulder through the back window—so I do. But by the time I turn, he's disappearing past the building across the street and out of my line of sight.

A rush of air escapes my lungs as I settle back into the soft leather of the seat, and realize how hard my heart is beating.

Sly Lucchetti has gotten under my skin all right, and it looks like he'll be making himself quite comfortable while he's there.

The Paladinos are a lot of things, but above all, we are loyal to each other. Our family is religious in the sense that Sundays are sacred, and seeing each other is mandatory.

Period.

It's been this way for as long as I can remember.

Sunday mornings, our family meets at Saint Sebastian's for ten a.m. mass, and from there, we return to my parents' house for brunch.

I say house with the utmost modesty.

My parents live on West 57th Street, smack dab in the middle of NoHo, in a home my father had custom-built for my mother. While still engaged, she insisted on raising their future children in a *house*, not an apartment, and had been adamant about finding a brownstone over a penthouse.

My father had just landed his first half-a-billion dollar contract and told the finest architects New York had to offer my mother's vision and that the sky was the limit.

After finding an available building to purchase on a prestigious Manhattan street, they promptly gutted and rebuilt it into a place that looked like a charming, upscale brownstone from the front, when in reality, it was a three-story mansion in plain sight.

It was ridiculous, and still, it was home.

And every Sunday, when I walk through the French door entry, a sense of contentment washes over me.

Nostalgia mixed with comfort.

That is, until my brother arrives.

Joseph is the reason I dread every family brunch. It's always something with him, and without fail, he'll be there to whisper idiotic ideas in father's ear.

My heart shatters every time I think about our strained relationship and how things used to be.

Often, I wonder at what point he stopped thinking of me as a sister and started thinking of me as an enemy. I've never wanted any of the things he *assumes* I want.

My father's business.

Our family's wealth.

Recognition and fame.

The only thing I've ever wanted is the love of my family, and, one day, a great love for myself.

"Hello, baby sister," he greets, singsonging through a sneer. It's an act he puts on in front of our parents. Pretending as though he's a doting big brother.

He bends down, leveling himself to where I sit, and presses his lips to the top of my head.

Cecilia and I share a look.

"I see you've brought the help along with you again," he says, pulling his linen napkin into his lap as he sits. His eyes meet mine, and behind them, I can see the malice.

"Joseph," my mother chastises. "Cecilia has been with us for more than a decade—she's family. Treat her as such."

"As have others we've had on payroll for longer, yet I don't see them sitting with us."

"Joseph, that's enough. Show some respect," my father interjects. He glares at Joseph, and Joseph glares at me.

Sighing, I add this to the long list of times my father has taken my side, giving Joseph more ammunition for his disdain.

"How has your week been, Sunshine?"

Offering him a tight smile, I take in the way he holds my mother's hand on top of the table while awaiting my answer, genuinely wanting to hear about my week.

From the corner of my eye, my brother pretends not to notice as he cuts into his quiche.

"It's been fine. Since we're creating a fully in-house space for authors, I hired another agent to join my team, and a fabulous editor. We received more than a hundred and fifty submissions between Wednesday afternoon and Friday morning. It's thrilling to watch something you started from nothing hit a patch of success."

"I have no doubts it'll continue to flourish," my mother remarks. "Independent authors are taking publishing by storm, and you're doing something no other publishing house is, by offering them royalties that rival what they make with self-publishing. It's remarkable."

"Well, it only makes sense," I continue. "And it's not quite as much as they'd make with some of the self-publishing platforms, but they get the benefits of a publishing house while still retaining the majority of their rights and royalties."

My father nods his head as he chews. "It's phenomenal—truly, Sunshine. I'm so proud of you."

"Thank you." My heart warms, and I look down at my plate, scooping a bite onto my fork.

"And you, Joseph? What type of havoc did you wreak this week?" Luciano asks, his voice dripping with amusement. Surely he can see the jealousy etched into our brother's features from my father's praise directed at me.

My oldest brother, Luciano, has always instigated

Joseph's foul moods, knowing he is liable to snap at any moment. I've always hoped my father would catch it in action and finally say something, which I think is why Luciano continues to push Joseph. Unfortunately, my father holds us all on such high pedestals—it would take a lot to taint the image he has of any one of us.

I'm a little convinced he *does* see it though and chooses to turn a blind eye.

Our father's love used to be distributed equally, but over the years, I've noticed him overcompensating after Joseph's true colors peek through.

Dabbing his mouth with the corner of his napkin, Joseph's devilish smile shines as he lowers it. "Well, I had the honor of attending the Reid Family's Annual Masquerade on Friday—"

"Oh, my goodness! How was it, Vincenza? I can't believe I forgot to ask!" my mother interrupts, turning the conversation back to me.

Thankfully, I have a mouthful of food and can't answer, which hardly matters because Joseph ignores her question and continues.

"August and I attended together. Father, did you know he's finally considering settling down?"

"Yes, you told me that not too long ago. Good for him. Commitment would do New York's most eligible bachelor some good, I think."

"He's quite picky though, looking for the perfect woman to call his wife—"

"Vincenza, were there any men at the ball who you

found attractive?" my mother asks, then squeals again. "I'm so glad you went on our behalf, darling!"

"I danced with many men, Mother, but I'm sorry to report there was not a spark in sight."

"I don't know, Sister, you looked pretty cozy in August's arms," Joseph taunts, and I can see the mockery in his eyes. "August was quite pleased after your dance together."

Through gritted teeth, I bite out, "August is your best friend, Joey. Practically family. I could *never* date a man who's considered family."

I watch as his hand that rests on the table balls into a fist.

"Oh, I don't know, Vin! Sometimes it's the most unsuspecting friendships that grow into love," my mother gushes, leaning forward on her elbow to rest her chin on her hand. She practically has hearts in her eyes.

"He seems very interested," Joseph prods.

He's baiting them—encouraging the very thoughts I wish to squash, but I can see my mother is already planning a wedding in her head, and my father is more focused on his brunch than listening to the exchange— at least, I think he is.

Luciano's eyes are beneath the table, responding to a text, or an email, on his phone. Samuele is ignoring everyone and shoveling food into his mouth.

The only person on my side is Cecilia. My fingernails bite into her wrist beneath the table as I hold on to one of my best friends to keep myself from exploding. I know she'll end up with half-moon indents, but it's the furthest from my mind as I try not to react outwardly.

Inside, I'm screaming, throwing a fit, begging for my family to rip the curtain back so they can see Joseph for what he really is, but on the outside, I am the product of my upbringing.

Calm. Dignified. Proper.

Perfect.

"I've heard the Lucchetti boy has returned stateside?" my father half states, half asks, as he finally inserts himself back into the conversation.

Looking at him, I see he's turned his attention to my brother.

Joseph scoffs. "He has. I saw him at the masquerade, too, with Sullivan Rochester."

"Oh, Vins, Sullivan is quite handsome!"

I simply shake my head at my mother and listen to the conversation my father and brother are having.

"You've had issues with him in the past, son. It's not to happen again. I expect you to eliminate the problem before it becomes one, by any means necessary."

A lump forms in my throat. It's the first time I've heard my father speak so brazenly in my presence. A quick glance in my direction confirms he didn't mean for it to happen, and he looks away quickly, not wanting to meet my eyes.

My thoughts flit back to the interactions I've had with Sly, and aside from the fight he got into with my brother when we were teens, I can't recall a single time the Lucchettis have ever been a problem. Then again, the Paladino men love to hide things from us women.

Still, I know the rivalry runs deep, and it's because of that deep-rooted dislike for the Luchettis that I find Sly so infuriating.

It's still hard to wrap my mind around the fact that I've now had interactions with him two days in a row, when I've gone years without having to see him.

My father's voice pulls me back to their conversation mid-sentence. "...long time since I've had a conversation with Antonio, perhaps I should pay him a visit myself and remind him."

"Darling, I wish you'd just end this long-time feud with that family. Valentina and Andrea have been very prominent members of the Kepner Foundation for years, and I just thi—"

"And I wish you would have stepped down from your position the moment those filthy Lucch—"

"Enough," I hear myself say, although I have no idea why.

All eyes snap to mine—except Sam's. He couldn't still care less about what's going on around him. I hesitate, now under complete scrutiny from my family.

Cecilia muffles a cough, no doubt subduing a giggle.

Time to dig myself out of the hole that outburst just put me in.

"We're all adults, are we not? How many years are we going to feud with a family who wants nothing to do with us, just like we want nothing to do with them? Has the bad blood not run dry yet? Can we just go about our lives and let their family do the same? Mother said it herself—the women of that family sit on the same board as her, and there has yet to be a problem. Clearly, the problem lies in the testosterone."

My mother sucks in a sharp breath, and I know I've said too much. But it feels good to speak out, even if this may not have been the subject to speak out on.

As though Joseph can see right through me, he asks, "Is there something we should know, sis? Something you're not telling us?"

My eyes meet Luciano's curious ones, then Father's. Shaking my head, I toss my hands into the air. "No, I just think it's stupid, that's all."

Father's lips purse, but I can tell he believes me. He has no reason not to.

My brother, on the other hand, analyzes me with complete distrust. His long fingers steeple in front of his mouth, saying nothing as he taps them against his lips.

Taking another bite of my quiche, I then place my napkin down next to my plate and push my chair back. As Cecilia stands, I round the table and place a kiss on my mother's cheek.

"Sorry to eat and run today, Mother, but I have an appointment I don't want to be late for."

"No problem, darling. I'll see you on Thursday at the agriculture committee luncheon."

Saying goodbye to the men in my family takes only a few more moments, so while Cecilia gets our purses from my mother's library, I step outside onto the stoop for some fresh air. The street is bustling with activity, the

July air surprisingly crisp, contrasting against the warmth of the sun.

Ross waits patiently by the car, having seen me walk out of the door, with his hands clasped behind his lower back.

When Cecilia emerges, she hands me my purse with a smirk playing on her lips.

"What?" I urge, walking with her down the steps.

She says nothing, and as Ross opens the car door for us, I ask again. "Well, are you going to tell me or just look at me with that coy smile of yours?"

Her eyes dart sideways to Ross, and I take the hint, turning to slip inside the car. She follows me in, and as he closes the door, she settles back and clips her seatbelt in. Once we tell him where we're headed—back to my apartment, because I don't actually have an appointment today, I just wanted to leave—she presses the button to close the partition.

Quirking a brow, she asks, "End the feud, huh?"

Sighing, I turn to look out the window. "It just seems silly at this point. It's been over a decade. What's the point?"

"The point is, my dear Vincenza, I think you're more interested in Mr. Lucchetti than you care to admit."

But she's wrong. My interest in the Lucchettis—in *Sly*—begins and ends with the simple fact that the man infuriates me, and any connection to them is a connection none of us want to have.

Chapter 9

Sly

Sweat drips down my brow, my lungs burning as the soles of my shoes carry me through mile seven on the treadmill. Grabbing my water bottle, I squeeze some into my mouth and keep running, watching as the machine counts me into my eighth.

Running is my preferred way to channel my anger and frustration.

I hate it—running.

Hate the burn in my lungs, the tightness I sometimes get in my calves. Hate the way my feet sound every time they touch the machine's walking belt. Or the sidewalk. Or the dirt, for that matter.

Regardless of my location, I hate the exercise.

Still, I do it because it allows me to think. It gives me the mental clarity I need.

And at this moment, I *need* the clarity.

This morning I saw three patients, all with varying

needs for their care, yet none with the resources to get it.

The first, a young mother with her four-year-old son. He's had a high fever for days, his throat so raw and red with white patches he can't even speak. His tears have dried up, none left to cry, the pain has been so great.

But his mother works odd jobs to get by, none of which offers insurance. Even if one did, she couldn't afford it. She's doing the best she can, but just can't quite get the help she needs.

Thankfully, I have antibiotics on hand. After a full assessment of his health, I hand her the medicine, a treatment plan, and a card with my phone number on it in case she needs to reach out regarding her son. Within twenty-four hours, the antibiotics will begin to do their job and the little guy should be feeling significantly better.

My other two patients were adults, but that didn't make seeing their struggle any easier. It eats at me that there is such a divide between affluence. Even the difference between middle class to lower class is astonishing. And lower class to poverty level?

Heart-shattering.

So badly, I wish there was more I could do.

In my periphery, I see Sully approach, wiping his face with a towel. Ignoring him, I keep going, but still his voice pushes through my headphones. "Really, Sylvester? Eight miles? Why do you have to be such a show-off?"

When I don't respond, he continues. "Eight miles seems excessive, Lucchetti. Hello? Can you even hear me through these?" He reaches over and plucks the headphone out of my ear. A grin rivaling the Cheshire Cat widens across his face.

With a huff of annoyance, I punch the buttons of the treadmill to slow it down, taking my pace to a walk. "Are you done with your workout already? Why are you interrupting mine?"

"Oh, someone's cranky. How long has it been since you've gotten laid, buddy?"

I shoot him a glare. I'm not *cranky*, nor does my mood have any correlation with having sex. I'm stressed. Angry at the uneven and unfair systematics of this country. Of this *world*.

"Well, I have a solution for that," he continues. Somehow, his smile widens, despite the frown I know is scrawled across my face.

Grabbing my towel, I swipe it over my forehead before stepping off the treadmill. "I'm not in need of one."

Passing rows of exercise machines, weight benches, and squat racks, he follows me through the gym and into the locker room.

"I have a date with the heiress on Friday—"

"Doesn't she have a *real* name you should be using?"

"She wants to bring her friend along, too. You know, like a double date? Turns out, this friend was also at the masquerade, and *apparently* someone by the name of Sly Lucchetti piqued her interest."

"No," I say instantly, dismissing his request.

His shoulders deflate. "No?"

Stowing my water bottle and towel in my locker, I peel my shirt off, followed by my running shoes and socks, and step into my slides. Once everything's inside, I shut the wooden door and reset the dial on the lock. "No."

I can feel his eyes on my back as I walk away, pulling open the sauna's door and stepping inside. Dry, hot air clings to me as I relax onto a cedar bench, leaning back against the wall with my eyes closed.

For about ninety seconds, I'm alone with my thoughts before the door opens. Sully hasn't even passed the threshold before he's yammering at me again.

"How could you possibly deny my request when I haven't even asked it?" He sits down next to me with a thud.

"Because I already know it involves me spending an evening as a fourth wheel, pretending to show interest in some poor girl who bores me, all so you can go home with the heiress you're attempting to impress. What *is* her name, anyway?"

My eyes are still closed, but Sully hasn't taken the hint.

"Hera. You wouldn't be a fourth wheel—you'd *very* much be the second half of a twosome."

"I'd rather not be any part of the equation." Bringing my hand to my face, I rub my eyes with my thumb and pointer finger, pressing harder than necessary, but the pressure is welcome, combating against the headache Sully is giving me.

"You're coming. You still owe me, remember?"

"Owe you for what?" Finally, I open my eyes and give him a pointed look.

His eyebrows shoot up to his hairline. "Oh, don't tell me you've already forgotten!" Sully crosses his arms over his bare chest, and tosses me a lopsided grin—the very grin that he calls "the panty dropper" because of the effect it has on women.

I have no idea why he would think it would work on *me*.

"There is not a single thing I can think of that *I* would owe *you*. You're the one with the favor list a mile long, amico mio. So please, enlighten me."

"I didn't tell on you."

"Tell on me? We haven't been in grade school for nearly two decades, Sullivan. Please. Do elaborate."

A hearty chuckle rumbles through him. "I could have easily told Enzo about you chasing after Vinnie Paladino at the masquerade. But I'm a great friend, therefore, I kept my lips sealed when I easily could have ratted your sorry, traitorous ass out."

All it takes is for him to say *her* name and my thoughts carry me back to this past weekend when I ran into her twice.

A spiral of annoyance, and something else, settles in the dead center of my chest. Quickly, I push the thoughts—and that *feeling*—away.

"Had you told Enzo, I would have sent you to meet

the Lord and Savior well before your time. Not that there was, or *is*, anything to tell."

"Aw, Sly! You think I'll end up in Heaven? I love your optimism." Sully's tone is mockingly playful. Of course, that's the part he honed in on.

Standing, I reach my arm across my body, pulling on it with the opposite hand to stretch the muscles. "The answer remains no."

"It's just dinner, Sly. I'm not asking you to put a ring on the girl's finger. You can leave right after we eat."

"*Just* dinner?" I question, switching arms to stretch. I don't believe him for a second.

Sully doesn't do anything simple. Everything is elaborate and grand. Ostentatious, even. There's no way all he has planned for the daughter of the biggest hotel chain on the East Coast is *just dinner*.

With a wicked smile, Sully stands and stretches his arms overhead. He knows he has me right where he wants me.

On the verge of saying yes.

In fact, I know Sully well enough to know that he turned the word *just* into the word *yes* and heard me say 'yes dinner', instead.

Bastardo.

"Yep! Dinner. I'll pick you up at eight, then we'll go get the girls together. See you in a couple days, buddy!" he says, tugging open the sauna door as he practically runs out, no doubt so I can't change my mind.

"Wonderful," I mutter to myself as the door shuts.

Sitting back on the bench, I kick my legs out in front

of me, crossing my feet at my ankles. My hands come to rest behind my head, elbows sprawled as I lean back and once again allow my eyes to close.

Only this time when I close them, I see piercing gray-blue eyes, dark hair, and a gorgeous, angelic face.

A face that belongs to my enemy.

Chapter 10

Vinnie

"Are you sure you can't come today?" I ask Cecilia through the reflection of my vanity mirror as I put on my diamond stud earrings.

She's behind me, fluffing the pillows on my bed, even though I've told her countless times she doesn't need to do the typical tasks of a maid. Just helping me around the apartment is more than enough, but I've stopped arguing. She never listens anyway.

She stops mid-fluff to give me a pointed look. "Vinnie, you know I'd rather cut off my left tit than go to an *agriculture* luncheon. It's a glorified homeowners' association meeting."

"Essentially, yes. But at least there'll be tea sandwiches and macarons."

"Served with a side of drama," she muses, taking a seat at the edge of my bed. "You'll have to fill me in on it later."

"Of course I will." Turning in my chair to face her, I ask, "So, what am I wearing?"

Cecilia's lips purse as she thinks about what's in my closet. "It's supposed to be warm and sunny today."

"Yes, but the luncheon is on the rooftop terrace of Chez Quatre. It might be cool up there."

"Still, you don't want anything too stuffy. Oh, wait! I know!" She shuffles off my bed and rushes to my closet.

The metal hooks of the hangers scrape across the rod as she moves things around, and I take the spot she just occupied on my bed while I wait. Seconds later, she appears with three garments hung over her arm, and my brand new nude peep-toe Louboutin's looped through her fingers.

She hands me my shoes as I stand to let her lay each piece of clothing down on the bed. Light pink cropped cigarette pants, a loose fitting three-quarter sleeved navy and cream button-up, and my navy blue fitted blazer.

It's a little more business casual than I'd prefer, but I know I'll be comfortable in it. It's one of my power outfits—I can command a room and lead in this outfit.

Not that I'll need to today, but at least I'll feel confident, regardless of what this luncheon throws my way.

"Good choice," I commend Cecilia, running my hand along the pants. "It's been a while since I've worn these. I forgot I had them."

"They'll look lovely with the Louboutin's."

"Yes, they will. Thank you, Lia."

I slip my robe down my shoulders while she returns to my closet, then dress myself. By the time she returns,

I'm sliding my feet into my heels. Wordlessly, she walks out of the room while I finish getting myself put together.

Grabbing my phone off my vanity, I click the side button and see Raina has texted me.

RAINA

See you soon?

In about an hour, I type, then push send. By the time Ross stops to pick up my mother, it'll be about that long.

Leighton Paladino is notoriously late. She takes her time getting ready, wanting to present herself as picture perfect one-hundred percent of the time. Which isn't a rarity for Manhattan women, but my mother has no regard for the clock.

Sending a quick text to Ross, I let him know I'll be downstairs in a few minutes, and step out of my bedroom. Cecilia is finishing switching my handbags, putting everything in my powder blue Dior clutch.

"It's perfect, thank you," I say as I air kiss her cheek.

"Have a great afternoon, Vinnie. I may or may not be here when you get back."

"I hope you're not," I tell her with a smile, and I mean it. She works too hard. Some time off and away from this apartment would do her some good.

Cecilia is thirty-six years old and has hardly dated throughout the time I've known her. She's gorgeous, and longs for a family of her own, but won't take the steps to actually go meet someone.

Playfully, she swats her hand at me, then practically

pushes me inside the elevator that's just opened. "Good-bye, Vinnie!" she says with sass.

And as the elevator doors are closing, I shout, "Go get laid, Cecilia!" and I practically hear her laughter the entire ride down.

My mother loops her arm through mine as we step out of the elevator and onto the rooftop terrace of Chez Quatre.

It's beautiful up here.

Rich with greenery all around, an elegant table practically spans the entire roof, set neatly with place settings and extravagant bouquets. Some women are already in their seats chatting, while others congregate around high-top tables placed around the space.

On the far left, a string quartet plays, basking us all in their soft melody.

"Wow, isn't this lovely?" my mother chirps, giving my forearm a little squeeze.

Looking around for Raina, I hum my agreement, quickly catching sight of my best friend. She's standing with her back to me at one of the tables, champagne glass in hand.

"Mother, I'm going to go say hello to some friends. See you when we sit down?"

Instantly, she slips her arm from mine and turns to air kiss my cheeks. "Absolutely, Darling. Enjoy yourself."

Then she walks away, calling out to someone she knows as she waves in their direction.

Walking up to Raina, I place my hand on her back to get her attention, and she wastes no time handing me the champagne flute she has in front of her.

"Thought you might be thirsty." She grins before taking a long sip of hers. We cheers, and I do the same.

Cold, crisp bubbles hit my tongue and I welcome them. It'll take a glass or two to get through today.

"Do you remember the Barron twins?" she asks, nodding in the direction of women across the table.

Smiling, I extend my hand to the twin closest to me. "Of course. How are you?"

They both greet me and limply squeeze my hand. I'm thankful they didn't come around the table for a hug or air kisses. I can only handle so many of those at one event.

Meaningless conversation overtakes the better part of the next thirty minutes before the soft clinking of metal on glass garners our attention.

"Lucky us, a word from the modern day Effie Trinket herself," Raina mutters so only I can hear.

Stifling a laugh, I look at the woman she's referring to. Meredith Rochester is standing at her seat at the head of the main table wearing a floral boatneck dress that flares slightly at her waist, accompanied by a large headpiece with what appears to be a fake bird on it. Thin meshing peeks out to create a birdcage veil effect.

It's a lot, and my eyes widen at the sight.

"Thank you all for coming today!" she exclaims

loudly, projecting her voice so we can all hear her. "If you could all take your seats, brunch will be served shortly! Unfortunately, I left my notes for our meeting portion at home, but my wonderful son, Sullivan Junior, should be here shortly with them. So, let's enjoy a beautiful meal together, then get down to business, shall we?"

"Let's get this over with, shall we?" Raina mocks, grabbing two more champagne flutes from a passing waiter's tray. She hands me one, then tosses hers back like a shot.

Laughing, I sip mine as she steers me by my elbow to the furthest end of the table. I spot my mother near the middle, but she's already talking animatedly with the women around her, paying me no attention as I pass.

We take our seats while others do the same, and I help myself to a stick of celery on the vegetable tray in front of me. It's bland and slightly bitter, and I instantly regret my choice.

"How's your week been?" I ask Raina while I grab a carrot instead.

"Meh. Aside from me PMSing and literally hating the entire human race, it's been whatever. Honestly, I'm getting a little old to be an intern. If Shelby doesn't promote me within the next month, I'm just going to quit. It's not like I *need* to work." She swishes her hand with annoyance.

Raina works for a fashion designer, Shelby Tomè, interning as her junior designer, which is a more dignified way to say she's Shelby's errand girl who occasionally gets to do important things like choosing textiles and deciding on potential upcoming trends. She loves it, but after *six years* of being an intern, the position has run its course.

"Has she hinted at it? Why a month?"

"She hasn't, but I sure have. Subtly. Not so subtly. Even outright asked for it. And I don't know, a month just sounds good, right? Another solid four weeks, and if she hasn't given me a promotion by then, I'll give her an ultimatum."

"Think that'll work?"

She pops a cherry tomato into her mouth, chewing slowly as she looks at me, as though giving it some thought. "If it doesn't, I have nothing to lose, anyway."

"You can always come intern for me," I tease, nudging her softly in the side.

"Not my field of expertise, babe."

We both quiet down as a waiter sets plates down in front of us. They're filled to the brim with the most beautiful display of breakfast foods.

I practically salivate.

Fresh grapes and squares of cheese. A croque madame made on a buttery croissant, rolled French toast, a buckwheat crepe smothered in sautéed mushroom gravy. And as though that isn't enough, two perfect, miniature beignets topped with powdered sugar sit perfectly on the edge with a small sprig of mint leaves between them.

"Oh, my gosh, Cecilia is going to be devastated that

she missed out on all of this." I don't wait before diving in, cutting into my rolled French toast first.

"How is Lia doing, anyway? I feel like she hardly leaves the house. Would it be rude of me to just pick this up?" she asks, poking at her croque madame with her fork. "It *is* a sandwich."

"Depends on who's watching. Some of these women won't even notice, while others will act like you personally offended them."

She glances around, shrugging, before placing her fork down and picking up her croissant.

"She's good," I continue. "Same as always. I've been trying to encourage her to get out there and meet someone, but you know how she is."

"Lia doesn't *need* to meet someone, sis. She can have a baby without a man. Modern technology is pretty amazing."

"She doesn't *just* want a baby, she wants a family. A life with someone."

"Well, she won't find that by sitting in your apartment all day."

"Exactly why I told her to go out today and get laid."

She laughs around a bite of her sandwich, earning her a few side-eyes. "Good. I hope she listens to that advice."

"She won't," I murmur, suddenly distracted. My attention shifts to a conversation happening across the table.

Actually, it seems as though several of us have had

their attention stolen by Hera Whitney, as multiple women have completely abandoned their food to listen, Raina included.

"He tried so hard to get my attention at the masquerade—it was *so* charming. But of course I made him work for it!" She giggles, swishing her auburn hair off her shoulder. "*Then*, when he finally did get my number, he put it to use. The man hasn't stopped texting me in days!"

Her friend next to her audibly *swoons*. Full-on deep sigh, palms settling on either side of her face as she watches Hera intensely.

"We have our first official date tomorrow night! Norah is coming with us, and Sully is bringing his best friend. It's so circa two-thousand fourteen, and I personally couldn't be more excited."

"Wait, Sully Rochester?" Raina speaks up, butting into the conversation. "As in, New York's biggest play-boy? *That's* who you're excited to go on a date with?"

Hera's head snaps toward us, her brown eyes sharp-ening into a glare. "I'm sorry—who are you again?" she asks, feigning boredom.

Classic mean girl, that one.

Raina laughs loudly before taking another bite of her food. She doesn't bother finishing it completely before answering her, talking with food still in her mouth. "All I'm saying is, that charm is sweet for now, but the man is a stage-five clinger."

My brow shoots to my hairline as I turn my head to look at my friend, confused, because I've never once heard her mention the name Sully Rochester to me.

"Sounds like you're jealous," Hera volleys back, trying to hide the fluster in her tone.

Raina waves her hand in the air dismissively. "Ew. No. Honey, one of my family's maids is married to his father's driver, or something like that. The maids gossip. One of my favorite breakfast pastimes is to listen."

Hera's demeanor instantly changes as she relaxes with Raina's explanation. "Oh," she giggles again. "I'll keep that in mind."

Beside her, her mousy friend pipes up, and suddenly all the tension Hera was carrying transfers to me. "I'm so excited, too! Sure, Sully is handsome, but his friend? Drop. Dead. Gorgeous. I'm still on cloud nine to be going on a date with Sly Lucchetti!"

It was the wrong time to take a sip of my cappuccino because I choke on the hot liquid at the mention of his name. Before I can stop myself, I loudly and wholly inappropriately shout, "Sly?"

Attempting to cover my screw up, I fake cough and look away. It's too late, though. The mousey one, and everyone else around us, heard.

She smiles triumphantly and nods, seemingly oblivious to my negative reaction.

Sighing like she's madly in love, she says, "I know, right?"

"Right." I smile as broadly as I can manage. Dropping my voice, I say to Raina, "If you find arrogance attractive."

Raina snorts, at the same time the mousy one says, "Excuse me? Maybe *you're* the jealous one. Sly Lucchetti is a catch, and I'm going to make sure I'm the one who reels him in."

Fishing puns from an Upper East Side socialite wanna-be who's probably never held a fishing pole in her life.

Not that *I've* held one in years, but yes, I've been fishing. Once. In Central Park.

And now I'm being catty for no reason.

Still, I can't stop the sarcastic laugh that flies from my mouth. "*Please.* I'd rather be single forever than spend five minutes with that man, let alone go on a date with him."

Hera cocks her head, assessing me with narrowed eyes. It makes me uncomfortable. "She *is* jealous. Look, Norah. She's blushing."

I want to deny it, but I feel the heat on my skin.

Glancing at Raina, I try to mentally signal for backup, but instead she looks awestruck as she watches me.

Just then, a collection of *aws* and *gasps* float into the air, and I turn in my seat to see an attractive man in an impeccably tailored navy suit saunter out of the elevator. He looks to be mid to late twenties, with chocolate brown hair cropped on the sides and perfectly styled on top, and light brown eyes that practically sparkle.

Sullivan Rochester *is* handsome, there's no denying that.

"There he is," Hera says brightly, her eyes glued to him.

Seeing this as my cue to avoid an already awkward situation, I stand, ready to spend some time in the ladies' room, then in the restaurant's lounge while I wait for my mother. She can give me the CliffsNotes version of the meeting.

"Ladies, it's been wonderful to catch up, but I must be going. Unexpected problem at work."

Raina looks at me with her lips turned down, her eyes trailing from mine to my clutch, then back. I can read her expression: *Problem at work? You haven't even looked at your phone.*

I try to communicate back that I just *can't* deal with this today—I don't have the mental capacity to—but I'm not sure if it articulates.

"*So* nice to see you," Hera says, still looking over my shoulder, presumably at Sully. But I don't miss the sarcasm in her tone.

"Enjoy your date," I say to both her and Norah, ignoring the bitter taste it leaves in my mouth.

"Their *double* date," a playful baritone says from right behind me. "Me, Hera, Nova, and *Sly*."

"Norah!" she corrects, frowning for just a split second.

Slowly, I turn, and end up standing practically chest to chest with—apparently—Sly's best friend. The smirk on his face tells me what I already need to know.

He knows who I am.

And he knows about my run-ins with Sly.

Instinctively I take a step back, but there's nowhere to go as my thighs nudge the edge of the table.

Sully stares at me with a smile that makes my stomach churn—not because it's creepy or anything, but because it makes me feel like he's privy to something I'm not. And considering he doesn't know me *at all*, it's unsettling.

"Norah! My bad." Finally, he pulls his gaze and looks behind me, tossing a wink in Hera's direction. "I'm looking forward to tomorrow night, ladies."

Reaching around me to wave the leather-bound portfolio in his hand in their direction, he tells us, "Better get these to Meredith before she realizes I'm delaying her luncheon more than necessary."

As he shifts his body again, his voice drops and through the smile plastered on his face he practically whispers, "You know, I suspect he'd rather go on a date with *you*, Miss Paladino."

Then as quickly as Sully appeared, he's gone, walking toward his mother without so much as a glance behind him.

I don't even realize that I'm dumbfounded, watching him go, until Raina reaches for my hand and gives it a squeeze, pulling me out of my daze.

"Call me once you diffuse the problem at work?" she asks, giving me an out even though she doesn't even know why I need it.

I haven't had a moment to tell her about Sly. She's completely in the dark.

Shaking my head, I give her a smile that doesn't reach my eyes. "Yes, absolutely. Love you."

"Love you," she assures me, and releases my hand.

The second it's out of her grasp, I take off toward the elevator, having to mentally remind myself to walk, not run to it, like I'd rather do.

No need to draw attention to myself.

My body constricts the air in my lungs, refusing to let it go until I'm out of the restaurant and back on the busy Manhattan street. The doorman gives me a look of question, but bites his tongue as I inhale air like I've been underwater for too long.

I don't bother texting Ross to pick me up, instead opting for a walk in Central Park. Fresh air and alone time will be good for me—it'll give my heart time to stop thumping.

The park is busy, as per usual, but I take my time moving along the path until I reach an empty bench and take a seat.

Pretending as though it won't mess up my makeup, I lean forward, elbows on my knees, and press my hands to my face. It feels good to close my eyes, even if for just a minute.

My mind hasn't stopped replaying the last twenty minutes of brunch. The way I felt when Norah said Sly's name. The way I *reacted*. The things I said.

Sly's best friend showing up like an unwanted apparition. Then, what *he* said.

"He'd rather go on a date with you."

Ha! Unlikely. He *hates* me, and I'm not exactly the biggest fan of his either.

And I meant what I said. I'd rather be single than spend any amount of time with him.

I don't care what he does.

Don't care if he goes on a date with a mousy woman who's going to 'reel him in'.

Not one bit.

Then why do I feel so flustered?

Chapter 11

Sly

"Explain to me again why you're dragging me along on your date?" I'm sitting on my couch with a glass of scotch in hand, sipping it while Sully checks his reflection in the mirror for the third time. My best friend and I couldn't be more opposite, but I suppose that's why we get along so well.

We need to leave in the next five minutes if we intend to make it to the opera on time.

Yes, the opera.

The shiesty bastardo made dinner reservations for after the opera.

The only silver lining is that because it is opening weekend of Roméo et Juliette at the Metropolitan Opera House, the soft opening showing begins at six, rather than the eight o'clock showing it will move to tomorrow.

Still, the performance is three hours long.

Then I have to make it through dinner.

"Because you owe me." He grins in the mirror.

"You are mistaken."

My phone vibrates in my hand, Enzo's name illuminating across the screen.

ENZO

Have you jumped out of the moving
vehicle yet, cousin?

Across the room, Sully pulls his phone from the pocket of his slacks and peers at the message, barking a laugh as he reads it.

SULLY

Stop giving him ideas.

"He's not, I assure you. The thoughts are already there," I say to Sully without looking up from my phone.

"Norah is cute, Sly. At least use tonight as a way to get back onto the scene with New York women. You haven't been on a date since we were in Verona."

"That wasn't that long ago."

"We were in Verona over *six* months ago."

"Things have been busy." Lifting the glass to my lips, I take a long drink of my scotch, finishing it completely.

"Mmhmm," Sully hums, adjusting his tie once more.

Standing, I move to the kitchen and rinse my glass

before placing it on the drying mat. Resting my palms along the edge of the counter, I let my eyes fall shut as I mentally prepare myself for this evening.

It's the last thing I want to do, but for Sully—and Enzo, for that matter—there's not a lot I'll say no to.

Behind me, footsteps on my marble floors alert me that Sully's approaching. "Are you ready to go get the girls?" I ask without turning around.

Opening my eyes, he comes into my peripheral, leaning on the wall next to where I stand. His arms cross over his chest as he settles in. "You know, I saw her yesterday."

My stomach dips, instinct telling me exactly *who* he saw. Tilting my head toward him, I keep my expression stoic. "Who?" I ask through the lump in my throat.

With curious eyes, Sully watches me, looking for any crack in my armor he can find. Luckily, he can't *see* the questions racing through my mind.

Pushing off the wall, he gives me his back and walks away. Following him, we head toward the door, and he grabs his coat from the arm of my couch.

Wordlessly, I pull my coat from the closet, then move to the credenza next to my door to get my keys and wallet, stowing them in my pocket. As I turn around, I see Sully shrugging on his jacket, a small smile playing on his lips.

He hasn't answered my question, and I suspect he won't.

Grabbing my phone, I return to the group chat and

respond to my cousin, knowing if I've had enough of tonight and need an out, he'll be just the man to help me.

Sully looks down at the incoming text message, shaking his head slightly as he reads it. Looking up, he nods at the door. "Let's go. We wouldn't want to be late for Romeo and Juliet."

As much as I had not looked forward to this date, I have to admit the opera is wonderful. I've always been a fan of Shakespeare, and though three hours is a little longer than I care to sit through any sort of performance, at least it's enjoyable.

My date, on the other hand…not as enjoyable.

Norah Dayton is one of the most surface-level people I have ever met. Our conversation while in the limo lacked substance, and I tried—truly, I did try to get to know the girl. There is zero depth to her. Nothing more than the latest fashion trends, city gossip, and trending cat videos.

She is a literal parrot of her friend Hera, harboring the same reactions throughout the opera, the same tone of laugh, and even the same hand gestures.

And as if that weren't enough, throughout the

whole performance, I've had to physically remove her hand as it inched closer to my cock. I would lift her appendage from my body, depositing it back onto her own, and what seemed like moments later, she'd try again.

Over and over.

For more than three hours.

Intermission came and went too quickly, and I excused myself to visit the men's room and take a walk around the beautiful venue. Couples looked exquisite as they meandered around, taking a walk to ease the stiffness of sitting for so long.

Now as I check my watch, I see that the performance is due to have only twenty minutes left, and remove my phone from my pocket. Keeping it low by my thigh opposite of Norah, I type a quick message.

> 9-1-1. 20 minutes.

Tucking my phone back safely into my pocket, I peel Norah's fingers from me once more.

With a deep sigh, I return my focus to the show. The actors playing Romeo and Juliet are so convincing —their chemistry so strong—I find myself completely enamored with the final act. The songs, the *tragedy*. The hushed audience basking in it all.

It makes me feel—lonely.

In all my years, I have yet to experience a love so passionate it's all-consuming. A love where you would die for the person without hesitation—risk it all just to be with them.

I find myself...*yearning.*

The feeling settles into my chest just as I'm jolted by heavy applause. Realizing the curtain is closing, mechanically I stand with the rest of my party and clap, watching as the cast takes their bows. The joy on the faces of those on stage is tangible. Clearly, they worked hard, and the standing ovation from the audience puts it all in perspective.

When the stage clears, the audience begins to leave as well, and I turn to look at Sully. He's staring dreamily at Hera, smiling as she says something to him.

Moving away from our seats and into a more open space within our box, I'm taken by surprise when warm fingers lace with mine. Looking down, I see Norah holding my hand.

It's off-putting, and my whole body goes rigid. Not even my fingers know how to react as they stay stiffly straight.

"That was beautiful," she admires, smiling brightly at me.

I look down at our connected hands again, and I know I should close my grasp around hers. It's the polite thing to do, yet I don't.

"Are we ready for some dinner?" Sully asks, clapping my shoulder with his hand as he comes up behind me. It's sobering—pulling me out of the trance I'm stuck in.

"We're starving," Norah answers for the both of us. It immediately upsets me, leaving a sour taste in my mouth of how presumptuous this woman is.

Disconnecting my hand from hers, my lips are glued shut as I turn my gaze to Sully, speaking to him with a simple look. He stifles a laugh and leads the way for us to exit the auditorium and walk through Lincoln Center Plaza.

Norah winds her arm around mine as we head to 65th Street, where Sully's limo is idling, waiting to take us to dinner. About halfway there, my phone vibrates in my pocket, and I pull it out and see Enzo's name flash across the screen.

The hint of a smile pulls at my lips as I answer it, and Sully glares at me.

"Pronto," I greet my cousin.

"You know if you use this as an excuse right now, Sully will hold a grudge for about, mmm, three days, give or take, right?"

"Sì, ma procedi, per favore." *Yes, but please proceed.*

"You know I don't speak Italian." Enzo's voice feigns boredom, but I know him well enough to hear the hint of amusement shining through.

Playing into the ruse, my lips part in mock surprise, and I bring my hand to my chin, rubbing it lightly before pushing my fingers through my hair as though I'm in distress. "Oh no. Sì. Sì, naturalmente. Sarò lì." *Oh no. Yes. Yes, of course. I'll be right there.*

Pulling the phone from my ear, I hang up quickly to

hide the caller's name, and push the phone back into my pocket.

Turning to Norah, I take her hand off my arm, kissing the top of it, before letting it go. It falls limply, as though she has no control of her body. "I'm so sorry, but I must go. That was mia madre, and she requires my assistance immediately."

Sighing, Sully butts in. "It's after nine o'clock. What could Valentina possibly need?"

Above Norah's head, I shoot him a glare before looking back down at my date. "I apologize, Ms. Dayton. It is not my intention to cut our night short."

It's actually always been my intention, but she doesn't need to know that.

Her expression looks sad for a moment before she claps her hands together triumphantly. "I'll go with you!"

Immediately, I shake my head no. "Family matters, I'm afraid. You stay and enjoy dinner. I'll hail a cab."

"No," Sully says, shaking his head. "Take the limo. The restaurant is only a few blocks away. We can walk there and Stephen can come back for us later. I insist."

Hera huffs impatiently. "But I'm wearing six-inch stilettos, Sully."

"You'll be fine," he responds quickly, giving her his infamous smile. "I'll carry you if I have to."

"I don't want to be a third wheel," Norah pouts, giving me doe eyes. She's still fishing for an invitation that won't be extended.

Forcing myself to refrain from rolling my eyes, I offer, "I could have Stephen drop you off on my way?"

Her eyes light up, and I momentarily feel guilty. "That sounds great, thank you!"

Nodding, I close the distance with Hera and politely kiss her on each cheek, thanking her for including me in a lovely evening, then turn to my best friend with my hand extended. He takes it with his opposite hand, and pulls me in by the shoulder with his other.

"You're lucky Norah's going home too, or you'd be in big, big trouble, my friend," he whispers, then gently pushes me away.

Keeping up the charade, I give him a small smile and say, "Thank you, Sullivan. I will let you know how everything works out with my family. I'll call you tomorrow, amico mio."

When Norah and I are in the limo, she gives Stephen, the driver, her address, which to my dismay is about twenty minutes away with this late evening traffic.

Leaning back, I get comfortable against the leather and pull my phone out. My messages with Enzo and Sully are the first tab I swipe to, so I type out a quick message to my cousin.

Grazie

Immediately, my phone vibrates with an incoming message.

SULLY

You suck

But also, thanks! Maybe Hera will
suck too…

ENZO

It's baffling how often you actually get
laid with such an eighth-grade outlook
on life.

> I'd say he has a face only a mother can
> love, but he's proven that to be untrue.

SULLY

Y'all are just jealous.

ENZO

Y'all? This is New York, not Alabama.

SULLY

But I love a reverse cowgirl.

ENZO

You continue to prove my point.

> Yee haw.

Chuckling to myself, I tap the button on the side to put my phone into sleep mode, lowering it from my line of sight. As I do, I'm surprised to find Norah on the floorboard, kneeling in front of me. My eyes move to the partition, which I now see is up, closing us off from the driver. I hadn't even seen her move, or heard the partition rise, which proves how little I'm invested in this evening.

"What are you doing?" I ask, hoping my assumptions aren't true. But the way she's settled back on her legs, looking up at me as she attempts to slyly press her breasts together, tells me exactly what she's doing.

She's trying to seduce me.

It's not working.

In fact, my flaccid cock feels even more limp than normal.

"You seem stressed, Sly. I'm sorry your family needs you and we can't finish our date." Again, her hands inch up my thigh, and I gently push them away.

"All will be fine, don't worry," I assure, but she's stopped listening.

It's startling how quickly she can move when she is trying. Quicker than I can process, Norah has undone my belt, lowered my zipper, and has taken my cock into her hand.

"Norah, please—this is not necessary." My hand covers hers as I attempt to pull her fingers away. She mistakes my touch for encouragement, though, and begins to stroke me.

"Shhh, let me make you feel good," she says, and before I can tell her no again, her mouth descends.

Her warm, wet tongue licks up the underside of my cock as she repositions her hand at the base. Pushing further onto her knees for leverage, she takes it in her mouth completely, bobbing up and down as she uses her fist to tug and twist in a way that is meant to be pleasurable.

Watching her go down on me so brazenly goes

against every fiber of my being. It goes against every-thing I stand for as a lover.

I *give* pleasure. And I receive it only when my partner can no longer take any more. It does not matter if it takes three orgasms or twenty. Giving pleasure brings *me* pleasure.

This girl's mouth on my cock brings me nothing.

Letting her continue, I watch out the window as we drive down the busy Manhattan streets, trying to get into the mindset where I can mildly enjoy what Norah is doing.

Fisting her hair, I turn to look down at her as she moves up and down my cock, concentrating on the task at hand. Her face is concealed, hidden behind a mass of wavy light brunette tendrils that she kept loose.

My mind drifts to a deeper hue. Thick, wavy, deep brown hair, cascading down. Long, languid strokes of her tongue followed by playful swirls and flicks to the slit at the tip.

Instantly, I feel myself harden between her lips, and a heady moan floats from her as she hums with approval.

I wind my hand tighter in her hair and begin to guide her movements, tilting my head back against the seat of the car and closing my eyes. Envisioning blazing gray-blue irises looking up at me, I groan appreciatively as her lips suction around the head of my cock, then slowly push down toward the base while her tongue massages every place it touches.

Breath hisses past my teeth as I lose myself to her

movements. "*Fuck*," I mutter, then my eyes jolt open as I realize the name that almost came out of my mouth after that curse.

Vincenza.

It's been the thought of her—*her* hair, *her* eyes, *her* lips—that's gotten me so hard. That's brought me to this point. Anger slowly blooms inside my chest.

But I'm too close to stop now.

Between my legs, Norah lets my cock *pop* from her mouth, letting some of her saliva drip before sliding her fist back down the length. With steady strokes, she watches me, gauging my pleasure.

Pulling me back inside her mouth, she works it at the same tempo as her fist.

Closing my eyes, my teeth clench together the moment the darkness transforms into visions of my enemy. My *rival*. The *one* person whose family I hate.

Norah moans, grasping my cock tighter. "Damn, Sly. You're *so* hard."

I grind my teeth, lifting my hips to push into her mouth more. Letting go of my cock, she places one palm on the seat on both sides of my legs and takes me as far into her throat as she can.

With every thrust of my hips, she slides further down until I reach the back of her relaxed throat. She whimpers, causing me to slow, but she pulls at my hips and shakes her head around my cock. I let her continue guiding the movements, and once her hand reaches to my balls, I lose all control, having already been at the edge for far too long.

With a grunt, I hold her down on my shaft as I spill down her throat, coming with pictures of the wrong woman in my head.

My ragged breathing is the only sound in the back of the limo as she pulls off my cock and presses her thumb against the corner of her mouth, cleaning up the saliva and cum that's leaked from the side.

She smiles at me, fixing her dress as she slides into the seat next to me. Leaning over, she kisses me on the cheek.

I can't even look at her. My stomach churns for what just happened—all of it feeling so wrong.

The intercom sounds, the driver letting us know we're about to arrive. I lower the partition as Norah curls close to my side, not saying anything, but the unspoken expectations I know she's thinking practically scream through the silence.

White hot shame courses through me as the car stops in front of Norah's building.

Shame for using her.

Shame for thinking of *someone else*.

For *whom* I thought of.

Stephen exits the driver's seat, walking around to open the door for Norah.

"Thank you so much for an amazing night," she says in a seductive tone. "I can't wait to do it again soon. Call me?" She kisses my cheek and steps out of the car.

The door closes before Norah gets through the

doors of her building, and I'm grateful for that. My hands are fisted at my sides, my jaw tight.

"Where to, sir?" Stephen asks once his door closes. He's looking at me through the rearview mirror, waiting for an address.

All I want to do is go home and wash the memory of Norah's lips off my cock.

"The Kenna," I say.

If only I could scrub the memory of someone else, too.

Chapter 12

Vinnie

Work has been a nightmare this last week.

A nightmare of my own creation, but still a living hell.

Since the luncheon, I've done everything I can not to think about what Sullivan Rochester said, and if there was any truth behind it.

I don't *want* to care whether it was true. But I still find myself wondering.

Maybe I'm a glutton for punishment—inappropriately pining over a man who's completely off-limits. Or maybe it's because Sly Lucchetti is the only man in years who's managed to spike my heart rate with a simple glance in my direction.

Either way, I've thrown myself into work.

Meeting after meeting. Saying goodbye to one of my in-house agents. Interviewing people to take their place. Training two new interns. Reading manuscripts.

Taking an extra look at the slush piles, just in case something was missed.

I do it all—wear every hat when it comes to my business.

It's been non-stop chaos, and I've barely had time to breathe, let alone do anything else. Minimal time to really *think* about anything else.

Thank God for Cecilia, and my personal chef, Theo. If it weren't for the two of them, I probably wouldn't even remember to eat—although having Cecilia pack me lunch is a little childish, I'm grateful nonetheless.

But today I need a break, if only for an hour or two. There's a gap in between meetings, giving me the perfect excuse to slip away unnoticed, hail a cab, and have a little time to myself. I've been dying to try the new coffee shop connected to Haven Market on the other side of the park.

Switching out of my heels and into a pair of flats, I neatly place them in the small closet of my office and grab my favorite cream peacoat, shrugging it on over my polka-dot button-up shirt. There's been a chill in the air, the weather acting strange, despite it being the middle of summer.

Not wanting to bother with my purse, I put my wallet into the inside pocket of my coat.

It takes only a minute to hail a cab before I'm tucked safely in the backseat, letting the driver know where to take me. Traffic is light for an afternoon in Manhattan, and it only takes fifteen minutes before I'm back out of the car after paying and thanking the man for the ride.

Haven Market is bustling with people as I step through the automatic door. Taylor Swift plays over the speakers, clashing with the clatter of patrons shopping for groceries or their mid-day meal. To my left, I see the open alcove that leads into Revival, their new coffee shop.

The scent of espresso wafts around me as I approach, following a group of young men into the coffee shop. As I take my place in line behind them, and unfortunately, about six other people, I strain my eyes to look at the menu from afar, but it's just a little *too* far for me to make out most of the drinks.

Sighing, I resolve to wait until I'm closer, when one of the men in front of me hands me a chic paper menu.

"Thanks," I tell him, taking it from his hands. Then, he reaches to hand the person behind me one too.

My fingers run down the front of the menu, appreciating the small detailing of the embossed foiling. I'm impressed, and I haven't even tried the coffee yet.

The line moves slowly, but eventually, I reach the counter.

"Hi," the barista greets. "What can I get for you?"

Looking up at the menu board behind his head, I skim the options again, still not entirely sure what I want. "I can't decide! What do you recommend?"

Behind me, I hear a groan, but I pretend like I don't. I'm grateful for the patience of the barista, unlike those in line behind me.

"My personal favorite is the honey oat milk latte, but if you're not a huge fan of oat milk, I'd recommend trying the hazelnut cappuccino."

My lips purse as I find those options on the board and quickly read the descriptions. "Let's go for your favorite," I tell him with a smile. "The honey oat milk latte."

Hopefully, it won't disappoint.

"Great choice," he says as we complete the transaction.

While I wait, I look at the eclectic artwork hanging on the wall, curious who the artist is.

The drink smells like heaven when I grab it from the pickup counter, the light notes of sweet honey, espresso, and oat milk steaming from the small opening on the lid. Bringing it to my lips, I take the smallest of sips. Flavors explode on my tongue, along with a searing heat.

Wrapping my hands around the cup, I leave and begin my trek back to work. It'll take about thirty minutes on foot, cutting through Central Park, and I have a little more than an hour before I need to be back in the office to prepare for my next meeting with the design team.

Stepping outside, I turn to head down 97th Street, which will give me a straight path through the park. As I walk, I remove the lid from my coffee and blow on it, hoping to cool it down a little faster so I can enjoy it.

Steam floats into the air as I begin to lift my cup, and just as I do, I'm nearly knocked to the ground as a solid mass slams into me. My hot coffee immediately flies, spilling down my front, and tears sting my eyes from the searing heat that soaks through my clothes.

"Ow, ow," I chant, pulling my wet shirt away from my body as coffee drips from my skin, between my cleavage and down my stomach.

"My apologies, I didn't see you—*you*. What are you doing here, Vincenza?"

Still slightly bent forward, softly shaking the liquid from my shirt, my eyes snap upward at the sound of *his* voice.

"Me?" I squeak, absolutely dumbfounded that of the roughly one point eight million people who live in Manhattan, *he's* the one who's slammed into me. "What are *you* doing here?"

Sly laughs, deep and unrestrained. Tossing his hands into the air, he says, "Unbelievable." Then he turns and walks away.

I stare at his back for several seconds, reeling over the exchange, before I snap out of it and gather my thoughts. Bending to pick up my empty coffee cup that's rolling near my feet from the light breeze, I smash it in my fist before slamming it into the trash can a few steps away.

Looking down, I'm mildly relieved to see the majority of the coffee soaked my blouse and *not* my favorite coat, though it did take some of the splatter. At this point, I have no choice but to get a cab back to my office so I can change. If there's time, I'll send one of the interns to grab another latte from the cafe on the corner near our building—which is where I should have gone to begin with.

Once I'm back at the corner, I lift my arm to get myself a car, but find myself turning when I hear quick footsteps hitting the pavement behind me. My attention is drawn as I see Sly jogging my way.

It's then I notice he's in black jeans and what appears to be a black medical scrub shirt beneath his black leather jacket. It's no secret that Sly's father is one of the most prominent surgeons on the Upper East Side, but I hadn't realized his son was also in the medical field.

When he reaches me, his brows are furrowed with confliction. He reaches out as though he's about to touch my arm, but then, at the last second, he drops his arm. "I wasn't paying attention. I apologize."

His apology is short and to the point, but as he says it, his eyes sweep over me, looking at the devastation caused to my shirt.

I'm not in the mood for an insincere apology. In the few times we've met, his interactions with me have been rude, if not one step above hostile, and it's crystal clear that the hatred for my family extends to me—he's made that known.

So, curiosity be damned, I'm not engaging.

Turning back toward the street, I lift my hand again as a cab driver speeds by without stopping. Another is further behind, stuck at a stoplight. I'll try harder to get that one's attention.

"Vinnie." I hear my name between his lips, but I stay strong and pretend like I haven't.

The sound of the crosswalk chirps next to me, and to distract myself, I take another step toward the edge of the curb.

"Vinnie," Sly tries again, his voice louder this time.

Pushing up to my tiptoes, I look to see where the yellow cab went, leaning forward slightly in an attempt to see past the cars blocking my view.

In a split second, a passing car quickly switches into the lane I'm practically standing in—the speed throwing me off-kilter and causing me to waver on the edge. I nearly slip and fall into the street when a hand grabs my arm, pulling me out of the way.

Slamming back into Sly, my hands instinctively land on his chest as his grip on my arm stabilizes me.

"Christ, Vincenza," he breathes, his voice unsteady and thick.

Once again, I'm too stunned to speak—something that seems to be becoming a trend around this man. Realizing I'm still pressing my hands against his chest, I drop my arms and take a step back, putting some distance between us. The close proximity is too intoxicating.

Swallowing thickly, I lick my lips, readying myself to thank him, but I don't miss the way his eyes drop to my mouth when I do.

"I—thanks…"

"Try to be more careful. Why are you taking a taxi, anyway? Where is your driver?"

My brows stitch together for a second. "Why do you care?"

It's juvenile, but it flies from my mouth faster than I can stop it. His expression is stone while he waits for me to give him a real answer. With a dramatic sigh, I cross my arms over my chest. "I didn't use my driver. Grabbed a cab here to get a coffee, and was planning on walking back to my office to clear my head a little—it's been a long week. But now that my shirt's soaked, I need to catch a cab back."

"Where is your office building?" he asks, his vibrant hazel eyes staring into mine. The anger is gone from his voice, but his gaze is still as intense as always.

"Manhattan Valley. On Columbus and 97th."

"That's over a mile from here."

"Yes, and I'm fully capable of walking a mile."

"You're not wearing the proper footwear."

Looking down at my flats, I take in the shine of the black patent vegan leather shoes. They're not ideal for walking, but they certainly are better than heels.

"There's nothing wrong with my flats," I respond airily, brushing him off. "Anyway, it doesn't matter now. My walk is ruined, so if you'll excuse me." Turning back to the street, I look for any sign of a cab, but of course, there's not a yellow car in sight.

From behind, I hear Sly blow out an exasperated breath. "I can give you a shirt. I only live two blocks from here. You can change, then take your walk."

Over my shoulder, I eye him suspiciously. Borrow a shirt? Follow him to his *home*? The thought is absurd.

But the twenty-four-ounce latte soaked into the fabric of my shirt has now grown cold, and with every press of it against my skin, a smattering of goosebumps lines my arms and torso.

"What's the catch?" I ask, knowing there's no way he's offering out of the kindness of his heart. For the Paladinos, there is no kindness from the Luchettis.

Shoving his hands into the pockets of his leather jacket, he shakes his head, looking almost as defeated as I feel. "No catch. I understand the need for a long walk after an even longer week."

He leaves then, not bothering to see if I'm following. I'm torn in two—not wanting, but also *wanting* to follow. I don't *have* to. I can easily hail a cab and go to my office, but the curious side of me wants to see this through.

Staying ten steps behind, I let him lead the way back to his apartment, purposely never getting closer.

Every crosswalk is green as we approach, and the walk is quick. I'm a little surprised when he veers toward a gorgeous building, walking through the open door past a smiling doorman. He tips his hat at me as I walk in after Sly.

Sly holds the elevator door open, waiting for me, but I'm slow to reach him, taking my time to look around at the lobby of his building. It's beautiful— recently remodeled, I'd assume by looking at its modern fixtures.

Honestly, though, I'm stalling, too. Doubting whether I made the right choice by following him here and taking him up on his offer of giving me a shirt to wear. My heart's racing with every step closer to that elevator, knowing that once the doors close, we're no longer in a public setting. At least in public, there's no room for error. Any misstep from either side could be a tabloid feeding frenzy—it's already surprising that the local paparazzi haven't caught us in any of our run-ins. But in public, we're forced to hold it together, keep our voices down.

There's no telling what may happen once we're alone.

His expression is solemn as I step into the elevator next to him, as though he's walking to his execution. And maybe, in his mind, he is. Interaction with a Paladino, with *me*, could be as detrimental to his family's opinion of him as it would be to mine.

And maybe that's why, as the elevator doors close, shutting us out from the rest of the world, I find it hard to swallow the bittersweet emotion that's lodged in my throat.

Chapter 13

Sly

The moment she stepped into the elevator, I knew I made a mistake.

Offering a replacement shirt to Vinnie—allowing her to follow me to my home…

By far the most idiotic thing I've done in recent years.

But the frustration in her eyes after her coffee spilled down the front of her—the *defeat*, and hearing about how she had planned on a walk to clear her head.

I've battled those demons. I know the need to be amongst the fresh air simply to let your thoughts fade away.

So I did two things I never thought I'd ever do. The first: I *apologized* to a *Paladino*. And the second: I extended a semblance of goodwill their family doesn't deserve.

"It has nothing to do with me."

Her words still haunt me. There's some truth to them, but it doesn't rewrite the past.

I'm stiff as a board the entire elevator ride to my floor, and I practically run out the moment the doors open.

Leading the way to my apartment, I slide the metal casing of the keypad and step closer, making sure my body hides the code I am entering. A green light illuminates, indicating the door is unlocked.

A gentleman would hold the door and step aside to let the lady enter first. But as I enter my home, I don't bother holding it for her, nor do I look to see if she's following.

The gentle sound of the door clicking into place rather than slamming shut tells me she's behind me, but instead of acknowledging her presence, I move to the coat closet and shrug off my jacket.

I take my time hanging it up, disguising my hammering heart as aloofness.

My body is filled with a sensation that's become unfamiliar. *Nerves.* Something I've long since experienced.

Knowing Vinnie is in my apartment has the neurons in my brain going haywire. I can *feel* her presence around me. Every bone in my body, every instinct in my soul, has me tightening my hands into fists as I work ten times harder than I should have to just to push one single thought from my mind.

The most beautiful woman I've ever seen is standing inside my apartment.

I should hate her.

I *do* hate her.

At least, that's what I continue to tell myself.

The breath inside my lungs catches as I turn and see her wandering around my living room, her eyes trailing along my space, taking it all in.

The natural light shines through the windows and casts a warm glow on the side of the apartment she's on, making her appear ethereal and angelic.

But I know there is nothing angelic about her when the devil is her father.

"Did you just move in?" she asks, her eyes lingering on a box next to my nearly empty bookshelf. The box holds the majority of my books, still tucked safely inside. She cranes her neck a bit to see past the cardboard siding and into it.

"Not recently enough to justify still having unpacked boxes," I muse as I lean against the wall of my living room, watching her. Curiosity is written all over her face as her eyes draw a path from the box of books to the bookshelf.

Her eyes meet mine briefly, and I do my best to make sure my expression remains impassive.

Next, she ventures to the mantel of my fireplace, her fingertips trailing over the bottom of my picture frames—various photos that I cherish of my family, my old dog Polpetta, and even one of me, Enzo, and Sully back when we were in college. When she stops in front of the final frame, I hold my breath.

Before moving back to New York, my last patient in

Verona was a little boy whose mother I had to treat more and more frequently toward the end of my time abroad. She was the victim of domestic violence and had come to me at various times for a sprained wrist, a dislocated elbow, and severe stomach pain.

It was only when the violence turned to her son did she accept my offer to help her get out of her situation. When she brought him in, she was sobbing hysterically—absolutely beside herself in fear—and her son was bleeding from his forehead. His father had shoved him, and he hit his head on the edge of a wooden chair.

He required four stitches.

When his mother brought him back for me to remove the stitches, I presented her with new identities for them both, train tickets to Monaco, and enough cash for them to comfortably start anew.

After I gave her all of those things, her son handed me a picture he drew—a stick figure drawing of him, smiling from my exam table with a lollipop in his hand and a Band-Aid on his head, and a stick figure of me smiling at him next to the table.

Not prepared to talk about the meaning behind the drawing, I wordlessly push off the wall and walk into my bedroom to get Vinnie a shirt as promised.

My fingers flick the light switch in my closet so I can see which one to pick. My options are limited, being that I rarely wear any color other than black, but I decide to bring her a button-down, as it is like the one she has on.

Before I emerge from my room, I take a few deep breaths.

All I have to do is hand her the shirt, allow her a few moments to change, and say goodbye.

Another five minutes, maximum.

Then I can go back to my day, and my life, and *hopefully* not have any more run-ins with Vincenza.

Momentarily, I question why that thought causes a bleak heaviness within me before I shake the feeling away, pull myself together, and stride out of my room.

Rounding the corner, I see her back is toward me while she stands at my kitchen sink, the water on a low stream. Part of her cream-colored coat sits on the edge of the marble as she gently dabs and twists with a bundle of wet paper towels.

"Is it ruined?" I ask, coming to the edge of the kitchen.

She lets the water soak into the towel again before squeezing the excess, turning off the faucet, and returning to her coat. "I hope not. It's my favorite."

"I grabbed you a shirt." My voice is gruff, and a small twinge of regret for my tone sears through me.

"Do you always have a back stock of women's shirts at your apartment?"

With her question, which drips with sass and attitude, I cannot stop myself from stalking toward her—the need to close the distance is palpable.

My footsteps alert her to my proximity, and she turns around, her gaze connecting with mine as she abandons cleaning her coat.

When I approach, my hands naturally grasp the edge of the counter, caging her in. She attempts to take a step back, but there's nowhere for her to go.

I lean into her, invading her space. Our breath mingles, and I fight against my instinct to touch her. "Who said it is a woman's shirt? Maybe I want to see how you'd look in one of mine."

Vinnie's eyes widen as she sucks in a breath between her teeth, giving me the reaction I hoped for. With the turmoil she's causing inside my chest, I appreciate seeing it reciprocated.

She's quick to react, though, and surprises me when she tilts her lips into a smile and says, "How was your date with Norah?"

Laughing, I drop my head. So *this* is what Sully meant when he said he saw her. He told her about the date. The question is, why?

Perhaps you're not as good at hiding your attraction as you think, you idiota.

Looking back up, Vinnie is staring at me expectantly, truly waiting for my answer.

"She had beautiful lips," I say in earnest, a smile gracing my own as I remember—and choose to laugh about—how absolutely horrendous that date was. I can't even say I am pleased with how it ended.

Vincenza's face falls—her mask dropping enough that I can read my response was not what she wanted to hear.

Reaching up, my thumb ghosts her bottom lip before pulling it slightly so it drags away from where her perfectly white teeth sink into it. "Nothing like yours, though."

Beneath my touch, I feel her lips part, creating a lovely O shape. I tear my gaze from hers, taking in her reaction. Her cheeks have turned a beautiful shade of light pink, and her chest rises and falls a little quicker, much like my own. When I bring my eyes back to hers, they stay locked for several long, tortuous seconds.

The startling idea of kissing her enters my mind, and I realize I want nothing more than to do just that. To press my lips against hers, to taste her. Feel her body melt into mine as my hand fists her long, beautiful hair.

The daydream overtakes me, and immediately I take a step back. Pulling the shirt from where it lays over my shoulder, I hold it out to her to take.

"There's a bathroom adjacent to the front door," I tell her after I clear my throat.

She takes the shirt from my hands, careful not to touch me as she does, and races past me in the direction I said.

When I hear the door close, I run my fingers through my hair and turn toward the sink, leaning my elbows onto it while I try to get a grip on what just happened, and what I *almost* did.

Nothing in my life could have prepared me for the moment Vinnie steps out of my bathroom dressed in my shirt.

Leaving it halfway unbuttoned from the bottom to allow one side to tuck into her pants, she's rolled the sleeves to her elbows and kept the top few buttons open.

It's too big on her frame, but the way she's styled it to adapt to her is stunning.

She is stunning.

My mouth goes dry the longer I look at her, and I can feel my body react in other ways.

Heart rate quickening. Cock hardening.

What is happening to me?

The silence stretches between us as she eyes me with skepticism, still standing in the doorway.

For all intents and purposes, our interaction is at its end. She came for a shirt, and now she's wearing it, so it's time for her to go.

But I find myself not wanting her to.

"Would you like something to drink?" The sound of my own voice is foreign to my ears as I ask her to stay.

Her eyes narrow a fraction, and she takes a moment before answering. "Care to make me a latte since you spilled my last one?"

She must have seen my espresso machine to know that I have the capability to make her one. Sully bought it for me as a housewarming gift, though it was mostly for *his* benefit—the man has more espresso in his bloodstream than water.

"Sure, but you'll have to choose from regular sugar or honey as a sweetener." Walking to the kitchen, I turn the machine on. It roars to life, gurgling as it warms the water from the reservoir.

"Lucky for you I ordered a honey oat milk latte," Vinnie says as she comes to a stop at the kitchen island. Leaning into it, she rests her elbows on the marble and watches me.

As I reach for a mug, I turn my head toward her. "Are you lactose intolerant?"

If she is, I can't make her a latte. But there is a bodega on the corner…

No. I do not *owe* her anything.

Her head shakes, the loose curls bouncing. "No, I just wanted to try the drink."

I say nothing as I move to my fridge and reach for the whole milk inside.

When I complete her drink, I set it on the island in front of her and move to the other side, pulling out a barstool to sit on. She pulls the mug to her lips, blowing on the liquid as steam rises in front of her.

"This is delicious, thank you. And thanks for letting me borrow a shirt," she says, but she's not looking at me. Instead, she's still looking around my apartment. Or at least what she can see of it.

Silence stretches between us, and I'm surprised that it's not uncomfortable. While she looks around, I look at her, watching as she sips her coffee. Her hands are wrapped around the mug, holding it tightly.

For some reason, my heart begins to race.

"What do you do, Vincenza?"

Slowly, she returns her gaze to mine. "I own an independent publishing house."

"Ah, so that is why you seemed to have an interest in my books earlier."

She grins. "Yes. Books are my love language. I'd rather spend my time in the company of thousands of words than a group of people."

"Ironic for someone who's considered a socialite in the tabloids."

Her brow raises in question. "*You* of all people should know you can't believe everything you read in the papers."

"Sì, this is true."

Silence surrounds us again. Vinnie chews on her bottom lip nervously. I can practically see the wheels in her head turning. She wants to say something, but she's holding back.

"You look like you have something on the tip of your tongue." Curiosity gets the better of me, despite part of me not wanting to further engage. The more time I spend in her presence, the weaker my resolve becomes.

I should not be *this* intrigued by her.

She hesitates, but finally speaks her mind. "I was just thinking about this quarrel between our families. It's ridiculous."

Anger spikes within me. Ridiculous? My uncle was murdered at the hand of her father, and she's calling it *ridiculous*.

As they so frequently do, her words echo through my mind again. *"It has nothing to do with me."*

I can feel my nostrils flare as I force the oxygen from

my lungs, attempting to calm myself before I speak, in fear of what I may say.

"What do you remember of that day?" I ask through gritted teeth.

Setting the mug down, she thinks several long seconds before answering. "I was young, Sly…"

"As was I, yet I remember every moment. What do *you* remember?"

A sigh of exasperation leaves her lips before she responds. "I remember my mother coming into my bedroom, urging me to put on a dress I hated. I remember walking into the sitting room and seeing your family, then all of us moving to the dining room. After dinner, my father dismissed us, and we all left."

"And after?"

"I remember a loud bang, and my mother ushering me upstairs quickly. I know now that bang was a gunshot."

"Sì. Your father shot my uncle in the face before the dining room doors had even fully shut. I practically witnessed it."

She winces and looks away from me. From this angle I can see tears line her lashes—whether they're genuine or if she's a talented actress, I'm unsure.

"Until my late teenage years, I wasn't even aware of what my father did. I'd always grown up believing his coffee business was the reason for his fortune. I had no idea what else he was doing."

I search her face, looking for any indication that she's lying, but I sense she's telling me the truth.

Still, something gnaws at me. If she was as unaware as she claims, *why* does her brother despise her as much as he does? It feels like there's a piece of the puzzle that's missing.

So, I ask, "Why does your brother harbor so much animosity toward you, Vincenza?"

This seems to irritate her, and I finally see the fire in her eyes. The same fire she had the night of the masquerade.

"That's quite a personal question for someone who claims to hate me."

"Perhaps the hate is dwindling the more time I spend with you." As soon as the words are spoken, I wish I could take them back.

Yes, it's true. However, now I've shown her my cards. That I am thawing to her is now apparent.

Her head tilts, scrutinizing me through questioning eyes, but with it, I see her soften, too.

"We used to be close," she begins, a look of sadness washing over her features. "He's two years older than I am, but that made no difference throughout our childhood. He was my best friend…"

Her voice trails off, and a twinge of guilt hits me square in the chest because my question placed the sorrow on her features.

"Once we got older, Joseph began to notice the favoritism our father awarded me. But our father was my hero—my favorite person. I was daddy's little girl… At first, Joseph was jealous because of the attention, but when we became young adults, he assumed that because of how close we were, Father would want me to take over his business—well, businesses—someday. And from jealousy, stemmed hatred."

My head bobs in understanding as she tells me about her relationship with her brother. It makes sense now—that the bastardo would turn against his own sister. *Of course* he would. Joseph Paladino is the most deplorable man I have ever met.

I open my mouth to speak, to offer a sense of comfort and apologize for his bad behavior even though it isn't my place, but she cuts me off.

"I don't need your sympathy. You've made it very clear how you feel about my family—about *me*. Honestly, I'm not even sure why I'm still here." She stands abruptly from the barstool she settled on long ago, its legs screeching against the hardwood floors.

Pulling her coat from the counter by the sink, she's through my kitchen, and I don't stop to think—I just react—following her through my apartment and to the front door. She's there faster than I can fathom, grabbing her phone off my entryway table.

As she reaches for the doorknob, I catch her wrist and pull her toward me.

Everything inside of me crumbles the moment she's in my arms. The anger, the hatred—gone.

My arms circle around her lower back as I pull her close—much closer than we were earlier. Pressing her hands against my chest, she doesn't fight me holding her, and instead surprises me when she leans against me.

As though they have a mind of their own, my fingers brush rhythmically against hers.

Touching her—comforting her—feels natural.

Feels right.

I let my mind wander back to the day we met as children and the curiosity I felt toward her then. The same curiosity I feel now. It's as though years have passed, but the wonder has not faded.

"I wasn't offering you my sympathy, Vinnie."

She breathes me in, shifting in my hold. I wonder for a moment if she's going to step away, but she doesn't, so I continue.

"Your words from the masquerade have stuck with me. You told me this feud between our families has nothing to do with you, and I think about that often."

"Because it *doesn't*," she argues, but my statement was not an argument to begin with.

Reaching between us, I use my thumb and pointer finger to grasp her chin, tipping it back so she's looking me in the eye. "Sì, it does. We cannot ignore who we are. Where we come from. La mia famiglia is the most important part of my life, and I can't just pretend like they aren't."

"I've never onc—"

"But I also cannot pretend like I feel nothing when I'm around *you*."

Vinnie's breathing hitches with my admission, sucking in a breath as confusion blankets her face.

For a moment, I look up at the ceiling and urge

myself to continue. I'm at war with myself at this moment, blurring the lines between right and wrong.

Everything as I know it could go up in flames if I've misread her at any point.

"I should hate you, but I don't. I should recoil from your touch, from your scent, from your very *being*. I should be strong enough to stay away from you, but when you're near, I find myself wanting to do the very opposite."

"You don't even know me," Vinnie whispers. She's still standing in my arms, giving me her full attention even though my hand has returned to grip the other, resting on her back.

"No, but I *want* to. And that's a problem for me, Vincenza, because I'm *supposed* to loathe you."

The words linger between us, echoing through the magnetism that zips in the air. I swallow thickly, and her tongue peeks from between her lips to wet them, my eyes dropping to track the movement.

Then suddenly, the spell is broken.

Vinnie gently pushes her hands against my chest, breaking the chain my arms have created behind her, and she steps back, out of my hold.

"We can't," she says quietly, shaking her head.

"I know."

"I have to go." She takes a step, her hand wrapping around the doorknob to leave.

My stomach falls, and I hate that every fiber of my being wants me to beg her to stay.

"I know," I agree, but she's already gone.

Chapter 14

Sly

Four days have passed and I'm surprised I have yet to go into cardiac arrest with the way my heart has been aggressively racing behind my rib cage.

My mind has replayed the day Vinnie came to my apartment over and over, scrutinizing every detail, my brain raging a war between whether I made a colossal mistake or simply a naïve one.

I should have never spoken my mind about my interest in her. It was foolish, and I had let myself fall into a moment of weakness. A fleeting moment where I removed the rivalry between our families and took a step back, looking at the woman in front of me and allowing myself to think about what could happen if she wasn't a Paladino.

To deny my attraction to her would be an outright lie. Still, these last few days have been eating me alive.

"Sylvester, amore mio, sembri teso." *Sylvester, my love, you seem tense.*

Mia madre has her arm looped through mine as we stroll together through Central Park. It's a beautiful day, the sun is brightly shining through the trees, the air warm. But Mamma is perceptive. She can read me like a book.

"It's just been a long week, Mamma. I am okay."

"You may fool the world, mio figlio, but you cannot fool tua madre. Tell me, what is plaguing your mind?"

Telling her is tempting, but I know I could never. She would keep my secret, but the disappointment she'll surely have is enough to keep my lips sealed. Her anger does not burn as brightly as the men in our family, but it's still there.

To admit that I am feeling even the smallest of feelings toward a Paladino would bring great shame. I can't even tell mia madre about my work frustrations, as that is another secret I keep.

They keep piling up, and if I'm not careful, I fear I may drown in them.

"There is nothing, Mamma." I place my hand over hers as it rests on my forearm, patting it lightly in reassurance.

Steering her to an empty bench beneath the shade of an oak, we sit. She unhooks her arm from mine and turns toward me, allowing one of her arms to drape across the back.

"I worry about you, my Sly. Since you have returned from Europe, you seem discontent. Perhaps you can explore a residency here in the city? Surely your father has some sway in his hospital."

I knew this conversation would arise at some point, but I still feel unprepared for it. How does one admit to their mother that they *do* practice medicine, just not in the traditional, legal way?

You don't, unfortunately.

"Sì," I tell her. "I've planned to explore my options." It's the best I can say at the moment. One day, I'll come clean about everything, but today isn't that day.

"All I want is your happiness. Guilio told me you had a date last week. How was it?"

For the love of all things holy, Guilio, I mentally curse my brother. Such a Mamma's boy, telling her everything unless he is explicitly told not to.

"It was…" I begin, my voice trailing off as I think back to that night, trying to think of something positive to tell her. "Well, Romèo et Juliette was wonderful. You would love it."

"Sì, but the girl?"

Sighing deeply, I give her a weak smile. "Vapid. Nice enough, I suppose, but there will not be a second date."

"That's a shame," she says lightly, patting my knee. "Perhaps the next one. How does that saying go? There are plenty of fish in the sea? Someday, you will meet someone who intrigues you and challenges you, amore mio."

My mind flits to Vinnie, the image of her sitting at my kitchen island drinking coffee, wandering into my mind.

I begin to see visions of her in ways I never have, my brain conjuring up new ideas. Her with her dark hair piled on top of her head, wearing my gray joggers, rolled at her hips to keep them up. Vinnie laying on my couch while we watch a movie, curled up with my pillow in her arms. Us holding hands as we round the corner to Di Mercutio, grabbing a late night bite to eat.

The visions are like a punch to the gut, knocking the air from my lungs.

Mamma takes my hand in hers and gives it a gentle squeeze, pulling me from my thoughts.

Giving her a tight-lipped smile, I nod once and squeeze her hand back. "Sì, Mamma, perhaps someday."

But I can't help but wonder if maybe I already have.

Chapter 15

Vinnie

"And you're absolutely positive you can't meet me there?"

Cecilia lets out a long sigh from the other end of the phone. "Vin, seriously? I'm going to a *funeral.*"

"For your second cousin's stepmother," I sass, but she knows from my tone I'm joking. Although, part of me isn't.

Sunday brunch isn't going to be the same without her.

Skyscrapers blur past as Ross weaves through the traffic, navigating us away from the busy roads until we can veer down a side street that leads to Central Park.

Brunch today is at Blankenship House, a posh restaurant on the edge of The Lake in Central Park. It overlooks the waters, and my mother keeps gushing about the ambiance and has been trying to get us all there for weeks now.

"Family is still family. You know that. I'll be back at your house before you know it."

"*Home*," I emphasize. "You'll be *home* later. I don't know why you insist on referring to it as mine when you've lived there since day one, too."

Because she still sees herself as the help, even though we're years and years past that.

"Mmhmm, I'll see you at *home*, Vinnie. Try not to have too much fun verbally sparring with Joey without me there to witness it."

"Ugh, don't hold your breath. You know how he is."

She laughs quietly. "Yes, unfortunately, I do. Text me if you need me."

"Have fun at the funeral."

"*Vinnie!*" she reprimands through her laughter.

"You know what I mean!"

The soft sounds of her amusement float through the phone as she ends the call. Looking back out my window, I set my phone down on my lap, and try to get in the right headspace for brunch.

I love my family. I do—*so* much—even Joseph. But my god, sometimes they're mentally exhausting.

Being the only daughter of Maurizio Paladino comes with responsibilities and expectations.

My parents love me, but growing up, they expected me to be the picture-perfect example of Manhattan royalty.

Oh, who am I kidding? They still do.

Talking about things that are still hypothetical—my wedding, my husband, my *children*—as if I'm not single and successful on my own, or perfectly content without any of those things.

Of course, I want them someday, but right now, I'm focusing on *me*.

Our family has three men who can carry out my father's legacy and take over the business. Continue the family name. Grace them with grandchildren. The latter still seems to fall onto my shoulders, though, which is why my mother absolutely loves to send me to galas, charity balls, and any event she can on her behalf.

She loves these events, but over the last year, she's been picking and choosing the ones to attend, and berating me into going to the others for her.

I know what she's doing.

She's hoping that I'll meet someone, fall head over heels in love, sell my company, and pop out a few kids.

Still, I find myself entertaining it—being a dutiful daughter and putting on a pretty dress for every one of them.

Clearing his throat, Ross meets my gaze in the rearview mirror. "We're here, Miss Paladino."

I hadn't even felt the car come to a stop, I was so lost in thought. "Thank you, Ross."

"Of course," he says before he slips out the driver's side and comes to open my door.

Placing his palm face up for me to grab, he adds, "I'll be parked nearby, so please send me a message about ten minutes before you're ready to leave."

"Sounds good, thank you, Ross. Enjoy your break."

Stepping onto the curb, I stare at the building, so

beautifully overgrown with ivy crawling up the sides and onto the roof. The lake peeks from behind, the dark blue glimmering from the sunlight that shines through the surrounding trees.

The park is quiet, and though from the windows I see the inside bustling with activity, Blankenship House seems like a picture from a fairytale on the outside.

I hardly take two steps before a doorman greets me, welcoming me in, where a waitress awaits.

"Right this way, Miss Paladino," she tells me with a bright smile, ushering me through the restaurant, toward a private section of the patio that overlooks the water.

As we pass, I see more than a few eyes wandering toward me, and unfortunately, a few cell phones point in my direction.

You'd think I'd be used to it by now, but the pit in my stomach never goes away. It's strange—being someone that people want to take photos of because they simply see them out in public. I couldn't imagine actually being famous in a country or worldwide capacity. Being well-known in Manhattan is anxiety-inducing enough.

"Vincenza!" my mother squeals as I step through the French doors and out onto the patio. She stands and greets me in a hug as I reach the table. Over her shoulder, my father smiles at me, while Luciano places his phone screen down on the table before standing as well. I go to him next, allowing my oldest brother to wrap me in a tight embrace.

"Hey, Sis."

"Hey," I greet, stepping out of his hold. Leaning over, I playfully punch Sam against his shoulder, since he hasn't bothered to look up. "Um, hello? No love for your sister, or what?"

Beneath his chin-length mop of dark brown curls, he pops an earbud out. "What?"

"Samuele, you're twenty-one years old. Stop acting like you're a teenager and show your sister some respect," my father barks from across the table.

"Show *everyone* some respect, Samuele," Luciano adds.

"Okay, okay," Sam scoffs, pulling the second earbud out. Popping open the case, he pushes each one into it without looking up.

Defeat rolls off of him in waves. As the youngest, he's often treated as such. Babied by our mother. Disciplined by our father, as well as Luciano and Joseph. It's a lot.

I try to keep our relationship playful and carefree, but often I see him disassociating and climbing back into his shell. He's overstimulated easily and needs to be left alone—especially in social settings—which I completely understand.

The others in our family aren't as understanding.

"It's fine. I was just playing with him. He smiled at me when I walked over, don't worry." Once again, I come to his aid, covering for him when it's a white lie. It rolls off my tongue easily, as I've said similar things many times over the years.

In our world, in *Manhattan*, you have two options: sink or swim. I vowed never to let myself sink, no matter how tumultuous the waves get. And as I watch my little brother barely tread water, I can't help but always extend a life preserver.

"So, Sunshine, how's your week been?" my father asks, as he does every Sunday.

Taking my seat, I pull my napkin onto my lap and smooth it. Nothing about my week stands out, except for my time spent with Sly, which for obvious reasons, I'll be taking to my grave.

A familiar surge of adrenaline spikes through my body as I think of him, though. "It was good. Busy, but that just made the days pass faster. How was your week?"

"Much better now that I'm seeing your smiling face."

My mother beams and reaches for his hand, giving it a light squeeze. She loves that he dotes upon me so much. On all of us. For every horrid thing he has ever done, being a bad husband or father isn't on the list. He loves us all fiercely.

"Well, I have a reason to smile," I coo as I deliberately look at the empty seats at the table, not so subtly referring to the absence of my middle brother. To my left, Luciano chuckles as he takes a sip of his ice water. "Just us today?"

"Oh, no, little sis, you know I wouldn't miss family brunch for the world."

Dread claws in the center of my stomach when I

hear the snide tone of Joseph's voice, but that dread turns to nausea when I look over my shoulder to see both him *and* August standing at the entrance to the patio.

"August!" my mother squeals, much like the way she did when I arrived.

"Leighton, always a pleasure," he says as he crosses the room to kiss her on the cheek. "I hope you don't mind that I've tagged along."

"Not at all," my father affirms, standing with his hand extended. August grips it, and my father pulls him in to clap his shoulder. "You're an honorary Paladino."

Hearing that makes my stomach recoil.

Joseph brought August around only a few years ago, and I've never had a good feeling about him. Still, he's weaseled his way into my parents' good graces and has held on like the leech he is. Despite voicing my concerns, I feel like I'm the only one who can see through his facade. He's a snake, and frankly, he makes my skin crawl.

"Hello, beautiful," he purrs as he slides against me, bending so he can wrap his arm around my shoulders in a side hug.

"August," I greet curtly. Attempting to shrug him off, I shoot a look at Luciano, silently asking for help.

Thankfully, my eldest brother can sense my discomfort. "August, perhaps you should keep your hands to yourself. It's clear my sister isn't consenting to you touching her."

August glares at my brother, shooting daggers from

his eyes before he pulls away. As he goes, he skates his fingers across my shoulder blades and twists a lock of my hair around his finger, giving it a slight tug before releasing it.

Luciano sees it and immediately stands, his chair scuffing loudly against the floor as he does. No words are exchanged as my brother stares him down, and August backs away slowly with a sinister smile playing on his lips.

"Oh, relax, Luce. August just has a harmless crush on our baby sister," Joseph comments, his smile as deplorable as his friend's.

Now, both Luciano and I glare at Joseph.

Are you kidding me?

From across the table, my mother shrieks a really shrill and giddy sound, and all heads snap to her. A wide smile overtakes her face as she holds her hands together in front of her. Excitedly she bursts, "Oh my goodness, isn't that so sweet!"

August chuckles as he and Joseph round the table to take the two empty chairs next to Sam.

"So, Joseph, what was it that you had to tell me?" my father asks when Joseph settles, without looking up from his menu.

Joseph scoffs, and I do my best to pretend like I'm studying my meal choices when I'm really listening intently.

"I think this is a conversation best kept private, Father."

"I trust all those in the room right now, do you not?"

"Of course, I do," Joseph snaps, though I know him well enough to hear the outright lie in his voice. He doesn't trust anyone but himself.

"Well then," Father urges, his voice flat. He waves his hand dismissively over his menu.

No sooner do the words leave his lips, does the waitress reappear. Time moves painfully slow as she attentively comes to each of us, taking our orders and confirming that we have everything we need for the time being. When she leaves again, Joseph surprises me by picking up where his and Father's conversation left off.

"That Lucchetti trash has been sniffing around again. My guy at the docks reported him showing up on the surveillance cameras two days in a row, after hours."

Heart sinking, my eyes bounce from Joseph to our father. The expression on Father's face is hardened, and he stays silent as though he's waiting for my brother to say more. When he doesn't, he gruffly asks, "And?"

For the quickest of seconds, Joseph's face falls, but he quickly returns it to his typical menacing scowl. "And he's a piece of shit who's sniffing around our territory looking for *something*."

"Which Lucchetti?"

"Lorenzo. Gabriele's son. You should just let me eliminate the problem like you did with his father—we can easily take care of it swiftly and unsuspectingly."

A small, shaky breath escapes my lungs when I hear the name Lorenzo.

They're not talking about Sly.

I shouldn't care.

"We cannot eliminate a problem that doesn't exist," my father snaps.

Joseph argues back like a five-year-old. "But he's—"

"He was caught on the cameras twice. Presumably, sniffing around a dead end because there is nothing he could have found. It is not your job to monitor the docks, Joseph. Whoever your informant is, tell him his job with *you* is done, or I will find out who he is and see to it that his *actual* job is over."

A tense thickness clouds us as my father's irritation hangs in the air. We all stay silent as he and Joseph stare at each other, awkwardly watching my brother attempt to assert his dominance and challenge our father.

He should know he'll never win.

Coming to his aid, August clears his throat, taking a small sip of his ice water and directing the conversation toward my mother. "So, Leighton. My aunt was asking if you'd be attending the Gallagher luncheon next month?"

I stop listening, because truly, I couldn't care less. Pulling my phone out, I scroll through the messages and see one from Raina. As my eyes skim the words, a smile pulls at my lips.

RAINA

> This isn't the same without you. Why did you decide that your job was more important than me again? Surely you're regretting your choices. We could be sipping coffee in a cafe on Rue Des Martyrs right now.

She's right, and I hate that she's right. This is the first year of many that I haven't gone with her to Paris for Fashion Week.

> Trust me, I regret the decision.
> Miss you.

Her response comes immediately.

> Miss you. I've got a date tonight with a hottie who's here from Spain, but he said his friend would be tagging along, too. Think I'll end up with a menage situation? When in Paris?

> Isn't the expression 'When in Rome?'

> Close enough.

A snort of laughter bubbles through me as my fingers fly over the on-screen keyboard.

> Turn on your location, okay?

> Yes, mom. Don't worry, I'll be under the protection of Javier and Felipe.

Who you literally just met.

Don't be such a buzzkill.

"Really, Sis?" Luciano elbows me in the arm softly. "Texting during brunch? You're lucky Leighton is distracted."

"You're lucky Father hasn't put you in an early grave for disrespecting our mother by calling her by her first name," I quip, typing out one last message to Raina.

Gotta go, Luciano's giving me grief. Love you. Be safe. Hope you get two dicks tonight.

Tell Luciano there's still room for one more if he wants to hop on a flight really quick. Love you!

Inwardly, I shudder. Raina has been goading me for *years* about how attractive she thinks my brother is.

Five years older than us, he always embodied that 'older, forbidden man' vibe to her, and for some reason, it's kept her interested. Luciano has never so much as batted an eye in her direction.

Stowing my phone back in my clutch, I look up in time to see several of the waitstaff step onto the patio with our plates in hand. The scent immediately fills the open air, and my mouth waters, realizing I'm much hungrier than I thought.

As like every Sunday, there's comfortable small talk

while we eat, and I do my best to dodge my mother's incessant questions about whether I've met anyone, the next event I'd be available to attend, or anything of the sort.

I'm grateful to Luciano for helping steer the conversation away from me by engaging our mother in any topic of meaningless conversation he can think of.

When my father's voice booms from across the table suddenly, I startle. "How're things at the firm, Luciano? I heard Gamble took the Hopper case?"

Luciano is a very prominent divorce lawyer in Manhattan. Funny that a drug connoisseur's son would become a lawyer, isn't it? He made quite the name for himself when he went into business with Simon Gamble, the top divorce lawyer in all of New York, and attached his name to the building.

The Hopper divorce has been the talk of the town for the last three weeks—one of the biggest cheating scandals to shake the Upper East Side in years. Mr. Hopper—whose name escapes me—came home early from a business trip to find his wife in bed with three of his colleagues.

Now, Mr. Hopper wants to make sure his wife is left without a dime to her name. Makes sense he'd have Gamble on retainer.

"Gamble won't stop gloating to anyone who will listen about how much of a slam dunk the case will be."

"Well, it's not like Liliana had a simple indiscretion. Her husband found her in bed with *three* men." My mother sounds horrified, and without her realizing it, she's clutching an invisible string of pearls as she brushes her fingers against her collarbone.

"I hope the man utterly destroys her," Father muses. "Both financially, and her reputation. Hopper is a good man."

Is he, though? Not from what I've heard.

"Mmhmm," Luciano murmurs, clearly trying to dismiss the conversation. "Attorney-client privilege—I can't say much."

"Well, any big case at the firm reflects positively on you. Excellent job, my boy," my father praises.

The scowl on Joseph's face deepens.

I'm grateful when we all finish our meals, ready to leave and get some distance. Even though we're outside, the air feels stifling.

"Aww, my sweet girl. Call me this week? We'll do lunch," my mother coos, pulling me in for a tight hug and a kiss on each cheek.

"That sounds good, Mother. I'll have my assistant pull my schedule first thing Monday, and I'll see which day works."

"You work too hard!"

"Price of owning a business."

When I've said my goodbyes to the rest of my family, I leave the patio, stopping to ask a waiter the direction of the restroom.

My stomach is full, and with no place to be, I decide to walk in the park for a while before texting Ross to pick me up. I'm not expecting to hear from Cecilia for the next few hours, and with Raina in Paris, the rest of my Sunday is wide open.

Taking my time at the sink, I wash my hands carefully and use a volcanic roller to absorb the excess oils from my skin. After applying a light layer of balm to my lip stain for hydration, I take a deep relaxing breath, thankful that brunch was actually pretty mild.

But I should have known I wouldn't get out of here scot-free. My happiness is short-lived when I exit the ladies' room and practically collide with August, who's leaning up against the wall with his arms crossed, like he has all the time in the world.

A run-in with August was inevitable. There's *always* a run-in when it comes to him. Why I thought otherwise is beyond me.

"Why are you hanging around outside of the ladies' room like a creep?" I ask, immediately regretting encouraging a conversation the moment the words are past my lips.

He smirks and reaches out to touch me, but I dodge it by taking a step back. Unfortunately, he takes one forward, crowding me again.

"Came to see you, beautiful."

"Stop calling me beautiful. It's not winning you any points."

"I don't need it to win me points. I could snap my fingers and make you mine right now, if I wanted to."

Rolling my eyes, I take a step to the side and attempt to move past him. He steps into my path, blocking me.

Deciding to engage, I ask, "Oh, really? How do you figure? It's twenty-twenty two. Last time I checked I am free to make my own choices in *all* aspects of my life."

"There are ways you can be persuaded. Trust me, I have plenty of ways to make you Mrs. St. Jean, even if it's the *last* thing you want."

"Planning on drugging me and dragging me to Vegas?"

"It could be arranged."

Rolling my eyes again, I step to the right and force my way past him, making it a few steps before he grabs me by the arm and spins me so rapidly, I slam against the wall. My head bounces against the drywall, and I wince on impact, my skull immediately aches at the base.

"You may think I'm joking, but I assure you, I'm not. The plan's already in motion, little Paladino. You're *mine*. And soon, there will be a rock on that finger that binds you to me in *all* aspects," he says with a mocking sneer. "You think Joe and I haven't been planning? Planting the seeds so daddy dearest thinks it's all his idea when he happily agrees to make you my bride?"

"He would never," I spit, turning my head to the side to put the smallest of space between us. He's too close. With every disgusting word, I can feel his hot breath on my face, and it makes me physically ill.

"Oh, he would. He's already halfway convinced that I'd be the best thing for you—the *perfect* husband. And let's be honest, Vincenza. He'd be all too happy to *sell* you to me if it meant it'd be good for business."

There's nothing I can even say back to that, because, at this moment, he's 'planting seeds', as he called it, of doubt into my head, and I can't help but wonder if my father would actually do that to his only daughter.

"Don't worry, Vinnie," August whispers, leaning closer. His hand reaches to brush a rogue curl away from my face, tucking it behind my ear. "I'll fuck you so good every night that your pussy will be throbbing. Are you one of those sluts who likes it hard, or are you going to be one of the little bitches who cries the whole time?"

His words send bile up my throat, along with a fierce need to fight back and get away from him.

"You're disgusting," I say, pressing both hands against his chest. Shoving him with all my might, I knock him back a couple of steps.

It's enough for me to get away, but just before I make it to the end of the hall, my brother rounds the corner.

"You'll get everything you deserve, sweet sister. Don't you worry. August will take good care of you."

I don't stop. I just keep moving, speed-walking through the restaurant with as much dignity as possible, holding in the nausea and fighting back the tears.

When I make it to the front doors, the doorman begins to open them, but I just want out and rudely push past him, throwing open the door myself.

Once I'm outside, I gasp for air, letting the tears fall freely.

I *hate* him.

I hate them both.

The thought of telling my father what just happened crosses my mind, but as my hand reaches into my clutch and wraps around my phone, I decide against it. I debate on calling Cecilia, or Raina, but they're both busy.

At this very moment, I feel absolutely alone.

Knowing I need to keep moving before they leave the restaurant, I briskly walk, not paying attention to which direction I'm walking or who's around me. I let the tears fall from my eyes, blurring my vision as I keep moving. Grateful I wore flats, I just let my subconscious guide me, moving through the park.

So many things are running through my mind—the brunch on a constant loop.

My chest constricts, a heaviness sitting dead center.

It's becoming hard to breathe.

My breaths are coming in short, rapid succession. The tightness in my chest feels like a snake wrapping around and constricting my organs.

"Miss, are you okay?"

I can't…I can't breathe. Everything inside my body feels like it's getting tighter and tighter.

"Miss?"

A hand on my upper arm jolts me, and I suck in a sharp breath. The city around me never slows, and from just feet away, the horn of a car blares as it slams on its brakes.

The feeling is surreal, almost as though I've been

dropped back into reality or woken up from a bad dream.

When I focus, I see a white-gloved man bent slightly to look at me, his eyes filled with concern, and I realize how crazy I must look.

Frantically, I wipe the tears from my eyes. "I'm okay. I'm so sorry."

"It's okay, Miss. I think you were having a panic attack. Are you okay? Can I call someone for you?"

"No, it's fine, truly. Thank you. I—this is embarrassing. Where am I?" I look up at the high-rise in front of me, then up and down the street, trying to get my bearings.

"The Kenna, Miss."

The Kenna.

I feel my eyes widen, and I take a step back to get a better look at my surroundings—at the apartment building looming above. The sun's reflecting off every window on the building, blinding me as I marvel at the fact that my subconscious led me here.

Led me to *him.*

The doorman steps away to go back to his post, but continues to watch me carefully, as though he's not so sure I won't go completely nuts again.

How could I have ended up outside of *his* building? I'm not even sure how far Blankenship House is from The Kenna. How long did it take me to get here? Why did I even come here to begin with?

Then a new sense of panic washes over me. What if

he comes out of his building and finds me here, lurking outside like some sort of stalker?

I need to go. *Now.*

I need to leave.

I need to text Ross and have him come get me.

Reaching into my clutch, I move the contents around until my fingers skim my phone.

But it's too late.

It doesn't make it out of my purse before I hear the smooth, deep voice I've been replaying through my mind, behind me.

"Vincenza?"

Exhaling a shaky breath, I squeeze my eyes shut before opening them and turning to face him. My breath hitches as my gaze sweeps over him, taking him in. He's in loose athletic shorts, a black t-shirt that's been cut at the sleeves, and a gym towel hanging from his neck, obviously on his way back from a workout. In his hand is a small duffle bag, and I can still see the sweat on his skin.

Immediately, concern etches his features as he takes me in, dropping the bag on the sidewalk and taking a fast step toward me. His large hands come up to cup my shoulders as he puts himself directly in my line of vision, forcing eye contact. His gaze hardens slightly as he waits for me to speak, growing impatient when I'm not instantly telling him my reason for being here.

It's only at that moment that I realize the reason why I'm here—the reason why I went into auto-pilot and was still able to make it to this building.

He makes me feel safe.

Even though I hardly know him—even though we've both been raised to hate each other, meant to be rivals in every capacity—I can sense he'd never hurt me.

"Vincenza…" he presses, still holding me by the shoulders.

His hand sweeps the hair away from my face, but it doesn't make my skin crawl like it did earlier, when August did it. Instead, I lean into his touch, if only briefly. For some reason I can't pinpoint, it steadies me.

I can feel a new wave of tears line my lashes as I look at him, swallowing thickly, before I tell him why I'm here.

Before I tell him the truth.

"I didn't know where else to go."

Chapter 16

Sly

er words break something inside of me, but at the same time, they ignite a rage unlike any other I've felt before.

As I stare at her—unshed tears, red cheeks, the look of sheer exhaustion in her eyes—I can feel in my gut something is very wrong.

But her showing up today is a surprise.

"I didn't know where else to go."

She came *here*. She came to me when she felt like she had nowhere else to turn.

Her words invoke a sense of possessiveness I have no right to feel.

But she came to *me*.

Which makes me think maybe our last interaction wasn't all in my head. She's feeling something too— something unknown and forbidden, something we *shouldn't* be feeling.

A part of me wants to ask her point-blank, but I can't. Not when she's here in distress.

For now, I do the only thing I can do. "Come upstairs. I'll make you a latte and you can tell me what happened."

Vinnie nods and follows me inside my building. The lobby is quiet—it's early in the day, just past noon, and the elevator doors open immediately after I press the call button.

Neither of us speaks as we ascend, but from the corner of my eye I can see she's closed hers and is blowing a silent breath through her lips.

Once inside my apartment, she heads straight to my couch, sinking down on it as though she's done it a thousand times. Her gaze remains on the floor, lost in thought.

After a few seconds of watching her, I clear my throat. "Will you be okay while I change out of my gym clothes?"

"Of course," she responds immediately.

Walking backward so my eyes never leave her, I take in the sadness she radiates. Crossing the apartment, I close my bedroom door behind me, changing quickly before heading to my en suite to toss my clothes in the hamper and wash my face to remove the sweat.

It's less than five minutes later when I reenter the room and take a seat on the couch next to her. She hasn't moved, but she does look up at me once I'm settled, her gray-blue eyes glassy with unshed tears.

"What happened, Vincenza?"

She sighs, leaning forward with her elbows on the tops of her knees, rubbing her temples. "Look, I'm sorry I showed up here. Honestly, I'm not even sure why I ended up here in the first place. Thank you for letting me come up, but I think I should go."

She stands, and the moment she does, I grab her wrist and gently pull her back down to the couch. "You came *here*, whether it was conscious or not. Tell me what happened, Vincenza."

Her eyes search mine, but I don't back down. I also don't let go of her wrist. Instead, I find myself rubbing her skin rhythmically.

Silence stretches between us, and I can see the inner battle she fights.

I'm fighting a similar one—the hesitancy to knock down the walls standing between us. But I feel like mine have crumbled almost completely, laying in a pile at my feet. The instinct to protect her—to be in her presence—is too strong for me to resist.

"Please, Vincenza. I cannot help if you don't tell me what's going on."

I want to help.

She relents. "My brother Joseph and his friend are scheming. For some reason, August has his sights set on me, and together they're laying the groundwork to have my father agree to him marrying me."

"Why would August want to marry you if you do not love him?" The notion makes no sense. August St. Jean is a wealthy man. A *desired*, wealthy man. He could pick any woman in this city and she'd sign whatever pre-nup he asked, just so she could become his bride. *Why* would he want someone who isn't falling at his feet in adoration?

"Business, I'm sure of it. Who knows in what capacity."

"And your father? Would he agree?"

"That's where your guess is as good as mine. My father loves me—we have a great relationship. But the relationship between him and his business undoubtedly runs far deeper. I wouldn't put it past him to at least strongly urge a marriage if he thought it was in his best interest."

"And would you agree to it? If your father urged it?"

"Absolutely not!" she snaps, pulling her arm out of my grasp. She stands and begins pacing the space in front of my couch. "The sky would need to be falling before I marry a man like August St. Jean. He's a disgusting, *revolting*, sexist piece of work."

The anger rolls off her in waves as she speaks. Her body language tells me she's still holding back—there's a piece of this story she's not sharing—but it's not my place to ask.

For whatever reason, she came to me for solace, and rather than dig for the information she is not freely giving, I can just bring her the comfort she seeks.

Standing, I reach my hand out hesitantly, before closing the final distance between us and clasping it around hers. Without our fingers laced, it feels less intimate of a gesture.

A *friendly* gesture, if you will.

Because that's all I can be to her—a friend.

I shouldn't even be that.

But I already crave to be *more*.

This is a problem—her and I.

Us.

In the same room.

She's a *piccola ladra*, a little thief. Already stealing pieces of my heart away with every glance in my direction.

I shouldn't *want* to help her—shouldn't care.

But I do. So quickly, I've done a one-eighty in my outlook on Vincenza Paladino, and quickly I feel the line of my loyalty blurring. Friendship shouldn't even be a thought in my mind, let alone more. Yet, it's all I can think of.

"Come," I say, pulling her toward the kitchen. "Let me make you that latte. Mia Madre always says a warm beverage can calm the nerves."

She slides onto a barstool and watches me as I make her drink, taking it upon myself to assume she'd want the same thing as last time. When I hand her the mug, her fingers wrap around the base as she brings it to her lips.

My eyes trail the movement. I shouldn't want her this badly, but the erratic pumping in my chest beats as though it has something to say.

Thump, thump.

You're screwed.

Thump, thump.

"Are you upset?" she asks, pulling me from my thoughts.

I can feel my eyebrows pulled together and realize I must look as though I've been scowling at her.

Shaking my head, I move around the island, taking the seat next to her. "No, piccola ladra. I am not upset. Why would you think that?"

Vinnie shrugs and brings the mugs to her lips again. After a small sip, she says, "This is twice now I've pulled you into my mess."

"I'm not sure how you figure. It was I who ran into you on the sidewalk last week."

A small smile ghosts her lips. "Yeah, you're right. You created that mess on your own."

It's impossible not to return the grin. "Sì. How is the drink?"

"Perfect." Her tongue peeks from between her lips to wet them, and once again my eyes catch on the movement. Not even trying to hide it, I openly stare, and when I meet her gaze again, I'm surprised to find her skin lightly flushed, and a curious look in her eye.

The moment severs when my phone begins to ring in my pocket. Pulling it out, Enzo's name flashes across the screen.

Silencing the call, I place my phone down on the marble, but no sooner does it ring again. I swipe to answer and bring it to my ear. "Che cosa?" *What?*

"That's no way to greet your cousin. We have a situation."

"Che cosa?" I repeat.

"Meet me at the clinic—it's an emergency. "

Fear ricochets through me, wondering what kind of emergency could have happened in the middle of a Sunday afternoon. "La famigilia?"

"Everyone's fine. Just meet me, *now*." Lorenzo ends the call, and I'm left with silence and a mild panic.

Scrubbing my palm down my face, I stand from the barstool and address the woman sitting next to me. "I have to go," I tell her, my stomach gnawing at me as I do.

I'm not ready for her to leave, and by the emotion that flashes past her eyes, I'm not sure she is either.

It's a bad idea, but the words flow from me before I can stop to consider what I'm offering. "Stay. I shouldn't be gone long. My television has every streaming service, the refrigerator is stocked, and I have an endless supply of espresso. Relax and ease your mind." Stepping forward, I reach my hand out, letting it hover between us before pulling it back. I have no reason to touch her. "No one will find you here, Vincenza. You're safe."

"Okay," she whispers, nodding as she glances behind me into the living room. "Thank you."

There's nothing left for me to say, so I simply walk away, stopping to grab my wallet and keys from the entryway, shoving them into my pocket.

Then I'm out the door, forgoing the elevator and racing down the stairs to see what kind of *emergency* my cousin has in store for me.

I make it down to my clinic in record time, finding Enzo and a man I've met once waiting by the door. The man has a bloody rag pressed against his arm, and my cousin looks pissed as he stands beside him.

"Took you long enough," he gripes, and I glare at him.

"It was hardly ten minutes."

Enzo tips his chin in his associate's direction. "Nathaniel's dripping blood by the front door. Got anything for me to clean it with?"

"Don't worry about it. Tell me what happened," I say, unlocking the door.

Once inside, I shrug into a scrub shirt and wash my hands before putting on sterile gloves and gesturing for Nathaniel to sit.

Expecting to find a bullet hole or a deep stab wound, I remove the rag and toss it into the open trash can to assess the injury. What I find beneath the rag immediately irritates me.

"This is hardly an emergency," I bark over my shoulder at Lorenzo, who's leaning with his arms crossed against the wall behind me.

Grasping Nathaniel's bicep tightly, I look over the gunshot wound, turning his arm so I can see it in all directions. "It's hardly a graze."

"I was *shot*," Nathaniel stresses.

Enzo pushes off the wall and comes to look at it. Our eyes meet, words silently exchanged so we don't have to speak them aloud.

It could have been worse.

It shouldn't have happened at all.

It's already stopped bleeding since we've come inside, which is a good sign. "What happened?" I ask again, walking to my cabinet to grab supplies.

"Intel gone wrong," Enzo says, his tone clipped.

"Intel on what?"

"Just a business situation," he snaps, and I take note of his annoyance.

"Don't be so casual about it, man," Nathaniel interjects. "Fuckin' Paladino assholes shot at us!"

My head snaps over to Enzo. "Paladino? Enzo, what are you doing starting a war with the Paladinos?"

"I'm not starting *anything*, cousin. I'm just gathering information. Seeing what they're up to."

"If Papà finds out—"

"He won't."

"But he will, and when he does—"

"He won't find out, Sly. I have it handled."

"They *shot* at you."

"It's fine, we were just spotted this time and—"

"IT COULD BE YOU ON MY TABLE RIGHT NOW," I scream, losing all control, my sense of levelheadedness completely gone. "Or worse, Lorenzo. You could be dead. And for what? *Information?*"

"I'm going to bring them down, Sly. If it's the last thing I do, the Paladinos will get what's coming to them. Maurizio will pay for what he did to my father."

"Then do it right. Talk to my father, come up with a plan together. Take them down the *right* way."

"Where's the fun in that?" Nathaniel chimes in.

Glaring at him, I squeeze the tape on his dressing unnecessarily hard as I adhere it to his skin. "Says the man on my table whose skin looks green from the mere sight of blood. I'd choose your next words carefully, amico mio, or next time I might not be as generous with my time and resources."

He swallows, recognizing the look in my eye. Nodding once, he hops off my table since we're finished. "Thank you. I appreciate it, man."

Ignoring him, my eyes connect with my cousin's. "Do things the right way, Lorenzo. Tell him of your plans, or I will. He will help. He *always* helps."

They move to the door, and as Nathaniel walks out, Enzo lingers in the doorway. He wants to say something —I can see the inner battle reflected in his eyes—but instead, he shakes his head, presumably shaking the thought away. Then, he says, "Thank you. For patching him up. Couldn't exactly take him to the hospital without questions being asked."

The entire situation annoys me, but I push the feeling aside. I would do anything for my family, including helping someone close to them. "You're welcome."

When they're gone, I remove my surgical gloves one at a time, throwing them away and washing my hands thoroughly, before sinking into the leather chair in the corner of my one-room clinic.

Propping my elbows on my thighs, I lean forward, my head hanging. My cousin was shot at today by a Paladino. Or at least the men employed by them.

Meanwhile, there's a Paladino doing God knows what in my apartment right this very moment.

So quickly, things have gone haywire.

The burning hatred lingers deep within, despising that family for what they've done to mine. What happens when you cannot forgive *or* forget? There seems to be no end in sight for the clash between us.

Frustrated, I gather peroxide and the other supplies needed to clean up the blood Nathaniel dripped outside of the clinic door. The last thing I need is for someone to see it and grow suspicious, or for a young patient to see it and become too scared to visit.

Knowing the cleaning process may take a while, I settle in and prepare myself to ease the chaos in my mind, ready to take out my anger by scrubbing the concrete floor.

I need time to think. So many problems persist, and the most pressing issue seems to be what to do about the woman in my apartment whose family just tried to kill a member of mine.

Again.

But I've come to recognize that it honestly has nothing to do with *her*, and that bothers me.

My anger is the only thing I have to hold on to. It's a living, breathing, tangible feeling I've harbored for so long, I'm not sure how she's begun to soften it so suddenly.

If I let the emotion completely fall away in her presence, there truly is *nothing* keeping me from exploring these new feelings that have taken hold of me. Ones *she's* put in there. Curiosity. Warmth.

Temptation.

Blooming inside, they've grown roots. And as much as the dishonesty to my family may kill me, there's nothing I want more than to water these feelings to see if they grow into something more.

Chapter 17

Vinnie

The sound of plates clattering jolts me awake, and for a moment I'm confused about where I'm at. Sitting up quickly, I scan my surroundings, recognizing the dark wood surfaces and muted color palette of Sly's apartment.

On the TV, a rom-com I don't remember putting on earlier plays. A plush blanket lays over my lap, and I realize I obviously fell asleep.

What time is it?

Rising from the couch, I drape the blanket across the back and walk into the kitchen, where I can now hear rustling. Sly's back is to me as he takes Styrofoam boxes from a large brown paper bag and sets them neatly on his kitchen island.

"You're awake," he states as I walk up beside him. "Are you hungry?"

The Di Mercutio logo on the side of the bag, along

with the rich scent of garlic and sauces, makes my mouth water. "Yes, thank you."

"I picked up food on my way back—I took longer than expected and thought you might want a decent meal. Figured this was a safe bet since I've seen you at this restaurant. But I wasn't sure what you liked, so I ordered a variety."

Glancing at the clock on the stove, I'm surprised to see it's nearing five in the evening. How had I slept *that* long?

"I didn't mean to fall asleep. I'm so sorry."

"There is no need to apologize. Both your body and mind were clearly exhausted. I'm glad you could find comfort from my couch."

Sliding onto the same barstool I claimed earlier, I smile as I watch him finish arranging everything on the island. He looks so domestic, completing such menial tasks with the sleeves of his black button down rolled to his elbows. The top three buttons are undone, and his hair is slightly disheveled, like he's been running his hands through it.

His entire demeanor at this moment makes my heart skip a beat.

"Could I bother you for a glass of water?" I ask, my mouth dry from my long, impromptu nap.

Wordlessly, he goes to retrieve a bottle from the refrigerator and hands it to me. As I drink, he goes back to work, opening all the containers, showcasing our food choices. He went a little overboard, supplying us with three different types of salads, two pasta dishes, chicken parmesan, Italian sausage, and two types of soups.

Everything looks amazing, and my stomach rumbles appreciatively.

"Please," Sly says, gesturing at all the food. "Help yourself." He reaches for a plate and hands it to me before picking up his.

We fall into a pleasant silence as we add to our plates—him loading up on meats and pastas, and myself reaching for the salads, and grabbing a bowl for soup.

As amazing as the rest of it looks, soup and salad sound deliciously comforting.

When we dig into our meals, my mind wanders, and I wonder where he went when he left. I want to ask, but I know it's none of my business, and I'd imagine he wouldn't tell me, anyway. Why would he? He doesn't owe me anything.

Suddenly I'm feeling nervous and unsure of what to ask or what to talk about. Every time I sneak a glance at him, he's looking at me, too, like he wants to say something but isn't sure what, either.

So I say nothing, enjoying my food and the company, no matter how quiet it may be. He doesn't seem bothered, so I take it at face value—we're just sharing a meal.

Then why is my heart running a marathon in my chest?

When I'm finished eating, I decide the silence has stretched long enough.

"So what do—"

But as I begin a sentence, so does he. "How did—"

Blushing, I look down at my empty bowl, fighting a smile. "You first," I say, peeking up at him from beneath my lashes.

He smirks, and the look sends heat through my veins. "How did you like your food, Vincenza?"

Every time he says my full name, I melt inside. I've always hated my name, but the way it rolls off his tongue has me wondering if maybe it's not so bad after all.

"It was wonderful, thank you. I've never had a bad dish from Di Mercutio. Oh! Let me give you some money for dinner."

I stand so I can go find my purse, and like earlier, Sly grabs my wrist. His touch makes my heart stop and my breathing go shallow from the electric tingles it sends through me.

"You will do no such thing," he growls, tugging me backward. I stumble and spin toward him. His hand moves to splay across my hip, stabilizing me.

"Okay," I breathe.

Sly's still sitting on his barstool, and my hands now rest in the space between his chest and shoulders. With our faces at the same level, there's no hiding from each other.

Desire pools low in my belly. This *feels* different from in the past when he's caught me and held me close. With him sitting and me standing between his open legs, his hands on my waist, it feels intimate.

It feels like a turning point.

The start of something.

And while that absolutely terrifies me, it also ignites my soul.

"Tell me why you came to me today, Vincenza. Why, of all people, you turned to me for comfort." Sly's voice is low, his heated stare glued to me, but his tone isn't angry, or in any way rude. It's curious and eager.

I'm at a crossroads now, and a decision must be made. Tell him the truth—*more* of the truth. Or backpedal. There are ways I can spin this and still make it out of here with my dignity intact.

He never needs to know that I've *always* had an interest in him—ever since I was a little girl. He doesn't need to know that ever since that night at the masquerade, he's been on my mind, parading through my thoughts on a constant loop.

It would be so much easier to apologize again, leave, and act like this entire day never happened. Go about my life, avoid this part of the city, and pretend as though I don't know what it feels like to have Sly Lucchetti's fingertips brush my skin.

But the way he's looking at me—the way he's holding me. How he took me into his home to make sure I was safe…

I may end up leaving here having made the biggest mistake of my life by admitting how I feel, but I'd rather live every day having made an ego-scarring mistake than survive one second with a soul-shattering regret.

"I told you, I didn't know where else to go."

His eyes search mine as though he knows that's merely a fraction of the truth, so I continue. "If I tell you the truth, it will shift things. I can already feel things changing between us, and if that feeling is one-sided, I can accept it, but saying my reason for coming here out loud is something I won't be able to take back. That's why I left last time."

Stillness falls between us, and a hint of adrenaline spikes through my bloodstream. Sly's chest rises and falls, and I'm about to take a step away, out of his arms.

I shouldn't have said that.

Even though I hardly said anything at all, it was still too much.

"And what exactly do you feel is changing between us, Vinnie?" His voice is shaky, but I feel his hold on me tighten a little, his fingertips biting into the small sliver of skin from where the hem of my shirt has shifted.

"Everything," I whisper. Closing my eyes, I take a small breath. "You make me feel safe. *That's* why I came here. I panicked, and even though I wasn't thinking straight—wasn't thinking at *all*, I somehow made it outside of your building."

He says nothing, just simply watches me, his eyes still searching mine as though he'll find the true answers in them, even though I am being completely honest.

His silence makes me keep talking—desperate to make him say something. Anything would be better than nothing. Even him coming to his senses and kicking me out of his home.

"We don't know each other—the only things we

know is the information our families have fed to us throughout our lives. And even though we've only had a few interactions, it's enough to know that I don't believe everything that's been said about your family, and about you. You're unexpected, Sly. You make me want to know more about you. I'd be lying to myself and to you if I said I wasn't interested, so maybe that's why I ended up on your doorstep today. Maybe that's why I didn't leave earlier when I should have."

The last word lingers between us, and as it does, his expression morphs into one I haven't seen yet. His eyes soften more than they already had, and his hand pulls from my hip.

As his knuckles skim down my cheek, I suck in a harsh breath.

"The hostility between our families runs much deeper than either of us can fathom, Vincenza."

My reaction is immediate, my shoulders sinking with the gentle rejection. My eyes close again. "Is this one-sided?"

More silence.

My heart begins to sink.

"It's not."

My eyes snap open, lips parting when I see his sparkling back at me.

"I cannot remove you from my head, Vincenza. You've embedded yourself within me from the very first time I saw you when we were just children. And when I saw you again at the masquerade, I could feel the trajectory of my life changing. I should have never chased after you that night, but I couldn't ignore the ache in my chest when I saw you upset. Just as I could not ignore the rage your panic ignited in me earlier today, knowing that someone put that feeling in you. I shouldn't *want* you, Vincenza, but I fear the regret of not knowing you would be greater than any other consequence."

Any coherent thought escapes me as his words sink in. A rush of emotion floods my senses, tears pricking my eyes as my heart rate accelerates. I'm overwhelmed by his confession, having prepared myself for the worst. I want to wrap my arms around his neck and beg him to press his lips against mine—to close the gap between us.

The air thickens and electrifies, and I take a fraction of a step forward. His hand moves to rest at the base of my neck.

"I won't kiss you, Vincenza. I won't kiss you unless you kiss me first."

My heart is beating so rapidly, it feels like it might explode within my chest.

"It has to be your decision. This is a line we cannot uncross."

He's right. There would be no turning back.

Everything our families have taught us to believe— years of hatred would be altered.

Kiss him.

I *can't.*

It would be the ultimate betrayal to my family.

They're our enemies.

"Kiss me," he whispers. Using the hand cradling my neck, he gently pushes against it, guiding my head forward until our foreheads rest against each other.

Blood rushes to my head, the thumping of my heart beating as loudly as a drum while it wages a war against my brain.

All because of a name.

A man with any other name would still be a man.

But he's a *Lucchetti.*

A small whimper floats from between my lips and I close my eyes, mentally begging myself to find the courage to do what he's asking.

I want to.

So badly.

"Kiss me, Vincenza. Kiss me until we forget who we are and the wall that's supposed to be between us. Kiss me until everything fades away. *Please*, piccola ladra."

His plea ruptures any remaining hesitancy I have, and with the smallest of tilts, our lips connect.

Our kiss starts slow, unmoving and gentle, before it blossoms into *more*. His tongue softly traces the seam, and when my lips part, everything intensifies.

Suddenly he's standing, lifting me by my waist until my backside hits the counter. Stepping between my legs, his lips never leave mine.

Our movements are rushed. My hands roam the hard planes of his shoulders while his grip the sides of my thighs, slide against my hips, then reconnect with the back of my neck. I'm seeing stars, lost in the moment, with every one of my senses in overdrive.

His lips are hot against mine, his hand tangling in my hair as he pulls me close, guiding me with every fevered nip and caress of his tongue.

Nothing in my life could have prepared me for this kiss.

I never want to come up for air.

Scooting closer to the edge of the counter, my body aligns with his. There's not a nerve ending that isn't electrified. Our bodies melt together as our mouths explore, while all thoughts fade away, just like he wanted.

Instinctually, my hips rock, the friction causing me to moan against his lips.

"*Fuck*, Vinnie," he groans, moving his hand back down to my thigh.

Swallowing thickly, the breath catches in my throat as his hand moves higher on my leg.

A plea for more is at the tip of my tongue, when suddenly the shrill ring of my phone sounds from the living room.

Startled, we break the kiss, but our foreheads remain together as we catch our breath. Seconds later, the ringing stops, but I don't let go of my hold on him, and he doesn't step away.

It feels like forever when he whispers two words. Two beautiful Italian words—neither of which I know the meaning of. "*Piccola ladra.*"

"What does that mean?" I whisper, my voice thick with desire.

His hand untangles from my hair and glides from

the back of my neck to the front. A chill rushes through me, my skin sensitive—heightened by his touch. I'm too afraid to open my eyes, not ready to wake up from this dream.

Brushing his thumb against my swollen lips, I can practically *hear* his smile. "Little thief," he responds simply, with no further explanation.

I want to question it and ask why he would call me that, but the words are forgotten when he tilts my face closer and kisses me again.

Chapter 18

Vinnie

I told Cecilia about the kiss with Sly a few days ago.

How could I not?

It's all I could think about—all I *can* think about—consuming my mind, body, and soul.

And I *trust* her. She'll never tell anyone.

When I left Sly's apartment last weekend, we made arrangements to see each other again the following Sunday, after my family brunch.

All week I've been like a teenage girl with a crush, practically doodling his name in a heart all over the manuscripts I've been reviewing at work.

It was only after I left that I realized we hadn't exchanged phone numbers. Just a time, date, and location.

Twelve o'clock, Sunday. His apartment.

"You're sure about this?" Cecilia asks as Ross pulls into the parking level of our building. "If your family were to find out—"

"I *know*, Lia." She's been questioning my sanity since I spilled my guts to her, reminding me of the implications this could have on me.

It's not only if my family finds out. If we're seen together, it would be a tabloid feeding frenzy. There's not a single person in Manhattan who isn't aware of the feud between the Paladinos and the Lucchettis. The press would lose their minds.

"I just worry," she stresses, and I take her hand in mine as Ross parks the car alongside the garage elevators.

Turning to her, I give her hand a squeeze. "I know, but I have to explore this. If it doesn't work out, then it doesn't work out, but I'm following my heart on this one, and my gut. It's *different*. I can't explain it because it doesn't even make sense in my own mind, but with a kiss, something changed."

"It was only one kiss, Vinnie…" her voice trails off, and she exhales deeply. "Okay, if you're sure. You know I support everything you do, even the things I don't agree with. Do you have a plan? You'll be safe?"

"Of course. And I trust he'll be discreet—he has a lot to lose, too. Don't worry, Lia. I know what I'm doing."

But do I?

Ross walks around the front of the car, coming to open the back passenger door for us to get out.

"Thank you," I say, taking his hand as he assists me out of the car.

"If you'd like to be taken somewhere at any point today, Miss Paladino, I'll be available."

Wanting him to always be close, my father pays the rent on Ross' one-bedroom here in the building as part of his salary.

Which is exactly why I will be leaving through the lobby while he's still in the parking garage—I can't risk Ross taking me to Sly's building and then relaying it to my father. He may be *my* driver, but he's in my father's pocket. Under these circumstances, it makes him untrustworthy.

When I join Cecilia in the elevator, she's holding the door, the button for the ninety-second floor already illuminated. As the door begins to shut, I press the L for lobby.

"If you need anything, or feel uncomfortable at any time, just call me."

"Of course," I promise, just as the elevator dings. "I'll see you tonight."

Taking a deep breath, I step out of the elevators, swallowing my nerves as I leave my building to hail a cab.

The cab driver drops me off a block from The Kenna, and even though the walk is short, I stand outside his building for five minutes staring up at it as I gather my courage.

Thankfully, the doorman on duty isn't the same

man as last weekend, so I'm able to avoid the judgment I'd no doubt receive, although this man keeps tossing me questionable glances.

Looking at my phone in my hand, I watch as the clock turns to twelve. Nerves swirl in my stomach, but it's now or never.

Nodding to myself, I'm about to take a step forward when the sound of tires pulling near me, coupled with another car's angry horn, pulls my attention.

Turning, I see a blacked-out Rolls Royce pull along-side the curb, with its passenger window rolling down.

When I look at the driver, a smile immediately forms on my lips.

"Get in, bellisima," Sly commands smoothly, leaning over the passenger seat to push open its door.

Instinctually, I look around to see who may be watching, and when I find everyone going about their day, I relax.

"You drive yourself?" I question, careful to push my leather skirt down as I use the roof's grab handle to hoist myself into the passenger seat.

"Sì. I prefer it. Although I prefer my Superleggara to this, I thought you'd appreciate the comfort my SUV offers."

My gaze falls to Sly's hands as they grip the steering wheel, expertly guiding us away from his building. He has beautiful hands.

Strong. Powerful. *Veiny.*

An image of his hands all over me flashes through

my mind, and my body reacts so instantaneously, I feel my toes curl in my boots.

"What's a Superleggara?" I ask, turning my focus to the road in an effort to regain my composure.

"My Ducati," he says with a grin. He looks over at me briefly. "You'll look amazing on the back of it, piccola ladra."

There are those words again.

Little thief.

"Why do you call me that?" I've been dying to know, mulling over it all week long, and it's been driving me insane.

His eyes never leave the road, the windshield now scattered with light raindrops from a passing cloud, but I can tell by his body language he's hesitant to tell me. His hands grip the steering wheel harder, but then loosen.

Tapping his finger against the rich leather, he gives in. "Because a little thief is what you are. You've broken down my walls and have begun to steal pieces of my heart without even realizing it."

Biting down on my bottom lip, I smile and look down at my hands that are settled in my lap. I can feel the heat rising from my neck and onto my cheeks, my heart inflating from what he's just told me.

"That might be the most romantic thing anyone's ever said to me," I confess.

"It is the truth, Vincenza. Though we have much to discuss this afternoon."

He reaches over and takes my hand—a gesture so

simple, yet so intimate. I can't downplay the smile it brings to my face, or the way my heart soars from his touch. This time, he laces his fingers through mine, stretching his arm across the center to settle both of our hands on my lap.

"Where are we going?" I ask, not really caring so long as I get to spend time in the company of this man.

He takes the on-ramp to the highway, sneaking a glance with a grin on his face. "Somewhere we can be alone without the watchful eye of others."

Forty minutes outside the city, we turn onto a long, tree-lined road and drive a little while longer before our destination finally comes into view.

Surprised, I suck in a breath, awestruck by the stunning, Gothic style mansion we're pulling up to. Built from bricks and stone in shades of gray, the building has beautiful cathedral style windows, old wooden shutters, stunning spires, and battlements.

A *castle*. He brought me to a castle.

And not just any castle, a castle with the most extraordinary views.

The grounds are rich in both color and plant life, with lush green grass and full, beautiful trees. The backdrop is equally spectacular, with views of the Hudson and other parts of the city.

As we pull up to the front entrance, I notice a black

and white sandwich board beneath the stone overhang that reads *"Sorry, closed for tours today."*

"I thought we could take a walk around the grounds and get to know each other," he says once the vehicle is in park. Unhooking his seatbelt, he rotates his body slightly to face me. "We have it all to ourselves today."

"How?" I ask, just as a man comes into view, exiting the castle doors.

"I called in a favor," Sly says, smiling as he opens his car door and hops out, moving around the front of his SUV to shake hands with the man.

Unbuckling, I watch their quick exchange. Sly listens as the man speaks, nodding along, and then they part ways.

Opening my car door, Sly closes the distance and extends his hand for me to take as I climb down.

"What would you like to see first? The castle? Or the grounds?" He offers his arm like a gentleman.

Looping my arm through his, I decide on the grounds and tell him such.

The air is cool, but any signs of rain have dissipated, leaving bright blue skies and fluffy white clouds in their wake.

With my free hand, I pull the edges of my peacoat, holding them together as we stroll.

Our conversation begins as comfortable pleasantries before we stray into everything from our childhoods to our ambitions and hopes for the future. The only topic we avoid is our families, which I know will be something to discuss later, but for now, I'd rather stay in this happy bubble with him.

When we reach a bench along the outskirts of where the greenhouse is, we sit beneath the shade of a line of large oak trees. The clouds have begun to gray again, multiplying in size.

"My head and my heart are at war, piccola ladra. How can this work when we must remain a secret?" Sly's voice is solemn as he asks, and it makes my heart sink a little.

His question is valid, though, and I take a moment to think before responding—my answer as weak as I feel.

"It won't be easy."

"No, it will not." He's quiet for several long seconds, as am I. Together we admire the architecture of the greenhouse, momentarily avoiding the rest of the conversation that is obviously inevitable.

"Secrecy is not a big enough reason for me *not* to pursue you, Vincenza. I cannot go against what my very soul is begging for, no matter the repercussions."

Conflicting emotions rush through me, and I can't say I disagree. I *want* him to pursue me. Being around him feels like coming home, which is insane because we hardly know each other. But I know I'm comfortable around him, and that's more than I can say I've ever felt around other men.

Still, there's my family to think about. My parents, particularly Father. The disrespect and the shame this would bring him—knowing my attraction to a

Lucchetti. How would he react if I were to be romantically involved with a Lucchetti, even more so than I already am?

Then there's my brother to think about, and whatever he and August are planning—if their threats are even credible.

But do I not even try? Do I walk away from this without seeing if it could be something real?

Because isn't that what fairytales and romance novels have taught us? That true love is worth fighting for?

Not that I love Sly—of course I don't—I practically just met the man. But how am I supposed to know if we have something worth fighting for if I don't allow myself to *try*?

"We keep this between us," I decide. "No one has to know, and it's nobody's business, anyway. We spend time together in private, and when we want to escape, we'll just have to find places to visit outside of the city. Like today. This is perfect."

"I cannot ask you to sneak around with me. You deserve to be wined and dined and taken to beautiful places. Not hidden behind closed doors."

"You're not asking me to sneak around with you, Sly," I tell him, grabbing his hand in mine. "I'm *telling* you I want to. Maybe I'm greedy. Our families have put each other through hell and there's a chance this will end badly, but I'm not sure if we were to part ways right now, I could just go and live my life knowing we weren't willing to take a leap of faith."

I can see the hesitancy between his eyes again—the guarded expression that tells me he's trying to do what's best.

The look written across his features seizes my chest, and suddenly I'm terrified he's going to end things before they begin.

I continue, knowing this could easily be the only opportunity I have to say my piece. All he'd have to do is say he couldn't do this, and we'd end up with an awkward car ride home. "For so long, I've had a feeling inside of me. An empty void I couldn't explain. I think you could fill it, Sly. Because already it doesn't feel as empty."

While my heart roars behind my rib cage, I watch as his gaze softens, and for a moment, I wonder if he's going to kiss me or if he's thinking of ways to let me down easy.

How did I let myself get to this point? Two weeks ago, I was running from his apartment after telling him we *couldn't* let ourselves go there. And now, I'm running full speed down the railroad tracks as the train speeds toward me.

Without warning, the sky above us opens up, the rain falling down quickly and violently. We both leap from the bench, and Sly laces his fingers through mine, setting off at a light jog, pulling me toward the greenhouse.

Within seconds, my peacoat is soaked through, the wool absorbing the water as we run. Droplets cling to our hair and skin as Sly opens the door and we rush inside, instantly hit with the warm, humid air inside of the greenhouse.

The sound of pounding rain amplifies through the clear glass roof as I shrug off my jacket, draping it over a wooden counter near the door.

When I turn back toward Sly, his lips are instantly on me, claiming me in a kiss that's absolutely carnal.

His tongue presses into my mouth, dancing with mine as he reaches down and grabs the back of my bare thighs, hoisting me into his arms.

As my legs wrap around his waist, he walks us until my back slams into the wall. His hands press against the glass on either side of my head, caging me in while his hips press into mine, keeping me firmly in place.

A moan pushes past my lips, and he catches it, groaning in satisfaction. Pulling away from my mouth, he trails kisses down my neck, softly sucking on my skin in various places, before moving onto the next, careful not to leave marks.

"You are the sweetest thing I've ever tasted, piccola ladra."

My hands cup around the back of his neck, and I gently run my fingers against his short hair, trying so hard not to rock against him as my body begs for more.

"Sly…" I moan.

His hands reconnect with my skin, running down the length of my body and to the back of my thighs.

With his fingertips digging into my skin, he pulls me away from the wall and walks us further into the greenhouse, never once disconnecting our kiss. He leads us to a bench surrounded by the gorgeous blossoms of cone-flowers and Japanese anemone, along with a variety of roses, sunflowers, and snapdragons.

It's me who pulls away as he sits with me in his lap, my knees touching the cool stone of the bench as I settle, straddling him with my hands placed gently on his shoulders. Looking around at the gorgeous rainbow of colors around us, their sweet fragrances filter through the air, and I can't help but admire the beauty as the sound of the rain begins to slow.

"I've never seen anything so beautiful," I say with appreciation.

"Neither have I."

Drawing my attention back to him, his focus is solely on me. His hand reaches to cup my cheek, and he pulls my face back to him for another slow, sensual kiss.

Our foreheads stay pressed together as it slows, and when our lips part, I whisper, "Can we stay here forever?"

Even though the rain has stopped, here in this greenhouse, it's like the world can't get to us. It's our own private hideaway, where we can just continue to get to know each other and pretend like our surnames don't matter.

"I wish, piccola ladra. I truly wish we could."

Weaving his hand into my mess of rain-soaked waves, he presses his lips against my forehead, then on my cheek, before claiming my lips again. I sigh against his lips, completely taken aback by how easily my worries melt away when he simply kisses me.

After a few more stolen moments, he stands with me in his arms before placing me gently on my feet. His hand moves easily from my hip to my hand as he takes it.

"Come," he says, leading me to the door. "Let's go explore the castle."

Chapter 19

Sly

"What's the rest of your week looking like?" Sully asks, making idle chitchat over a cup of coffee.

It's ten a.m. on Thursday, and he showed up at my house an hour ago, unannounced, per usual. After making himself a cup of coffee, he followed me into my home office, settling down on the black leather couch while I continued to scroll the florist's website, looking for an arrangement to send to my piccola ladra.

"A few patients scheduled throughout. Lunch with Mamma on Saturday." *And hopefully a date with Vincenza on Sunday.*

I keep that to myself.

"Anyone scheduled for today?" he asks, his tone attempting to be nonchalant, but I know him well enough to know he's fishing for information.

"No."

"Tomorrow?"

I pause, looking away from my computer's screen. "In the afternoon. Why are you asking about my schedule, Sully?"

Our phones go off simultaneously, a notification for group chat popping up.

ENZO

On my way.

My eyes meet Sully's. "Did we have plans I was unaware of?"

"Eh." He shrugs. "Figured you weren't doing much this morning, so…" his voice trails off.

"So, what?"

"Sooo…"

Glaring at him, I wait for him to finish whatever it is he's withholding.

"I might be kidnapping you and Enzo for the next twenty-four hours."

I arch a brow and lean backward in my chair, my arms crossing over my chest. "To go where, amico mio?"

"Well, I have a business meeting that my dad wants me to go to in person, but that should only last a few hours. So I figured, why not take the boys and have some fun after?"

"Again, I ask where, Sully?"

"Houston." He presses his lips together to hide his amusement.

I, on the other hand, am not amused. Dryly, I question, "As in Texas?"

Hopping up from his spot on the couch, he jumps forward, slapping his hand against my mahogany desk. "Go pack your boots, cowboy! We're heading to Texas as soon as Enzo gets here. The jet's being gassed up as we speak, and Stephen's waiting with the limo out front.'"

"I'm not going," I state simply, returning to the website I was looking at prior to Sully's travel ambush.

"C'mon, Sly, I knew you'd oppose. Just come with us. It's *one* day."

"I have patients."

"Not until tomorrow afternoon, you said it yourself. I'll have you back in plenty of time—we'll come back in the morning."

While clicking on a particularly beautiful bouquet arrangement, I ask him, "Why am I just now hearing of this? Enzo was clued in, but I was not."

Reading the description of the flowers, I note it does, in fact, include sunflowers, roses, and snapdragon, which are just a few of the varieties the greenhouse had. According to their website, same day delivery is an option, as is one-hour delivery.

Perfect.

"Because I knew you'd say no. So we gave you no choice," Sully says smugly, pulling my attention briefly back to him.

He's correct. But in my defense, since returning to the States, I've had to work to build my business, in secret, from the ground up, whereas Sully stepped right into his role at his father's company.

After making him wait in silence while finalizing my purchase, I power down my computer and stand. Apparently, I need to pack.

"I will go on one condition," I tell him as I round my desk, heading for the door.

"Name it."

"Give me two hours. I have some business to attend to before I'm able to leave."

"Done," he agrees eagerly, and I hear him already on the phone. "Michael—hey. There's been a delay…"

His voice fades as I go to my bedroom to pack, hoping he'll leave so I won't have to come up with an excuse as to why I need these next two hours.

The courier went inside Vincenza's office building five minutes ago, carrying a stunning bouquet that I hope she'll love. Sticking out of the floral arrangement was a bright white envelope, with a note saying, *"Come outside. -S"*, hoping she'd read it right away and come out.

I rode my Ducati here, leaving my full-face helmet on just in case someone sees me lurking in the shadows. Not many know I ride a motorcycle, a piece of information that helps me stay off the radar.

Crossing the street, I step into a recessed part of the building and wait.

When the courier leaves, I wait with bated breath until Vinnie steps through the doors just moments later.

As I step away from the building, she's looking around, and I grab her hand.

She gasps, and I don't say anything in greeting. Instead, I guide her just beyond the doors and through a covered breezeway. On the other side is a private parking lot, and looking around, I see another recessed portion of the building, this time with an overhang.

Gently pushing her into it, I step forward and crowd her space, letting my hands roam over her hips. The tight skirt she's wearing instantly sends me into a frenzy, loving the way it hugs her soft curves and forms so exquisitely to her body.

"Sly," she giggles, her hands coming up to grip the side of my arms. The smile on her face rivals the beauty of the sun.

Taking my helmet off, I hold it at my side and lean forward to kiss her. Her lips part willingly, granting me entrance to her perfect mouth and allowing me to explore. Bracing my palm against the stone wall behind her, I lean in, deepening the kiss.

She sighs against my lips, melting into me.

It pains me to pull away, but my time is limited.

Brushing a small piece of hair from her face, she smiles up at me.

"The flowers are gorgeous. Thank you."

"Gorgeous flowers for a gorgeous woman," I remark, bending to kiss her neck.

I can't stop.

Her head tilts to the side to allow me access, and I slowly kiss a trail against her soft flesh. Not bothering to remove my lips from her, I tell her about the overnight excursion I'm being forced to go on. "My best friend and cousin are stealing me away for the next twenty-four hours. I couldn't leave without saying goodbye."

"That sounds like fun," she muses, her hands sliding down my chest. They come to rest at my waist, so I remove one, and interlace our fingers.

"At least it'll be quick."

"You're not looking forward to the time away?"

"I'd rather be here with you," I say honestly. A faint blush touches her skin, her lips pursing in a small smile. "Speaking of which, I realized earlier that we have not exchanged phone numbers. And I'd like to see you again this week, but it's difficult to make plans when my only way to reach you is by courier."

"Well then, you should have my number. I can cook for you, if you want," she suggests. "Tomorrow, after you return home? Eight o'clock?"

"You cook?"

Her eyes fall to the concrete below us, then meet mine again. Laughing, she shakes her head. "Absolutely. I can make you the best bowl of cereal you've ever tasted."

The image of her in a kitchen surrounded by a plume of smoke flashes through my mind, and I begin to laugh, too. "Perhaps it would be better to order in."

"How about this? My chef, Theo, is absolutely amazing. I'll ask *him* to cook dinner."

Letting go of her hand, the backs of my fingers skim down her side and back to her hip, and I pull her closer. "How will that work, Vincenza? No one is supposed to know about us."

Tilting her head, her lips practically touch mine, and her eyes twinkle with excitement. "You'll come over once he's gone. No one but me will be home. You're just as safe at my apartment as I am at yours."

"I'm not so sure about that—my apartment doesn't have staff who might see us and report back to your father."

Vinnie's face flashes with a hint of sadness, and I sense I've struck a chord, but we need to think about this logically. I cannot pursue this attraction between us and risk my family. And neither can she. Not until we know if this can be something real or if it is purely attraction and curiosity.

"You're right, but I can assure you my staff is on *my* payroll and reports to me. But they will be sent home prior to your arrival."

"Okay, piccola ladra," I say before brushing my lips against hers. "I must go, but let me put my number in your phone, and I will send you messages tonight while Sullivan is dragging me around Houston."

"I left my phone upstairs, but I'll add my number to yours." Her palms pat against the front pockets of my pants, and she reaches into the one with my phone, pulling it out.

The innocent movement instantly hardens me, and even though she's simply holding my phone and looking up at me with her doe eyes, I groan and catch her lips with mine again.

"You're a little minx. When I have you alone again, Vincenza…"

I don't finish my thought, unsure if I should. My attraction to her is more than just physical, and I want her to know that.

There are also things about my sexual preferences we must discuss prior to us sharing a bed.

Winding her arms around my neck, she presses up on her tiptoes to give me a final kiss, then gently pushes me away. "Go. I need to get back to work anyway, I have a meeting in—" She glances at the diamond-banded smartwatch on her wrist. "Five minutes."

She hands me my phone so I can unlock it, before plucking it from my fingertips and adding her number into it.

"There," she says matter-of-factly. "Now you have it. I've got to go, and so do you. Have fun on your trip."

Stepping back, she starts to walk away, but I grab her wrist, tugging her back to me because I just can't get enough.

My lips collide with hers in one last kiss—one I'm hoping will keep the memory of me on her mind throughout the night, because I certainly won't stop thinking of her.

She smiles at me and walks away, glancing over her shoulder after a few steps.

The grin on my face rivals hers as I call out, "Addio, piccola ladra!" *Goodbye, little thief.*

Not hiding the fact that I'm watching her leave, I appreciate the gentle sway of her hips as she walks, and the way her body looks beneath her tight clothing. But I'm aware of the time, so I tug my helmet back on and follow her steps beneath the breezeway, crossing the street to where I've parked the Ducati.

I have fifteen minutes before I'm due to meet Lorenzo and Sullivan, and as I climb onto my bike, I bet myself I can make it to them in ten.

The motorcycle roars to life beneath me; the vibrations igniting a thrill within me as I steady the bike then jet off, weaving through the traffic on Columbus Avenue.

Chapter 20

Sly

The bass of electronic dance music does nothing for the headache that's clawed its way into my skull and is currently radiating pain.

Sitting on a black leather couch, I'm relaxed into it, legs spread wide while I nurse a bourbon. I watch the dance floor from the private balcony Enzo rented for us, suppressing a yawn that begs to come out.

Below me, Sully is in the center of the dance floor sandwiched between two women. His greedy hands wander the one at his front, while the one behind him looks as though she's too inebriated to function.

He's having fun, though. I can see the joy on his face from here, as he dances without a care.

His meeting went well, and we celebrated with a bottle of Mitcher's 25, sent over by Sullivan Senior as a congratulations to his son.

"Why do you look like someone pissed in your Cheerios, cousin?" Enzo asks from where he sits in a leather armchair to the side of the couch I sit on. A redhead is draped across his lap, her face buried against his neck, her hand slid partway through his slightly unbuttoned dress shirt.

"Not much in the party mood," I tell him, returning my gaze to the dance floor.

My mind has been elsewhere since boarding the plane early this afternoon. I haven't yet texted her, but my idle fingers have been itching to all evening.

"That's a shame," Enzo continues. "It's been a long time since we've partied together."

"Sì, it has."

Years, in fact.

I can't say I miss it.

"We used to share a pretty girl every now and then." I turn my attention back to him just as he pulls the redhead's hair aside, exposing her neck. There's a glimmer in his eye—one that says he's taunting me.

He's exaggerating. We've never shared a girl sexually—no more than allowing her to climb back and forth from our laps at parties, kissing us until one of us snapped and carried her to a bedroom.

But I was a different man back then. I struggled with women—not understanding why I never felt fulfilled both sexually and intellectually. It wasn't until my ex-girlfriend that I began to understand why.

Giving pleasure brings me pleasure.

But I have no interest in giving just any woman pleasure. She has to interest me. Intrigue me. *Challenge* me.

"That was a long time ago, Lorenzo."

The music is loud, so I cannot hear my cousin as he leans down and says something to the women in his lap, but she looks over at me with a shy smile spreading across her lips as she stands and sashays over.

Her black dress is like a second skin, clinging to her as she tries to pull it down slightly while she walks, but it still leaves little to the imagination.

She hardly slows as she approaches and leans forward, as though she's going to climb into my lap.

With the bourbon in my hand, I hold the glass upward, signaling for her to stop. "That's enough," I tell her, only feeling the smallest tick of remorse as her face falls. "I am not interested."

Embarrassed, she turns and quickly scurries back over to Enzo, who's glaring at me.

"Not tonight," I tell him, then lean forward, bracing my elbows against my knees, once again returning my attention to the dance floor.

Vinnie muddles my thoughts again, and I wonder what she's up to.

Succumbing to temptation, I pull my phone from my pocket and scroll through my contacts to find hers. She hid her phone number under an alias, but it's not difficult to find. She's labeled herself as *Thief*.

Clever pseudonym, piccola ladra.

I keep the phone in my hand, not knowing whether she's even awake to read the message. It's late, and though many would say the night was only beginning, others have been asleep for hours.

There are so many things I have yet to learn about her, one of those being if she is a night owl or early riser.

There's a flip in my heart when my phone vibrates in my grasp.

I thought you might appreciate that.

I just added you to my contacts as S.

S. My initial with which I signed the note from her floral arrangement with.

I can feel Enzo's stare as I ignore the club around me and respond to her.

How was the rest of your day?

She replies immediately, and it brings a smile to my lips.

Nothing special. How is your trip so far?

Uneventful. I am currently sitting at a club watching people make a fool of themselves. Not my idea of an exciting evening.

Sounds riveting. What would you rather be doing?

Anything with you.

"Sly," Enzo says, drawing my attention.

"Che cosa?"

"I asked if you wanted another," he says, tipping his head toward my glass.

Glancing around the balcony, I realize the redhead is gone.

"I'm okay," I tell him. "Thank you though."

His eyes wander to my phone, and instinctively I press the side button, darkening the screen.

Once he's gone, I unlock the phone again, and pull up my messages.

> Anything? You'll have to be more specific.

Her message comes off as flirtatious, the hidden innuendo behind it sending a spark of arousal through me as I think of all the things I would love to do to her.

Still, this is new for us, and I am hesitant to come off too strong or move things too fast. Though she strikes me as a woman who would let go of the perfect, proper exterior she exudes, and I hope to test that theory.

> Perhaps you should tell me what you would rather be doing, piccola ladra. I suspect you're not doing anything exciting, since you are spending your time messaging me. What other ways would you rather be spending your time?

To my dismay, her response is not immediate. My

phone idles, darkening to sleep mode from its lack of use.

Crossing my ankle over my opposite knee, I keep my phone in hand, but turn my attention back to the lower level. Sully and his women are gone, but this time I spot Enzo and the woman from earlier.

Scrubbing my hand down my face, I groan. It's never good when Sully disappears, but we're not too far from our hotel, so I'll walk if need be.

My phone vibrates again, and I waste no time reading the message.

> I'd rather be spending time with you.
> Getting to know you in many different
> ways.

The sound of a curtain being pulled lifts my attention from the screen and I look behind me, seeing Sully walk in. To my surprise, he's alone.

Swaying on his feet, he stumbles over to the couch and falls onto it, practically sitting on my lap in the process.

"Hiya," he slurs loudly, tossing his arm around my shoulder. "Why have you been sitting up here like a lonely boy?"

Laughing, I peel his hand from my shoulder, shrug out from under it, and stand. "It might be time to get you back to the hotel, amico mio."

Moving to the edge of the balcony, I pinpoint where Enzo is dancing and send him a text, letting him know it's time to go. Moments later, he pulls out his phone and reads it before looking up to where I'm standing. I gesture toward the entrance, and he nods in understanding, dipping his head to say something to the woman he's dancing with.

My eyes sweep the balcony, looking to see if any of us have left any personal belongings behind before I return to Sully, helping him to his feet. "Let's go."

"Noooo! One more drink. Where'd that chick go?"

He's dead weight against me as I sling his arm around my shoulder and help him move to the curtain so we can locate the elevators and leave.

"Shoulda known you'd be the party pooper, Sylvester Lucchetti."

"If you weren't such a sloppy drunk, maybe I'd be the one who could enjoy myself from time to time," I retort, but my tone lacks conviction. I have no interest in drinking heavily, nor do I have an interest in meeting random women in clubs.

"Where'd my date go?" Sully asks on the elevator ride downstairs. He's standing on his own, but leaning against the elevator wall, rubbing his temples. "Why's it so bright in here?"

"You did not come with a date, you came with me and Enzo. The women you entertained this evening are not joining you back at the hotel. I'm afraid it's just us tonight. Perhaps your hand will get lucky if you sober up."

I look forward to the day where Sully meets a woman who completely brings him to his knees.

Sullivan Rochester is a good man, unlike so many

of the men in Manhattan. He has a kind heart and genuinely cares about the people in his life. He doesn't use them as pawns in the game of greed.

But he's a partier. A womanizer.

Or as he's been called a time or two, a *fuckboy*.

The elevator dings, and when the doors open, Enzo is standing in front of them, waiting for us with a scowl on his face.

"Enzo!" Sully exclaims, stumbling out and into Enzo's personal space.

He wraps Sully's arm around his shoulders, taking over my position of assisting him out of the club. "You owe me, Rochester. That woman I was dancing with had just asked if I wanted to go back to her place."

Since we're only a few blocks from the hotel, we walk.

It's a disaster, but we make it back, and after depositing Sully in his suite—where he passes out on his bed fully clothed before we even leave—I retreat back to mine.

After a quick shower, I shut the lights off and climb into bed, not bothering to dress. The linens are soft and welcoming, immediately bringing my tired, aching body comfort. For a moment, I rest my head against the pillow and shut my eyes, letting the blur of black and white dance behind my vision as I relax.

But the guilt from not responding to Vinnie earlier worms its way into my chest, so I reach for my phone.

The screen is bright, and I squint as I read through our prior messages and decide what to say.

> I apologize for my delay. Unfortunately, I had to help a very intoxicated Sully back to his hotel room.

Her response is almost immediate.

> That's okay. Did you make it back to yours as well?

> Sì. Curled up in bed.

> Sounds cozy.

> It would be if you were curled up beside me. The space next to me could use some warmth.

> Still on for dinner tomorrow?

> I wouldn't miss it, piccola ladra.

As much as I wish I could stay awake all night and talk with her, my eyes are heavy, bouncing from open to closed with every glance at a word.

> I do not want to be rude and simply stop replying, so I must say goodnight, Vincenza. The exhaustion has crept up on me. Sleep well, bellisima. Send me your address tomorrow, and I will see you at eight.

Closing my eyes again, I think about earlier when I had her in my arms, my lips pressed against her soft skin. I recall the sweet sounds she makes when I kiss her.

I long to be holding her now, and imagine what it'd be like to pull her close, skin against skin.

Picturing her beautiful face, I smile to myself over the simplicity of our message exchange. There was nothing extravagant about our conversation, but there didn't need to be either.

I like that.

I like that beyond her outward appearance is a woman who is real and unapologetically herself.

Even though I am drifting in and out of sleep, I want to talk to her more—want to know what she has to say, and if she's responded to my last message, but before I can muster the energy to reach for my phone again, I fall asleep.

Chapter 21

Vinnie

Sliding my palms down the front of my red dress, I smooth the already pristine fabric. The sweetheart neckline of the ruched bodice hugs my breasts, accentuating them in a classy way, and the long sleeves balance out the short hemline. My feet are bare because I hate wearing shoes in the house, and as much as I love my slippers, they do nothing to add to the outfit.

Nervous, I look over the place settings on the table, re-straightening the utensils that don't need to be fixed.

Theo prepared chicken quarters with rosemary mashed potatoes and a green salad, with miniature molten lava cakes for dessert. Everything warms in the oven, with exception of the salad, which rests in the center of the table. Chardonnay chills on ice in a bucket so silver, it's practically mirrored.

I've been thinking about Sly all day. It scares me how much I want to be around him—how much I crave him.

All day, my fingers have hovered over my phone's keyboard, itching to type a message to him just to read his response. I've wanted to call him, just to hear his voice.

But I've refrained.

It terrifies me how quickly this has escalated from physical attraction to an emotional affair. Everything about Sly Lucchetti mesmerizes me. The way he speaks, the empathy he has.

He's perfect, and I can't help but hate him for it, if only just a little.

The man whose soul speaks to mine so clearly shouldn't be someone whom my family despises.

But maybe this is all a facade. Maybe I'm thinking with my heart more than my head.

There's so much about him I still don't know. What he does for a living, the relationship he has with his family.

He presents himself as an open book, answering every question I've ever asked without hesitation. It's my fault I haven't dug deeper. I haven't because I *trust* him, and I've put my faith into this.

Being with him could implode my entire life, and I've been so focused on seeing if *this* could be real, if it's worth risking *everything* for, that I've forgotten to learn the basics about the man I'm quite literally hoping to get into bed with.

That ends tonight.

Over dinner, or perhaps after, I'll ask the questions I

need answers to. I just hope he's willing to answer honestly.

My heart jolts when the doorbell rings, and I realize I've been lost inside my own head for who knows how long.

Once again, my hands smooth my dress as I approach the door, blowing out a shaky breath when I pull it open.

The moment our eyes meet, any uncertainty and fear rushes from my body. Seeing him instantly calms me.

"Hi," he says, a sexy smile on his face as he stands in front of my doorway. Waiting patiently, he doesn't walk into my apartment—like a gentleman, he waits to be invited in.

"Hi." Stepping closer, I look up at him, returning the smile.

Gone is the woman who was just allowing her thoughts to run rampant. My confidence has returned.

Grabbing a fistful of his shirt, I pull him inside, reaching my other hand out as far as I can to push the door shut behind him. Once we're secluded from the outside world, my hands wrap around the back of his neck. Pulling him to me as I press up onto my tiptoes, I finish closing the distance between us. Through the kiss, I hope my body can show him what my words aren't ready to articulate.

That I *missed* him.

We kiss until we're both breathless. Bracing his

hands on my hips, Sly smirks, and the happiness I'm feeling mirrors in his eyes.

"That was sure a welcome," he teases.

"What can I say?" I laugh. Stepping back, I slide my hand to his wrist and tug him further inside my home. "I hope you brought your appetite."

"Oh, you have no idea, *piccola ladra*."

I don't miss the suggestive undertones in his voice, and it sends a wave of tingles through me.

As he takes in my apartment, I watch him quietly, appreciating the way he seems to notice all the small details of my home. The muted, neutral color palette with hints of a blush pink so light, it's nearly white. My collection of rare first editions, and the shelf that houses recent best-sellers. The simple layout of my furniture—understated, but elegant.

While he looks around, I grab the food from the oven and place it onto the waiting hot-pads on the table.

"You have a lovely home, Vincenza. It suits you."

"Thank you," I tell him as I walk over to the table. Reaching for the bottle of wine, I ask, "Would you like a drink?"

"Sì, grazie."

The weight of his eyes is heavy against my back as I pour us both a glass, trying to hide the shake in my hand.

Tonight feels different.

Important.

Pivotal.

Having him in my home feels like I'm fully opening the door that we've been gently nudging open for weeks.

After passing Sly his glass, I swirl mine and take a sip, letting the crisp tang of the fruity notes settle on my taste buds before swallowing it down.

He does the same then takes both of our wine glasses and places them on the table. The moment they leave his grasp, he turns, and both of his hands cup the edges of my jaw, his fingers weaving into my hair as his lips descend to mine.

This time when he kisses me, I feel it too. He missed me just as much as I missed him.

Expertly, he claims my mouth, holding my face in his hands as he throws every ounce of passion he possesses into his kiss.

Or maybe I'm wrong. Maybe he's just a phenomenal kisser—but something tells me it's more than that.

After a few moments, he breaks the kiss, leaning his forehead against mine. "It feels as though you were made for me, *piccola ladra*. And I've never been more torn between right and wrong."

"I feel like we're on a runaway train," I whisper. "I'm terrified we're going to crash."

"What is it exactly that makes you so scared?"

"*This*," I stress. "You and I. My family finding out. *Your* family finding out. They'll rip us apart."

Standing up straight, he slides his hand to my cheek and rubs his thumb comfortingly against my skin.

"We're adults, Vincenza. Ultimately, they cannot decide what we do or who we love."

My eyes burn with unshed tears as I look up at him. "My father would never forgive me if he found out we were together."

For a moment, sadness sweeps past his eyes before it's replaced with a look of annoyance.

"Your father is a bastardo. The last person I care about—"

"He's my father, Sly. Like it or not, I love him. I love *all* of my family, even if the feeling isn't always mutual."

"Has he done something again? Joseph?" he asks quickly, pressing my hand between his. He places it against his chest, and I swear I can feel his heart racing.

"No," I tell him, and I can visibly see the relief wash over him.

Leading me to my couch, he sits and pulls me into his lap. "I don't want to argue, piccola ladra. I just want to spend time with you. I meant what I said before. I won't ask you to sneak around with me—"

"You're not."

"I want you to live the life you deserve. To be taken places. Spoiled. I cannot do that for you behind closed doors."

Pressing my hands against his cheeks, I mirror how he held me earlier, and look him deep in his eyes. "Listen to me, Sly. I don't care about being paraded around the city or going on lavish dates. I want to be right here, with you. I want *you*. Even *if* it's behind closed doors."

"But for how long, piccola ladra? We've already established that our families will not approve. There will come a day you want a man who you can go places with. Have a *future* with."

Thoughts of said future flit into my mind, and so clearly I can envision everything with *him*. A beautiful wedding and saying "I do." Children, Christmases, birthdays, lazy Saturday mornings.

The only thing that isn't clearly visible in that daydream is a life filled with our families.

"Let's just take it day by day," I whisper, looking down at my lap. I won't lie and say there isn't sadness in my heart.

Pushing the length of his finger beneath my chin, he lifts it gently, encouraging me to look at him. "Day by day, piccola ladra, is more than I should even ask for."

Pressing his lips against mine, he kisses me slowly. His touch instantly makes me melt—my sorrows disappearing into thin air. I wrap my arms around his neck, letting him guide the kiss.

Suddenly, it's like a fire ignites within me and I need *more*. Without allowing our kiss to break, I reposition myself so I'm straddling his lap, letting my body sit directly on top of his.

He groans when my center meets his groin, and I feel him harden beneath me as he fists the hair at the base of my skull. Deepening the kiss, I rock my body gently against him, slowly exploring, testing the boundaries.

My body buzzes with arousal, a neediness inside of me burning so brightly and begging for me to act on it.

Sly's hands roam my back as we kiss, and I become hyper aware when he moves them to my thighs.

A sound between a moan and a whimper pushes past my lips and onto his tongue as his hand slides under my dress.

The anticipation is killing me as he barely skims his fingers against the sensitive skin of my inner thigh; the tips brushing against the bend between my leg and panties.

Just knowing how close he is, waiting for his touch, feels almost as good as I imagine he'll feel. With my eyes closed, I sink my teeth into my bottom lip and tilt my head back. A small moan escapes and I fight against every instinct screaming at me to move against him.

"You look so gorgeous waiting for my touch," he murmurs, his voice low. "Tell me, piccola ladra. Where do you want my fingers?"

"Everywhere," I breathe, tilting my head back up to meet his gaze. Despite the butterflies swirling low in my stomach, confidently I say, "I want you to touch me everywhere."

"Show me. Move my hands."

Leaving the hand that's under my dress, I grab his other hand, positioning mine over his as I grab the edges. Placing it against my hip, I slide it up my body slowly, gently guiding it over my stomach and up to the swell of my breast.

Engulfing my modest B-cup, his fingers flex. He moans appreciatively as he squeezes.

With my hand still on top of his, I move my other beneath my dress and rest it over his. He hasn't moved it—his fingers still hovering right on the edge of my panties, and I can't take it anymore.

The slightest of movement connects him with my soaked panties, and I suck in a sharp breath.

Pressing one of his fingers against my clit, another grazes against my entrance, pushing the fabric into me slightly.

"You're soaked," he verbalizes through a shaky breath, stating the obvious.

All I can do is nod. I'm completely frozen on top of him, my skin blazing.

Like a rubber band snapping from tension, his hand flies from my breast to the back of my neck and he draws me to him, slamming his lips against mine.

In the same movement, his hand pulls my panties aside so quickly I hear the seams ripping, but they're lost on deaf ears as his thumb begins to stroke my slit, stopping only to circle my clit a few times before repeating the caresses.

"Oh my god," I moan, shamelessly rolling my hips against him. "*Please*, Sly."

"Please what?" he whispers against my lips. I can feel the upturn of his smirk.

As he circles my clit again, my orgasm starts to build.

"*Please*," I mumble incoherently.

"I *crave* you, piccola ladra. Your smile. Your skin. Your moans. All I want is to have you in my arms, always."

Pushing a finger into me, he immediately curls it upward and begins to stroke, then adds another. His ministrations are slow and steady—calculated, as though he knows exactly what my body wants and needs, building it up little by little.

I feel like I'm about to let go and fall over the edge, when he removes his fingers from me, and repositions my panties as they were.

My eyes snap open, and panic floods through me as I take in his stoic demeanor.

As I open my mouth to question what's going on, his hands settle on my hips and he lightly pushes me off his lap, scooting to the edge of the couch as I stand and take a half step back.

"I know you were close, and I apologize. But the first time I make you come, I wish to see the pleasure written on your face. And from that position, it was difficult."

"Oh…"

His smile calms me.

Sliding his hands up my thighs, they disappear under my dress, and his thumbs hook around the lace straps that rest at my hips. Tugging them, he pulls them down my legs and lets them fall to the floor once they've reached my knees.

With his eyes glued to mine, he leans down and reaches for them, waiting for me to lift each foot as I step out of them. Once in his hand, he leans back and lifts his hips, pushing them into his front pocket.

"I want those back," I remark playfully. They're one of my favorite pairs.

"Not a chance in hell, piccola ladra."

Bringing his hands back to my hips, he pulls me forward, positioning me to straddle him again, but this time on only one of his legs. Guiding me to sit completely, I find nervous, intrusive thoughts forcing themselves into my mind.

"Show me how you come, Vinnie," he rasps, his accent thick.

"Sly…I…your pants."

His thumb runs against my bottom lip, pulling it from between my teeth. "The messier, the better. If there isn't a wet spot soaked with your cum, I won't leave until there is. Ride my leg, Vinnie. Let me see what pleasure looks like as it dances across your face."

My body screams *yes*, but my mind keeps me frozen in place.

I'm not a virgin, but my sex life has never been adventurous. I've had a total of two partners, neither of which gave any mind to whether or not I had an orgasm. I gave up on that years ago, much like I gave up on trying to date.

This is new, uncharted territory. Completely out of my comfort zone, yet I'm not afraid.

Uncertain, but not afraid.

My face must reflect something I'm thinking

because Sly lifts my dress and places his hands on my butt.

"Move," he growls, nuzzling his nose against my jaw.

So I do.

My hips roll, rubbing myself against him. The black denim fabric brushes against my clit in a rough, delicious way.

I know I'm soaked, and I know my juices are rubbing all over his pants, but I'm forcing myself to push those thoughts away and just enjoy the moment.

He's kissing my neck, trailing rough, wet kisses up and down the column, as his fingernails dig into my bare skin where he holds me tight, urging me to keep moving.

It only takes a few seconds before I'm building again, my orgasm cresting even more powerfully than before. I'm directing my movements, allowing my body to rock in a rhythm I'm familiar with from my own exploration.

"You should see how lovely you look right now, riding my leg. Does it feel good, bellissima? It's taking all my restraint not to flip your dress up and sink into you."

Moving my hand from his chest, he lowers it on top of his hard length, still constrained behind his pants. "Do you feel how much I want you, piccola ladra? What you do to me?"

"Yes," I moan, picking up my pace. "I want you so badly, Sly."

"You have me, Vinnie."

His words draw another moan from my lips, and I toss my head back.

"Your body is so wound up—so ready for release. Come for me, Vinnie. Let me see you."

It takes a few more rocks of my hips, my clit brushing against his leg, before I'm spiraling—falling over the ledge as my orgasm cascades into me.

A string of moans erupts from me, and my hands leave Sly to connect with my breasts, grabbing at them as I continue to roll my hips against his leg.

When I feel myself float back down to earth, I still, keeping my eyes closed as my breathing evens out.

"Stunning," he declares. Reaching his arms around my lower back, he pulls me forward, embracing me as I relax into him.

My body is still tingling, settled in a euphoric state. I could easily fall asleep from how relaxed I am.

Sly gently presses kisses against my hair as we sit in contented silence for several minutes.

When the effects of my orgasm have dissipated, I sigh and sit up in his hold so I can look at him. I can't help but smile.

"Are you hungry?" he asks, brushing a loose tendril from my face. "You should eat—replenish your energy."

"I could eat," I say, pushing against his chest to scoot myself back until I'm able to put my feet on the floor. Grabbing his hand, I tug him to a stand, my eyes dropping to notice the place on his jeans where it's wet from my cum.

His eyes follow mine, and he grins. "You're beautiful when you come, but I can promise you next time, there will be much more of a mess."

My cheeks burn, and I bite my lip to keep from smiling. "When will that be?" I ask casually, feigning innocence and hoping it'll be sooner than later.

"I may be crazy about you, piccola ladra, but I still strive to be a gentleman, at least for one evening. Consider this the last night I will restrain myself around you."

Sly pulls out my chair at my dining table, and I take a seat, smiling up at him as I watch him walk around and take the one opposite of me.

"That sounds like a threat *and* a promise," I muse, pulling my napkin into my lap.

His eyes sparkle with something akin to mischief, my stomach flip-flopping with excitement as he says, "Oh, Vincenza. You have no idea."

Chapter 22

Vinnie

"Oh my god, you have no idea how much I've missed you," Raina squeals as she climbs into the back of my town car, pushing her sunglasses onto her head after she slams the door.

Tossing my arms around her, I hug her tight, resting my chin on top of her shoulder. "I've missed you too! You're never allowed to leave me for three weeks again, okay?"

"Don't worry, I won't let you bail on me again. Paris isn't the same without you."

She clicks her seatbelt into place as my driver pulls back into traffic. This weekend, we both have a charity gala to attend with an "all that glitters" theme. As soon as I read that on the invitation, my mind conjured up a vision of me in a floor length crystal gown with my hair curled and cascading down my back.

Hopefully 5th Avenue won't disappoint.

"How was it?" I ask. "Tell me everything you weren't able to squeeze into our phone calls."

"It was…interesting, to say the least."

"Oh no. What happened?" I ask, noticing the way she tries to hide that something's bothering her. But I know my best friend. There's something on her mind.

"Honestly, Vins. I'd rather not talk about it right now. What I need is some time with my best friend and retail therapy."

It worries me that she's not wanting to talk to me—she always does. Typically, she can't stop the words from flowing out of her, telling me every single detail, including the ones I don't particularly want to hear.

So having her do the opposite is concerning.

Deciding not to press her for information right now, I change the subject. "What's your vision for the gala?"

"Something drastic and fierce. And sparkly, obviously."

"So a bold color then?"

"Fire-engine red, preferably."

"I can see you in red," I say, smiling into my flute of champagne I just poured. As I take a sip, I pass Raina her glass.

"What's going on with you?" she questions, wrapping her fingers around the stem. "You seem… different."

Heat creeps into my cheeks and I look away, knowing I can't lie to my best friend.

Sly and I agreed to keep us a secret, but it's *Raina*. She's been my best friend since we were kids.

"You're hiding something. Spill it. *Now*."

"I'm not!"

"Are you really going to sit here and lie to me? Have you forgotten I know you? Sometimes better than you know yourself," she scoffs.

I roll my eyes. "I'm just happy you're home."

"You're such a liar." As she sips her champagne, she studies me. For several seconds, I think she's going to give up, then she gasps loudly, her manicured hand flying to her crimson lips. "You met someone!"

On instinct, I shake my head. "No! I—"

"Do *not* lie to me, Vincenza Mae Paladino."

The look in Raina's eye—equal parts pissed off and curious—reminds me she always gets her way. Sighing dramatically, I twist in my seat so that I'm facing her.

"Fine, but this needs to be taken to the grave."

Holding up two fingers, she says, "Scout's honor."

"I'm serious, Raina. This could ruin me. If anyone finds out—"

"When have I *ever* spilled your secrets?"

"Mason," I snap, glaring at her.

I'm not actually angry, but she did tell him I liked him when we were teenagers, after promising she wouldn't. Still, that's been the only "secret" she's ever repeated, and if I'm being honest, my feelings for Mason were so obvious, everyone knew about them without her meddling.

She swishes her hand in front of her while she takes another sip of champagne. "Ugh, please. Mason was a secret that needed to be spilled. You crushed on him for *years* before I finally told him. I thought it'd be a nudge in the right direction."

"Okay, well, what I'm about to tell you can never leave this car. *Ever*."

"Okay, okay, I get it!" Her eyes glance at the partition that's rolled up. "You sure driving Miss Daisy up there won't be able to hear though?"

"No, Father made sure the backs of the town cars were soundproof." I never asked why, but I can imagine.

My heart begins to hammer in my chest as I work up the courage to tell her. I'm not sure why it feels different than when I told Cecilia, but it does. Raina would never judge me or rat me out, but I still hesitate.

"Wow, Vins. I feel like you're about to tell me you're dating a mafia don, or something equally as dramatic."

"Sly Lucchetti," I croak, clearing my throat. Sitting up straighter in my seat, I say it again. "I'm seeing Sly Lucchetti."

"*Lucchetti*," she repeats skeptically. "As in, the *one family* your family absolutely despises?"

"The one and the same."

Her loud cackle echoes through the car. "Oh, babes. You're so screwed if anyone finds out. How did this even *happen*? Tell me every little detail, even the dirty ones."

"That's the thing!" I toss my hands into the air. "I don't even know how I let it happen! I saw him for the first time since we were teenagers, at the masquerade ball my mother made me attend back in July. After that, we kept running into each other. One of the times, quite literally."

"What does that mean?"

"He was coming out from somewhere and I was leaving a coffee shop. Neither of us were paying attention and ran right into each other. My coffee spilled down the front of me, and he offered to let me borrow one of his shirts..."

"You've been to his apartment?"

Biting my lip, I look down into my lap and smile. "A couple of times now."

"Damn. Then what?"

"God, I'm kind of embarrassed to say."

The car comes to a stop at a red light, and I notice that we're getting close to Bergdorf's. Turning back to Raina, I decide to just rip the Band-Aid. "When you were in Paris, we had family brunch and August showed up. He and Joseph both said some things, and I had a panic attack. Next thing I know, I'm outside of his apartment, not really having any recollection of how I got there."

After filling her in on the rest, on what feels like one long-winded run-on sentence—omitting the details of our time together a few days ago—she stares at me wide-eyed.

Rendering Raina speechless is something that doesn't happen often.

I rushed out everything I had to say while my driver found a loading zone to pull into. Now, Ross is standing outside of the car door after shutting it a few minutes ago when I told him we weren't ready.

He'll wait as long as necessary, but every passing moment spikes my anxiety.

"Say something," I beg, picking an invisible piece of lint from my jeans.

Surprising me, she punches me lightly on the arm. "You little harlot, you. You realize you two are a modern day Romeo and Juliet, right? Families who hate each other. Sneaking around. Forbidden love. Ugh, I love this. Someone should write another book about it."

"They ended in tragedy."

She quirks a brow, her demeanor quickly changing. "Do you expect this to end with your families forgetting the past and holding each other's hands while you walk down the aisle? Seriously, Vinnie. I've been around your family for nearly two decades, and not once has anything kind ever been said about the Lucchettis. You're playing with fire."

Tears pool in my eyes, her words a harsh reality that embody every fear I've been thinking. I didn't need the reminder, and it hurts to hear it aloud.

A bead of wetness rolls down my cheek, and I wipe it away quickly. "I know."

"I know you know. You're the smartest person I've ever met, but this is a terrible idea." Reaching out, she grabs my hand. I look down at them, blinking back the waterfall of tears that threaten to fall. "But regardless if it's a good idea or a bad one, I still support your decision. If Sly makes you happy—hell, if you don't even know yet and you just think he *might* make you happy—then I'll do whatever I can to help you explore this."

Swallowing back the emotion that's clogging my throat, I smile at my best friend. "Thank you," I tell her. "I really just think I owe it to myself to see if this is real. The way he makes me feel is unlike anything I've felt before. And it very well could just be unexplored lust, but Raina, I don't think it is. I think it's *more*, and that scares me. I don't want to ever have to choose between love and my family."

Placing her hand on the door handle, she says, "Well, for right now, you don't have to. Come on, let's go shop and you can tell me all about this unexplored lust you're feeling."

Then she pops open the door and steps out, pulling me out onto the busy 5th Avenue sidewalk along with her.

The soft leather of the couch beneath me feels like butter against my skin as I sit and sip champagne while Raina's in a fitting room.

I picked out my dress almost an hour ago—a floor-length beaded rose gold gown that sits off the shoulders and has a sweeping back that dips just above my panty line. It's stunning, and everything I'd been envisioning for the gala this weekend.

Raina hasn't been as lucky, tossing everything she

tries on aside for various reasons. Too tight, too loose, too short, too much train.

"Any luck?" I ask before taking another drink.

I hear her huff with annoyance. The stylist hears it too and shuffles over to the fitting room door.

"Miss Lancaster, I'd be happy to bring you another—"

The door swings open and slams against the wall as she emerges in a gorgeous floor-length lilac silk gown that hugs every curve of her body perfectly. It's simple with spaghetti straps and a dramatic draping neckline, and the dress trails out behind her as she moves toward me with a scowl on her face.

"I love it, but there's not a hint of sparkle on it, *of course*," she says, rolling her eyes.

"Then get the one you tried on before this." It was a gorgeous off the shoulder silk gown in the same color, that had a peek-a-boo layer of sparkles along the breasts. Very Julia Roberts à la *My Best Friend's Wedding*.

"It looks too similar to the one you're buying."

Literally, the only similarities are that they're both floor length, tight, and off the shoulder.

"Then dress this one up. We'll go to Cartier after we leave. All that glitters applies to beautiful jewelry, too."

"So diamonds really *are* a girl's best friend, then?"

The slimy gravel tone from behind me makes my spine stiffen.

I watch as Raina places her hands on her hips, stepping forward as she glares at the person behind me. "What are you doing here, August?" she demands.

Reacting, I quickly pull myself from the couch and turn so I'm standing by her side.

Ignoring her, August turns his attention toward me, a devilish smirk pulling at his lips. "What's the matter, Vinnie? I thought you'd be happy to see me."

"Am I ever?" I sneer. From the corner of my eye, I see the stylist watching the exchange, her eyes volleying between the three of us.

"Oh c'mon, Vin. I'm not so bad once you give me the chance." The way his hand trails against the back of the couch I was just sitting on absolutely disgusts me.

"Pigs will fly before I give you a chance, August. Please leave. No one wants you here."

August tsks in response, his head shaking slightly. "One day you'll feel different. I'll see to it."

"*Ugh.* Seriously, take a hint, August," Raina intervenes. "She's not interested." She opens and closes her hand a few times, putting attitude into a wave. "Bye bye."

He snickers, and his eyes sweep over to Raina. With malice in his tone, he glowers, "That color makes your complexion a little dull, don't you think?"

Instinctually my hand flies to her wrist, and I dig my fingernails into her skin in silent warning. She *will* bite back, and this will turn into a scene, which will turn into more ammunition for August and my brother.

August watches us for a moment longer, his eyes sliding between us, over the length of our bodies, then casually to the watch on his wrist.

Without another word, he turns on his heel and walks out of the store.

I don't relax until he's no longer in view, then I finally release the air in my lungs.

"God, I hate him," Raina mumbles.

"You have no idea," I agree, letting go of her wrist. "Sorry, I didn't mean to leave marks."

She shrugs, then looks down at the gown she's still wearing.

"That dress is absolutely stunning on you. Don't listen to a word he says."

"As if I would." Holding up her hand, she waves to the stylist, who hurries over to us. "I'll take this one. Thanks."

She saunters back into the fitting room to get undressed, and as she does, I head to the register, pulling out my black card while the cashier rings me up. "Add the lilac gown my friend tried on as well please."

"You don't have to do that," Raina says, coming up from behind me.

"Don't worry, my father's the one paying. I agree to attend these events on behalf of them in exchange for the fabulous wardrobe they expect me to wear. I'd be happy attending in my jeans, but Mother insists on the gowns."

Laughing, she glances at the cashier and says, "Well, by all means then, ring her up!"

"We'll have those delivered to your home within the next two hours, Miss," the cashier tells me, handing me the receipt. "They'll be steamed and ready for wear, pending you aren't in need of alterations?"

"Both gowns fit perfect, thank you."

"Very well. Expect delivery shortly."

"Thank you," I tell the woman, and Raina echoes the sentiment.

Looping her arm through mine, we exit the building and are met with the hustle and bustle of late-afternoon Manhattan.

"Where to?" I ask, looking left and right up the street to see which store speaks to me next.

"Well, we now need some *glitter*. Or at least I do. Cartier?"

Smiling, I nod and tug Raina in the direction of the store.

August's comment from earlier flits into my mind.

Yes, idiot. Diamonds are a girl's best friend.

But honestly, who in their right mind would say no to diamonds?

"How was your day today, piccola ladra?" Sly's deep, smooth baritone floats through my cell phone. With it, my body aches for him.

"Long," I sigh, exhaustion settling deep in my bones.

Now that I'm laying on my bed after a full day with my best friend, I find it hard to keep my eyes open.

The day was amazing, but exhausting, and I was

happy to get home, even if it was late in the evening by the time I did.

After showering, Cecilia blow dried my hair, using a barrel brush to style it as it dried. I told her she didn't need to do that for me—she had a long day herself—but she insisted.

Part of me thinks she holds onto the things she used to do for me when I was a child because she longs for a family of her own. Even though she's only ten years older than I am, she's been just as much of a mother to me as my own mom.

"Mmmm," Sly murmurs. "Tell me about it."

So I do, recounting the CliffsNotes version of the day, although I omit the part where I told Raina about him, and about August.

I'm not sure why I hide that August showed up, but I do.

"How was your day?" I ask, stifling a yawn.

"Vincenza, if I am keeping you awake, we can just speak tomorrow."

"No! I don't want to hang up. Tell me about your day."

He chuckles, and I hear what sounds like him getting onto his own bed. For some reason, it makes me snuggle into mine further. Putting him on speakerphone, I place the phone onto the pillow next to me and close my eyes.

When he speaks again, it's like he's there next to me.

"It was uneventful. I went to work for some time,

then met up with my cousin and friend for dinner. After that, I came home."

"You know, you still haven't told me what you do for a living," I say, remembering that I meant to ask him when he was at my apartment, but never did.

The other end of the phone goes silent for several seconds, so I tap my screen to see if the call's been disconnected. It hasn't, and I watch the seconds tick by before finally saying, "Hello?"

"I am here."

"Oh, I thought you hung up."

"I would never do that to you, Vincenza."

Tugging the blanket further up my body, I press again. "So, are you going to tell me or are you going to keep being all mysterious about your profession?"

My tone is playful and light, but the longer he doesn't answer, the more worried I become.

Finally, he sighs. "I am a doctor."

Surprised, my eyes fly open in the dark. "You're a doctor?"

"Sì, but Vincenza, there are things you must know. I do not practice in the most ethical of manners. The medical system is unjust. Not everyone can afford the healthcare they deserve, yet they still need it..." his voice trails off. "I have a practice, in a nondescript location nearby. My passion is to help people."

My mind is spinning with what he has told me—what he's admitted without flat out saying the words.

Sly isn't practicing medicine legally.

Something like this could ruin him if this got out.

Ruin his family.

And he's trusting me with it.

I shouldn't be focusing so selfishly on what he's said, but I am. Tears line my eyes, heavy with the reality of what he's just told me and the gratitude I feel for him entrusting it with me.

"That's risky," I tell him. "But so incredibly selfless and brave."

"Grazie, piccola ladra. I'm sure it goes without saying that no one can hear about this. In time, you will learn more, but I have already said enough over the phone."

"Of course. I won't breathe a word."

"So tell me." He changes the subject promptly. "Can I see you this weekend?"

Turning from my side onto my back, I rest the phone on my chest. "Maybe Sunday, after brunch with my family? Unfortunately, Saturday I have some work to catch up on at the office, and then I'm stuck attending the Venus-Hope benefit gala in the evening."

"Hmm, well, perhaps I will see you on Saturday, after all. I, too, will be in attendance at the gala. Sullivan's father arranged a table, and my cousin and I have been swindled into going."

"It's going to be difficult to avoid you."

"Sì, it will be. I will see what I can do to arrange somewhere for us to sneak off to." I can hear the grin in his voice.

I smile, and it turns into another yawn. "I'm so sorry! I didn't realize how tired I was until I got into bed. I absolutely hate when people yawn into the phone, and here I am doing it to you."

"Vincenza, you never have to apologize for being tired. Let us say goodnight so you can rest."

"We don't have to, really. I'm fine. I'm not ready to hang up, I want to hear your voice."

"If you insist on staying on the phone, then I must insist you rest. Plug your phone in, Vincenza, and lay it on the pillow. I will stay on the line until you fall asleep."

"You'd do that?"

"Trust me, if I could be by your side instead, I would be. Now, what would you like me to talk about?"

If I could melt further into my bed, I would. I wish he could be here. What I'd give to have him in my bed right now, laying beside me.

I have a feeling that if I asked him to come, he would.

But Cecilia is in the next room and I could never ask her to leave her home just so he could sneak in. It'd be so much easier if we were out in the open, but knowing I've now told two people when we agreed to tell no one, sends a pang of guilt through me.

"Tell me about your family. Or one of your favorite patients."

He dives into a story about his childhood, telling me about when his little brother was born, and what Italy is like. His detailing is so vivid, I can picture myself standing in the kitchen of the home he grew up in, seeing his story play out as though I'm a ghost in the room.

A smile touches my lips as he talks about his mother and the bond they share.

As he speaks, I picture us in another life, holding hands and smiling, sitting at a table with his mother, a newborn cooing in her arms as Sly presses a kiss against the side of my head.

It's startling how easily I can envision everything with him by my side—how badly I want it—and utterly heartbreaking to know that'll never be the future we have together.

A tear escapes the side of my eye, but I don't bother to reach up and wipe it away, because the comfort of his voice lulls me to sleep, even though a piece of my heart just broke off.

Chapter 23

Vinnie

A festering of nerves settles in my chest as I ride alone in the back of my family's limousine Ross picked up earlier today from my parents' garage. The Venus-Hope benefit gala is arguably the most highly profiled event of the year, put on by the Arison family, set up to pull on the heartstrings of New York's most prestigious.

It's the one event my mother insists I use the limo for. Even though they won't be in attendance, local press will be swarming the red carpet entry, and she wants the Paladinos to be "presented properly".

I just wish I wasn't arriving alone.

Pulling the small mirror from my clutch, I open it and check my lipstick, ensuring that it hasn't smudged. We're about five minutes away from the venue, and I know once I check my bag, I won't have it for the rest of the evening.

Just as I close the compact, my phone rings, and a

candid shot of Raina and me in Central Park overtakes the screen.

"Hello?" I answer, clicking the speakerphone button.

"Hey. I'm about fifteen minutes out. How far are you?"

"Less than five," I groan. "Remind me again why we couldn't just go together?"

"Hi, Vincenza," Raina's mother's voice floats through the phone while her father's gruff chuckle echoes behind it.

"Ah, that's right. Hi, Mr. and Mrs. Lancaster. Looking forward to seeing you shortly."

Raina laughs. "I'll be there soon, okay? Just grab a glass of champagne and relax. Tonight will be fun."

I'm not so sure about that. Being at the same event as Sly and not being able to talk to him, after not seeing him for a week, is going to kill me. But he *did* promise he'd find a way for us to escape together, so for now I'll hold on to that hope.

"See you guys soon," I say, before ending the call.

Moments later, the car comes to a stop, and from my tinted window I see the paparazzi lined up, cameras aimed and ready to catch whatever they can. The lights from the entry of the building are bright and inviting, and the red carpet they've rolled out looks plush.

The quiet hum of the partition rolling down catches my attention. Looking over, I see Ross looking at me through the reflection of the rearview mirror. "Are you ready, Miss Paladino?"

I turn back to the spectacle outside of my door, looking for a familiar face in the crowd. I'm not sure why I expected *him* to be there, but I wish he was, and I can't help but to deflate a little when I don't find his warm, hazel eyes in the sea of people.

"Ready as I'll ever be."

"Very well. I'll come around."

Taking a few steadying breaths, I gently pull my dress up to expose my feet, making it easier to step from the limo. The gown I chose fits me like a glove and makes me feel like a billion dollars. Just as I envisioned, my hair's styled down in waves, and I kept my makeup subtle, not wanting to take away from the beauty of the dress.

As soon as my door opens, camera flashes assault my eyes, and from all around, I hear the media yelling my name.

"Vinnie!"

"Miss Paladino!"

Placing my hand in Ross', he helps pull me from the car as I plaster on a smile.

I hate this part—it feels so fake.

Between my family's fortune and my thriving business, the press wants to know all about my life. I'd been coined *The Paladino Princess* by them my entire life, and it's exhausting.

Desperate to get this red carpet walk over with as quickly as possible, I take a step forward, only to be stopped in my tracks by a man stepping through the reporters.

A collective round of gasps slices through the air, and a large palm grips onto my waist before sliding to my lower back.

Before I realize what's happening, I'm being dipped backward as the cameras catch every second of it. Above me, August's smug grin is all I can see.

"Smile for the cameras, darling. You don't want to look miserable as they capture this moment."

"August," I sneer through gritted teeth. "What the *hell* do you think you're doing?"

He swings me upward to stand again, grinning for the cameras as he settles his hand on my lower back and guides me down the path toward the entrance.

"Making the media fall in love with us, obviously."

Anger grips me. Internally, I remind myself to stay calm.

Questions fly from the reporters, their cameras still clicking, flashes aggressively blinding me as we pass.

"Are you two dating?"

"When did you first become a couple?"

"Does this mean August St. Jean is officially off the market?"

The moment we reach the steps, I bound forward, stomping up them so I can put as much distance between us as possible.

I'm fuming—anger rolling off me in waves—by the time I make it to coat check.

To my dismay, August is still following me, sauntering behind with his hands in his pockets as though he has not a care in the world.

Slamming my clutch down on the coat check table, I turn to him and point a finger in his face. "You had absolutely no right to do that."

Swiftly, he grabs my hand and presses a chaste kiss to my finger, putting on a show.

"Quiet," he growls lowly, glancing behind me. "You're causing a scene."

Ripping my hand from his, I snap, "Stay the hell away from me, August," before I turn back to the coat check attendant and take the number from her.

While walking away, I discreetly shove it into my bra and continue into the ballroom.

Thankfully, a waiter is passing by as I enter, so I grab two glasses of champagne, downing one as I walk further into the room. My eyes sweep past the tables as I look around, keeping an eye out for any friendly face.

Unfortunately, I come up short.

Placing the empty champagne flute on a nearby high top, I retreat to a corner where I can watch everything and wait for Raina.

I want to cry. The bitter sting of tears burns my eyes, but the last thing I will do is allow them to fall. Not when I know August is still watching. And probably my brother, too, for that matter.

Tossing back the last drop of champagne left in my second glass, I see a man approaching from my peripheral.

"Miss Paladino!" he greets me when he makes it over. "I was hoping I'd see you here. How are you?"

My entire body sighs with relief to see Ansel

Emmons, a kind older gentleman I met at the masquerade ball in July. He's wearing a suit with tails, his round glasses sitting at the tip of his nose.

"I'm doing well, thank you, Mr. Emmons. How are you? How's your wife doing?"

"We're both well, child, thank you. She's holding our spots at the table. I saw you from across the room and wanted to come say hello. Abigail wanted me to pass along a request," he chuckles, beaming up at me.

"Oh?"

"Yes, well, she's asked me to request that you come rescue her from dancing at some point tonight. You see, she has two left feet, and I could dance for hours." His eyes wander across the room, pinpointing where his wife's seated.

Grinning, I wave at her, and she returns the gestures.

"The pleasure would be all mine again, Mr. Emmons. Please let your wife know I'd be happy to take you off her hands for a while."

"Please, call me Ansel."

"Then you be sure to call me Vinnie."

Taking my hand, he brings it to his lips and kisses the top of it. "I will, Vinnie. Looking forward to dancing with you later. Enjoy the party."

He walks off, and again, I look at his wife, who is beaming ear to ear at her husband as he meanders back to her, stopping to shake a few hands and clap a few men on their shoulders.

Having Ansel come say hello was a much-needed

distraction. This is twice now he's rescued me without realizing it. It's like he and his wife know when I need a savior.

"Hey!"

I nearly come out of my skin, jumping from the sound of Raina's voice.

"Oh my God, you just scared the hell out of me."

Laughing, she grabs my hand and urges me to spin for her. "This dress is absolutely phenomenal on you, Vins! You look like a goddess."

"You've already seen me in it!"

"Yeah, but not with your hair and makeup done. Seriously." She scrunches her fingers together and brings them to her lips, making a kissing noise as she flicks them away. "Chef's kiss."

"Well, you look amazing yourself. I'm so glad you went with this one. That necklace is a showstopper."

She picked out a Pluie de Cartier necklace with over thirty carats set in white gold. I found it hard to stomach the price tag, but she swiped her black card without blinking.

"Thanks! I'm glad I went with this one. It ended up being perfect. What was up with that old guy?"

"That's Ansel Emmons. He's a sweet older gentleman who always seems to know when I need an angel on earth."

"Emmons, as in, Emmons Technologies?"

The light bulb in my head clicks on, and I can't believe I didn't realize it before.

Emmons Technologies is one of the biggest tech

conglomerates in the country. They're known for buying tech companies that are going under, but keeping on the staff, therefore winning them praise around the country and being known as a company that cares. It's been all over the news that they just bought out a company called Skyline Tech out of some small town in California.

Raina starts laughing—clearly the look on my face reflects me connecting the pieces.

"I can't believe I didn't make that connection."

"You crack me up, babe. You know, they have three sons." She lightly nudges her elbow against mine.

I flash her a pointed look. "Have you already forgotten our conversation from earlier this week?"

A waiter passes by and she plucks two flutes of champagne off his tray, passing me one.

"I haven't forgotten." Smiling, she brings her champagne close to her mouth and over the rim says, "Look, there's your man now."

Following her gaze, I see Sly step into the ballroom, looking gut-wrenchingly handsome in a black tuxedo. Following his usual fashion trend, everything he's wearing is black—from the black-collared shirt to the black tie. His hair is impeccably styled, his facial hair trimmed and groomed.

Just looking at him makes me weak in the knees.

I watch as his eyes wander the room as he scans the crowd, his gaze piercing and sharp when it finally lands on me. Even though he's far, I can see the desire in his eyes as they graze my body, drinking me in.

Beside me, Raina whistles lowly. "God damn, that man looks like sex on a stick, Vinnie. No wonder you're breaking all the rules for him."

Sly's gaze is heavy against mine, neither of us wanting to look away. "Damn, and his cousin looks fine as hell, too. Those Lucchetti men have good genes, don't they?"

Coming up beside him, Enzo's presence severs our stare, causing Sly to look away. Knowing it's for the best, I loop my arm through Raina's and say, "C'mon, let's go find our table and hope this night flies by."

Tonight's no different than the last two times I've attended events on my parents' behalf. A delicious meal, boring speeches, and a parade of men keeping me on the dance floor until my feet are numb.

The only difference is all throughout tonight I've felt *his* eyes on me.

I've tried not to look over to where I know he's sitting, failing time and time again. He's always engrossed in conversation with the people across from him, knowing just how to make it look like his eyes are on *them* when really he's *actually* looking over their shoulder at me, slowly sipping on an amber liquid.

The man I'm dancing with—the CEO of some company I can't remember the name of—spins me outward. Laughing, I wind back into him and he grabs my hand, continuing to lead. He's a nice guy, one of the few I've danced with tonight who hasn't tried to woo me into going on a date. When we turn back in the direction of where Sly is sitting, I immediately find him again.

Subtly, he meets my gaze, then drags his eyes from me, looking to the far door of the ballroom, then back to me.

A smile overtakes my face before I force it down, sinking my teeth into my bottom lip as I look away.

"It's been lovely to dance with you tonight, Miss Paladino," the man I'm dancing with says, drawing my attention back to him. The song is in its final chords, and we're slowing along with it.

"Thank you for asking me to." I'm polite, but all I want to do is bolt to the exit.

Sneaking yet another glance to the table that Sly has occupied all evening, I notice he's gone.

The man in front of me bows low and kisses my hand before walking away. I do the same, spinning on my heel and crossing the dance floor.

"Miss Paladino!" An older man steps through the crowd, greeting me with an awkward wave. "May I have this dance?"

"Perhaps the next one, I was just one my way to the ladies' room."

"Oh! Of course, of course. I'll seek you out shortly."

Wonderful, you do that, I think to myself as I weave my way through the tables.

As soon as I step through the threshold and into the

large lobby of the building, the air changes. What was once warm and slightly humid from all the bodies in such close proximity is now cool and still.

Nearby voices echo against the marble flooring, so I begin to walk in the opposite direction. My heels clicking with every step, the sound ricocheting from the walls.

It's quiet in this secluded area of the venue, with abstract paintings at least six-feet high lining the walls. Although the lighting is dim, I stop to admire them, not sure what else to do while I wait for Sly.

It's only another few moments before the deep, smooth timbre of his voice sends a wave of tingles down my spine.

"I underestimated how difficult it would be to keep my eyes off you tonight, piccola ladra." He stops right behind me, only leaving a sliver of distance between us. "How much of a challenge it would be to not touch you." Brushing my hair away from my cheek, his finger-tips graze my neck. "How badly I want to rip the hands off every man who has had the opportunity to dance with you, when it's one I may never have." His lips press soft kisses to the curve where my neck meets my shoulder.

Sighing, my body melts against him. "I hate this. I want nothing more than to be out there with you."

"I know. As do I."

His hand drifts up the length of my arm before he circles it around my neck, lightly brushing his thumb rhythmically against the side. Dipping his face lower, he skims his nose against my cheek. "Come home with me tonight," he whispers.

Turning my face, our lips are a hair's breadth away from touching. My eyes close, and I gently bump my nose against his.

We stand there still—unmoving and silent.

Breathing each other in.

Getting lost in the moment.

"Yes," I say, but it comes out throaty.

"Watching you and not being in your presence is killing me. I will give you thirty minutes to say your goodbyes, and then we're going home."

My heart flips at the ease in which he said *home* as though it's ours together. Pushing the feeling away, I start to nod, but he catches my lips with his, stepping slightly to adjust where he's standing.

I moan as he deepens the kiss, using both of his hands to tilt my head back. Our tongues meld, dancing wildly together in a way that instantly ignites my lust. Warmth pools low in my stomach, desire coursing through my veins.

When he breaks the kiss suddenly, I try to pull him back, but he doesn't allow me to.

"Piccola ladra, our time right now is limited, but I want nothing more than to rip this dress from your body." His hands find their way to my sides, and slowly, he begins scrunching fistfuls of the dress into his grasp, shortening it with every grab.

"Please?" he asks. There's a sparkle of mischief in his eye that I'm drawn to.

Looking up and down the hallway, I see that we're completely alone in this corridor, so I nod my head in agreement.

Without hesitation, Sly sinks to his knees. "Hold your dress for me, bellissima."

My hands find his, and I take the dress from his fists. The crystal beads are rough against my palms, but I hold it up exactly where he had it.

Just the smallest part of my nude lace panties show and he wastes no time tugging them down my legs, leaving them to pool around my feet. His hands drag up my bare thighs, and I shiver even though I'm anything but cold.

"Wondering what you taste like is turning me into a desperate man."

He takes his time, his soft touch caressing my upper thighs, his fingertips tracing the curve of my backside.

"How so?" I ask, my voice surprisingly steady now, considering I'm turning into putty in his hands.

"You're all I can think about. From the moment I wake until my very last thought when slumber takes me. And now that I know the sounds you make when you come, it plays on a constant loop in my mind."

As he tells me this, his hands slide against my outer thighs until they rest just below my hip bones. His thumbs spread the lips between my legs, and he leans forward, swiping his tongue against my exposed clit.

A moan erupts from my throat, echoing off the walls. On instinct, I drop one of the fistfuls of my dress and slam my hand over my mouth.

"Oh god," I moan again, but it's muffled by my hand.

Soft vibrations from his low laugh bounce off his mouth and straight to my clit, and my knees buckle.

Pushing my dress back up on the left side, he keeps it firmly in his grasp as he lifts my leg, bracing it over his shoulder as he leans in deeper to apply more pressure with his tongue.

When his finger pushes into my warmth, I lose all control. My hips roll to chase his touch, and I can't help but dig my stiletto into him while my shoulders lean against the wall for leverage.

"I love to see my finger disappear inside of you, Vinnie. I cannot wait to watch my cock slowly sink in as you take me inch by inch. I'll fit perfectly inside you. You were made for me."

Pumping into me with his finger, he swirls his tongue around my clit, swiping it down to meet his finger before refocusing his attention back on that bundle of nerves. Pulling it into his mouth, he creates a suckling rhythm that has me seeing stars within seconds.

I can't formulate a thought to string together a sentence, but so badly I want to agree with him. I *was* made for him. That's what it feels like.

Before I realize it's happening, I explode, coming so blindsighteningly hard my body slides down the wall a few inches. I cry out—the sound muffled behind my hand—as my orgasm crashes into me like a tidal wave.

But he doesn't stop. Instead, he adds another finger

and looks up at me with devilish eyes, removing his mouth from me long enough to say, "Another."

Impossible, I think. It's never happened before. Then again, no man has ever aimed to make it happen.

"I can't," I part whine, part groan as sparks shoot through my body.

My head tilts back to meet the wall as Sly works his fingers, pumping, and curving and, stroking inside me while his mouth presses rough, demanding kisses on my skin.

"You absolutely can, piccola ladra. Nothing brings me greater pleasure than watching you embrace yours."

When he reaches the inner part of my thigh, he sinks his teeth into my skin hard enough to leave a bruise on the soft flesh. I whimper as he contrasts his bite with soft kisses, soothing the sting he left behind.

As his lips reach my clit again, all is forgotten as my eyes roll backward. I'm sensitive, and instinct tells me to fight against his tongue, but I quickly learn there's a fine line between too much and losing control.

"Oh my God," I moan as another orgasm washes over me and Sly increases the thrusts of his fingers.

"*Fuck*, Vinnie. I cannot wait to take you home." His fingers slow as my orgasm levels out, my breathing evening.

Looking down at him, he doesn't abandon where he kneels on the floor, nor does he remove my leg from his shoulder, or drop my dress.

Instead, he returns to pressing, soft kisses on my

thighs, his fingers brushing against the spot where he bit.

"I apologize. I got carried away."

"Don't," I breathe, still in a state of euphoria. I slide my leg from his shoulder, the position starting to become uncomfortable.

"It will likely bruise."

"Then I'll wear it proudly."

His eyes blaze and he stands quickly, letting my dress fall as he reaches around the back of my head and pushes me up against the wall. As he kisses me, I taste myself and a night full of passion on his lips. He pins his hips to me, gently rubbing his erection against me.

Suddenly all I want is to leave.

Voices drawing closer force us to break apart, my heart rate sparking even more than it already is, realizing we're moments from being caught.

We could have been caught while his face was between my legs, too.

We're both breathy as we listen, waiting for the footfall to either get closer or retreat.

When the corridor grows silent again, Sly places a quick kiss against my cheek.

"Come," he says. "Let's say our goodbyes and you can meet me in front of my apartment."

He helps smooth my dress, and as we're looking down I realize my panties are still around my feet.

"Leave them," he growls.

Looking into his smoldering eyes, I suppress a smile. "I might be a little longer than we'd both like. I need to have my driver take me home, then I'll need to leave again."

"Whatever it takes, piccola ladra. Just make sure to stay in that gown. I'll be the one taking it off you tonight. Now go, we've been gone too long."

Stepping out of the delicate fabric of my panties, I take a few steps before glancing back to see Sly reach down and pick them up.

"You know, that's the second pair you've stolen. Are you sure *you're* not the thief?"

He chuckles, opening his coat and slipping them into the inside pocket. "I assure you, what you have stolen from me is far more valuable than the two scraps of lace I have stolen from you."

The underlying meaning of his words makes me grin. "What are you doing with them?"

"Probably not what you're thinking. What do you take me for?"

Laughing, I shake my head. "A man, Sly. I take you for a *man*."

Then I walk away, heading back in the direction of the ballroom. When I make it to the bend, I look back just in time to see Sly disappear in the opposite direction and I wonder if he's seeking out another exit or if I'll be able to sneak more glances at him before we go.

Chapter 24

Sly

I make it back into the ballroom several minutes before Vincenza does, thanks to my knowledge of this building. Cutting through the parlor, I walk back into the crowd with purpose, crossing to where Enzo and Sullivan have made themselves comfortable at the open bar.

"Where've you been?" Sully asks, gesturing to the bartender for service. "We thought you may have gotten lost."

Enzo watches me with scrutiny from over his crystal lowball, holding it at his lips but not drinking.

The lie slips from my tongue with ease. "I ran into an associate of Papà's out in the foyer."

The bartender approaches, and Sully orders himself and me another bourbon.

"Enzo and I were discussing going to Metamorphosis tonight. This party's a little dull," Sully says, turning his body to look back into the sea of people.

The majority have retreated to the dance floor, while others are engaged in conversation within small groups around the room and at their tables.

"It's a benefit gala," Enzo retorts dryly.

"Yes, but is lively music too much to ask for?"

Personally, I've enjoyed the music this evening. They've instrumentally covered popular songs and given a nice variety throughout the decades.

"You know," Enzo says to Sully. "Not every event needs to be a party. It baffles me how your father is preparing for you to take over his company when you can hardly manage an evening among his associates."

"I'm managing just fine, thank you very much. I just like to have a good time."

"Which is why I brought you to Europe," I cut in. "So you could get it out of your system, Sullivan. It seems as though it's very much still *in* your system. Perhaps you should heed our advice, amico mio."

"Wow, what is this? Gang up on Sully night?"

"Not ganging up, just reminding you that you're an adult with adult responsibilities and expectations." Enzo flashes me a look that says *'he'll never get it.'*

Gripping Sully's shoulder in my hand, I tell him, "We just want you to succeed, amico."

Getting frustrated, Sully shrugs out of my grip. "Enzo and I were *both* discussing going to the club tonight, not just me. Your reminders are unwarranted— you're my friends. Stop treating me like I'm a child or you'll find yourself with one less friend."

He tosses back the remainder of his drink and slams

the glass onto the bartop a little too hard before walking away.

"Oops, did we do that?" Enzo says sarcastically, rolling his eyes.

"He'll get over it. He always does."

Enzo signals to the bartender again, so I turn my back to the bar, my eyes sweeping through the crowd. It only takes seconds before I find Vinnie. The beads on her gown sparkle in the light as she laughs with the groups she's conversing with.

She's breathtaking.

The taste of her still lingers on my lips, and coupled with the sight of her, my cock begins to harden again.

As to not seem obvious, I continue to look around the room, appreciating the time and effort that went into such a beautiful event. Light shimmers off every crystal in the ballroom, creating tiny kaleidoscopic rainbows that dance across any open space. The women are impeccably dressed, dripping in jewels and beaded gowns, while the men selected tuxes that show off their affluence.

I hope the gala raised millions for the Venus-Hope foundation, which was set up to provide childhood cancer patients with the funding needed for their treatments and anything they feel would cheer them up. Parents should not need to worry about whether their insurance will cover the chemotherapy their children need, and the children should be able to request something that will make them happy during the most difficult time in their life, and be able to receive it.

Each year the Lucchettis donate upwards of five-hundred thousand dollars. This year we doubled that figure, as I matched my parents' donation.

"I'm going to hit the road soon," Enzo says. "You coming?"

"Soon."

I seek Vinnie out again—she's with a new group, completely unaware that everyone is giving her their full attention, admiring her as she speaks with them.

As I openly stare, a nagging sensation prickles my awareness, drawing my gaze elsewhere. On the wall opposite of where I am, stands August St. Jean, watching me with far too much interest.

Anger flashes through me as I meet his stare, silently challenging him.

He smirks, then turns to look to the exact spot I was just looking in. I don't give him the satisfaction of following his line of sight—I know he is looking at Vincenza.

When he pushes off the wall and heads in her direction, I toss back the bourbon the bartender just dropped off, giving August my back as I set the glass down. Every instinct tells me to intercept him, but I refrain, knowing it'll only draw suspicion.

"You good?" Enzo asks. "You look pissed all of a sudden."

"Sì," I snap, then realize my tone. I'm digging myself a deeper hole by reacting this way. "I think the day has finally caught up with me." Turning back to face both him and the ballroom, I speak to my cousin, all while watching August. Thankfully, they're practically aligned now and I can do both.

August approaches Vincenza, reaching for her hand. Bringing it to his mouth, he kisses the top of it.

The women in the group have dreamy looks on their face, as though they're falling in love with him for simply being in their vicinity.

Vinnie flinches slightly, shaking her head before he pulls her out onto the dance floor.

Whatever Lorenzo is saying falls upon deaf ears. August brings their hands above Vinnie's head and spins her dramatically before pulling her in close.

Leaning down, her scowl turns into a smile from whatever he said.

He spins her again, and suddenly he's the one facing me, and all I can see is how his hand descends behind her lower back, lingering too close to her backside, and the way he closes his eyes with a serene look on his face —all for show.

My blood is boiling from the exchange. Not knowing whether she's in distress or is enjoying the dance. Knowing I cannot step in but desperately wanting to.

She hates him. She's putting on a show.

Spin her, I mentally beg of August, needing her to make eye contact with me. I know she will.

Every passing moment is a battle within, talking myself off a ledge and ordering myself to stay put.

Needing a distraction, I look over at my cousin. He's staring down into his drink, swirling it gently.

"Are *you* okay, cugino?" For the first time this evening, I realize something is off about his demeanor.

It takes a second before his eyes find mine. Behind them I find pure exhaustion. "Yeah, I've just filled my quota for dealing with the public." Reaching forward, he pats my shoulder. "See you on Tuesday?"

Momma has planned a dinner for Aunt Andrea's birthday.

"Of course."

He smiles, then walks away, leaving me alone at the bar.

On the dance floor, Vinnie is still in August's arms. There's a small smile on her face that looks more cordial than truthful.

Like magnets, her eyes find mine. She must see something reflected in my face because she subtly shakes her head then looks to the ballroom doors.

Gritting my teeth, I rip my eyes away from hers. It takes everything I have to listen to what she's just silently asked me to do, but I do it regardless.

Heading back to the table where I sat, I take a quick glance to make sure I haven't left anything behind, then I leave the gala.

My mind is somber the entire drive home, plagued with the vision of Vinnie in the arms of a man I loathe. Seeing the smile on her face was like a knife to the heart

—a feeling that seems to have buried itself deep in a short amount of time.

Jealousy is a toxic trait I normally do not exhibit, but it seems as though my *piccola ladra* has stirred a new emotion within me.

Worse than that, I can't shake the thought of what it might be like to come clean to our families and tell the world that we're together.

After the disaster it would inevitably cause, would there be an opportunity for us to rise from the rubble? Or would the pressure become too much for us?

Or we could do the opposite.

Pack our bags. Run away and never look back.

Disappear and start anew.

Wherever she wants—Paris, Italy, Barcelona. I'll follow her anywhere.

But I know she would never agree. And would I truly want that? To be away from *la mia famiglia* again?

Dropping my keys and wallet onto the credenza by the door, I leave it cracked, knowing she won't be too far behind me. I don't bother turning on the lights as I unbutton my tuxedo jacket and shrug it off, tossing it over the edge of the couch as I continue further into my apartment.

Loosening my tie, I pull it over my head and drape it over the dining chair, then begin to unbutton my shirt as I head to the bar cart.

Pouring two fingers of whiskey, I take a swig and relax into the leather chair that sits by the floor-to-ceiling windows.

The city shimmers, twinkling with its evening beauty and promises. My view overlooks Manhattan and part of Central Park, although some of it is blocked by other high-rises. Still, I pay enough for the view, and tonight feels as good of a night as ever to sit back and admire the cityscape.

My thoughts bounce around from thinking about my cousin's strange behavior, the upset we caused Sully, and back to Vincenza.

Always back to Vincenza.

Expelling a shuddering breath, I picture her clearly, seeing her future in my mind like a movie. Walking down the aisle on her wedding day. In a hospital bed giving birth to a child, a sheen of sweat glistening on her forehead as she holds the hand of the person next to her. At the park, chasing after a small child as they run toward a flock of geese.

What's startling is that while I can picture her, I cannot see the man in which she shares these moments with, but I have the unsettling weight in my gut that the man isn't *me*.

And it never can be. Not under these circumstances.

They say if you love something, set it free.

Do I love her? I certainly can't fathom the thought of walking away from her, even though I know that would be the right thing to do—to give her the chance at a future with a man who can give her everything that I can only give her behind closed doors.

Just the thought of this ending sends a stabbing pain

through the organ within my chest. It only took me weeks to fall in love, but it will take a lifetime to let it go.

I *can't.*

Tossing back the rest of my whiskey, I finger the glass, running my pointer across the grooves as I stare out at the city.

My attention is drawn to the crack of the door, where the sound of heels in the hallway nears closer.

"Sly?" her voice floats through the air as her fingers wrap around the edge of the door. She pushes it open further, her head peering inside without entering.

"Come in, piccola ladra," I rasp, staying in my chair even though I'm drawn to her like a moth to a flame.

She does and shuts the door quietly behind her.

"Why are you sitting in the dark?" she asks, but as she does, her eyes immediately fall to the window, caught on the sight that's held my attention for the last forty minutes or so. "Wow. The city looks beautiful from this angle."

I say nothing, still stuck in my head. But she's perceptive, and walks over to me.

Reaching out to touch my shoulder, she says, "Hey. Are you okay?"

My hand reaches up and covers hers, my gaze following to look at her face.

She's come straight from the gala, her hair and makeup still done to perfection, with the dress I admired all evening still clinging to her body in the most beautiful of ways.

"Sì," I tell her, wishing I truly felt it.

She stares at me, searching my face, but I remain stoic. "I can leave…if you want?"

Her offer is like a punch in the gut after my harrowing thoughts of her future. The *last* thing I want is for her to leave. I want all the time I can get with her —selfishly and greedily.

"That is the last thing I want," I growl. Her eyes widen, and I take her hand from my shoulder and hold it, motioning with it for her to come stand in front of me. "Come here, piccola ladra."

Her body moves elegantly, as though her half turn toward me is a dance move she's perfected in my arms. Stepping in between my widened legs, she drops my hand and crosses her arms over her chest, telling me with her body language that she's unsure of my mood.

I'm allowing a *thought* to dampen the evening.

That ends *now*.

Moonlight streams through the windows, making beads of Vinnie's gown shimmer, as the low-light illuminates off her radiant skin. She's mesmerizing, but as much as I adore this dress, I am confident it will look much better on the floor.

Straightening in my seat, I reach behind her and find the hidden zipper that rests above her backside, unzipping slowly. When I reach the base of it, I allow my fingers to wander back up against her exposed skin, and my touch is rewarded with a small shiver.

"Take it off," I murmur, removing my hand from her body and placing it back in my lap. Her eyes shine from the glow of the moon, the uncertainty I caused no longer visible.

With careful movements, she shrugs one side of her dress down, followed by the other. Once the straps no longer rest off her shoulders, the gown slips from her body quickly and pools at her feet.

I can't help but suck in a sharp breath at the sight of her in front of me, completely bare, with the exception of the intricately strapped heels she still wears.

"Sei la cosa più bella che abbia mai visto." *You are the most beautiful thing I've ever seen.*

Starting at her thighs, I drag my knuckles up the sides of her body, moving as slowly as possible to savor the moment. I watch her face, taking in each expression and shallow gasp as I explore with light touches.

Goosebumps scatter across her skin, her nipples transforming into hard peaks before my eyes.

"*Sly,*" she moans, standing perfectly still despite clearly fighting against her instinct to move.

Once I have gone as high as I can reach without standing, I brush my knuckles down, dragging across the front of her body, over the swell of her breasts, until I reach her waist. Using one hand to grasp her hip, I skim my fingers between her legs and groan with appreciation.

"You're so wet, piccola ladra. Have you been thinking about this moment all evening like I have?"

"*Yes,*" she moans.

Fingering her entrance, my thumb finds her clit and begins to play with it softly.

"Tell me what you were thinking. Did you envision me doing this?" I curve my finger, stroking her G-spot. "Or were you thinking about me inside of you? Filling you up. Uniting as one."

"Yes. *That.*" Her inner walls clench around my finger as her hips roll into my hand.

Her pleasure, as it paints across her face, is the sexiest thing I've experienced in my lifetime.

"Use your words, Vincenza. In this room, here with me, you can be as crass as you'd like to be. There is no one here but the two of us. No one to judge you for the things you say or the manner in which you say them. Don't hold back—not with me. Tell me what you want."

"I want your cock," she breathes, her knees buckling from the pressure I'm using on her clit. "I want you to fuck me."

And I've become a lying man. The sexiest thing I've experienced in my lifetime are the sentences that just flowed so naturally from her mouth.

As if her own words possessed her, she bends down, my fingers never relenting inside her as she begins unfastening the remaining buttons on my shirt.

Once open, she pushes it off my shoulders, reaching over to my free hand to pull the fabric from my arm.

For the briefest of moments, I remove my fingers from her and rip the fabric from my other arm, throwing it onto the floor before I shove two back in, perhaps a little more roughly than needed. But she moans in response, her head tipping back on her shoulders as she places one hand on mine to brace herself.

Leaning forward, I press kisses to her stomach, pumping my fingers as I do.

I'm going out of my mind with need, desperate to be inside of her.

But I won't allow that until she's come at least once, preferably by my tongue.

Without warning, I remove my fingers again and stand quickly, grabbing her arms to turn her before pushing her lightly so she drops onto the chair I was just in.

Sinking to my knees, I tug her to the edge, shoving her legs apart, before I descend on her pussy.

Her juices spread into her slick folds, allowing me to feast between her legs as I push them wider. Her wanton cry pierces through my silent apartment. The only other sound is the lapping of my tongue against her.

From this angle, with her legs spread and her back arched, I am able to admire the soft curves of her body, and the way it trembles with pleasure.

I've quickly learned the signs of her body nearing the height of its pleasure and she's right there—on the cusp of seeing the stars that glitter in Heaven.

When I suction my lips around her clit, she free falls.

Her fingernails dig into my skull as she rides through her orgasm, her hips rolling into my face. I don't stop or let up the pressure. Instead, I add two fingers back inside her and give her more friction.

When I stroke her G-spot, a second orgasm crashes into her, and a sound between a moan and a screech leaves her lips, as her hips jump upward from the intense stimulation.

"Oh my God, *oh my God*," she chants in between incoherent moans.

As tempted as I am to continue to work her body to see if I can expel a third, the selfish side of me is dying to feel her against me.

Gently, I guide her hips back down to the chair and unlatch my belt buckle, leaving it hanging open as I unbutton and unzip my dress pants.

Standing, I scoop Vinnie into my arms, urging her legs to wrap around me. She winds her arms around my neck and slams her mouth to mine, kissing me with abandon as I walk us closer to the window. Her pussy is soaked, her wetness smearing onto my bare stomach.

The sensation is intoxicating.

Pressing her against the window, I give just enough space between us to push my pants down enough for my cock to spring free. Her body slides down slightly, aligning us perfectly, and without any further hesitation, I pull my cock through her juices, coating the tip, then push into her.

Our lips leave each other as I fill her to entirety. A slur of curses flees my lips in Italian, and she gasps as I bottom out within her.

For several seconds, I don't move, I simply *feel*.

Pulling back, I look at her, taking in the sight of her disheveled hair, and the flush on her beautiful light-olive complexion, against the backdrop of the city we both love.

And then I begin to move.

Rolling my hips, I find a rhythm that allows me to thrust deep inside her while still anchoring her between me and the window. I grasp at her breasts, kiss any inch of skin my lips can reach, and whisper things in my native language that I know she won't know the meaning of.

Things I'm not ready to say aloud in the language she understands.

Hoisting her onto my hips a bit more changes the angle, and within seconds her hand curls into a fist, the flat part slamming into the window above her head as she writhes in my arms, panting and losing all control once again. The bite of her stilettos digs into butt with every thrust, creating a slight tinge of pain mixed with my pleasure.

When she comes, her pussy tightens around my cock, milking it tightly as I fight to hold my own release in. The sweet sounds of her crying out flood my senses, beckoning me to follow suit.

Reaching beneath us, I pull my length from her so I can relocate us.

My hands clasp under her thighs, and I carry her through my apartment. My pants fall and get kicked off within the first few steps, so by the time we make it to my bedroom, we're both completely nude.

Tossing her to my bed, her breasts bounce as she lands and I follow her onto it, placing my knee between her legs as she crawls up further to fit us both.

"Do you have any idea how exceptionally beautiful you are, piccola ladra? Both inside and out." I unbuckle her left shoe, sliding it from her foot and letting it fall off the side of my bed, before repeating the process with the right. "Such a little thief, Vincenza. You've stolen my heart. Can't you see that you're holding it captive now?"

"I could say the same about you…" Her voice trails off as I kiss my way up her body, exaggerating each open mouth kiss into a lingering caress.

When I reach her pussy, I kiss it as I did the rest of her, worshiping it and taking my time.

The way her body seizes beneath my hands tells me she's still reactive. Changing my technique, I use my fingertips to spread her as I did while at the gala, and begin to massage her clit.

Alternating between the tip and the pad of my tongue, I play with the pressures as I hold her open, learning which makes her squirm and which makes her tense from it being too much.

It only takes a few minutes before she's writhing beneath me, on the brink of another orgasm.

When her legs snap around my head, I feel the quake of her body before she screams out in pleasure.

This time, I don't help her through it, but I jump to my knees and position myself on top of her, slamming into her as she rides through her orgasm.

Lifting her leg, I thrust into her, bringing it higher and higher until I'm hitting her at an angle that keeps her whimpering.

"Holy shit," she moans. "Right *there*. Right there, right there, right there."

Vinnie pushes her foot against my hip, keeping the angle as I let go of her leg and reach between us, rolling her clit between my pointer finger and thumb.

I'm close—no longer wanting to fight it off—but I'm determined to watch the pleasure of her orgasm dance across her face one more time before I allow myself release.

"I can't," she whines, her eyes rolling back as her back arches.

"You can, piccola ladra, and you will. Come for me, Vinnie, and I'll chase you into the stars."

She moans, slamming her eyes shut as she pushes her foot into my hip more.

Then I feel it. Her walls clench around me again, the breathing pattern of her chest shallowing into tight gasps. And then she plummets, letting the pleasure overtake her.

It hits her harder this time, her body shaking as her moans fill my bedroom. Her foot falls from my hip, though just in time, because I quickly pull out of her and grasp my cock in my hand, pumping it rapidly from base to tip as I finally allow myself to ejaculate.

Ropes of cum cover her stomach, the first fall spurring her eyes to open so she can see the rest.

She presses up on her elbows, watching me as I

groan in pleasure. My hand slows, but I continue to stroke my cock, observing her as she studies the movements.

When I stop, I stay kneeling with her beneath me, and we both take a moment to catch our breath. As we stare at each other silently, I know there are so many things I could say, but our bodies have just spoken everything for us in a way words may never be able to articulate.

Vinnie smiles up at me, and it's like the heat of a thousand suns are shining their warmth.

Crawling from the bed, I move to my en suite and run the faucet, allowing the water to heat, washing my hands as I wait. When it's hot, I run a towel beneath the water and squeeze out the excess, cleaning myself quickly before doing the same with a clean towel for Vinnie.

She looks content as I walk back into my bedroom and rejoin her on the bed, pressing the towel between her legs. Gently, I soothe her with its heat before bringing it to her stomach to clean her up.

"Are you thirsty?" I ask when I've finished, walking back over to the en suite to toss the towel into my laundry basket.

"A little."

Walking back to my bed, I pull the duvet back on my side and smile. "Get inside. I'll be right back."

When I return with two cold bottles of water, I'm pleased to see she's curled up under the covers, lying on my pillow.

She sits up, scooting over when I pull the duvet open and start to climb inside. I pass her the water, and she takes it, greedily drinking down more than half.

"Thank you," she says, grinning at me.

"Of course. It's my pleasure to care for you, Vinnie."

I drink my water down, then place it on my bedside table before taking hers from her hands and setting it down, too. Together, we sink further into the blankets, and I pull her close.

"There are things you must know about me," I tell her, trying to think of how to start this conversation. "And there are parts you may not want to listen to, but you need to hear them."

As I speak, I trace circles with my fingertip on her arm. "Until two years ago, I found sex to be unfulfilling. It was enjoyable, but always left me with an ache for more that I never understood. It took many years for me to realize why. When I was in Europe, I met a woman who helped me discover my true self in the bedroom. Our connection was purely physical—she allowed me to explore the part of me I hadn't realized existed until *she* put the puzzle pieces together. I am a Pleasure Dominant, Vinnie. And although I do not actively practice the lifestyle, I now know what fulfills me."

Her brows scrunch together, processing all I have said. I do not know whether it is a term she is familiar with, but I hope she will allow me to explain further.

She's quiet for what feels like several long minutes, but she doesn't move away, and I allow her to think.

"What questions are going through that beautiful mind of yours?" I ask, pulling her closer, even though she's already flush against me.

"So many," she whispers. "What exactly does that mean? A *Pleasure Dominant?*"

"I assure you the term is nothing to build fear around. In a short answer, it means that bringing my sexual partner pleasure is what ultimately brings *me* pleasure. The more orgasms you experience by my hand—or my tongue, or my cock—the more sexual gratification I obtain. Does that make sense?"

"Yes," she says, though her tone wobbles slightly with uncertainty.

"Some Pleasure Dominants enjoy mixing pain with pleasure, in the form of edging or sensation play, but I simply seek to fulfill my partner's every sexual desire. I do not wish to do anything with you that you do not ask for, nor do I expect you to change your sexual preferences or interests to appease me. Just know that I will be at your beck and call, happy to do whatever it may take to achieve your pleasure."

"This is a lot to take in," she admits bashfully, but still she doesn't look away. "You said you discovered this about yourself a couple of years ago… How many partners have you had?"

It dawns on me then that we did not use protection tonight, and naturally, she is probably feeling some panic.

"Prior to my realization, I had been with possibly eight to ten women, chasing an emptiness I could never figure out. But since? Only the woman who taught me my desire had a name. She lives in France, and since my time with her, I have not been with anyone else. Only you, and I realize that we just slept together without a barrier, but I want to assure you I am clean. I am a doctor, Vinnie. I would never put your health at risk."

Her eyes narrow quickly, sharpening her gaze as I finish my sentence. "My health is not the only one at risk, Sly."

After kissing the side of her head, I smile against her hair. "I *trust* you, Vinnie. You would have said something if there had been anything for me to consider."

She relaxes in my arms, settling her head against my chest. "So what can I do? To make sure *you're* sexually fulfilled? I want you to enjoy this as much as I do."

"That's the thing, piccola ladra. Your physical satisfaction brings me both mental and physical fulfillment. I get off by you getting off repeatedly. The only thing I ask is that you tell me if it's too much. Many Dominants —of *all* varieties—use a safe word. I want to encourage you to choose one, and if you are ever uncomfortable, in pain, or simply want to stop, you use it, and I will stop."

I pause to gauge her reaction, searching her eyes for any sort of discomfort or uncertainty.

"As I said earlier, my tastes do not include causing pain, but there may be times where you are so overstimulated the sensation turns into it, and that is something you may choose to use your safe word for. While on the contrary, you may choose to explore it. I am here for your desires, Vinnie. Any and all."

"Locket," she says matter-of-factly, lifting her chin to see my face better.

"Excuse me?"

"Locket. That's my safe word."

"So you're okay with everything I've said? You have no questions? Concerns? I am an open book, Vincenza. Please talk to me about anything."

"I trust you too, Sly. If I think of anything along the way, I'll ask, but you've explained everything I need to know and there's nothing overly shocking about it. I read books. I watch movies. I may not know the exact, *accurate* terms and practices of this type of lifestyle, but from what you're telling me about your preferences, I understand."

I press another kiss to the side of her head, breathing in the smell of her cherry blossom scented shampoo. "You continue to amaze me, Vincenza Paladino."

I close my eyes, happy and content in the moment.

But it's also hard to ignore the pang in my chest as her last name rolls off my tongue.

Lingering emotions from my spiral earlier flood me, but I force them down, disregarding the way they're trying to make me feel.

Tonight has been too amazing to let them back in.

"Why locket?" I ask, refocusing on the random word she selected as her safety net.

She laughs, her head bobbing against my chest as she shakes it, like the question I just asked was so out of pocket.

"*Piccola ladra*. Little thief. Thieves steal jewelry, and a locket is a type of jewelry." She shrugs, and I laugh at how quickly she thought of a word that made so much sense for us. "Yes, that's the connection my brain made."

"It's perfect," I tell her, turning my body so I can reach her lips. "And so are you."

Kissing her, I slide my arm under her body and pull her on top of me. Our bodies line up perfectly, and she's already wet, gliding against my length, moving slowly. I harden beneath her as our mouths move together and our tongues explore.

Pushing up on her knees, Vinnie wraps her hand around my cock and lines it up with her entrance, slowly sinking down until I'm filling her completely once again.

As I did earlier, she stays still, not moving even though both of our bodies demand it.

We kiss slowly, our hands both wandering as we do. She sighs against my lips, content as one of her hands settles in my short hair, pulling against the strands near my scalp when she deepens it.

Then we begin to move as one.

Chapter 25

Vinnie

Warm rays of sunshine kiss my bare skin as I lay on my stomach, admiring the man asleep beside me. The glow of his olive complexion—the rippling of his muscles as he sleeps with his hands beneath his head. Everything about him is captivating.

Soft puffs of air expel past his lips while I lay there and daydream about the night we shared.

I'm falling in love with him.

I can feel it in every bone in my body—recognize the sweet sensation of butterflies fluttering every time I simply think of his name. Feel it in the way my heart inflates when I see him, and the emptiness I feel whenever he's not near.

Under different circumstances, I should be inherently happy, but I find myself so frequently ignoring a glaring red warning sign illuminating in my mind, reminding me of everything that could go wrong. It sits like a weight in the pit of my stomach and crushes the spirit of the butterflies.

The clock illuminates the digits, telling me it's seven in the morning, and reminding me the more time I spend laying in this bed, the more I risk when I eventually sneak out of it. With August's garish display last night, I have no doubts that the media will be watching us both like a hawk now. And the last thing I can afford is for them to catch me leaving *anywhere* in last night's gown.

As gently as I can, I turn over onto my back and sit up, pulling myself out of bed to search for my phone.

The floor is cool beneath my feet as I tip-toe through Sly's apartment, finding my clutch by the front door where I let it drop last night.

Digging through my purse, I locate it and open my messages to text Raina.

Can I borrow your driver?

Walking to the window, I pick up my dress that's laying in a heap next to the leather armchair. The beads are scratchy as I hold the gown close to my body and stare out at the city, letting the memories of last night play like a movie in my head.

Every groan that left his lips, the look on his face when he finally shuddered his release. The way he held me in his strong arms, cradling my head against his chest as he whispered things I couldn't understand in Italian. I should have asked him what they meant, but the beauty of the language bewitched me, and the safety of his presence allowed me to drift off to sleep.

My phone vibrates in my hand, pulling me from my thoughts. Raina's name flashes across the screen as an incoming call and for a second I hesitate. The apartment is silent, but I decide to answer anyway. "Hello?"

"Hey," she croaks, her voice thick with sleep. "Do you still need the car?"

"Yeah, is that ok?" I whisper, turning my body away from the direction of Sly's room, shielding my mouth with my hand to try to contain my voice.

Air assaults the receiver, and the unmistakable sound of a man in the background asks, "What time is it?" His voice almost sounds familiar, like I've heard it before.

"Shh," Raina chastises, but she sounds muffled, like she's covering the speaker.

"Of course," she says, sounding normal again. "Hang on." The rustling of the phone being readjusted is loud against my ear, before a clicking begins, from what I assume is her typing a message. "Where are you?"

"The Kenna."

More tapping ensues, then stops. The phone line goes silent for a beat before she says, "Okay, he's on his way. ETA is ten minutes."

"I owe you one," I tell her, cradling the phone against my shoulder so I can step into my dress. "The last thing I need is for the press to catch me hailing a cab in last night's dress, especially after that stunt August pulled."

"I still can't believe he did that."

I reach behind and zip up my dress. "Yeah, well, unfortunately I can. I swear, if he's at brunch today, I might need to call you for backup."

"Don't hesitate. I'll be around all day."

"Thanks. I have to go. Thanks for lending me your driver."

"Anytime." She blows a kiss into the phone, then ends the call.

Stuffing my phone back into my clutch, I walk back toward Sly's room. My heels are still on the floor by his bed, but I leave them there. I'll say goodbye first, then deal with putting them on.

As I approach, a smile touches my lips as I look at him—sleeping peacefully, unknowing how sexy he is without even trying. He's *sleeping*, and still he looks like a demigod. My body flushes with conflicting emotions—my heart tugs with affection, while there's a rush of desire that leads straight to my core.

Stopping at the edge of his bed, I reach out and run a finger down the curve of his cheek and against short beard. Even in his sleep, he turns toward my touch.

"Sly," I say, running my finger down his cheek again, rousing him softly. "I have to go."

He stirs and reaches for my hand, weaving his fingers through mine. "Mmm, don't go. Stay."

"I can't. I arranged for a driver to pick me up. I have to go."

Grinning, he pulls me forward, and I have no choice but to land on top of him. His eyes finally crack open, his free hand tangling in my hair. "You put the dress back on. Perhaps I need to peel it off of you again."

I use this angle to my advantage and press my lips to his chest, peppering kisses to his skin as I work my way up his neck to his lips. When I reach them, I kiss him slowly, and he immediately grants me access, tangling his tongue with mine.

He groans, and beneath the few fabrics that lie between us, I feel him grow hard beneath me. It sends a spark of need directly between my thighs.

Sliding his hands over the curve of my butt, he anchors me to him.

"Are you sure you have to leave? We can stay in bed today and pretend the world ceases to exist."

Wiggling my hips, I simultaneously break free of where he holds me, and drive us both wild.

"I can't. It's Sunday—I have to meet my family." And as much as it pains me, I slide off him, but he refuses to fully let go, keeping our hands laced.

Lightly, he tugs me forward again so he can bring my hand to his lips and kissing the back of it. "And after?"

"You want me to come back?" I question, but I can't ignore the flutter of my heart, or the way his eyes sparkle up at me.

"Amore mio, I never want you to *leave*."

Leaning down again, I press another kiss to his lips. "I'll be back this afternoon, then."

He watches me go, sitting up in his bed so he can see me better. The sheet rests over his lower half, but I can see the way he tents it. It makes my core ache with a need that's igniting slowly within me.

My heart pangs, reminding me I don't *really* want to leave—not yet—and I glance over my shoulder again.

Stopping at his doorway, I pull my phone from my clutch and type out a quick message to Raina.

On second thought, I'll find another ride home later. So sorry, and thank you!

I'll figure out my ride situation later, but right now, I can't ignore the precious moments I have with the man who's looking at me like he'd hang the moon for me if I ask him to.

Without turning around, I drop my clutch. It hits the floor with a soft thud.

Reaching around, I find my zipper and lower it slowly.

When I peek over my shoulder again, Sly's eyes shimmer in the reflection of the sunlight as a smirk plays on his lips.

"Change of heart, piccola ladra?" he rasps, his throat bobbing as he watches the movement of my fingers.

The dress slips from my body.

Stepping out from where it lies at my feet, I saunter toward him. When I reach the edge of his bed, his hand instantly curls around my thigh as I climb on top of him, bracing myself with my palms pressed against his headboard.

"I never want to leave, Sly." Then I kiss him.

Hard.

It's unrestrained and lustful, not just because I want him, but because he makes me feel reckless.

An inferno blazes through me. A rush of desire sparking and pooling low in my stomach, aching deep in my core. I moan against his lips as he takes charge, his fingers finding my opening.

He pushes two inside me. "Your moans are my favorite sound. Let me hear them."

I moan again, but it turns into a whimper when he expertly finds my G-spot, knowing exactly where I need him. As though he's known my body forever.

He kisses me harder.

Deeper.

Allowing himself to unravel with me.

"I need more," I whimper against his lips. "I need you inside of me."

I don't wait for him to respond. Instead, I reach beneath my body and move the sheet off him so we're skin to skin. His cock springs free and I curl my fingers around him, pumping from root to tip.

His head tilts against the headboard as his fingernails drag against my thighs, finding their way to my hips, and he lets out a moan so carnal, I lose control.

Positioning him against my entrance, I sink onto him, inch by delicious inch, gasping from the way our bodies fit perfectly together—as though they were made for each other.

"Che cazzo" he mutters under his breath, his eyes fluttering closed.

Once he's completely filled me, I begin to move, riding him until I find a rhythm. He holds onto my hips, lifting me as I slide up and down his length.

"You ride me so well, Vinnie. Look at us." He presses his fingers and thumbs against my chin, tipping it down until I'm staring between us, where our bodies connect. He moves his hand back to my hips, guiding me slowly up his length.

"Perfetta," he groans.

Fusing our mouths together again, he sits up, readjusting our angle as he wraps his arms around my back. Thrusting his hips upward, he dips his head, reaching to kiss the swell of my breast before he takes a nipple into his mouth.

I cry out when his teeth skim it, building the pleasure within me.

"More," I beg, my voice raspy with need. "Harder."

Bracing one hand on the bed, he uses it as leverage to intensify his thrusts, spearing me as I hold onto his shoulders.

"Yes. Right there, Sly." My moans fill the room, echoing against his guttural sounds. I wind my arms around his neck and kiss him, focusing on the pleasure building and the sounds of our skin slapping as we chase the feeling of our bodies together as one.

Pleasure vibrates through my body, intensifying so

quickly it slams through me, pushing me over the edge. "There! God, I feel you *everywhere*. Harder. I'm coming!"

Sweet euphoria overtakes my body, my walls tightening around him as my orgasm rains down like a lightning storm.

I feel feral.

Alive.

Slowing his movements, he gently presses kisses against my chest while his hands move to my hair, gathering it until he transfers it all to one hand, holding it in a ponytail to get it off my neck.

"You're everything I want and need, piccola ladra," he rasps.

Then he pulls out—the movement so sudden I'm not ready for it, and I wince from the feeling of him leaving me—and flips me onto my back.

Sinking further down the bed, he grins up at me as he hitches my legs over his shoulders.

"Wait, you didn't—"

"Your pleasure *is* my pleasure, remember? I'm nowhere near done with you yet, and when I feel you've had enough, *then* I will find my release." His fingertips drag across my slit, gathering the wetness before he smears it around, his eyes never leaving mine as he does. "Lay back, piccola ladra."

And then he worships at the throbbing between my thighs over and over again.

"You're late, baby sister," Joseph sneers as I breeze through the front door of my parents' home. I hand my clutch to a nearby housekeeper and shrug my coat off, glaring at my brother.

"And?" My patience has run thin for him and his disgusting friend.

He says nothing, but smirks in a way that says far more than his words could.

"Oh my gosh, Vinnie!" My mother bursts into the room, clutching a newspaper so tightly it's completely crumpled. "How could you not tell me!"

God, I'm not in the mood for this. Leaving Sly's apartment after *six* orgasms had been blissful. The last thing I want to deal with is *this*. Not when his touch still lingers on my skin, his scent still clinging to me beneath the cover of my perfume.

I hadn't had time to shower when I arrived back at my apartment, and instead, I washed quickly between my legs, threw on a clean outfit, and applied a light dusting of makeup and a spritz of perfume. Because I *was* running late.

But wow, was it worth it.

"Not tell you what, Mother?" The irritation comes out much more intensely than I intended, but I'm irritated all the same.

Thrusting the newspaper into my hands, she taps the photo on the front page with excitement. "That you and August are a couple! Oh, honey, you two are stunning together!"

My eyes widen with horror as I see a photo of me

and August from last night plastered on the front page of the paper with the headline *Who's Falling for Who? Manhattan's most eligible bachelor, August St. Jean, spotted out with Vinnie Paladino!*

Below it is a half-page photo of me in August's arms as he dips me low. One of his hands cradles my lower back while the other holds my hand as he smiles down at me—a position far too intimate for what I was feeling in the moment. But the worst part of the photo is that it captured the brief moment *I* smiled before I truly realized what was going on.

Guilt claws in my stomach, absolutely hating how this photo portrays us. No part of me enjoyed that moment, I only smiled because who doesn't instinctually smile when they're being moved in a fun way? What woman doesn't like to be dipped?

"Mom, we're not—"

"That serious yet," Joseph cuts in. "But August won't shut up about your time at the gala last night, sis. He's *very* smitten." The smirk he's giving me sends a chill down my spine, but my mother doesn't seem to notice. She just visibly melts from the news, looping her arm through my brother's as she looks up at him adoringly.

"And when are you going to meet someone, sweetheart?" she asks, leading him into the dining room.

My feet are rooted to the floor, watching them as they go, completely unaware that I'm forcing myself not to lose all control. I want to scream, cry, and hurl my anger at them. Demand answers from my brother about why he hates me so much. Curling my hands into fists at my side, I close my eyes.

"Vinnie," Luciano's smooth voice floats through the foyer.

For a moment I consider ignoring him, finding the woman I handed my clutch to, and leaving. It's tempting, but I know the utter chaos it will cause if I do.

Opening my eyes, I see him leaning against the archway of the sitting room.

"Are you okay?" he asks, his brows knitted with concern.

Luciano and I have never been very close due to our age difference, but he's always been protective over me. He's always had my back more than my *other* older brother has, and although I know he won't openly speak to me about family affairs I have no part of, I trust he won't lie to me, and because of this, I make a snap decision.

"Can we talk?" I ask. I hold my breath, even though I know he won't tell me no.

He nods his head, then gestures at the sitting room, walking back into it.

The soles of my ballet flats squeak against the freshly polished marble floors as I follow him.

The room is chilly from the open window. Its sheer curtains billow from the breeze.

My brother takes a seat on the couch, picking up a book that was left behind on a cushion. Placing a bookmark as close to the spine as possible, he shuts it and sets it down beside him. I sit next to him in the warm sunlight that envelopes part of the couch.

"What's going on?" Luciano asks simply, his tone cold, but not mean. Just...unamused, perhaps even a little bored.

I recognize this side of him as his lawyer persona. He's assessing me—gathering all the information he needs for this conversation.

It strikes me as odd, since he has no idea what this conversation will be about, but then again I learned not to underestimate my brother years ago. He's highly intelligent, and can easily read people. It's one of the reasons why he's such a successful divorce attorney.

"I need you to explain to me why Joseph hates me so much."

Luciano's mask slips as he winces.

So it's true, then. Joseph *actually* hates me.

"Vinnie," Luciano starts, but I hold up my palm to stop him.

"Stop. Don't you dare try to sit here and sugarcoat things for me, Luce. I'm not a little girl anymore."

He sighs deeply, rotating his body so his arm can rest along the back of the couch. His eyes catch on something outside, and he stares at it. I can see the wheels in his head turning, carefully selecting what he wants to tell me.

"Joseph," he says quietly, then he stops again, his lips pursing in thought. "Joseph has always had a deeply rooted fear that Father will overlook him when it comes time to carry on his legacy. He knows I don't want it.

Not with my own career thriving. Truthfully, the last thing I'd ever want to do is take over Father's business—coffee, or otherwise. But you've always been Father's favorite. Daddy's little girl, and all that."

Irritation spikes through my blood. "I don't want his business. Like you, I have my own."

He turns to me, his cerulean eyes colliding with mine. "I know that, and you know that, Vinnie. But Joseph doesn't *believe* it. He thinks when it comes time to pass the torch that Daddy Dearest will pass it directly over his head and straight into your hands."

His words resonate within me and I fold my arms across my chest in a very child-like way. Tears prick the back of my eyes as a flood of memories overtake my thoughts—moments from when Joseph and I were children and best friends. I let myself internally mourn for a moment. "So that's it then? Joseph just hates me until the day that Father finally does step down and he realizes the business has always been his?"

Luciano shrugs, then claps his palm against my knee. "I wish I had more to say about the matter, V. I've had numerous conversations with him, but Joseph is stubborn and refuses to see anything outside of his own thoughts and opinions. Give him time. He'll change his outlook eventually."

"And the bullshit with August? I'm just supposed to give that time, too? They're scheming, Luce. My gut's screaming at me that something isn't right."

"I haven't heard you curse in a long time, sister." He stands, buttoning his suit jacket. "I'll see what I can find out about August and why he's pursuing you, because you're right, those two are up to something—I can see it clear as day."

Bending down, he kisses my cheek. "Don't worry, sis. At least you have one brother who will always love you."

He cracks a smile, meaning his words as a joke, but they invoke immediate sadness throughout me.

Vibration pulls both of our attention as his phone rings in his pocket. He pulls it out, discreetly looking at who's calling. "I have to take this," he says, immediately turning to leave. "Hello?" he says as he walks through the alcove, his footsteps disappearing down the hall.

Mirroring how my brother sat earlier, I turn toward the window and drape my arm across the back, leaning my head against my hand as I look out to the street.

Worry lines my brow, my brain running rampant with thoughts of what August and Joseph might be conspiring. I want to talk to Sly. I want him to hold me in his arms and tell me everything will be fine and he'll protect me against whatever my brother and his friend are planning.

Because they *are* planning something. I can feel it. I just don't know what it is.

"Miss Paladino? Brunch is served, and your mother is requesting you," a housekeeper says from the edge of the room, offering me a small smile in apology for interrupting my thoughts.

I look over at her and nod before turning back to the window.

My mother is requesting me.

Of course she is. She probably wants to gush more about this morning's paper.

Oh, God. The paper. I need to speak with Sly before he sees it—explain to him that the smile was not what it looked like.

My stomach twists into knots.

"Miss?" the housekeeper asks again, a sympathetic look etched into her features. Clearly under instruction to make sure I join my family.

Blowing out a deep breath, I stand and ready myself for the next forty-five minutes of my life, where I have to act like everything's okay.

Lie to my parents about not having met someone. Pretend that I'm not falling in love with him and I haven't been sneaking around with the son of a man my father considers an enemy.

Convince them the photo with August means *nothing*.

Most importantly, though, it's time to go play the role of the perfect daughter until I can get out of this house and finally breathe again.

Chapter 26

Sly

Green is not a color I consider myself to look good in, so I'm completely bewildered as to how I keep wearing a very particular shade of it—jealousy.

Seeing my woman in the arms of another plastered all over the front pages of Manhattan newspapers and gossip stirs the darkness inside me, forcing me to push it down. White hot anger coursing through my blood, nipping at my insides until it consumes me so wildly, it overtakes my whole being.

I hadn't expected to see it in print, and I sure as hell don't expect to see it on my walk to work, as I pass by the newspaper vendor on the corner. My neck narrowly survives whiplash with how quickly my muscles snap back when I see Vincenza on the front page.

And the way my stomach sinks…

I practically rip the paper in half as I pick it up, gripping it so tightly in my hands my knuckles turn white, and the edges crinkle from the pressure.

It takes me several minutes to snap out of it.

Tossing a bill at the vendor—I can't even tell you the denomination, perhaps it is a twenty, or a hundred—I rush down the street, weaving through the hordes of people blocking my path, until I reach the plain door to my clinic.

Once inside, I slam the newspaper down on the examination table and let my eyes fly over words.

Who's Falling for Who? Manhattan's most eligible bachelor, August St. Jean, spotted out with Vinnie Paladino!

Women all over the city are drying their eyes after seeing Manhattan's most eligible bachelor, August St. Jean, holding Vinnie Paladino in a cozy clutch as he dips her in greeting at the Venus-Hope gala last night. Are the two dating? A source close to St. Jean told us the two have been growing closer and getting to know each other, but that St. Jean is "smitten" with the Paladino Princess.

Rage erupts at the article, my fingers curling around the monotone pages, crumpling it until it's no longer legible. Tossing it into the trash, I lean over the countertop, grabbing the edge with as much force as I can.

All I see is red.

The monster within trying to claw through the walls of the box I've stored him away in, begging to be set free. He's taunting me about how easy it would be to pay August a visit. Send him a message.

Doing so would compromise everything I've worked toward, everything I fight to keep locked tightly within me.

I'm not that man.

But for *her*, I consider the consequences.

Vinnie hadn't mentioned this to me. She hadn't mentioned anything that night, nor last night when she was in my arms and in my bed.

But there's no mistaking that something *did* happen.

There's no mistaking the dress she's wearing in the photo. The same one I had the pleasure of watching fall from her body.

Her smile…

She looked surprised, but not unhappy.

Could I be misreading the signs of our relationship?

I squash that notion the moment it filters through my brain, remembering the day she showed up at my apartment in *fear* of him.

She hates him just as much as I do. She had to have been caught off guard.

But why didn't she tell me about it?

A knock at the door startles me, pulling me from my thoughts. Glancing at my watch, I notice that it's nearly thirty minutes before my patient is supposed to arrive.

My long strides have me at the door quickly, and as I pull it open, I'm greeted by the familiar, and entirely unwelcome in this moment, face of my best friend.

"Sully." I glower at him, eyes narrowing as he stands in my doorway with a shit-eating grin on his face.

"Invite me in?" He winks, then pushes past me.

Settling in the leather guest chair, he crosses his foot over the opposite knee and looks at me with scrutiny in his eyes.

We haven't spoken since the gala last night and I

can't tell if he's still upset or if, in true Sully fashion, he's brushed it under the rug.

"Why are you here, Sullivan?" I lean against the counter, crossing my arms over my chest.

"I need to ask you something, and I know this might seem a little out of left field, but it's been on my mind."

I can't help but narrow my eyes at him, intuition telling me whatever his question is will piss me off even more than I already am. "What's that, amico?"

"Is there something going on between you and Vinnie Paladino?"

A rush of endorphins drops through my body, spiking my heart rate. My stomach somersaults as my jaw locks. I feel like a child who's been caught doing something they shouldn't have. "Why would you ask me that?"

I don't want to lie to him, but if I have to, I will.

Sully has never betrayed me, but the idea of someone finding out about Vincenza and I, in any way other than on my terms, sends a stabbing pain through me. I *will* protect her, even from my own best friend.

"I saw the way you were looking at her at the gala, man."

When I couldn't keep my eyes off her. Of course, *someone saw.*

I attempt to hide it. "Like she is the enemy?"

He smirks. "Like you wanted to rip the clothes from her body and fuck her right in the middle of the dance floor."

Fuck.

I waver, torn between coming clean or lying to him. Still balancing on the line between trusting him with this secret or protecting it at all costs. The thought of getting it off my chest is appealing, but if anyone found out. If my family—*Enzo*—found out.

"Look, you don't have to say anything," he relents, putting his palms up as though he's backing away from the subject. "I can understand that if there is something going on between you, it could be detrimental for your family dynamic. But, if you *do* want to talk about it, you have someone who's not in the Lucchetti bloodline who can lend an ear."

It's the most mature thing he's said since we came back to the States. Perhaps his outburst at the gala last night pushed him in a direction to think and reflect about his life.

Running a hand through my hair, my voice is strained when I finally respond. "Grazie, amico mio."

"Plus," he continues. "She's hot as hell. I bet you could have stripped her naked and let her bounce on your dick on the dance floor and not a single pers—".

"ENOUGH," I boom, seeing red at the mere thought of that happening.

Immediately, Sully starts laughing hysterically. "Shit, man. You've got it *bad* for her. How long have you two been sneaking around right under my nose? Does *anyone* know?"

"No," I bark, giving up the secret. I should have known Sully would have seen the truth all over my face. Now all I can do is beg him to keep his mouth shut.

"And it needs to be kept that way. If this gets out, I don't need to tell you the implications of what could happen. Enzo may never speak to me again. And Papà—"

"Your pops will support you, eventually. Enzo, on the other hand…"

"Exactly." I rub my hand through my hair and cross the room.

Defeated, I sink into the seat next to him. Memories of the gown slipping from my piccola ladra's body instantly infiltrate my brain as I sink against the soft leather.

"Your secret is safe," Sully vows. "Sixty-nine years of friendship and I've never stabbed you in the back once."

"Perhaps you should go back to school for some extra math classes, amico."

"It's billionaire math. You know, when we're so rich, we have other people handle the numbers for us?"

"You worry me."

"Not the first time I've heard that. Listen, I need to get going. I'm supposed to be at my parents' house in thirty and I have a feeling traffic's going to be a bitch. Keep me updated on the dirty details of your love life, though, okay? A man could use a little excitement from time to time."

"Finished with Hera so soon?"

"Please, that was weeks ago. You know commitment isn't in my vocabulary."

Sighing, I lean back in my chair and pinch the

bridge of my nose to relieve the headache Sully is building.

"We will talk soon, amico. Tell your parents I said hello."

"Will do." Sully stands and leaves my clinic, the door slamming closed behind him.

Leaning forward on my elbows, I rub my eyes, digging the heels of my hands into the sockets.

Idiota.

Obviously I haven't been as discreet as I thought. Then again, Sullivan has been my best friend since we were children. He knows me well. Knows my tells, and has seen me around women. I should be less surprised that he picked up on my feelings and more concerned that perhaps he wasn't the only one.

My mind wanders back to the look Enzo had given me a few times throughout the night. Had he been paying closer attention than I thought? A small tinge of panic sends a soft wave of tingles through my body as I consider the implications of my cousin knowing, but I squash the nerves, knowing I'd do whatever necessary to keep Vincenza safe—even if that meant protecting her from my own flesh and blood.

Chapter 27

Sly

Voices carry through the foyer of la mia famigilia's brownstone before I even shut the door behind me. An overwhelming sense of home settles itself in my soul. It doesn't matter if I was nine when we moved to the States, this comfortable Manhattan house became our home.

The argument coming from my father's office is muffled, but my curiosity of who is behind the closed door overshadows the delicious smell wafting from the kitchen. Which is a shame, because there's nothing like Mamma's cooking.

"They've been going at it for fifteen minutes," she says flatly, emerging from the kitchen before I can go to Papà's office. She shakes her head, eyes flitting to the closed door. "Lorenzo is unhappy."

"Unhappy about what?" Shrugging off my coat, I hang it on the coat rack by the door, then slip off my shoes and into the wool pantofoles kept by the door for me.

Her lips purse. "It's always something." After running her hands down her apron, she pats my chest, then returns to the kitchen.

When I reach Papà's office, I stride into the room as though I'm not interrupting whatever the hell is going on in here.

Enzo's voice booms as he leans over my father's desk, his back to me. "I'm tired of this, Zio Antonio. They've been getting away with this shit for far too long, and it's time we do something about it."

On the couch against the wall, my younger brother Guilio sits with his foot crossed over his opposite knee, taking in the scene with relaxed posture, which tells me Papà is relaxed too, though I cannot see his face. Guilio has a habit of mirroring our father's emotions.

"We will do no such thing." Papà's voice is firm but soothing, trying to diffuse Enzo's anger while he speaks. "There is only conflict because you've poked the bear."

"There has *always* been conflict. I want their family to finally pay for their sins, like ours has over for almost two decades."

From where I stand in the doorway, I can see Enzo's fingers flex against the mahogany of Papà's desk.

"What happened this time?" I interject, knowing that it must be serious if Enzo took it to my father. Last time he had come to me for medical attention for his friend, but as I scan what I can see of his body, he holds no injuries that need to be attended to.

Then slowly, Enzo turns toward me, his face full of a sneer…and physical pain.

His left eye is swollen shut, his upper lip is split, and the majority of his face is an angry red with bruises that are settling beneath his skin.

"Oh, hello cousin," he greets, his voice dripping with sarcasm. "You came just in time. Your father and I were just discussing the best course of action for retaliation on the Paladinos."

My eyes take inventory of every wound on Enzo, assessing how I might be able to help him heal, and while the only evident injuries are that on his face, I suspect there is bruising beneath his shirt as well.

"We will *not* retaliate." Papà slams his hand against the desk as he flies up out of his seat, standing to his full height to face Lorenzo eye to eye. "*We* are not *them*, Lorenzo. You are a Lucchetti, and we Lucchettis *choose* to take the high road. Forgetting who you are would be a disappointment to your father. It sure is one to me."

Lorenzo's shoulders sag for a split second before he raises them again, drawing his eyes away from mine to turn back to my father.

"Can somebody fill me in on the details of what happened?" I ask, wanting more information, but also wanting to diffuse the situation as much as possible.

From the couch, Guilio snickers. "He got his ass handed to him."

"You shut your mouth, Guilio," Enzo snaps.

"Gesù Cristo," I mutter, swiping my hand down the

front of my face in frustration. My voice raises. "What the hell happened?"

"What happened?" Enzo yells back. "I'll tell you what *fucking* happened. That piece of shit Paladino is too much of a pussy to handle his own wars and instead had three of his men jump me while he watched."

"What I still don't understand, Lorenzo, is why you were even in their vicinity," my father counters, sitting back down behind his desk.

"The *why* is not important, Zio."

"Sì, it is, Enzo," I interject. Striding over to the couch, I take a seat with my brother. "It has been clear for many years that our families strongly avoid each other. Yet, this is twice you have set foot behind enemy lines."

The admission falls from my lips, and Enzo glares at me, his eyes narrowing into dangerous slits.

"Twice?" Papà questions. His tone has slid into an icy malice. "Explain."

Enzo stares at me, and I can read his expression. I must undo the damage.

Looking over at him, I leave it as vague as possible. "Nothing to be concerned with Papà. It was a misunderstanding at best." My gaze cuts back to Enzo. "Are you hurt elsewhere?"

"I couldn't care less about the state of my body. I'm more worried about what our family will do to send a clear message that we will not tolerate their bullshit."

"And you don't think a retaliation would add fuel to the fire?"

"I don't give a rat's ass what it adds to the fire so long as they know who the fuck they're messing with."

Everything about the way Enzo is acting right now is pissing me off. He's clearly reached his breaking point, but the way he's lashing out at Papà and attempting to call for a retaliation that could land us *all* in hot water with the Paladino family is upsetting, to say the least.

"And what exactly do you propose, Lorenzo?" I retort. "I have yet to hear a solid plan. Just you whining about how you want to get back at them."

"*Whining?* You think I'm… Alright." The sarcasm is thick in his voice. "A solid plan. How about we stick it to them where it really hurts? Fuck Joseph. Fuck Maurizio. We send a message with a member of their family who they'd *never* expect for us to target."

My blood turns to ice, my mind instantly conjuring an image of Vinnie asleep in my bed.

"Lorenzo," Papà warns, his tone conveying that he also doesn't like where this is headed.

With a smirk that makes my stomach turn to knots, Enzo crosses his arms over his chest and leans against my father's desk. "They have a younger son—can't remember his name. We could rough him up a little, send him back in just slightly worse shape than what I'm in now. Show them we won't just stand here and take it. Eye for an eye, and all that."

I expel a small breath of relief, but the feeling is gone the moment Enzo opens his mouth again.

"*Or* there's always Vinnie Paladino. She seems like she'd be an easy one for us to grab and—"

I'm off the couch and lunging for my cousin faster than I can comprehend, losing all composure as I yell in his face. The monster in me aches to enclose my hands around his neck and squeeze the life out of him for the mere suggestion of hurting Vinnie. "You will not touch her, Lorenzo."

My outburst sends an instant wave of silence over the room, so quiet you could hear a pin drop. The air is tense, and for several seconds, no one speaks or moves, but Enzo cocks his head to the side, watching me closely.

Inside, a war rages. The urge to snap my cousin's neck is so strong I'm not even sure I would feel remorse. But I have to get my emotions under control. My reaction is entirely too telling of my feelings for Vinnie, and although I'm confident I didn't reveal my entire hand, I have no doubt that my cousin now has suspicion of the cards I hold.

"You will not touch her," I repeat, calmer this time —my voice deadly flat as I shove my emotions into a box within my mind and lock it. "How could you even imply that you would harm a woman?"

His eyes narrow like he doesn't quite believe my words. "Who said anything about harming her? Had you let me finish, you would have heard me suggest that we grab her and take her on a little joy ride to scare her father before returning her."

"So kidnapping then? That's your suggestion?"

"How can that even be a thought in your mind, Enz? Are you really *that* desperate for revenge?" Guilio looks at Enzo like he's a complete stranger.

And to be honest, right now he is. My best friend and closest family member is not the same man I'm seeing at this moment.

He's let his monster out.

"I don't even recognize you right now," I mutter, shaking my head

My father clears his throat. "Lorenzo, perhaps it's best that you take a moment and collect yourself before your mother arrives for her birthday dinner. I'd hate for her to see you so vengeful. Sylvester, could you take him somewhere? Come back when the dust has settled?"

My father's eyes cut to mine and I nod, standing so I can do as he's asked. Coming to stand in front of Enzo, I place my hand on his shoulder. "Come."

He shrugs me off, shoulder checking me as he moves past. "Don't fucking touch me, Sly. I can see I'll have to do this on my own. You know, my dad would be disappointed in all of you for letting the Paladinos run our lives after they murdered him in cold blood."

He stomps from the office, grabbing onto the door as he passes through the threshold so he can slam it behind him.

My father exhales loudly, running both hands through his hair as he leans his elbows against his knees. "He's right. His father would be disappointed. But not in us. He'd be disappointed in *him*. For all his faults,

Gabriele was a caring man. He wouldn't have wanted this."

"How can we fix it?" Guilio asks.

Crossing the room, I return to my seat next to him, sinking down into the cool leather of the sofa.

"I'm not sure there is a way to fix it," I tell him. Digging my thumb and finger into my eye sockets I massage the headache that's filtered its way into my skull. "Enzo is out for blood, and he won't stop until someone aside from him is feeling the pain he's feeling."

"He still grieves his father," Papà adds.

"Should we worry about his threats?" Guilio asks. "Would he actually kidnap Paladino's daughter?"

"No," I say without hesitation. Not because I wouldn't put it past Enzo to do something stupid, but because I would never let *anything* happen to Vinnie.

Guilio nods, and from my periphery Papà gives me a look I can't read.

We fall silent again, and moments later, the ringing of the doorbell echoes through the halls.

"That'll be Aunt Andrea," Guilio says to no one in particular. Standing, he crosses the room and leaves, letting the door click closed behind him much softer than Enzo had.

As soon as he's gone, Papà pierces me with a heavy gaze. "I've been meaning to speak to you."

"Oh?"

"I want you to reconsider your residency. Re-enter the program and come work at my hospital—hell, any hospital."

Internally, I groan.

I am not prepared for this conversation.

The last thing I want is to lie to my father, so I opt for the truth. Or at least a form of the truth.

"Papà, as I have told you, I am not sure a residency is the right avenue for my long-term goals."

"Which are?" He leans back against his leather office chair, his arms crossed over his chest. The look on his face tells me he is serious about this conversation, but over the years I have come to realize that although I hold the utmost respect for my father, I am also an adult.

"Not in the confines of a hospital, Papà." Adjusting the cuff on my shirt, I roll it to my elbow before repeating the process with the other. "Now, if you'll excuse me, I think I'll go say happy birthday to Andrea."

My father's eyes burn a hole through the silk-like cotton of my shirt as I leave his office. On the other side of the door, I can breathe a little easier.

Keeping my occupation from him feels like slicing a knife through my own heart—painful and wrong—but I fear the reaction he may have if I tell him I *am* practicing medicine, just not in the way he would want me to.

Despite the years-long feud between our family and the Paladinos, Papà is very much a "by the book" type of man who holds himself to a very high standard of ethics. He's always led with his moral compass, so if I were to tell him his son was illegally practicing medicine in an unmarked clinic, he'd lose his mind.

When I reach the kitchen, I find the women of my family leaning against the large kitchen island, sipping glasses of wine as they chat. My youngest brother, Federico, is rummaging through the refrigerator, but Guilio is nowhere to be found, nor is my cousin.

"Happy birthday," I tell my aunt, bending down to kiss her on the cheek. Her dark brown hair is in a sleek twist at the nape of her neck. She's wearing a hunter green dress that brings out the golden flecks in her eyes. "How old are you today? Thirty-one? Thirty-two?"

Her boisterous laugh fills the kitchen. "How dare you! I'm not a day over twenty-eight, thank you."

"Ah, yes, that's right. I forgot we're so close in age."

"You're damn straight we are." She takes another sip of her wine. "Where's Enz? You two are never too far from each other. Is he not here yet?"

From my peripheral, I see Mamma grip the stem of her glass tighter. I'm sure she saw Enzo storm out mere minutes before Andrea's arrival.

"He should be back any time," I answer simply, giving her a curt smile before I head into the attached dining room.

My eyes are on the bar cart when I feel my phone vibrate in my pocket.

Before I reach for it, I carefully pour myself two fingers of whiskey, swirling the glass as I meander into the study and take a seat in front of the roaring fire.

It vibrates again once I'm seated, and with my eyes

transfixed on the flames dancing against the brick fire-box, I pull my phone from my pocket.

Two messages await, one from Vinnie and one from Enzo. It's no surprise which message I open first.

> I'm free Thursday evening, but tomorrow I have back-to-back meetings and don't anticipate leaving the office until late.

She's responding to my dinner invitation, and I smile at the way she offers an immediate solution when she cannot accept my original proposal.

> Thursday is great. Meet me at Di Mercuitios at seven.

Switching to my conversation with Enzo, I read what he said.

> Has my mom shown up yet?

My phone vibrates as a notification banner appears across the top.

> Yes, about ten minutes ago. Have you regained your composure?

I swipe back to Vinnie's messages.

> Dinner out?

> Don't worry, piccola ladra. I have a plan.

I toggle over to a new message from Enzo.

Fuck off.

No sooner do I read it, does the echo of the front door slamming rattle throughout the brownstone. Annoyed, I sip the whiskey, and settle back into the soft wingback chair and watch the fire.

The heat from the flame is intense enough to warm my body, even though the chair sits several feet from it. It's a welcome feeling—an appreciated luxury in contrast to the turning air outside.

October is one of my favorite months in the city. Not quite cold enough to produce snow, but the air is crisp and refreshing. The seasons have noticeably changed throughout the colors of the plant life, and the promise of festivities for the upcoming holidays swirl in the air.

Approaching footsteps pull me from my thoughts, and I take another drink, watching the doorway to see who's coming.

Enzo steps through the open threshold, refusing to look at me as he sinks down into the chair adjacent to where I sit. Leaning forward, he rests his elbows on top of his legs, steepling his hands against his mouth as he stares into the fire, lost in thought.

The crackling of wood, and the far-off clanging of dishes, are the only sounds that settle in the study. The air thickens with tension—neither Enzo nor I speak the first word.

I have nothing to say that won't end in regret, either of my words or my actions.

I'm *angry* at him, and I can't even explain to him why.

It's better to go.

Standing, I toss back what's left of my whiskey, casting a glance at my cousin as I walk toward the door. Just before I make it there, he decides to break the silence.

"Why did you have such a reaction to me suggesting we take Paladino's daughter?"

My reaction is instantaneous—my heart rate spikes, palms twitch, wanting to curl into fists. There's a lump in my throat I can't quite swallow, as I force myself to remain impassive and not let my facial expressions give me away.

"I'm not sure what you mean," I put forth, buying myself a little more time.

From over his shoulder, he scrutinizes me. His eyes narrow, then he shakes his head.

Pushing his hand through his hair, he hangs his head in defeat.

Just then, my phone vibrates in my hand. Vinnie's name catches my eye, so I turn my attention to the message.

I trust you.

My lips upturn, heart inflating once again, simply

because of her words. She's talking about our dinner plans, but I take those three words as so much more.

Pushing my phone into my pocket, I look back at Enzo, and our eyes meet. Although he doesn't say anything, his look speaks volumes.

I know you're hiding something from me.

But he doesn't know what.

And after his "suggestion" to take Vinnie, he'll never have the privilege of knowing.

Keeping my mouth shut, I realize that my gut is telling me the truth—this interaction will only end in regret.

I used to be able to talk to my cousin about anything, but now I feel the rift between us is so vast, we may never return to how things were when we were younger.

Turning my back to him, I leave the room to seek out the rest of the family.

Today's intentions are to celebrate my aunt, so I plan to do just that until I can make an excuse to go back to my apartment and put the much-needed distance between me and my cousin, because now I need to figure out how to keep him away from amore mio.

Chapter 28

Vinnie

"What are you getting all dolled up for?" Cecilia asks, watching me from my doorway.

Our eyes meet in the mirror. She looks adorable, in an oversized fuzzy gray sweater coupled with distressed black jeans and her hair pinned back. I love seeing her in such casual clothing. It suits her.

Smiling, she quirks a brow, waiting for me to answer.

"Where'd you just come from?" I counter, knowing she just returned home from another mystery appointment. I've been trying not to pry, but her being so secretive about her whereabouts lately has my curiosity piqued.

"Are you helping your mom get ready for the Halloween ball next Friday?"

My eyes narrow in the mirror. "Yes, after brunch on Sunday. Don't deflect."

She shrugs and asks me another question. "Are you meeting Sly?"

I apply a thin layer of gloss over my lip stain for hydration. "Are you going to keep avoiding telling me where you've been disappearing to lately? You've had more appointments than I can keep up with."

Lia sighs and walks over to my bed, sinking down onto the edge. Turning in my seat, I face her.

"You really want to know?" She looks down at her lap.

I'm out of my chair and sitting next to her in a blink, pulling her hands into mine. "Of *course* I want to know," I stress. "Lia, if there's something going on, you don't have to face it alone."

"There's *nothing* going on, and that's the problem. I'm tired of waiting for my happily ever after, Vin. And I realize I say I'm waiting for it, and not actually doing anything to find it, but it's not for lack of wanting." She looks up at me. "I'm ready to become a mom. I've been meeting with doctors and sperm banks and adoption agencies to figure out what my best course of action is."

My heart swells and simultaneously aches for her. "Oh, Lia, that's amazing! Why didn't you tell me?"

I reach for her neck and wrap my arms around it in a tight hug. She squeezes me back, but pulls away quickly. "Because it's embarrassing? I'm in my late thirties, and I haven't been in a serious relationship for at least a decade. And now, I'm so desperate to start a family, I'm going to do it on my own."

"That's *not* desperate, Cecilia. You don't need a man to get what you want out of life, and if that's a family and babies, then there's no reason for you not to."

"I know," she sighs. "I just thought things would be different, you know? I want the love story too."

"It'll come. Sometimes things happen out of order, that's all."

Looking across the room, she focuses on the wall. "I know."

We sit quietly for a bit, her hand in mine, and my mind starts to spin—wandering as I waver on a thought that could tip the scales either way.

"You're fired," I say to her, my voice getting lodged in my throat as I utter the words.

Her head snaps to me. "Wh—what?"

Lifting my chin, I meet her gaze. "You're fired, Lia. I want you to live your life, find your love story, and create your family. You've been by my side for so long, you've forgotten to take care of *you*. And I can't let you keep doing it. I love you too much to allow you to be stuck here with me when you need to be living for *you*."

"But you can't fire me. I have nowhere to go—no other job lined up." She panics, her eyes welling up with tears.

"Shh, shh," I console. "You're not going anywhere. This is your home, and I wouldn't dream of asking you to leave. You don't need another job. I'll give you three years salary up front as a severance, that way you have time to plan for your future without the rush or stress.

But Lia—I've been holding you back. You can't tell me you disagree."

Her mouth presses together in a thin line.

"That's what I thought," I quip. "I've had you on my staff for as long as I can remember, and now it's time for you to just be my *friend*."

Cecilia swallows thickly, and wipes a wayward tear from her cheek. "I can't accept a three year salary severance. That's insane."

I shake my head. "No, it's not. Not after everything you've done for me over the years. I want you to take the time to focus on yourself and whatever it takes to give me a niece or nephew. Okay? The apartment could use the pitter-patter of tiny feet running around."

This makes her smile. "I don't deserve you."

"I think it's me who doesn't deserve you, yet you've stayed by my side." Standing, I give her shoulder a squeeze. "Now it's my turn to stand by yours."

I go back to the vanity to finish getting ready, picking up the diamond studs sitting in my jewelry tray and putting them on.

"Are you going to tell me what you're getting ready for or are you going to keep me in the dark? I *do* follow your location on your phone, you know. I can just look for myself whenever you get there."

"I have a date tonight," I tell her, biting back my smile. "Sly's taking me to dinner."

Her eyes widen. "In public? Vinnie."

"He says he's taken care of it," I say with a shrug. "I'm not sure what the plan is, but I'm meeting him at

Di Mercutio in—" I look down at my diamond Rolex. "Shoot, in twenty minutes. I need to go. Can you call Ross and tell him… Nevermind, not your job! I'll call him myself."

Cecilia rolls her eyes, pulling her phone from her back pocket. "Just because you fired me doesn't mean I don't still love you. Finish getting ready, I'll call Ross and tell him to bring the car around."

"Thank you," I sigh, but she's waving me off, already talking to Ross.

"Miss Paladino will be ready to go in five minutes, Ross. Please have the car ready. Yes. Yes, she'll need transport to Di Mercutio. Yes, I know you know, I'm just reminding yo—oh shush, just get your ass to the car so you can drive her. Kay, thanks!"

I start laughing as soon as she hangs up the phone. "What was that about?"

"You know him. He started going off on a tangent about how he knows where you want to go and all that."

"He's not wrong." Picking up my hunter green peacoat, I go to my full-length mirror.

Di Mercutio isn't an overly fancy restaurant, but the feminine urge to get dolled up for Sly was too strong to ignore, so this morning I decided to go buy a new outfit.

After a quick excursion to Bergdorf's, I found the perfect black long sleeve mini dress made from a soft cashmere that hugged each of my curves gently. Paired with black nylons, high-heeled boots, and my hunter green peacoat, I felt like the perfect combination of beautiful and sexy.

"You look amazing," Cecilia compliments as I pull my hair from beneath the collar of my coat. I left it in soft waves down my back, which is my go-to hairstyle. Just then, her phone pings and she looks down at the message that flashes across her screen. She smiles, handing me my clutch. "Car's ready. Go get your man."

Di Mercutio is packed when Ross pulls in front of it, idling alongside the curb. I've never seen it so busy—through the window, every table looks full.

A rush of nerves spikes through me, settling like a rock in the depths of my stomach. I hate that the article about me and August has made me paranoid to leave my house—scared I'll be seen by paparazzi and questioned as to his whereabouts or my so-called relationship with him. But most of all, I'm scared of being caught on camera as I sneak around with the man who I can only have in private.

When the hostess stand looks clear of other patrons, I slip out of the car. I told Ross on the drive over that I could handle getting out on my own, wanting to call as little attention as possible to my car and driver, with the intention of getting in the restaurant undetected.

Thankfully, my timing is perfect and my surroundings are empty as I open the door to the restaurant and immediately turn to face the host stand. The man behind it smiles at me.

"Welcome, Miss Paladino. I've been instructed to escort you to your table upon your arrival. If you'll follow me, please." He moves from behind the podium and leads me through the restaurant, taking a straight path to the back.

I keep my head down as we walk, my eyes glued to my shoes, avoiding eye contact with anyone. I seem to go unnoticed, and when I look up at where the host has stopped, he's in front of a thick velvet curtain I didn't notice the last time I was here, pulling it open so I can step inside.

The private dining area is no larger than a six by six room, with ornate sconces on the walls, flickering with soft candlelight that bounces off the soft cream color paint. There are no windows or alternate exit—aside from the curtain, the room is completely secluded.

A table for two is set with a maroon tablecloth and a beautiful candle centerpiece. A bouquet of red roses lays across one of the place settings.

"Grazie, Elijah. I'll take it from here." Sly steps out of the shadows on my left, his hands deep in the pockets of his black slacks, as he saunters toward me. His gaze is heated as it sweeps over my body appreciatively.

"Very well, sir. Your waiter will be in shortly. Enjoy."

He walks out, letting the curtain fall from his hold as he leaves.

As soon as we're alone, Sly's lips fuse to mine, his

hand cupping the nape of my neck as he deepens the kiss.

"I missed you, piccola ladra," he groans, forcing himself away by taking a step back.

"I missed you too." I grin, letting him take my clutch from my hands. He tucks it under his arm as I turn, then helps pull my coat from my shoulders. "I didn't realize they had a private dining area."

"They don't," he says simply, pulling out my chair so I can sit down.

"Then how—"

"I told you I had a plan," he explains, pushing me in once I've sat. "I frequent this restaurant often, so I simply spoke to the manager and asked him how I could rent a private space for us."

Rounding the table, he wears an alluring smile. He sits down and I watch attentively as he pours us each a glass of wine from the uncorked bottle.

I try to hide my disbelief as I ask, "All this for dinner?"

He places my glass in front of me. "You deserve a proper date, Vincenza. This is the best I could do while still allowing our anonymity and privacy from the public eye. You look absolutely stunning tonight, by the way."

"Thank you. You look handsome as well." I subconsciously lick my lips and his eyes immediately lower.

Sly's wearing his signature color—all black everything—but the button down he wears has a subtle off-black design, giving the shirt a visual texture and elevating it. His sleeves are rolled to his elbows and the top has two buttons unhooked, leaving me wishing the entire shirt was unbuttoned instead.

He looks good, and the more I openly stare at him the more my core aches with longing.

"You must stop looking at me like that, *piccola ladra*, or I'll lay you across this table and enjoy you as my meal instead."

His words ignite the desire within me, setting fire to the gasoline trail leading straight to my panties. A rush of arousal floods me, and immediately I feel myself dampen, soaking through the thin fabrics I'm wearing.

"*Damn it*," he groans, obviously sensing how much I want him. Something must have shown on my features —I've never had much of a poker face.

Squirming in my seat, I clear my throat and pick up my menu. "So, what are you having tonight?"

My eyes scan the words, but I'm not comprehending them. Nothing registers in my brain aside from the heaviness of Sly's eyes on me.

"You," he growls. My eyes rip from the menu and meet his. The tension in the air is palpable, practically crackling with electric bursts as we stare at one another.

Just as he pushes his chair back to stand, our waiter pulls open the curtain.

"Good evening, folks. My name is Edward. I'll be your server tonight. May I start you off with an antipasto, or perhaps our delicious balsamic bruschetta?"

Sly never takes his eyes off me as he addresses our server. "We will take both, *per favore*." His eyes slide down to my lips again briefly. "What would you like to eat, piccola ladra?"

"Risotto, please." I bite my lip to conceal a smile, and shift in my seat a little to ease the pressure building between my thighs. Sly notices.

"Risotto for the lady, and Bistecca Fiorentina for myself."

"Excellent choices, excellent choices," the server, Edward, muses as he writes down our order, seeming completely unphased that neither of us has looked at him once. "I'll get the order in with the chef and those should be out shortly."

"Edward, we are not to be disturbed for a minimum of thirty minutes." Sly reaches into his front pocket and pulls out a folded hundred-dollar bill, holding it between two fingers. "Grazie, amico mio."

"Understood, sir." He takes the money from Sly's outstretched hand and leaves the room without another word.

Once the curtain falls back into place, Sly stands and prowls around the table to me. Pushing my chair, he positions it so I'm facing where he stands, then drops to the floor in front of me, kneeling.

Running his hands up my legs, he looks up at me with nothing but raw desire in his eyes. "We have things to discuss, piccola ladra, but they can wait for now. Lift your hips." His fingertips brush the hem of my dress, bunching the fabric in his fists.

My stomach dips, knowing exactly what we need to discuss—he saw the article.

I should have told him about what August did the night of the gala, and I intended to, but got distracted.

Several times.

Then I didn't want to ruin everything that had happened between us by recounting the evening's events. So I pushed it aside. I shouldn't have—I *know* that.

And now…well, he's about to distract me again when I know the healthy thing to do would be to discuss everything first, but when he looks at me how he's looking at me, it's hard to care about much else.

Still, this doesn't seem like the best place to be intimate. "Sly, we're in a restaurant…"

"Lift. Your. Hips," he growls through gritted teeth.

I do as he instructs, thrusting my hips upward slightly. Reaching beneath the fabric of my dress, he hooks his thumbs in the waistband of my nylons and pulls them—and my panties—down my legs.

Once they're mid-calf, he fixes my dress and presses against my thigh to lower me back to the chair.

"You're lucky we're in a public setting, Vinnie. I can think of nothing more beautiful than edging you to the brink of explosion, over and over, until your legs are shaking and you're begging for release, for holding information of that magnitude from me." He slides his hands up the inside of my thighs, stroking the soft skin. My legs widen as my breath quickens, anticipating his touch while listening to his words. His voice is low, dangerous, even. But I'm not afraid. I know he'd never hurt me, and I *can* see how badly he wants me. "But when it comes to you, I am a weak man, and I'd do anything to bring you happiness and pleasure, even if that means allowing you to have your secrets."

That last part shocks me. "I don't have—"

But my thoughts are lost when he pushes two fingers inside me without warning and begins to stroke my G-spot. His thumb finds my clit, and he begins to strum my body like his favorite instrument.

"Sly," I moan, tilting my head back to the back of the chair.

"Shh, piccola ladra. We may be concealed visually, but we are only separated from a full restaurant by a curtain."

My body slides down in the chair, chasing his touch as he pumps his fingers slowly, his eyes never leaving my face.

"Sly," I moan again. "We shouldn't do this…in a restaurant."

"If I do not make you come at least three times prior to our meals, I have not done my job as your lover." He presses against my clit harder, circling it with precision.

My toes curl in my boots as the pressure of my orgasm builds.

"You're…so much more…than that," I breathe, my eyes fluttering closed. My hands grip the edges of the chair tightly, white knuckling it with the anticipation of my orgasm.

I'm so close…it's right there. My breaths come in shorter and faster as I teeter on the edge. "Sly…I'm—"

"I know, I can feel you, piccola ladra. You're clenching around my fingers so beautifully." He changes the rhythm of the thrusts of his fingers and that's all it takes before a wave of pure euphoria crashes into me.

It takes everything in me to not cry out in pleasure, but impossible to conceal every moan that pushes past my lips. Sly continues to rub me as I ride his hand, and he stands without removing it, bending to kiss me.

His lips are firm against mine, commanding as he guides the kiss.

It's possessive.

Passionate.

I whimper against them, unable to push back the emotion he elicits.

Ripping his mouth from mine, he falls to his knees and pulls me by the backs of my legs to the edge of the chair. He pushes my dress up with one hand, pushing the other against my thigh as he descends.

In one languid stroke of his tongue, he has me seeing stars.

When he suctions his lips around my clit, sucking the sensitive nub like he's drinking from a straw, I lose all function of my body.

A second orgasm rolls into me so hard and fast I *do* cry out with a sharp, high-pitched gasp, as the back of my head slams against the back of the chair. My hips roll into his face, silently begging for more of everything he's doing as my body trembles and my thighs beg to close around him.

I feel him everywhere, even the places he isn't touching.

Kissing my thighs, he unzips my boots and removes them from my feet before peeling off my stockings and panties from where they've been hitched around my calves.

"Sly," I whimper, because it's the only word my brain will form.

He's up on his feet and pulling me to mine quicker than I can process, turning us before he sits down in the chair. Pulling me to his lap, he tangles his hand in my hair, bringing me to him.

Kissing my neck, he groans. "Say it again, piccola ladra. Say my name again."

His other hand finds its way between my legs, and he strokes the wet flesh gently.

"Sly," I repeat, opening my eyes just in time to watch the way his slam closed, his head tilting back on his shoulders as though simply saying his name brings him the greatest pleasure.

"Music to my ears," he mutters. The low, gravelly tone coupled with his accent does something indescribable to my insides, provoking a salacious reaction.

Frantically, I grab his jaw, tilting his head up so I can kiss him. It's messy and wild, and I can't get enough of it.

"More," I demand. "I need you. All of you."

My hands work his belt buckle, unhooking it and leaving it slack so I can unbutton his pants. Once loosened, I reach inside. Immediately, my fingers wrap around the smooth skin of his hardened shaft, and I pull it out.

He groans, wiggling his hips, so I stand just enough to give him room to push his pants down slightly. His erection springs free, leaving him bare and ready before me. I practically salivate at how perfect he is.

Big, but not *too* big.

Gripping him at the base, I lower myself onto him, inch by inch, taking him slowly so my body accommodates to the stretch.

Once I'm seated with him fully inside me, he catches my lips again, tangling our tongues together in a kiss so deep it steals my breath away.

As we kiss, he skates his fingertips over my body until they reach my hips, and he begins to guide my movements, sliding my hips forward and backward so that I'm riding him slowly.

"Is this what you wanted, piccola ladra? All of me?"

I nod a few times before tossing my head back, my eyes rolling from the slow, methodical way our bodies are inducing pleasure. "Every piece."

"Every piece of me is yours. Take it. Anything you want, take it, Vinnie."

Bracing my hands on his shoulders, I move up and down on him, and take exactly what I want. His groans spur me on, giving me the encouragement and confidence I'm craving.

A thin layer of sweat coats my body, pooling at my lower back. There's too much fabric on me—on him— and I want nothing more than to rip everything off us.

Sliding my hands down his chest, I push them beneath the hem of his shirt and onto his abdominals, tracing my fingers across every ridge and plane of his muscles. My fingernails bite into his skin as he grips my hips and starts to move me faster.

Once we're in a steady flow, he moves his hand to between my legs again, his thumb effortlessly finding my clit. "Come for me, piccola ladra. We haven't much time left alone."

He knows the way my body responds and uses it to his advantage, applying the perfect amount of pressure combined with the right movements to have my orgasm cresting within seconds.

"You too," I rasp. "I want you to come too. I want to feel you seeping from me throughout dinner."

My words surprise me, realizing just how comfortable in my own skin I am, thanks to Sly. Never in my wildest dreams would I have said something like that with a past lover. But with Sly, I can explore sides of myself I haven't even known to exist.

"*Sarai la mia morte*," he groans, then his lips are on mine, his tongue in my mouth.

Whimpering, my eyes snap shut, and I focus on his touch. It's blinding, the way he turns my body into putty in his hand. He has the ability to watch me crumble in any way he sees fit.

"I'm coming," I whisper, but I'm not even sure it's audible. Speckles dance behind my lids, like stars in the New York sky, hiding behind the skyscrapers but desperate to be seen.

As I come, my moans transfer into Sly's mouth and he catches each one, swallowing them as they meld with his own. I feel him chase his own release, bucking his hips beneath me with shallow thrusts, each movement matching his groans.

We ride the high for as long as we can until finally Sly reaches his hand into my hair again and leans his forehead into mine. "And here I was thinking if I took you somewhere public, I'd be able to behave myself long enough for a proper date."

Laughing, I pull back to look at him, my head shaking slowly. "So far, this date is perfect."

"It will be once we enjoy our meal and I can take you home and worship your body for the remainder of our evening."

Grabbing a handful of my butt, Sly playfully nips at my lower lip before he gives me a long, slow kiss.

He lifts me off him and reaches down to where he left my nylons and panties on the floor. Righting them so they're no longer inside-out, he hands them to me, and we both dress quickly.

"So, how has your week been, piccola ladra?" Sly asks conversationally—with a hint of laughter in his tone—as I take my seat and pull it toward the table. He readjusts his seat so instead of sitting across from each other, he's next to me.

"Oh, now it's time for pleasantries?" I tease, running my hand along the inside of his thigh. He catches it at the wrist and pulls it to him, kissing my palm.

Behind us, a throat clears and I turn to see the server tentatively pulling open the curtain. When he sees us at the table, he beams and gestures to someone beyond the threshold. Two additional waiters arrive, one holding a large tray with our entrees, and another holding a corked bottle of wine as though it's his prized possession.

"Mr. Lucchetti, the owner wants to extend his finest bottle of merlot to accompany your meal tonight. If it's to your satisfaction, we will uncork."

Sly looks at me and I nod, accepting the offer.

"Very well, grazie," he tells the servers, and they get to work, uncorking the bottle, then distributing our plates, before standing in a uniform line before us.

"Is there anything else we can get for you?" our main server, Edward, asks.

"Not at the moment, grazie."

"Thank you," I chime in.

As they leave, I smile at Sly. He nods to my plate, and we both begin to eat. A silence settles between us, and with each passing bite, a heaviness also settles.

The next mouthful I swallow hardly goes down.

"So," I start hesitantly, breaking the ice and spearheading the conversation that needs to take place. "The only reason I didn't say anything is because once we were together, nothing else mattered. I pushed the memory of what'd happened far into the recesses of my mind—not because I had something to hide, but because I was present in the moment with *you*. I'm sorry."

Sly sets his fork down, then lifts his napkin to wipe his mouth, before laying it back on his lap. He takes his time before he says anything, which does nothing to ease my nerves.

"You do not owe me an apology, Vincenza. I recognize our relationship as challenging. We cannot be seen in public together. We cannot allow our loved ones to know what we're feeling for each other. If you're seen in public with another man, the only man I can be upset with is myself for not being able to give you that."

"The only man I want to be seen with is *you*." My heart plummets through my body. The words are hardly a whisper, but as I say them, I'm not sure I mean them. *Of course*, he's the only man I want to be seen with, but I also don't want us to be seen.

"Then we should go public." He lifts his chin, showing me he stands by his suggestion. "Our families will learn to live with it or they learn to live *without* us."

I shake my head, then look down at my lap to stop the tears. "We can't."

"But we *should*."

"It's too soon." I force myself to look at him. Suddenly, I'm inundated with emotions. "There's too much risk. My family… I can't betray them like that. I won't. Please don't make me choose." Thick, silent tears pool at my lashes before one falls, rolling down my cheek.

We stare at each other for several long seconds before he nods, reaching up to wipe away the wet river the tear left in its wake.

"Okay. I apologize, piccola ladra. As I have said before, I would rather have you in private than not at all." He leans forward and kisses my forehead. "Let's finish our meals. They are already cooling."

We go back to eating, speaking conversationally with surface level topics for the rest of our meals and through dessert. We smile, and laugh, touch, and kiss, but I can't help but to hear the little voice in the back of my mind that tells me the night's already been ruined.

Chapter 29

Sly

Pushing open the door to Vincenza's office building, I walk in with confidence, completely ignoring the risk of being here. My helmet is on, concealing my entire face, but I still scan the room as though I may run into a member of her family.

The woman at reception greets me with a warm smile, her curly hair sitting on top of her head in a wild bun. "Good afternoon, sir. Who are you here to see?"

"I'm just dropping this off for Ms. Vinnie Paladino," I say in my best American accent, throwing my voice. "Please make sure she gets it before she leaves for the day."

Reaching over the counter, I hand her a full-face helmet. Her eyes widen as she takes it from me, purposely brushing her fingers against my leather gloves.

"With pleasure, sir. Does she know to expect it?"

My head bobs in a nod. "She should, yes."

"Very well then." She grabs a sticky note and jots Vinnie's name down on it, pressing the paper against the top of the helmet before she sets it aside.

"Gra—thank you." Turning on my heel, I leave and head back to where I parked my Ducati half of a block north of here.

Checking my watch, I confirm I have about fifteen minutes before Vinnie should be down.

We'd agreed last night at dinner to meet at two the next afternoon. The place I want to take her is a bit of a drive outside of the city, and with the sun setting so early now, we'll be on borrowed time.

After a few minutes of people watching, Vinnie walks out of her building, and immediately I can't take my eyes off her.

Everything from her smile to her outfit, and the way she carries my spare helmet under her arm like she was born to ride, sends me into a frenzy that I force myself to conceal, but I can feel my cock lengthening behind my black jeans.

She's wearing a tight black turtleneck that has a cutout above her breasts, displaying them just enough for me to appreciate her figure, with a black leather jacket for warmth. Her skirt is a black-and-white pattern that flows around her and reaches mid-calf, covering her boots, which perhaps are the same ones she wore last night. Her hair is twisted back, but when she sees me she reaches behind her and unclips it, allowing the dark brown wavy tendrils to fall as she shakes them out, attaching the clip to the strap of her purse.

My eyes rake over her appreciatively, although she can't see it from behind the helmet I never removed.

"Hi," she says when she stops in front of me, reaching for my hand and squeezing it.

"You look absolutely fantastic, piccola ladra. Put your helmet on—I have a surprise for you." I know my voice is muffled, so I speak louder than necessary.

She pulls her helmet over her head, adjusting it once it's on so it fits comfortably, then follows me to the bike, climbing on after I do. Scooting her hips forward, she presses her front into my back, turning her head so it rests against me. Once I feel her tight grip, I know she's ready.

The Ducati roars to life, and with a quick glance over my shoulder, we take off. Even over the noise, I hear her squeal behind me.

As we gain momentum, swerving through the midday traffic, her arms tighten around my midsection.

There's an accident on the freeway that delays us as we leave the city, heading toward Staten Island, but we make it to our destination in just under an hour.

Pulling off onto a dirt road, I pick up speed in an attempt to avoid the cloud of dust we kick up, until we make it to a small make-shift parking lot. I stabilize the motorcycle and climb off before helping Vinnie down. We both peel off our helmets, and I take hers from her, setting both down on the seats of the bike.

"Where are we?" she asks, looking around. There's

an old sign that hangs off a square wooden archway, and just past it, a small house that acts as a ticket stand. "Gillespie Farms?"

"Sì," I say with a smirk. Reaching down, I lace our fingers together and lead her over to it.

When we arrive at the window, an older woman sits on a stool, knitting with bright green yarn. She's deep in concentration and doesn't notice us, so I knock gently against the glass.

"Oh, great Heavens!" she startles, looking up with wide eyes. "I didn't see you there!" Placing her project down, she hops from the stool and closes the distance to the window, pushing it open further. "Hello! Welcome. Are you the Lucchettis?"

I glance at Vinnie, who looks down at the floor with a faint smile on her lips at the woman's assumption.

"Yes, ma'am," I say.

"You have the place to yourselves until five thirty, after which we'll be reopening to the general public. Our vendors are stationed around the farm and available for any assistance you may need, including the hayride. Pumpkin patch is to the right, marigold fields are to the left. Any questions for me?" She speaks quickly, reciting her monologue as though she's done it a thousand times before.

She hands me two wristbands for admission, but instead of putting them on I stuff them into my pants pocket.

This morning I spoke with the owner and offered them an exuberant sum of money to shut the place down for two hours so Vincenza and I could enjoy it alone. He was more than willing to accommodate my request, so the wristbands aren't necessary. As she said, we have the place to ourselves.

"No, grazie."

We take the dirt path toward the center of the farm, and as Vinnie steps gingerly through the soft ground-cover, it occurs to me that I should have warned her to wear flat shoes.

Letting go of her hand, I step in front of her and squat down. "Hop on."

"What?" she asks with surprise.

"Hop on my back, I'll carry you."

"You don't have to do that."

"I know I don't, but I want to, so hop on, piccola ladra."

Gripping my shoulders, she leans forward onto my back and as I come to a stand, her legs wrap around my waist.

"Perfetto. Now, to the patch or the marigolds?"

We're at a fork in the path, and a decision must be made. I know which I would choose, but it's in her hands. As are other decisions in our relationship, but the choice between pumpkins or flowers carries less weight.

"Surprise me," she says, tightening her hold around my neck as she leans around to kiss my cheek. "I love your surprises."

And I love you, I think to myself.

But there will be a better time to tell her.

For fun, I veer right, then turn dramatically to the left, before zig-zagging my steps and curving right again, taking her to the pumpkins. She laughs as we stumble around, and a carefree feeling settles within me.

We continue trudging through the dirt, looking for the row with the best pumpkins to go explore.

I am anxious to show her the flower fields, but I can imagine their beauty will be much greater at sunset when the light reflects against the vibrant colors.

For the next forty minutes or so, we continue to wander through the pumpkin patch, stopping after a while to take a hayride that tours the farm, then share a slice of freshly baked apple pie that's still warm, with rich and creamy homemade ice cream melting on top of it.

Our time spent together is simple and so relaxed I forget all the stressors this relationship harbors.

The thoughts of my family, and hers, float away as though the world ceases to exist but us.

Paparazzi and newspaper reporters embellishing stories are not a worry.

The future doesn't seem so bleak.

At this moment, it's just us. I am just a man. She is just a woman. And we can just love one another.

In a perfect world, this would last forever.

By the time we make it over to the marigold fields, I'm carrying her shoes and she's walking nearly barefoot through the dirt as though she was raised in the country and not in one of the most prominent cities in America.

The stockings she's wearing tore when they snagged on a rogue pumpkin stem, but she paid it no mind, never once fussing over the ruined clothing or that they were uncomfortable.

"Wow," she breathes when we stop in the middle of the flowers, taking in the shades of orange and yellow that surround us like an infinite sea. They go on and on, their bright colors vibrant and so full of life.

As I suspected, the beauty of the sunset only enhances our spectacular surroundings.

But as beautiful as everything is, I can't take my eyes off *her*.

She spins slowly with her hands outstretched as if the flowers transport her to a place of pure happiness. When she stops and faces me, I drop her shoes and take a step forward, closing the distance between us.

Bringing my hand to her hair, I weave my fingers through the tendrils at the nape of her neck and bring her body flush with mine. The soft scent of her cherry blossom perfume envelops me as the breeze catches her hair.

"I love you, Vincenza." The words slide easily from my tongue, feeling them wholeheartedly and deeply.

A wave of relief crashes into me. I've felt it for so long and have bit my tongue, but finally saying the words aloud feels incredibly right.

Kissing her softly, I coax her mouth open and trace her tongue with my own. She sighs and relaxes in my hold, kissing me back, but never changes the tempo.

When we break apart, she stares up into my eyes

and I see a thousand things dance across her gray-blue irises.

"I love you too." She presses up on her tiptoes to reach my lips again, and I meet her halfway.

In the middle of the marigolds, we allow ourselves to speak silently through our kisses, long past when the sun sets.

It's only when the voices of other patrons entering the farm sound in the distance that we force ourselves apart, but my hand never leaves her body, sliding from her neck to her hand. "We should go, piccola ladra. Come home with me? Stay the night. I want you in my bed when I sleep and when I wake tomorrow."

"Okay." She smiles, then looks around strangely, like she's about to get caught doing something.

My brows knit together as I try to figure out what she's doing, before she reaches beneath her skirt and pulls her stockings down her legs, stepping out of them once they're at her ankles. "Can I have my shoes, please?"

I bend down to grab them and hand them to her, watching as she balances on one leg to slide them on. When she's done, winks at me.

"Can I have another ride?"

Laughing, I squat down and allow her to climb back onto my back. "You can have whatever you want, piccola ladra."

The sky is dark as we ride back to the city, veering in and out of traffic before we finally have a straight shot on the freeway, at least for the next ten minutes or so. Our route is a shortcut of sorts, one that I learned years ago when I was far more impatient than I am now.

With every tilt of the bike, Vinnie's thighs clench around me and I hear her gasp. It shouldn't turn me on, but I grow impossibly hard thinking about her bare skin around my hips and how the vibration from the bike must be making her feel.

A thought trickles into my mind, but I'm hesitant to act on it. It's reckless, but the closer to The Kenna we get, the more desperate I become to try it.

Leaning forward, I press my elbows against the handlebars of the motorcycle and pull the glove off my right hand and stow it in the pocket of my riding jacket.

All day, I've longed to touch her in ways that should only be done behind closed doors, but in the darkness of the night I can't resist any longer. Careful to focus on the road, I slide my ungloved hand up Vinnie's leg, feeling the softness of her skin beneath my fingertips.

Twisting my arm, I maneuver the fabric of Vinnie's skirt until my hand is beneath it, and since she's so close, it doesn't take long to find the fabric of her underwear. I'm not gentle when I yank it aside and plunge two inside of her, knuckles deep.

It's too loud to hear any noises she makes, but the way her helmet slams against my back and her hips scoot forward into my hand, tells me what her words cannot.

Gripping the handlebar with one hand, I seamlessly multitask as I drive down the freeway while my other hand works her body, fingering her with two digits.

My fingers slide in and out as slowly as I can, alternating between curving upward to stroke her G-spot and mercilessly pumping into her.

Her thighs widen slightly as I push harder into her.

From this angle, it's difficult to rub her clit as I know she likes, but it is fine because right now, my end goal is not to make her come, but to wind her up.

Her hand slips from my waist to my thigh, and I feel her nails press against the fabric. Her helmet rocks against my back again.

She's incredibly wet, her juices coating my fingers as I pull onto 1st Avenue. Traffic is thick again, forcing me to slow the speed at which I'm driving.

I anticipate Vinnie removing my hand now that more people are around, but she surprises me when she squeezes my side and rolls her hips, chasing more of my touch.

Reaching around to my cock, she grabs it through my jeans, keeping me against her hand. I groan, but I'm certain she hasn't heard me over the noises of the street.

As we pull into the underground parking garage of The Kenna, I speed to my parking spot, killing the engine and settling the bike before I hop off. She hurries off too and reaches for her helmet.

"No," I growl. "Leave it on. There are cameras in the elevator, piccola ladra."

I want to kiss her so badly—to watch the expressions on her face—but until we're tucked behind my apartment doors, the helmets will stay to conceal our identities. It doesn't matter how many times she has been to my apartment—that was before the paparazzi painted her to be in a relationship with another man. If we were to be caught on camera, it would create a media frenzy that we're not ready for.

She cocks her head to the side in question but leaves her helmet on, letting me guide her with my hand on her lower back as though it's not still slick with her arousal.

Once we're inside the elevator, with the call button for the forty-seventh floor lit up, I pounce as the doors shut behind us.

Turning to her, I grab both of her wrists in my hand and pull them above her head, pressing them against the wall as my dominant hand finds its way back between her legs. Immediately, I circle her clit with the exact amount of pressure I know will have her writhing within seconds.

"I have pictured what you'd look like in my motorcycle helmet and the reality is much, much better than the fantasy. You have until the elevator pings to come, amore mio. I know you are close."

She moans as I change how I massage her, her knees buckling slightly.

"You are so beautiful. Even when I cannot see your face, I know what expressions dance across it. The rise and fall of your chest. The motion of your hips. Come for me. Let go, let me hear you."

On instinct, she moves against the hold I have on her wrists, but I keep her pinned in place, rubbing her clit while I tease her entrance with another finger. Soft mewls reverberate from her lips before she lets go, crying out in pleasure as I hit just the right spot and her orgasm ricochets through her body.

I continue to massage her through her climax, enjoying the sounds she makes and the way her body trembles, until the elevator doors open with a soft *ping*.

Letting go of her wrists, I wrap my arm around her lower back, hoisting her into my arms as hers encircle my neck. Her legs lock around me and I carry her out of the elevator and toward my apartment.

Quickly, I unlock the door and slam it shut behind me, not bothering to turn on any lights and go toward my living space.

With one hand, I pull the motorcycle helmet from my head and drop it onto the couch before I do the same for Vinnie, pressing my lips against hers in a frenzied kiss the second it's off her head.

"Where are we going?" she asks breathlessly against my lips as I continue to move through my dark apartment with her in my arms.

Stepping into my room, I readjust my hold on her and walk until my shins hit the edge of my bed, tossing her onto it.

Even though all I can see is her shadow in the dark, I can't help but smile as I place my knee between her legs, crawling up to where she landed. "To bed, *piccola ladra*. I'm taking you to bed."

Chapter 30

Sly

Sweaty and spent, we lay in a heap of intertwined limbs with the sheet tangled between us. Dusting my fingers against Vinnie's bare shoulder, she curls into me further, a soft breath of air expelling from her lips with a deep sigh.

The warm light from a lamp splays dimly across my bedroom, casting a serene glow through the room.

"Are you tired?" I ask, glancing over at the clock on my bedside table. It's not particularly late, but she seems content, and on the verge of sleep.

"Not really. Could we watch a movie?" Her head lifts from my chest to look at me with a hopeful gleam.

A smile touches my lips. She wants to watch a movie.

It's such a simple request, but it humbles me. Reminds me of how well we fit together, like two pieces of a puzzle that were always meant to match together.

Reaching my arm out, I pat the wood of the table in search of the remote. "Of course."

The TV comes to life at the press of a button, the ten o'clock news opens up to a story about the Manhattan Bridge closing two lanes next week to conduct roadwork. The newscaster has a green-screen image of the bridge behind her as she reads the prompter.

I'm about to switch to a streaming site when they switch to their local celebrity segment, and August St. Jean's photo appears behind her.

Immediately, I freeze.

"And now for the story we've all been waiting for—Manhattan's most eligible bachelor may not be a bachelor for long! August St. Jean was spotted on Fifth Avenue today shopping at both Cartier and Tiffany & Co."

The TV cuts to footage of August peering into the counters at Cartier, walking around with a smile on his face, his hands in the pockets of his tweed suit.

"Mr. St. Jean, can you tell us what you're shopping for today?" the reporter's voice sounds from behind the camera.

"You've got to be kidding me," Vinnie mutters from beside me, sitting up, then leaning forward to see the screen better.

Her hair falls down her bare back, and if I wasn't so transfixed on the screen, I'd admire the soft curves of her body. Instead, I push myself up, resting my back against my headboard.

On screen, August looks up and shakes his head, giving them a boyish smile. "I plead the fifth." He laughs, then continues strolling around the store.

Vinnie's hands curl into fists on my sheet.

They cut to another video of him, this one filmed from outside the store. It's grainier and darker from being zoomed, but you can clearly see August standing at the jewelry counter with a showcase of rings on a velvet slab. He picks one up and inspects it, nodding his head to the woman before placing it back down. Then the frame cuts back to the newscaster.

My blood turns to ice. Every bit of anger for August that I've been holding back rushes to the surface, engulfing me into a raging inferno. I grip the remote control so tightly in my grasp the plastic groans under the pressure.

"Based on the photo we saw just last week of August St. Jean and Vinnie Paladino getting cozy on the red carpet, we now have to wonder if there's been a love affair happening right under our noses. Stay tuned for more updates as this story continues to unfold."

They move into talking about another socialite who was caught with a wardrobe malfunction that caused her to flash the camera, but I turn it off, slamming my thumb onto the power button just to make it stop.

My self-control is hanging on by a thread—only because I know Vinnie is just as stunned as I am.

I will myself to relax—to bottle the onslaught of emotions—but as much as I try to hold it in, the anger wins. Rearing back my arm, I hurl the remote across the room and it slams into the wall before clattering to the floor.

"Is he shopping for a ring for you, Vincenza?" My tone is icy. I see red, the anger coursing through my veins like molten lava erupting from a volcano that's laid dormant for centuries.

"I have no idea," she says, her voice breaking as she stares at the dark screen of the TV. "He set this up."

"Does he think you will accept a marriage proposal, Vinnie?" I question, insecurities thick in my voice.

"I wouldn't."

"That's not what I asked. Does *he* think you would?"

"I don't know why he would! I've never given him any flicker of interest. You know I hate him."

"Sì, but it is a thin line between love and hate, Vincenza. A man does not just shop for rings without intentions."

I think of the smile on her face in the snapshot that was all over the front page news not so long ago.

My stomach churns.

She gasps, rearing back as though she's been slapped. Looking at me with widened eyes, her hand floats up to her mouth. "You think I knew about this."

It's a statement, not a question, and it makes my heart dip within my chest.

I cannot deny the doubt that has crept into my head and my heart.

But I trust her. I *love* her. So I shake my head.

"No, piccola ladra, I don't think you knew."

At the same moment I say the words, Vinnie's off

my bed, naked as the day she was born, rushing to her pile of belongings sitting in my oversized reading chair.

"What are you doing?" I demand with far too harsh of a tone, but I am struggling to control the feelings swirling within me. I stand and come around to the side of the room she's on, raking my hand through my hair in frustration.

"Looking for my phone," she snaps, rifling through her small purse. When she finds it, she presses a few things on the screen before pulling it up to her ear.

She begins to pace.

Sinking down onto the edge of my bed, I force myself to regain my composure, shutting my eyes for a moment so I can get control of myself.

"Don't you dare *sister* me," she seethes into the phone. "What the hell was August doing shopping for rings, Joseph?"

She stops moving and tosses her hand into the air. "Bullshit you have no idea. You and him have something up your sleeve—don't think I'm too naïve to see it."

Pausing, her eyes dart over to where I sit watching her. Her nipples are erect, her skin pebbled with goosebumps.

Despite the adrenaline coursing through her, she's cold.

"You're unbelievable. August would *never* hold an interest in me unless it was for some greater reason. No! I absolutely do *not* believe that, Joseph."

I stand and pull my top sheet from the bed, then

wrap it around her shoulders. Her eyes soften as they connect with mine, and she pulls it around her.

"You're both clinically insane if you think I'm buying your act. You can both go to hell."

She hangs up the phone and tosses on top of the pile of her things. When she looks at me, her eyes are full of tears. "I hate him."

Wrapping my arms around her, I bring her to my chest and hug her tightly. "I would kill him if you ask me to."

She tenses briefly, then relaxes against me again, likely assuming I don't truly mean my words.

But I do.

I would kill Joseph Paladino—and August St. Jean—without hesitation or regret if she asked me to.

She wouldn't even *need* to ask. A simple look from her would have me checking that I had enough rounds in the magazine of my Glock and I'd be on my way to them.

Instead of following that urge, I hold her tighter.

"What did he say?" I ask, kissing the top of her head.

"He claims August has a genuine interest in me. That he'd be a shoo-in with my father and a great choice for a husband." Her eyes connect with mine. "He speaks about my life as though I'm not in control of it."

Scooping her into a bridal carry, I take her to my bed and climb onto it on my knees before sitting back, settling her in my lap.

"He seems to think he has a hold over your choices," I agree. "And your father? Have you spoken to him about your suspicions?"

"He'd never believe me."

"If what you've told me is accurate, your brother holds so much anger toward you, it must be evident in your family, in which case, your father *should* believe you. But I think your brother is counting on your doubt as well. It's the only insurance they have that you won't say anything. It's what Joseph and August are hoping for."

She lays her head against my chest, chuffing with defeat.

As much resentment as I hold for her brother, I know this is not a time for me to express it. Vincenza needs me for comfort. She needs me to be her safe space. Not to encourage the anger.

Kissing the top of her head again, I change the subject. "Tell me about your weekend plans, piccola ladra. And what you have going on next week. When can I see you again?"

She flinches a little, a scowl knitting her brows together before she gives me an apologetic look. "Tomorrow I've dedicated the day to Raina, and after Sunday brunch I promised Cecilia we'd catch up. Things have been so crazy with work, and I've wanted to spend every free moment with you...I need to spend some time with them."

Tucking a piece of her hair behind her ear, I nod. "There is no need to explain. It is important to maintain your friendships, especially with your two best friends. Don't ever feel guilty for that."

My mind trails to Enzo and Sully, and how I've been neglecting their friendship. It is hard not to become consumed by this woman, and I've let myself completely succumb to the spell she's put me under.

Her hand lifts to catch mine as it brushes against her cheek and she holds it there. "Part of me would rather be here with you."

"All the more reason to go. Whenever you have some time, I will be waiting. Next week?"

"Swamped at work, I'm afraid. We have two book releases and countless meetings with prospective clients and existing ones. There'll be several late nights at the office. Then on Friday, I have to attend my parents' annual Halloween costume ball."

I have heard of that event—it's one of the most talked about events of the year in Manhattan. Every Halloween, the Paladinos host a costume party with a silent auction. They rotate charities to donate the proceeds to, and every important citizen of New York society is in attendance.

Except the Lucchettis.

I hate the thought of Vinnie being in the arms of who knows how many other men, being trotted around the dance floor like she's a prized horse. I've seen it first-hand at the galas we've both attended. Only this time, I won't be there to intervene if absolutely necessary.

The thought makes my palms twitch.

"Next weekend?" I ask, already feeling desperate to

see her. "I'm not sure I can go a full week without seeing you, amore mio. I may need to sneak by your office for a few stolen moments."

"I'm all yours. Except for Sunday brunch, I'll have to sneak away for that." She tilts her head back and I lean down to kiss her.

"Next weekend it is," I mutter against her lips.

Our lips fuse once more, but this time, the kiss is frantic. I can feel her heart beating wildly in her chest as she pushes into me. Reaching between us, she grabs my length in her hand, pushing up on her toes to allow space between us.

Her eyes speak a million words as she lowers herself onto me slowly.

Emotions grip my heart as I watch her, taking in how stunningly beautiful she is. I'm overwhelmed by how much I love her—how she has imprinted herself into my very being.

Her lips form a perfect O as she continues inch by inch. She's so wet, her warmth gripping my cock like a vice, as she slides herself down.

Once she's taken me entirely, she stills, a sweet moan floating past her lips, matching my own soft groan.

Neither of us moves, nor do we speak, as I hold her close. We're simply united as one for several heavenly minutes.

Having her on top of me is a vision I have seared permanently into my mind, but right now, I wish to look at her and watch the pleasure dance across her face as I make love to her.

In one fluid motion, I flip us so Vinnie is lying on her back. Her legs fit around my hips as I support my weight on my forearm, using my other hand to tame her wild hair as it's scattered all over her face from my movement.

It becomes difficult to breathe.

My heart squeezes in my chest, and I want nothing more than to protect Vinnie from everything bad this life tries to throw at her—to shield her from any pain she may be caused.

I want to be the person she *always* turns to, not just in secret.

There is no doubt in my mind that we are approaching a crossroads. She's afraid to tell her family of us, as am I, but we must take the leap if we're to continue to move forward.

And I want to. I *ache* to.

She's my present, and my future. My *forever*.

I'm just not sure if I am hers.

My fingers brush softly down her cheek as she looks up at me with nothing but affection in her eyes, and for a moment, I am filled with hope.

"Ti amo, piccola ladra. Giuro di amarti sempre."

I love you, little thief. I vow to always love you.

Chapter 31

Vinnie

"Oh, Vinnie, darling, you look gorgeous!" my mother singsongs as she walks into the ballroom where I'm standing, admiring the details the staff put into the decor.

Candles hang from the ceiling giving the illusion of them floating. Vintage sconces have been added to the walls with votives sitting on top of them, their wax already melting. Black tapestries are hung, interlaced with lighter black fabrics such as tulle and gauze to add texture.

Servers stand next to large cauldrons that have vapor floating from the dry ice inside, ready to pour drinks into the arrangement of crystal drinkware sitting on the tables beside them.

The lights in the ballroom are dimmed low, but warm twinkle lights have been added around the room to add to the ambiance, intertwined with orange and purple lights to give off a Halloween glow.

Turning toward my mother, I smile warmly at her costume. Marie Antoinette, if the slice of cake on a plate in her hand paired with the luxuriously large ball gown and wig is any indication.

"It looks beautiful in here," I muse, turning to watch some of the staff add the finishing touches to the tables around the room. "You've really outdone yourself this year."

"We were going for a subtle yet glamorous look. Halloween chic, if you will."

"Well, you've accomplished it," I laugh politely.

She reaches toward me and touches the skirt of the ball gown I'm wearing. "Is this custom?"

"It is. Raina helped me make the idea come to life." I look down at the dress, admiring it with her. The delicate gold fabric has a slight shimmer without being reflective. It fits tight at the bodice, beautiful beads embellishing every inch, and the straps cascade down my shoulders, sitting lightly against my skin. At my hips, the fabric flares, the large petticoat beneath it amplifying how much undercoat there is.

Cecilia did my hair and makeup, giving them both a dramatic look. My hair is wound in curls that hang down my back, but is pulled half up with a small, tight bun sitting at the back, while smaller pieces frame my face. Red roses are woven in between the locks, matching the crimson she painted on my lips and the rouge on my cheeks. My eyeliner is pointed in a perfect cat eye, sharp and pristine.

"Now all you need is your prince," my mother says coyly. "Perhaps you've already found him, though?"

I feel the smile curl my lips as I picture Sly with his hazel eyes and seductive smile.

My mother gently touches my cheek and walks away, heading over to a server who is placing mini cakes on a platter in the middle of a nearby table.

Within the next hour, the ballroom transforms, filling with guests in lavish costumes of all types. Fairy-tale characters to horror movie villains portrayed in a tasteful, high society way, mixed with silly interpretations of political figures and inanimate objects. If you can think of a costume, it's probably at this party in some form or another.

The music is lively, a mix of songs from every decade, and the dance floor is packed with couples enjoying themselves.

Raina bumps her shoulder into mine, cradling a glass of champagne as I stand and watch from along the wall. "Having fun?"

She's dressed as Barbie, with her sleek blonde hair in a high ponytail. Her pink satin skirt sits high on her waist and has a slit clear up the side of her leg, showing off miles of bare skin and her beautiful strappy black heels and French painted toes. Her matching cropped tube top accentuates her breasts, and even I can't help but admire them.

"I am." I smile weakly.

The truth is, I miss Sly desperately. I only saw him once this week when he came by my office and we snuck away to the hidden alcove behind the building for ten minutes of time alone. It wasn't enough, and as much as we've been texting and talking on the phone in the evenings, falling asleep together from separate sides of the city, it's not the same.

It's not *enough*.

"I can see right through you," she chastises. "So I don't know why you're lying to me right now."

I don't have time to answer her before she's gripping onto my wrist, her manicured nails biting into my skin. "Holy shit, it should be illegal for your brother to look that good."

My brows scrunch together as I follow her stare to the open doors Luciano just walked through. Rolling my eyes, I turn my head back to her and glare.

"His costume is appropriate for him too, don't you think?"

"If he's who'll take my soul when I die, I'll willingly go now." She's practically drooling, her eyes glued to my brother as he moves further into the room, greeting people while he walks toward the bar.

Dressed in all black, a floor length cape rests around his shoulders, the hood up, and he carries a scythe. The Grim Reaper has been his go-to costume for years now.

"You disappoint me," I tell her jokingly as she continues to ogle my brother.

While she watches him, I scan the room, taking in everyone's costumes and the joyous energy that fills the space. There's a few people wearing masks that I don't recognize, but one in particular catches my eye.

From across the room, a man dressed as The Phantom of the Opera, in a Victorian era tuxedo and a cape, leans with one foot pressed against the wall behind him. He has his arms crossed, and appears to be looking in my direction, but it's hard to tell for sure from the full face, white mask he wears.

Still, prickles of awareness coat my skin, and my mind wanders, wondering for the briefest of moments if it could be Sly.

I shake the feeling off and chalk it up to me missing him, then go back to people-watching.

I freeze momentarily when my eyes trail over August, who's schmoozing a group of men near the center of the room. He's dressed as a prince in a full dress uniform, sash and all.

Of *course* he is.

Annoyance erupts through my bloodstream, hating that he's here. It makes it worse that he's dressed like a prince when he's anything but. Especially since I chose a princess for my own costume.

What are the odds?

Removing my phone from the hidden pocket in my dress, I text Sly, knowing he's the only person who can calm my irritation.

I wish you were here.

His reply comes through immediately, and instant relief washes over me.

Are you missing me, piccola ladra?

So much. This week has been torture.

As I stare down at my phone, awaiting the text bubble to appear, a man steps in front of me.

"May I have this dance?" he asks, placing his hand out for me to take. When I glance up, I realize he looks vaguely familiar, though I can't recall why.

Hesitantly, I tuck my phone back into my pocket and place my hand in his. "Sure."

Raina winks at me as he guides me away from her, clearly approving.

"Thank you for agreeing to this dance," the man says, turning to face me. We get into a slow dance position as the song changes. "My name is Alistair Emmons. My father has told me a lot about you."

It dawns on me why this man looks familiar—he has the same sparkle in his green eyes as his father does.

"And how is my good friend Ansel?" I ask, glancing around to see if I spot him. "Is he here?"

"Unfortunately, my mother has a head cold, so they've stayed home. My younger brother and I are here on their behalf, and I promised my father I would seek you out for a dance. He said—and I quote—'if you see her standing on the sidelines, or in the arms of a man she clearly is not interested in dancing with, you must go to her.' So, true to my word, here I am."

"Your father thinks I'm a damsel in distress," I quip as he spins me.

Alistair is extremely handsome, dressed as a super-hero, in a leotard that leaves little to the imagination. He looks to be in his mid to late thirties, with emerald eyes, and milk chocolate hair, with sun-kissed lighter pieces, whose strands are longer on top and styled back perfectly. He has a dusting of facial hair, as though it's just growing back after being clean-shaven for so long.

"I can see that you're not," he tells me, dipping me low before pulling me back to a stand. "You command the room—it's very obvious to see."

I blush, even though it doesn't feel like he's *trying* to flirt with me, and change the subject. "You said you're here with your younger brother? What is his name? Ansel hasn't told me much about his life, other than he has three sons."

"Well, you have the pleasure of dancing with the oldest right now." He winks. "As I said, my youngest brother, Jasper, is here with me. Our other brother is out of the country right now. His name is Ledger."

"And what is it that all of you do for a living, Alistair?"

His lips purse, and he gets a mischievous look in his eye just as the song changes. Suddenly, the man dressed as The Phantom of the Opera appears to our left, his hand outstretched in my direction.

He says nothing, but as our gazes collide, my heart stops. A gasp of air leaves me and I bite my lip to keep the emotion off my face.

Alistair looks from me to the man in the mask, then takes a step back. "It seems as though you have a new suitor." He bows and kisses the top of my hand. "It was a pleasure dancing with you, Miss Paladino. Thank you for allowing me to keep my word to my father."

Then he's gone, sinking into the crowd as The Phantom steps closer. His hand engulfs my hip while the other clasps around mine, holding it outward as we start to move.

"What are you doing here?" I breathe, my voice barely above a whisper. I trail my hand lightly down the front of his tuxedo, just enough to touch him, but not enough to raise suspicion if someone was to see.

"I needed to dance with you, piccola ladra. To hold you out in the open for all to see, at least once." Sly keeps his smooth voice low, speaking only to me. "You look breathtaking."

There's no way to keep the smile off my face from the happiness I'm feeling. The risk of him being here is unimaginable, but now that I'm in his arms, none of it matters. I pretend as though the repercussions cease to exist—that we're not standing in the same room as my entire family, and that I'm not falling even deeper in love with him than I ever thought possible.

I feel utterly giddy as he holds me in his arms, slowly swaying with me to the music.

"This feels like a dream," I murmur, shifting my arm around his neck. It pulls us closer together, and the grip he holds on my hip tightens.

"It is a dream I wish to never wake from." Through his tone, I hear the conflict of emotions—the happiness mixed with sadness.

We're reaching a point where we need to make a decision together, and knowing this makes the room feel like it's caving in.

I want to be with him more than I've ever wanted anything in this lifetime, but the thought of revealing who the love of my life is to my family feels like a hundred knives stabbing into my gut.

For the remainder of the song, neither of us says a word, but we hold each other close, slow dancing while the world around us ceases to exist.

It's a beautiful moment.

Romantic and lovely, but somehow also filled with sorrow.

As the song ends, my stomach clenches when he bows low and presses a long kiss to the top of my hand.

"Ti amo, piccola ladra," he whispers, then backs away, never taking his eyes off me as I stand frozen in place, watching him go.

It's difficult to breathe, and as the song changes to an upbeat melody, I swallow thickly and go to find a drink.

The server submerges a large ladle into the cauldron and fills a crystal glass full of spiked punch. I take a sip just as my father comes to stand next to me.

"Are you having a nice time, sunshine?"

A shiver runs through me, fear slicing through my core as I wonder if my father recognized Sly.

"I am," I tell him a little too enthusiastically.

"The best of the night is yet to come," he muses, kissing my temple.

He walks away before I can ask what he means, leaving me what can only be described as a bewildered expression.

Sipping my drink, I go back to watching the party, looking everywhere to see where Sly disappeared to.

Knowing he's here fills me with peace, but also an eruption of nerves.

Another slow song plays, its soft melody filling the room as couples stand and head to the dance floor, while others already on the dance floor break apart and find new partners. I watch the shift, wishing Sly would have allowed me one or two more dances.

"How fitting that you're dressed as a princess when I'm here as a prince," August's slimy voice rumbles far too close to my ear.

I stiffen, but keep my chin held high. "Funny, it looks to me like you were a courtier, not a prince."

He hums in a snide tone, not having a comeback to hurl at me.

"Come dance with me," he says, encircling his hand around my wrist.

"No." I pull against his grasp, but he doesn't let me go.

"It wasn't a request," he sneers, and tugs me so I have no choice but to move, until we're walking in step and he's wrapped my arm around his.

He's forcing my hand, strong-arming me into putting my fake smile into place under the watchful eye of those around us.

Once on the dance floor, he pulls me into his embrace, and we start to glide.

"Things don't have to be so unpleasant between us, you know. I'm not as unfavorable as you think I am. I could make you very happy, Vinnie."

I rear back, looking at him like he's grown another head. "You're kidding me, right? August, you disgust me. You've cornered me numerous times, threatened me with unspeakable things. Portrayed us as in a relationship in the media without my knowledge or consent. And that's just to name a few things. You are the last person I would ever consider having in my life more than I already am forced to."

"There are ways I can persuade you to reconsider." He dips me suddenly, just like he did that night of the gala, then pulls me back upright, holding me closer to his body than before.

Over his shoulder, it seems like all eyes are on us, watching us move and sway.

"You could never persuade me to change how I think of you," I seethe through a strained smile. With all eyes watching, I must remember to control the anger brewing within me.

He snickers, nuzzling his cheek against mine. His voice is low and dangerous as tells me, "I know who's behind the Phantom mask, Vinnie. Perhaps I should tell your brother?"

Every molecule in my body stands on edge, electrifying with fear as soon as the words pass his lips.

A wave of nausea crashes through me.

I stop moving, but he forces me to continue, pressing his head against mine. "Keep dancing, darling. Everyone is thrilled to see us together right now."

Looking out into the crowd again, it seems as though time has stopped around us. Every head is turned in our direction, and it's then I notice the crowd has dispersed from the dance floor, and a wide circle has formed around us.

Women fawn over us adoringly, while the men watch on intently as though they're waiting for something to happen.

I scan the crowd, looking for one face.

One mask.

It takes a minute, but I find him standing at the back of the crowd, watching from over everyone's heads. Our eyes connect, but they're impossible to read from this far, and I can't see his expression behind the mask.

I can only hope my expression conveys the way I'm feeling.

Silently, I tell him, *this isn't what I want—he's forcing this dance.*

I'm acting, only keeping up appearances for the sake of my family and our image in the public eye.

I love you.

But I'm not sure if any of it comes across.

The song comes to a close and applause rings out around us, deafeningly loud.

August slides his hands down my arms until he reaches my hands, and at the same moment, I realize the music has stopped completely.

With my hands in his, August lowers himself to one knee.

The applause becomes muffled in my ears as I look at him in wide-eyed horror.

Time moves in slow motion as he releases my hands and pulls open his costume jacket, reaching into a concealed pocket.

I swallow down the bile in my throat.

In the next instant, he's holding a teal box, cracking open the lid.

"No," I gasp as my eyes connect with the enormous diamond ring, but the sound of my voice is overpowered by the cheers of the crowd.

Peering over him, my eyes search for Sly in the crowd, but I can't find him—I can't make out anyone's faces as the blur of tears blocks my vision.

"Vinnie Paladino," August's voice booms, immediately hushing the crowd. "From the moment I first laid eyes on you, I knew I had to make you mine. And now I hope to keep you forever. Will you marry me?"

A lone tear falls from my eye from the absolute devastation I'm feeling inside. More threaten to fall, I can feel them collect at the bottom of my lashes, but they are as frozen as I feel.

There's no way to describe the storm of emotions— the chaos and fear that's sinking to the very bottom of my stomach.

On instinct, my hand covers my mouth and I look down at the diamond ring August is presenting, screaming at myself internally to shout the word that my mind won't stop repeating.

NO.

NO, I will not marry you.

NO. I would rather die *than marry you.*

Over my dead body, will I marry you.

But I'm in complete shock.

Hundreds of eyes are on me, waiting with bated breath for me to accept a proposal from a man who, to everyone in the room, is a saint.

Little do they know I loathe him with every fiber of my being.

August's eyes narrow so slightly, I almost think I imagined it. Then, he's taking the ring from the box and sliding it on my ring finger.

"She said yes!" he shouts, rising to his feet.

I said nothing.

He lifts my hand into the air triumphantly, pulling me into a tight embrace.

Why didn't I say no? Why couldn't the words form?

Behind him, I can see my parents both looking completely elated, my mom bouncing excitedly as much as she possibly can in her stilettos.

"I know who's behind the Phantom mask, Vinnie."

Sly.

"Your secret is safe with me, fiancée. For now," August whispers as he presses a kiss against my head. "By the way, I received your *entire* family's blessing."

As he tells me that, my eyes connect with Joseph's. A

look of sick satisfaction is etched into his smirk as he watches the spectacle his best friend is putting on.

For whatever reason, it snaps me back to reality, and I step back from August's hold.

Frantically, I whisk through the crowd, searching every face for the Phantom mask. Fear locks itself into every piece of me the more people I push past, not seeing him anywhere.

"Vinnie," I hear someone say my name, but I'm too tunneled to pay it any mind, walking around the edge of where everyone is congregated, congratulating August.

It's interesting how no one tries to congratulate me. Perhaps my performance has stalled and they can see how manic I feel.

"Vinnie," the voice says again, this time grabbing my wrist. The contact breaks my focus and I look down at the touch, then lower to the ring that sits on my finger. Another wave of nausea hits.

Finally, I look up at the face of the person touching me. Raina is staring back with raw concern in her eyes. "Vins," she groans sympathetically.

"I didn't say yes," I croak, my voice scratchy and raw with emotion.

"I *know*."

"Sly." The tears fall with just the mention of his name.

"Go. I'll cover for you if I have to."

Shaking my head, she pulls me in and hugs me

tightly, only furthering the tears. "I love you, and more importantly, *he* loves you. It'll all be okay."

Then she pushes me from her grasp and I turn, running through the doors of my parents' mansion and into the frigid Manhattan night with only one concern on my mind.

Finding Sly.

Chapter 32

Sly

"*She said yes.*"

August's triumph reverberates through my mind over and over until I'm questioning my sanity. White-hot stabbing fury courses through me in a rush so powerful it threatens to bring me to my knees.

The moment he held Vinnie's hand in the air, the diamond glistening in the light as he displayed it for all to see; I turned my back and left, practically running out the doors.

I can't breathe—it's like the devil himself has torn through my body and is gripping his hands around my lungs, squeezing them as his heat scalds me from the inside out.

Ripping the ridiculous mask off my face, I toss it on the sidewalk and jog to my Ducati, which is parked a block away. I need to get out of here—to get as far away as possible before I turn back around and shove that ring down August's throat then kill him with my bare hands.

Have I been played for a fool?

Surely the things I feel for Vinnie are real for her, too. Every moment. Every kiss. Every time we've made love.

A connection this powerful cannot be faked.

Or can it?

I feel numb as I climb onto my motorcycle and bring the engine to life. The second my helmet is on, I'm flying down the road toward my home, fighting against the cataclysm building inside.

The speedometer creeps up as I veer around the cars on the road.

Seventy.

Seventy-Five.

Eighty.

Ninety.

I exhale a shuddering breath, releasing one handlebar to push the face shield up, needing the bite of the cold air against my skin.

One hundred.

One-Ten.

One-Fifteen.

The pain increases with my speed.

Moisture rolls down my cheeks, and I'm unclear if my eyes are watering from how fast I'm going or if I'm crying.

One-Twenty.

The Kenna comes into view, forcing me to decelerate.

I'm numb, silently screaming curses to myself, wondering if I've wasted my time by putting my love and my trust in someone who doesn't feel the same.

Memories crash into me, blasting through my mind in rapid succession. At the masquerade, speaking to her for the first time in years. Her sweet scent of cherry blossoms seeping into my pores and becoming my favorite scent. Our first official date at the castle, and the thrill of running through the rain, only to be wrapped in each other's arms.

Stolen moments.

Longing glances.

Saying *I love you.*

I have no idea how I make it into my apartment, but the moment I slam the door behind me, the noise in my brain begins to fade.

Leaning against the cool wood, my chest heaves as I catch my breath. My heart is racing, and as I peel off the jacket of my tuxedo and loosen the bow tie, I realize my face is still damp.

I don't bother wiping my tears.

Tossing the bow tie onto the floor, I go straight to my bar cart, pulling the top of a crystal decanter off, and chug straight from the bottle.

It burns going down, reminding me a liquor of this quality is meant to be sipped—savored—but right now I choose to see it for what it truly is: a means for getting drunk.

As I lower the decanter, my gaze lands on the leather chair that faces the window, and an urge so powerful overtakes me, whispering for me to go destroy it.

Instead, I stalk toward it, glaring at the piece of furniture like it is the one who stole my future.

My fingers connect with its back, feeling the soft leather as I grip it tighter, tilting it so it teeters on its back feet.

Then I let it go.

It lands back in place with a thud as I move to the front and sink down into the welcoming, traitorous cushions.

I take another swig of bourbon.

This is the first place me and Vinnie made love.

Where I watched her dress fall from her body, the moonlight illuminating the soft curves of her skin as she stood before me in nothing but her heels.

The recollection burns worse than the drink.

I take another swig to drown the pain.

Tilting my head against the back of the chair, I close my eyes, replaying our earlier dance. She had nothing but excitement in her eyes when she realized it was me behind the Phantom mask.

It had taken me far too long to think of a costume where a full mask would be appropriate, but when she mentioned the Halloween party, I knew I had to be in attendance, if only to surprise her with the ability to hold her for a few stolen moments in public.

"She said yes."

How could she?

The next mouthful of alcohol doesn't burn so badly.

"Sly!"

Pounding on the front door rattles through the apartment, snapping my eyes toward the frantic, feminine voice that accompanies it.

"Sly! Please. Are you in there?" She sounds as heartbroken as I feel, her voice cracking when she says *please*.

Simply hearing her voice begins to mend my heart.

"*Sly.*" It's desperate and sad. It hurts to hear—the pain in her voice is almost too much to bear.

Yet, I can't bring myself to say anything or alert her of my presence.

Vinnie knocks again, gentler this time.

I watch the door, seeing the exact moment she tries the handle. It gives way, having never been locked after I arrived home.

"Sly?" She pushes the door open further and walks in, looking around my apartment. The moment she sees me sitting across the room and our eyes connect, she slams the door closed behind her and is on her way to me.

Her golden ball gown somehow shines even though the apartment is dark, as does her tear-soaked skin.

When Vinnie reaches me, she sinks down on her knees. Her dress balloons out around her as she grabs my hands. Taking the decanter from me, she sets it aside before lacing both of our hands together.

Immediately, I can feel the metallic band around her finger.

Ripping my hands from hers, I stand and step over her, careful not to harm her as I do, and move further down the wall-length window.

"Sly, *please*. Talk to me," she pleads, catching my arm.

"What is there to say?" My voice comes out strangled, as though she's holding her hands around my throat.

It feels like she is.

Her eyes fill up with tears. "It wasn't what it looked like!"

Those words hit me like a sucker punch to the gut, physically knocking the wind from my lungs.

Reaching down, I grab ahold of her wrist, yanking it until her hand is eye level between us.

The diamond glints in what little light streams in through the windows.

Taunting me.

Taunting us both.

"YOU'RE WEARING HIS RING, VINCENZA!"

Dropping her hand like it scalded me, I take a step back and rake my fingers through my hair, furious at myself for shouting at her.

But it hurts so fucking bad I can't contain my rage.

"I…" She looks down at her hand, her eyes widening as if she's just realized the ring is on her finger. Tugging it off, she shoves it into the pocket of her dress. "Everything happened so fast, I went into shock. I didn't know what was happening… I didn't say yes!"

My head snaps up, eyes locking with hers. "You said no?"

"I… I didn't say anything… I was in shock."

Her words barrel into me like a wrecking ball. Knowing she said nothing is somehow almost worse.

My jaw tics as I choose my words carefully, forcing myself to suppress the exasperation that wants to fuel my speech.

The silence rings deadly—the calm before the storm.

Rivers of quiet tears stream down her face as she looks at me, not knowing what to say. I'm sure she can see the monster within me now, the savage demon that reminds her of all the other men in her life.

"Please leave, Vincenza," I mutter, the words sour on my tongue.

A small gasp leaves her, and she takes a step toward me. "What? No. *Please*. Let's talk about this."

"Anything I say now will be words I regret in the future. I can hardly look at you right now. Please allow me to process this before I end up saying something we cannot come back from."

Her eyes search mine as her tears fall one after another, ripping the last fragments of my heart into shreds.

She opens her mouth like she's going to say something, but I cut her off—the fragile organ behind my rib cage barely beats as is.

"Please, just leave, Vinnie. I will seek you out in a

day or two, and we can talk then." Then, as much as it kills me, I turn my back on her.

Looking out the window at the Manhattan skyline, I focus on an incoming plane, its flashing lights barely visible in the distance.

Tears burn my eyes while I stare at it, listening to the sound of Vinnie's heels click against my floor as she crosses the apartment.

The sting intensifies when she closes the door behind her, the *click* barely audible over the blood rushing through my ears.

Every fiber of my being screams to chase after her, to work this out right here and now. She's the love of my life, and if she didn't accept his marriage proposal, perhaps there is still hope for our happily ever after.

But I ignore the instinct, curling my hands into fists as I stand my ground, staring at the plane's lights becoming slightly brighter in the sky.

The longer I stand here, the more abundantly the tears multiply in my eyes, but rather than give into temptation and allow my body the release of emotion it so badly craves, I refuse to let them fall.

Not anymore than they already have.

Instead, I begin to sort through the madness in my head so I can think clearly and problem solve as I have been taught to do my entire life.

Because one thing is for certain, I will never love another as I love Vincenza Paladino and I must do everything I can to ensure that she knows that.

Even if that means getting my hands dirty.

Chapter 33

Vinnie

Today has been the longest day of my life. The pit in my stomach has been a permanent fixture since I walked out of Sly's apartment, reluctant to give him the space he asked for.

It hurt to walk away, even if it was only for a short time.

I know he's hurting—and I am, too. What August did was cruel and horrible, and like an idiot, I didn't even have the quick-wit to shut him down on the spot.

Not with the eyes of hundreds of people on me, watching through rose-colored glasses.

What's that saying about going into shock?

Is there even a saying? There should be.

Foolish. That's the only word I can use to describe myself.

My eyes burn, red and raw from the constant tears that have flowed. My sinuses ache. My jaw hurts from gritting my teeth. It should go without saying that I slept horribly last night—tossing and turning in between tears, crying myself to sleep as I replayed the events of the evening in my head.

How could I have been so stupid?

How had the words not formed to shut August down?

Cecilia cried with me when I recounted everything that had happened, rubbing my head in a motherly way as I lay in bed sobbing.

It's late afternoon now and I've been curled up on an oversized chair, wrapped in a blanket, as I stare out of the window blankly, watching the city below me.

I'm too high up to see the faces of those who are out there living their lives as though mine isn't falling apart, but the busy city never wavers as people go about their Saturday.

"Are you hungry?" Cecilia asks, handing me a steaming cup of tea.

I take it, my hands wrapping around the warm mug, bringing me the smallest bit of comfort. "No, not at all."

"You need to eat."

"I need to speak to Sly."

"Still no response?"

Looking down at my lap, I shake my head no.

I've sent him countless messages, all of which have gone without a response. Each one making my heart feel more and more like a hollow vessel.

> I know you asked for time, but can we please talk?

> Please call me.

> I love you. While you take the time to think, please just remember that.

> I hate this.

There is no way for me to tell if he's seen them and is just ignoring me, or if his phone is off and he hasn't yet received them.

It's killing me—the not knowing.

But I'm not brave enough to actually pick up my phone and call him. Hearing his voice might shatter me.

Meanwhile, *my* phone has been ringing off the hook, but not a single call or message is from the one person I *need* to hear from.

My mother.

Raina.

Various media outlets.

The only call I felt guilty denying was Raina's, but hearing her voice would break me too.

"Give Sly some time. From what you've told me about him, he doesn't seem like the type of man to make an irrational decision, and he seems to really care about you. You'll hear from him. You may just need to make peace with the fact that you might not hear from him *today*."

The thought of not hearing from him today makes a new rush of tears fall.

"Oh Vins," Cecilia coos, rushing forward to wipe my tears. She holds my face, tilting it up so I'm looking at her. "Things have a way of working themselves out, okay? I'm going to call your mother and tell her you've been sick all day and won't be attending brunch tomorrow, and that will be one less stressor for you to deal with this weekend."

I nod in her hold. "Okay," I croak. "Tell her I'll call her for lunch next week."

She nods her head and reaches down to squeeze my hand. The gesture is reassuring. "I'm going to go get us some dinner. I know you're not hungry, but Fraîche just opened their 'home-cooked' section of the market and I've heard wonderful things about their soups and fresh-baked breads. I'll go get us some comfort food, alright?"

Despite the lack of appetite, soup *does* sound cozy. I can't promise I'll eat it, but I'll at least try.

"Thank you," I mutter.

She walks away as I bring my mug back to my lips and sip the hot liquid, tasting the light notes of chamomile and honey.

The sky is darkening, thick gray clouds coming in from all around. It feels symbolic of my life. One moment, things are calm and beautiful, and the next, a storm is swirling.

I sit and watch the clouds roll in, removing every trace of blue skies from the city. My tea cools quickly as I take small sips, slowly drinking it.

A while after Cecilia leaves, the doorbell rings and I startle, so captivated by the clouds and the silence I had almost forgotten I was at home.

I'm not expecting guests, and frankly don't have the mental capacity to speak to anyone. The list of people who could potentially be behind the door makes my stomach fall as though it's weighed down by lead.

Deciding to ignore it, I continue to look out the window, quiet as a mouse, while I wait for them to leave.

But the person knocks, their firm fist rattling the door.

"Vincenza?" Sly's smooth deep voice calls through the wood and my heart skips a beat as I push myself out of my chair.

Setting my mug down on a side table as I pass, I rush to the door, flipping the lock and pulling it open as quickly as I can.

The moment our eyes collide, I feel like I can breathe again, but another freefall of tears cascades from my lashes.

"*Piccola ladra,*" he sighs, closing the distance between us. His hand immediately slides into my hair, resting at the nape of my neck as he brings me forward and presses his lips to my forehead.

"I'm so sorry," I cry, not knowing what else to do but apologize.

Stepping forward, he forces me to take a step back so he can come in, closing the door behind us. His arms wrap around me, holding me tightly.

"We need to talk," he says, his voice strained.

I take a step away from him, my eyes widening in fear.

Please don't end this, I beg to myself. *I'll never survive it if you do.*

But instead of articulating the words, I hold my breath and lead him to the couch.

Once we're seated with our bodies turned so we're facing each other, he reaches out, cupping my cheek. "I hate when you cry."

Every unimaginable fear has surfaced—all the worst-case scenarios and the what-ifs. I'm terrified of losing him. Petrified that he will walk away from me right now.

From across the room, a light smattering of rain hits the windows, the soft pelts tapping across the glass. I shiver on instinct, my skin erupting in goosebumps as I watch the rain for a breath, before finally pulling my gaze back to him.

"I'm so scared, Sly." The words are hardly audible to my own ears, but my voice seems lost at this moment.

His brows knit together, almost as if he's confused. "Of what, Vincenza?"

"Of losing *you*. Of all of this ending. I would *never* marry him, Sly. I hate August, and he set me up. Him and my brother have been planning this up for weeks—months even. Can't you see that?"

"Sí, piccola ladra. I can. Which is why I am here now."

"You believe me?"

"Of course I do." He reaches out and takes my hand. Bringing it to his lips, he kisses my palm. "But still, we must have a serious talk. Things have changed. The entire city now thinks you're engaged to August St. Jean. Your family believes this. He may have set you up, but he did so in a way that will only make himself look better when you end it."

"I don't care about that. The only thing I care about is *you*, and being with you."

"I am yours, amore mio," he says, brushing his thumb over my lower lip. He stares at me, eyes softening as he leans forward and kisses me gently. All too quickly, he pulls away, but leaves his forehead pressed against mine.

His voice is strained when he speaks again. "I am a slave to your emotions, controlled by a simple look on your face. When you are sad, I want to kill the one who puts that feeling into your heart. When you are happy, I want to bottle that emotion and save it for all the times you are not. You own me, Vinnie. I love you more than words will ever express, but I won't watch you marry another man. Not when the only man who will ever love you wholly is me."

"I'm *not* marrying him, Sly."

"Then you need to tell your family that—tell everyone. And then we need to tell them we're together. It's time to confess to everyone that *we* love each other. I cannot continue our relationship behind closed doors.

August has already stripped away my ability to be the man who proposes to you. He will not take *you* as well."

My heart seizes in my chest, thinking of how my family will react if we tell them. I want to—God, so badly do I want to tell the world that I love Sly Lucchetti, but the fear of my family's reaction still grips me.

And then there's August.

His words rattle through my mind. He knew it was Sly behind that mask…

"I can't—"

"Can't, or won't, Vincenza? Because if you allow me to slide a ring onto your finger and throw his into the East River, I will do everything in my power to always protect you, our families be damned."

"You know I want that." Tears slide down my cheeks as he brings my hands to his mouth and kisses my knuckles. A sob catches in my throat at the sweet gesture. "But you don't know my family like I do. My father… Joseph… I can't be the reason *you* end up hurt. Because they will come after you, Sly. You and I both know it."

"You forget, I *do* know your family and their capabilities. I witnessed it firsthand as a child. Still, I am not worried. Loving you is worth any risk."

"I could never live with myself if anything ever happened to you."

He shakes his head. "If your concern is with my safety, then let's leave together."

My eyes widen at the suggestion. "Run away?"

"Sì, *piccola ladra*. We can go to my home—to Verona—and start anew. Or Paris. Madrid, even. Wherever you decide, we can be together, *amore mio*. *Really* be together."

"They would find us," I whisper, staring down at our connected hands. A numb feeling has settled deep inside, my head at war with my heart. "My *father* would find me, eventually."

"Let me worry about that. It is my burden to shoulder, not yours. I will *always* protect you. I have no fear of my life when it comes to your family." Hope shines in his hazel eyes. It makes my heart flip-flop in my chest, inflating my own sense of optimism. He presses a chaste kiss to my lips. "Run away with me," he whispers against them.

I squeeze my eyes shut, wanting so badly to say yes. "I—"

"You don't have to say anything now," he interrupts. "Think about it. Think about both options. We don't have to leave, we can simply tell our families. I know you love New York—your loved ones, your business. We can stay and weather the storm together. Just think about it. If you decide I am worth running away with, and leaving all of this behind, I will be waiting. Or if you choose to tell our families, we'll devise a plan—figure it out together. But if you do n—"

This time, I'm the one who cuts him off. "I'll be there. Wherever you say to meet, I'll be there."

Not isn't even an option.

A life without Sly is not a life I want to live.

"Wait, let me get this out, amoire mio." He slides from the couch, crouching with one knee on the floor, and takes both of my hands in his. "If you decide a life on the run is not one you are willing to live, or that you simply cannot tell your family about me, then I will respect that. I love you with the heat of a thousand suns, but I also understand the gravity of what I am asking you to do. And even though I would do anything, earth side or heaven far, to keep you, I will not ruin your life just to do so."

He pauses, shifting his weight slightly. "Think on it. If you want to leave with me, pack the things that mean the most to you. If you'd rather tell our families and allow ourselves to love another in the open, then we will. But if you don't arrive, I will understand. It may kill me, but I will understand that you had to choose *your* happiness over ours."

"I'll never be happy without you," I stress. "I don't need the time to consider it."

"You do. I want this decision to come as easily as breathing, piccola ladra, and decisions as such need *time*. Meet me tomorrow in Central park. I'll be at the staircase in Shakespeare Garden at one p.m.."

One p.m.

He's giving me the chance to have one last *normal* brunch with my family, even though I've already decided I won't be there. Still, I know he's chosen one o'clock to ensure I get that time with them, because regardless if I choose for us to run away or to tell our families, things will be forever different.

I'm just not sure which path I'll choose to take for us.

He grabs my face with both hands and pulls me to him, his lips smashing against mine hard. There's no tongue, no wandering hands, but the words spoken through the kiss speak louder than any we've ever spoken out loud.

Sly and I break apart when my front door opens, the sound of keys jingling and bags shifting, following the sound of footsteps. We both turn to see Cecilia standing in the threshold with two large brown paper bags, soaked with raindrops, in her arms. She looks like a deer caught in headlights as her eyes bounce between us.

"Oh my gosh, I'm so sorry!" she gasps, using her foot to shut the door.

Without a second thought, Sly stands and goes to her, taking the bags from her hands. "There is nothing to apologize for. I am in *your* home. To the kitchen?"

"Yes, please. Thank you." She looks back at me, a smile on her lips as she follows him into the kitchen.

"I am Sly Lucchetti," he tells her, extending his hand after he's set the groceries on the counter. "It is nice to meet you."

"Cecilia." For some reason, she seems a little awestruck as they shake hands.

He offers her a warm smile, then crosses the room to me. "I must go now, but please, think on it, amore mio."

"I'll be there," I reaffirm, nodding my head through the tears that just won't cease to end. They're lighter now, but still tumble down my skin from the mayhem inside.

With his thumb and finger on my chin, he tilts my head down, pressing one last kiss to my forehead. Another lump builds in my throat as he releases me. "Ti amo, piccola ladra."

He leaves without another word, closing the door quietly behind him as he goes, and I'm left alone with my thoughts and heavy decisions to make.

Either path I choose, I end with the same outcome: Sly by my side.

But how do I choose between leaving my family and telling them something I know will drive us apart?

There's no way in which I win in terms of my relationship with my family.

But Sly… my third, unspoken option is to walk away from him, and that's not something I could ever do.

I love him too much to let him go.

He means more to me than anything in the world.

My thoughts are spiraling, my chest tightening as each minute passes. But I continue to stand here, unable to move from this spot, staring a hole into the wood.

"Vins?" Cecilia's voice is soft as she approaches. "Do you want to talk about it?"

I do, but I'm not sure where to start, so I just nod.

She moves to the couch, curling up with her feet under her in the same place Sly sat just moments ago.

I take the seat I sat in.

"He wants to run away together," I tell her, almost

robotically. "Run away together or come clean to our families."

Always the voice of reason, she asks, "What do *you* want?"

"Him," I croak, my voice raw. "I just want *him*."

She sits quietly for a few seconds, and I can practically see the wheels in her head turning. "You've had him, Vins. You *have* him. But August spun your world upside down last night and now Sly is asking for you to take a stand and show him your love is worth fighting for."

Our eyes meet, her words resonating somewhere deep in my soul.

Holding my gaze, she lifts her chin, and reflects the confidence I know she wants me to feel. "Your love is worth fighting for, isn't it?"

It is—there's no doubt in my mind.

I love him, and as much as I've said it, I know it's time for me to *show* it.

"Of *course* it is," I say firmly, wiping the tears from my eyes and sitting up a little straighter.

"Then *fight*."

Her words stop the tears from falling, lifting the cloud from my brain that my sorrow has put there.

She's right. She's absolutely right.

Who cares what our families think?

Why am I wasting time on the fear I have that's ultimately holding me back from true happiness? I *deserve* happiness.

And *screw* August and whatever game he's trying to play—I'm not playing it.

It's time for me to show Sly that I'm going to fight for him. For *us*.

Because our love isn't just worth fighting for.

It's worth starting a *war*.

Chapter 34

Sly

"Alright, Mr. O'Neil, your lungs sound good and your vitals are perfect. I think it's safe to say you've beat the pneumonia, and everything else from your physical looks as it should. There's no need to stress. However, I will prescribe you one last thing before you go."

"What's that, Doc?"

The eighty-seven-year-old man sits on my exam table, his feet dangling from the edge as though he's a small child, looking up at me through the round bifocals sitting on the tip of his nose.

When his wife brought him to me two weeks ago, I had been extremely nervous about the best course of action for his care given his age, but we caught his pneumonia very early, and with the right antibiotics and the role of attentive bedside nurse his wife played, he pulled through quickly.

"I'm prescribing you a date night with your wife at a

delicious Italian restaurant. Di Mercutio is my favorite spot in the city and if you'll allow me, I would love to treat you and Bernice to a meal."

Immediately he shakes his head, holding his glasses as he does. "No, no, we couldn't possibly—"

"Please," I stress. "It would be my pleasure."

His wife looks up from her knitting and beams at me. "That would be lovely, Doctor Lucchetti. It's been years since we've had a proper date night."

Mr. O'Neil sighs, tossing his frail hands into the air in defeat. "Fine. We accept. Thank you, Doc."

With my assistance, he gets off the exam table and I hand him his cane.

"I would still like for you to rest and make sure you are drinking plenty of fluids. Keep yourself warm. Go to bed early."

"I'm in bed by seven every night."

Chuckling, I continue my monologue. "Take your vitamins. Go on a short walk at least once a day."

He waves me off. "Yeah, yeah. Eat my vegetables, spend plenty of time in the sun to help with Vitamin D."

"Precisely."

"Thank you, Doctor," his wife says, standing to shake my hand.

"I am happy to help. I'll give you some privacy. Pop the door open when you're dressed and I'll see you out."

The door closes behind me, and I pull my phone out, looking down at the time. I have forty-five minutes before I'm due to meet Vinnie, which is just enough time for me to finish up with this patient, sanitize the clinic, make a quick stop for flowers, and get to Shakespeare Garden.

There's a small part of me wondering which Vincenza will choose—to run away together or tell our families—though my instincts tell me she will choose to tell our families.

She loves them, and I cannot see her willingly walking away from the people she loves.

There's a pit in my stomach as my mind conjures a scenario in which we sit down together and speak to *my* family, seeing them all sitting in my family's living room. With time, my parents will be supportive.

Mamma does not have a malicious bone in her body, and while the shock may cause her to seem closed off for a moment in time, she will one day welcome Vincenza with open arms and love her deeply.

Papà will be indifferent. I suspect he will be saddened by the news, to know the woman his son loves is the daughter of the man who killed his little brother, but again, with time, that feeling will pass.

Guilio won't have a care in the world. Nor will Federico.

But Lorenzo... I am fearful of my cousin's reaction and can only hope my news does not ruin our already fragile relationship.

"Thank you again, Doctor Lucchetti," Mrs. O'Neil's voice sounds from the doorway as she helps her husband through it. "We truly appreciate your care and compassion."

"I will call right now and make your dinner reservations for Di Mercutio. Would you prefer tonight or tomorrow?"

"We have some leftovers to finish up tonight," Mr. O'Neil tells me. "Better make the reservations for tomorrow. Four o'clock is preferred."

"I'll see to it that it's arranged. Would you like me to have a car sent for you?"

"We can find our way," Mrs. O'Neil insists. "You're already offering us too much."

I nod, not wanting to argue with the woman. I know pride when I see it, and I am already thrilled they accepted my dinner offer.

Mr. O'Neil had confided in me in our last appointment that he was afraid the pneumonia would take his life before he could take his wife on one last date. I promised to not let that happen.

He squeezes my hand on the way out, his eyes shining with unshed tears as he gives me a brisk nod. I return it and watch them until they're tucked safely in a cab, then call the restaurant to make plans for their dinner.

"Whatever they want, charge to my card," I instruct the manager as I wipe down the exam table with a disinfectant wipe, holding the phone to my ear in my other hand. "Make sure they're treated like royalty, please. This couple deserves the very best."

"We'll do just that, Mr. Lucchetti. We look forward to seeing the O'Neils tomorrow at four."

With thirty minutes to go, I lock up the clinic and hop on my motorcycle, knowing there's a flower stand off West 81st, which is where I'll have to park, anyway.

I need to be quick—the last thing I want is to be late and for Vinnie to think I am standing her up.

Leaning against the old wood rail of the staircase in Shakespeare Garden, I take in the beauty of the grounds.

It's been many years since I've visited these gardens. My mother used to love to bring me and Guilio here as children, but the tradition was lost the older we became, no longer interested in looking at flowers or walking in the park.

All around me, plant life flourishes. Vibrant flowers to thick bushels of herbs, every inch of the unpaved land-scape filled to the brim with vast colors and textures. Gold plaques sit on the edges, highlighting famous quotes from William Shakespeare, celebrating his beautiful words.

Across from where I stand is the Swedish Cottage, a historic building built in the late 1800s, that now houses a theater. The architecture is stunning, and with the way the sun illuminates behind it, it brings a certain splendor to the gardens.

Pulling out my phone, I see Vinnie is now ten

minutes late to meet me. It builds the nerves in my system, but I force them down.

Perhaps she hit traffic or had a difficult time getting a cab. This is New York—any number of things could be the result of a late arrival.

Adjusting the bouquet in my hold, I focus my attention on a family nearby, watching as their toddler chases a duck that has waddled over from Turtle Pond. The child has a mop of curly blond hair on top of his head and a plethora of drool spilling from his mouth, but he looks overjoyed to simply be chasing a duck.

The child's parents watch from a few steps behind, and though their backs are to me and I cannot see their faces, I can only imagine their contentment.

I then realize how much I long for that—a family of my own.

My mind returns to Vincenza. She should be here by now.

Twisting my wrist, I read my watch, frowning at the time.

One twenty.

The flowers go slack in my hand, hanging by my side as I sink onto a low step of the staircase. As I sit, I pay close attention to the people around me, searching every face for hers.

The clock creeps later, and by a little after one thirty, the bile has risen in my throat, nausea settling deep in my stomach.

When the sound of gravel crunches, I whip my

head up only to feel like I've been kicked back down when I meet my cousin's eyes.

"Lorenzo?" I question, but my tone lacks nuance. "What are you doing here?"

"I should ask you the same, cousin. Who are you waiting for?" He stands in front of me, practically toe to toe, towering above me.

It's difficult to swallow, my airway feeling as though it's being suppressed with emotion. "No one."

"I hoped you wouldn't lie to me, but you have been for a long time, haven't you?"

I rise, not liking the position we're in. With him standing over me, he feels like he's in control. But he forgets we are equals.

Rising to my full height, I look him straight in the eyes. "What is it that you want me to say exactly, Lorenzo?"

"How about the truth?" he spits. Taking the flowers from my hand, he waves them in my face, his temper rising. "Who are these for?"

"The love of my life."

The answer is honest, even if it's now obvious I'm not the love of hers.

She didn't show up.

And true to my word, I will respect her decision, even if it kills me.

So why fight with Enzo on this?

Holding his gaze, I decide there's no point. I shake my head, walking past him to leave.

"You're not as smart as I thought you were," he calls

over his shoulder. Immediately, my footsteps falter as I listen. "If you thought she cared about you."

I turn slowly to face him. He hasn't moved, but he now leans against the wood rail, settled in as though we're going to be here a while.

When I don't respond, he keeps going. "She's engaged, Sly. August St. Jean is a powerful man, and every woman in Manhattan would move mountains to be with that son-of-a-bitch. For you to think Vinnie Paladino would be any different, makes you a fool."

"You don't know anything about her," I growl, taking a step forward.

"I know enough, and pictures don't lie. Every photo of them I've seen together, she looks over the damn moon." Pulling a magazine from his back pocket, he walks toward me until he's close enough to slam it against my chest.

Taking it, I unfold it and look down at the photo of August proposing. Vinnie's mouth is covered by her hand, but the camera captured the unshed tears in her eyes as she looked down at him on one knee, Tiffany & Co. box wide open to display her ring.

"This proves nothing." I shove the magazine back into his hands. "He set her up. *We're* in love, Enzo. Not them."

"Then where is she, Sly? Because you're supposed to meet her here, aren't you?"

"Why are you here, Enzo? How did you find me?"

"I followed you because you've been off lately. Ever since my mom's birthday, you've been avoiding me. It didn't take much for me to figure out what you've been hiding—you've had the same tells since you were a child. I just hoped I was wrong about it."

"So you came here to, what, exactly?"

"To see for myself. You're a fucking traitor to this family, Sly. A Paladino? You've been sleeping with the literal enemy. What happened to family loyalty?" His voice raises with every word, each syllable enunciating through his gritted teeth. "My dad would be disgusted with you."

His words slice like a dull knife through my heart, sawing slowly with intense pressure just to make a cut.

I feel vulnerable in front of him, aching from the absence of her arrival, and conflicted from the things Lorenzo is saying.

My fear from before circles back, settling deep in my bones.

What if I was wrong? What if she and August played me for a fool?

"I love her," I tell my cousin, because it's true. I feel it as naturally as breathing. She's a part of me, ingrained in my soul.

His eyes darken as he looks at me, as though he's seeing me for the very first time, and doesn't like what he sees. Still, I cannot find it in me to care. Not when my heart is breaking.

Seeking her out, hoping one last time that she's going to show up and is just incredibly late, I look around the gardens.

When I've fully circled and my eyes return to Lorenzo's, he shakes his head. "You might love her, but I'm telling you, she doesn't love you. You've been played, Sly. Because that's what Paladinos do. You shouldn't have trusted her."

Then he walks away, leaving me alone without a second glance.

His words weigh heavy as I watch him go until he's completely out of sight. Once I'm truly alone is when the world finally feels like it's breaking around me.

Looking at the bouquet that sits on the ground where Enzo tossed it, I fight back the anger that rises within me. This time, I'm not so sure I'll hold back the monster when he shows his face again.

But one thing is abundantly certain, like a neon light flashing in a dimly lit room—I can't be here.

I can't stay in New York.

Not unless I want to succumb to the darkness inside, which is what will happen if I am forced to watch amore mio in the arms of another man. Even if Lorenzo is correct in saying she had planned this, I cannot turn off my feelings overnight.

Or perhaps at all.

I wasn't lying when I vowed to always love her. My heart has only spoken the truth when it comes to Vincenza Paladino.

I need to leave.

Racing down the path, I turn to the one person I know, despite the annoyance he causes, will always help me.

Pulling my phone from my pocket, I pull up my recent calls and press the number.

Sully answers on the second ring, but true to his nature, he says nothing.

"Sullivan?" I growl, quickening my pace down the path. All I want is to get back to my bike and get out of here before I boil over and cause a scene. Regardless of being outside, the air feels thick around me.

"What's up?"

"I need to borrow your jet."

He coughs as though he's choking on something. "My jet? Right now? Where are you going?"

"Yes, now. I need to get away for a while. May I borrow it or not?"

"Of course. Let me just make a few calls. Do you want me to meet you on the tarmac? I can come with you if you need a wingman."

For the briefest of moments, I consider inviting him along, ultimately shaking off the thought. This isn't like leaving after med school. I have no idea when, or if, I'll return to New York.

"No, I need to go alone. Can you make sure it's ready within the hour?"

"I… Yeah man, no problem. Will you at least tell me where you're going?"

"As far away from here as possible."

Once I'm on the plane, I'll flip a coin onto the west coast portion of the map and whichever city it lands will be where I land, too.

As long as it's far away from this city, I don't care.

My Ducati comes into view, parked exactly where I left it. It calls to me like a beacon—offering only the slightest of comfort as I kick my leg over the soft leather cushion and balance it between my legs.

"International?" he asks, and I can hear the unease in his voice, craving the details I'm refusing to tell.

I never knew until this moment how fragile a heart could be, like it's made of glass. From the outside, it's strong and made to withstand many hardships, but when its exterior is splintered, all it takes is one thing to shatter it completely.

So I'll head west and leave the fragments behind.

I won't need them anyway—I could never love anyone like I love Vincenza—and I sure as hell won't be here to watch her marry another man.

"No. California."

"These violent delights have violent ends."

Act 2, Scene 5 - Romeo & Juliet
William Shakespeare

Chapter 35

Vinnie

Thirty minutes earlier

"**I**'m in here!" I shout from my bedroom as the front door slams closed.

It's earlier than I expected Cecilia to return home, but I'm happy she did. I have to leave in less than five minutes to meet Sly and still have no idea what to wear.

It's the most trivial detail, but I've hyper focused on it because it's either stewing over the dress or doubting my decision to tell our parents.

All day, I've been running scenarios through my head, and no matter which way I spin it, there's always a fallout between me and my father. I just pray he can learn to love me again with time. I'm still his little girl, I just happened to fall in love with someone he will deem as the wrong person.

But Sly is not only the *right* person, he's *my* person.

If my father can't see that, then so be it.

I'm choosing *me*.

My life. My future.

I'm choosing love.

Cecilia's footsteps grow closer.

"I have two outfits on my bed! Could you pick one for me?" I call, smiling in my vanity's mirror.

My smile falls as my bedroom swings inward and August is the one pushing it open.

"What are you doing here? How'd you get in?" Immediately I stand, tightening my robe around me.

"You weren't at the family brunch." He leans against my door frame, crossing his arms. In one hand, he holds a manila folder.

"Well, aren't you observant? Last time I checked it was *my* family's brunch. I decided not to go today, if you must know."

"So my warning at the Halloween ball wasn't enough then? I need to make myself more clear?"

He sneers, pushing off the frame and stepping further into my room. Folding back the folder, he tosses it onto my bed.

Hundreds of photos scatter across the outfits.

Photos of me and Sly. Of just me. Of just Sly.

My stomach sinks. "You've been following us?"

I walk to my bed, pushing photos aside to reveal more.

Private moments captured from countless angles. Entire dates seemingly stuck in a freeze frame.

Under other circumstances I'd be grateful for the memories captured.

But under *these* circumstances, I feel physically ill.

I haven't noticed how close he is to me until his breath is hot against my cheek. "This bullshit affair you've got going on with Lucchetti ends now."

"How did you even know we were together?" I'm still pushing through the pictures, trying to piece together a timeline.

Not *every* moment was captured. Not the early weeks. He found out somehow.

Recently. Within the last six weeks or so.

He ignores my question, wrapping his hand around my upper arm. "Are you hearing me? You will not be another man's whore when you are to be *my* wife. You are mine, Vincenza, and one day you will love me."

"I could *never* love a man like you," I spit, trying to pull my arm from his grip.

His eyes narrow, and he tightens his hold. It hurts, he's deliberately pushing his fingers in deeper in a way that I know will leave bruises. "You can, and you will. Keep testing me, sweetheart, and your little lover boy will end up with his head severed and as the centerpiece on our dining room table."

Tugging my arm harder, I try to break free. Tears begin to blur my vision. "I hate you, August, and I will never *willingly* be your wife. Now get the hell out of my house."

He laughs—a sinister sound I've never heard from him before—and lets go of my arm. I stumble back, catching my balance.

"It's a little late for that, isn't it, love?" He prods.

"Your father practically sold you off to the highest bidder. Didn't take much to get his blessing. You're *mine* now, and nothing can change that—not even you crying to daddy and begging him to change his mind. You may hate me now, but one day you will come to accept our arrangement and your title as Mrs. St. Jean."

Instinct tells me to leave, to get the hell out of there and put as much distance between us as possible.

The look in his eyes is scaring me, but I know if I run, or show any signs of weakness, it'll only make things worse.

He'll look at me as prey, even more than he already does.

Still, I can't keep my mouth shut, wanting to somehow prove to him how deep my hatred runs. Walking past him, I lift my chin with confidence and have the last word as I stride from the room. "I would rather die than be your wife. I'd rather die than be anyone's wife but *his*."

What I'm not anticipating is his quick reaction when he runs after me, hurling me around so I'm facing him. He raises his hand, backhanding me across the face. The room falls sideways as the back of his hand collides with my skin so forcefully, the impact throws me into the corner of my bedside table. As my head bounces off it, I hear, "Be careful what you wish for, Vinnie, because I might just give you exactly what you ask for, only it won't be *you* who dies."

Then everything goes black.

Dear Reader,

Thank you, sweet reader, for taking a chance on Sins of Sorrow. I hope you enjoyed the first part of Sly and Vinnie's story as much as I enjoyed writing it.

Sly's story began with him as a side character in Marked By Cain, but it wasn't long before he started whispering his beautiful Italian accent in my ear, telling me his own life story. Thus, the With a Kiss Duet was born.

But… I quickly realized that still wasn't enough, and as the pieces of the duet began to fall into place, so did the rest of his story. If you want to read more about Sly, please follow the suggested reading order below. If you're content with picking up right where we left off, Sins of Bliss, book two of the With a Kiss Duet, releases in June 2024.

Suggested reading order:
Sins of Sorrow (With a Kiss Duet Book 1)
The Sinners (With a Kiss Duet Bridging Novella, releases April 2024)
Marked By Cain (Available Now)
Sins of Bliss (With a Kiss Duet Book 2, releases June 2024).

Acknowledgments

Thank YOU for reading this book.

A huge chunk of my heart and soul were poured into writing Sins of Sorrow and I adored every second of it. So many personal touches were added to this story, from the names of characters, to sprinkles of some of my favorite things. As my mom said, I dug into my Italian roots for this book and I could not be more proud of how it turned out.

I'd like to extend a very special thank you to Jess & Bee with CopyCats Editing, as well as Virginia Tesi Carey and Nicole Bucciarelli for being such an amazing team of editors and proofreaders.

To my friends and family, thank you to always having my back and being such a tremendous support throughout my writing process, especially DeLynda and Amanda who help me form each and every story to what it is.

Thank you so much to my amazing PA, Cassie, and the dedicated readers on my street team, ARC team, and influencer team!

I love you all.

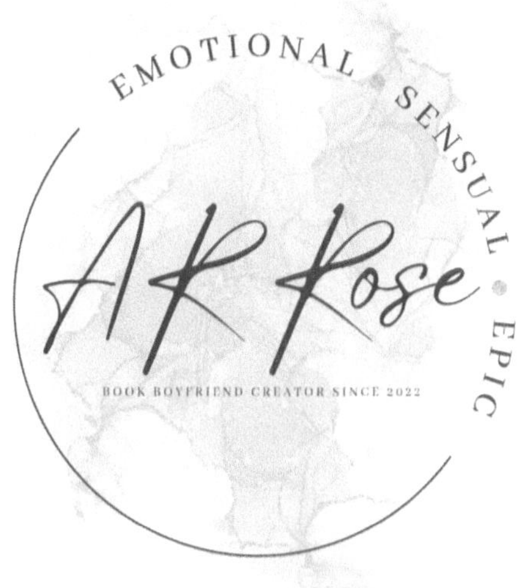

A.R. Rose's greatest job in life is being a mom to her two boys. She is a born and raised California native who loves to hang out at home with her kids and her dog.

A.R. realized her passion for writing in the third grade, although it wasn't until early 2022 when she began to pursue it. Now, if she skips a day of writing, she feels as though her day is incomplete.

On any given day, you will find A.R. toting around her laptop and her Kindle, with a coffee in hand, daydreaming about the characters and worlds she's building. She is grateful to have the opportunity to bring her stories to life and is excited about her journey as a romance writer.

CONNECT

Join A.R. Rose's newsletter for info & updates
https://www.authorarrose.com/email-subscribe

Website
www.authorarrose.com

Reading Group
https://www.facebook.com/groups/authorarrose

Facebook
https://www.facebook.com/authorarrose

TikTok
https://www.tiktok.com/@authorarrose

Instagram
https://www.instagram.com/authorarrose